TALES OF LOVE
AND WAR

TALES OF LOVE AND WAR

Julian Fane

The Book Guild Ltd
Sussex, England

First published in Great Britain in 2002 by
The Book Guild Ltd
25 High Street,
Lewes, East Sussex
BN7 2LU

Typesetting in Palatino by
Keyboard Services, Luton, Bedfordshire

Printed in Great Britain by
Antony Rowe Ltd, Chippenham, Wiltshire

A catalogue record for this book is
available from The British Library

ISBN 1 85776 640 7

CONTENTS

THE THIRD TIME

PART ONE

Nobody worried in the summer of 1938. Cath Allen and her friends seemed not to have a care in the world. Of course they were not so carefree as they appeared to be – who is? But they were oblivious of the particular worries that creased the brows of their parents and caused more experienced hearts to sink.

Catherine Mary Allen was seventeen. She was emerging from the cocoon of her girlhood, though she could hardly be compared to a butterfly as yet. She was strong-boned and rather overweight; a dark brunette, she wore her hair that gleamed with health in page-boy style, and the goodness of her nature expressed itself more often than not in giggling. Her giggles were never shrill, nor were they noticeably frivolous and exclusive of sympathy; they were harmonious, gentle, happy, infectiously happy – they put things in a perspective of happiness. In more earthy terms, they bubbled up from deep inside her, irresistibly, while the moral message they conveyed was that we must learn to laugh at nothing, since often there is nothing to laugh at.

Opinions differ as to which feature of the female form establishes a claim to beauty. Some say a face, others a figure. Every millimetre of a woman's countenance has earned the epithet beautiful, eyes, nose, lips, chin, a short upper lip, the angle of an eye, a temple, a cheekbone. Cath Allen's complexion spoke well of her digestion and nervous system. But, all her charms considered, she was no exception to the rule that a pretty smile takes a lot of beating. The teeth she showed when she giggled, when she smiled, the front teeth in her upper jaw, were a fine, white, perfectly graduated set that cancelled faults and made her lovely to look upon.

Not that she was interested. She was even less interested in her looks than her girlfriends were in theirs. She dressed not to kill but to be decent and to keep warm. Seductiveness was almost a closed book to her, along with English grammar and other esoteric and, in her case, unnecessary studies: she did not see the opposite sex in a sexual light, having herself been a tomboy in earlier days. The male members of her young group were simply friends who were either fun or not much fun, and grown-ups were sweet or grumpy.

Her marked differences from the continental model of budding womanliness, expected to know love from A to Z at the age of fifteen, and from modern misses who may have borne children by the time they are fifteen or even younger – her innocence amounting to ignorance had its own attractions. She was as fresh as dawn, as the dews of dawn, she really was the pristine wax tablet waiting to be scratched upon by life. Older women glanced more ruefully than enviously at her purity, and the adult majority was kind to a girl who had good manners and always time to smile at and listen to them.

No wonder Cath was apparently carefree. She was on friendly terms with the world. She had swanned through school, passing exams in her sure-fire middling way and not doing badly at games. Popularity gave her confidence, yet never tempted her to be anything but modest and diffident. No doubt the rock on which her character was founded went by the name of her home and its address, Shelford Grange, Shelford, near Bath, Somerset. It was also like a lodestar to her, a sort of guiding principle rather than

a place, an exemplary accumulation of the joys of her childhood and the love of both her parents.

Mary Allen was in her mid-forties when her only child
Cath was seventeen. She was a large woman, yet not
unwieldy, grey-haired, and not much made up. She was a
countrified type who had obviously settled for somewhat
premature retirement from the competition to turn heads.
She was also, and unmistakably, that rare bird, a lady, a
lady with refined manners, dedicated to the cause of making everyone she met feel better, brighter and more amusing than ever before. The paradox of what might be called
her spectacularly unassuming persona produced the effect
that in the eyes of many she was a figure of romance. She
was certainly raised on to a large number of pedestals by
various friends and acquaintances, by shop people and her
servants, by her husband and even by her daughter, now
that Cath was emerging from the common anti-maternal
phase of her development.
    She had married twice. Her first husband, Theo Grenchard,
perished in the Great War: they were only husband and
wife for a few months, and there was no issue. Theo was a
lord, he would have inherited the Earldom of Grenchard
and considerable estates; he and Mary, who was the grand-
daughter of another aristo, Lord Bethany, were out of the
same social drawer. She survived her bereavement by working as a VAD nurse just behind the front line for the rest of
the war: she had occasionally told Cath stories of that heart-
breaking time of her life. Then, when the war finished, she
succumbed to the patient courtship of Jack Allen.
    They had known each other for several years before she
said yes. She had nursed him – he was brought into her
hospital in a terrible state after performing some gallant
action for which he was awarded his M.C., and almost as

7

soon as he was able he proposed to her. She began by laughing at him, but gratefully. Next, she could not help admiring his spirit and his decisiveness. In due course she was touched by his perseverance. Eventually she admitted that he had worn down her powers of resistance.

The marriage was nonetheless happy. They were responsible people and kept their promises and did not forget to count their blessings: he, that he could rely on her absolutely, she, that she was prized and provided for and allowed scope and freedom to be herself. They refused to feel cheated by their sexual communing, they had so many other shared interests, and anyway they soon called sex a day – or a night. They were the best of friends, and could never thank each other enough for the gift of Cath.

Jack was five years older than Mary. Despite the wounds of his youth he enjoyed pretty good health. He was a couple of inches shorter than she was, pink-faced, smooth-complexioned, with a snub nose, clear blue eyes, a steady regard and a kindly expression. By a sad coincidence he lost both his parents in the lethal flu epidemic that followed the Great War, and Mary's father also died of it. Jack therefore inherited Shelford Grange and its two hundred and fifty acres and became a farmer in accordance with his family's tradition. He farmed more for pleasure than profit, he turned his fields and woods into extensions of his garden – luckily he could afford to pour money down the drain. Although he did not go in for remunerative work, he was always busy, attending to squirearchical duties as J.P., Chairman of his Parish Council, reading the lessons in church and taking a lead in community affairs. He was a sociable hospitable gentleman of leisure. In spare moments he would beat the bounds of his property, on summer evenings with a shotgun tucked under his arm and one of his yellow Labradors trotting along at heel.

The Grange was the big house in the hamlet of Shelford.

It was a manor made of Cotswold stone, stone-tiled, sash-windowed. Wisteria was artfully trained across its front, it had a useful back yard between outhouses, and a walled kitchen garden, a tennis court, undulating lawns and fine views. It nestled in a dip of the Mendip Hills with its farm manager's house and farm buildings situated at a discreet distance.

The rest of Shelford consisted of a church like a barn and thirty or so dwellings, some very old, others newer, and several owned by the Allens. There was no shop, which was bad for older people, and no pub, which was bad for the young. Three times a week a bus drove people to the larger village of Upper Shelford, and once a week to and from Bath. Half the population served Jack and Mary in diverse capacities, and approval of the Allen family was general.

They were conservative by habit and inclination, but often forgot to vote in elections. They took *The Times* and *The Mendip Echo*, the local daily, and *The Field* for Jack. Breakfast at the Grange started at nine o'clock, late enough for the housemaid May to do the reception rooms and Cook to get going in the kitchen and the papers and post to arrive.

Mary was the first down to breakfast. She would help herself to weak tea and eat a slice of toast and marmalade. She would put on spectacles to read her letters and at the same time talk to her parlour maid Nellie, whose husband Bill was cowman at the farm. She could not be compared to an ostrich by any stretch of the imagination, but in the August of 1938 she wished *The Times* did not carry another threatening headline and Nellie did not ask again if there was going to be a war. The summer sunshine streamed through the open dining-room French window and wood pigeons cooed in the sycamores.

9

'Oh Nellie,' Mary said, 'I'm going in to Bath this morning, and I'll buy the things you need for the house. Will you let me have your shopping list?'

Jack appeared, wearing his customary corduroys, tweed jacket, blue shirt and tie. His chin was smooth and shiny after shaving, and his face rosy from his bath.

'Morning, Nellie,' he said, 'and a good one for a change.'

He helped himself to fried egg and bacon and white coffee, scanned the front page of *The Times* with a sudden scowl, and took his breakfast, his letters and *The Mendip Echo* to the table and sat down in the chair at the top, facing the window.

'Anything in your post?' he asked.

'There's a letter from France.'

'Ah,' he commented, an exclamation denoting uncertainty, and picked up his paper.

'We're off to Bath, you know – Cath'll have to have something more to wear if she goes abroad.'

'If's the word. What does the lady say in her letter?'

'I haven't read it yet.'

'We'll have to wait and see.'

'I hope we won't have to cancel, Cath would be disappointed – but I mustn't talk like that, I mustn't be petty.'

'No.'

'I'd like to buy her the clothes anyway. Do you think it would be wrong?'

'No.' He raised his eyes from his paper opened at the agricultural page and suggested: 'No need to worry the girl. Why don't we read and discuss the letter when we're together later on?'

'That's it! That's the best idea. What about your letters?'

'They look like bills,' he replied, and set to work on the egg and bacon.

Cath was always last. She entered sleepily and apologetically, eyes half open and with a hint of contrite giggle. She kissed her father and mother, calling them Pa and Ma, and helped herself to the cooked breakfast, which, in her case, included a slice of fried bread. She took her place on her father's left and began to eat in her quietly businesslike manner – Cook's spoiling provision of the fried bread elicited no comment from her parents, although they privately discussed her puppy fat.

'Oh,' she addressed her mother, 'I forgot to tell you, I've asked people to play tennis this afternoon.'

'How lovely!' Mary exclaimed, and Jack inquired over the top of his paper: 'Is it your gang again?'

'I'll do the tea, we'll do it – we won't want anyone to bother about us,' Cath said.

'Would you rather we kept out of your way?'

'Oh no, Ma – I don't mean that – everybody loves to see you and you know how they love your teas – would you like to play? Pa, will you play tennis this afternoon?'

'Probably not, we'll probably come and watch you for a bit.'

'Would we cramp your style, darling?' Mary asked, and Cath giggled.

'I haven't got a lot of style to cramp. Do join us for tea and tennis! Ma, aren't we meant to go to Bath quite soon?'

'Yes, if ... if that suits.'

'I should say it does! You're giving me clothes and stuff for France, aren't you? What a summer! This time last year I was getting ready for the foul winter term at school, and now every day is fun and treats. And going abroad with Helen and Jenny is the best bit – we can hardly wait. Golly! But I do know how lucky I am – girls at school didn't have parents like you.'

'Thank you, darling. Shall we be off in half an hour?'

'Super! Did you hear what I said, Pa?'

'What did you say?'

'Nothing. Ma'll tell you.'

*　*　*

After lunch Cath's gang arrived at Shelford Grange. Jenny Holton and Helen Lestair bicycled the four or five miles over from their respective homes in the depths of the Somerset countryside. William Douglas-Holt came on his anti-social motorbike with the bust exhaust pipe, and Fred Bannerman on his new Triumph Twin with Peter Sengall on the pillion. Sheila Topps drove her brother Timmy in the Topps family's stuffy Lanchester. And Danny Ware had walked across the fields from the Ware farm that marched with the Allens'. They were nine – even numbers were not a prerequisite of their meetings.

They assembled in the old schoolroom with its untidy shelves of Cath's books and sat-out sofa and chairs. Music played on the radiogram. Greetings were informal – not much kissing and no handshakes. They carried rackets and some had changes of clothes and shoes – William Douglas-Holt's motorbike invariably spewed oil on his trousers, so he had taken to wearing overalls for riding it, then on arrival hurrying to wash and make himself more presentable. The two bicyclists, Jenny and Helen, said they were whacked and pretended to mop their brows as they lolled on the chairs. Fred Bannerman boasted that he had touched seventy on his Triumph, and Peter Sengall, his passenger, said it had been delightful. Sheila Topps was overdressed as usual and wore a green eye-shade even indoors, while Timmy swiped his racket back and forth, practising air shots. Danny Ware, a perfect specimen of farmer's boy, strong, russet-cheeked under his thick black curly hair, sat in a composed attitude on the arm of a chair, not saying a lot but smiling.

They were not in a hurry to reach the tennis court. The general conversation was playful. Fred Bannerman told the story of one of his funny dreams, in which he became a

Wimbledon tennis ball in dread of being served. In response to the inquiries of Jenny and Helen, who knew everything that happened to Cath and vice versa, Cath described in accents of tolerant resignation the shopping expedition with her mother, who had been shocked and saddened by the suggestion that a pair of slacks might come in useful. Jenny went further for a joke and said her mother had bought her a brassiere that was like a breastplate. Peter Sengall asked the three girls who were heading for France if they were taking corsets. Sheila Topps broke things up by stalking out through the open French window – the house had two such windows.

They followed her, straggling across the stripey lawns, past herbaceous borders, up and down steps, towards the kitchen garden. The sky was cloudless, and the still silence was interrupted by the zooming flight of a bee or the bark of a distant dog, no doubt Jack Allen's Snipe, asking to be let out of her kennel.

The young friends did not comment on the horticultural pleasures or the weather. William Douglas-Holt said he was staying on an extra year at school because he was completely in the dark about his future. Fred Bannerman and Peter Sengall were bound for university, Oxford for Fred, somewhere up north for Peter, who said it specialised in dunces and theatricals. Timmy Topps hit his prim sister on the bottom with his racket, and she chased him, shouting 'Rats must die!' Cath, Jenny and Helen were all giggling over whether the French for lavatory was *lavabo* or *toilette*. Someone called to Danny: 'Why aren't you harvesting?' and Danny called back: 'Tomorrow, *mañana*!'

They were united by geography, children's parties, auld lang syne, and by scarcely noticed sexual bonds and simpler loyalties. The Toppses gave dances for Sheila, Jenny's people organised Christmas outings to the panto in Bristol, Fred Bannerman's contribution to the fun and games was outings to skate at the Bristol rink, and the Wares offered days on the farm, helping to stook the corn in summer, learning to milk cows in winter, rabbiting, bonfires. Helen Lestair had a difficult widowed mother and dared not invite anybody into her home. William Douglas-Holt had divorced parents, did not get on with either of them, and lived in a cramped flat in Bath with a maiden aunt, his father's sister. But materialistic rewards were not the aim of the gang, and the ability to provide or not to provide entertainment hardly figured in the picture, although young people are so impressed by luxury.

Again, social distinctions made no difference. It was generally known that Mary Allen had grander connections than some, and that the Toppses were *nouveau riche*. That Fred Bannerman's father sold cars in London, and Danny Ware's called Jack Allen sir, were facts stored at the very back of minds. Worldliness had yet to invade the land of their friendship, ruled by congeniality.

Of course divisions existed, favouritism reared its head, squabbles were not barred – the friends were human after all. Intermittently the majority hated Sheila Topps, who made herself up for tennis as if she were going to a Court Ball. After a dance at the Topps', Jenny Holton necked with Fred Bannerman and then would not speak to him for a few weeks. And Cath temporarily took against poor William Douglas-Holt, who smeared one of her dresses with his motor oil. But Danny never did wrong in anyone's eyes – he was a self-contained sort of person and would not stoop to changeable behaviour; and the triumvirate of Cath and Jenny and Helen held firm without interruption.

At about five o'clock on the day of the tennis party refreshments were borne up to the players by Jack and Mary Allen in person. He carried the tray with the home-made iced lemonade and glasses, and she the tray with the plates of heaped cucumber sandwiches, the scones spread with butter and strawberry jam, and the jam doughnuts bought that morning in Bath. Cath's parents were always popular with her friends, who sensed that they were loved for Cath's sake; moreover Jack's undemanding jollity and Mary's lack of any trace of snobbery were appreciated. And youth's appetite for food, at any rate, was satisfied in full at Shelford Grange.

The older generation departed tactfully and the boys and girls clustered round the wooden seat on which the trays had been deposited. The plates of food were soon cleared and the jugs of lemonade emptied. Tennis was not resumed for a spell. Instead the players stretched out on the lawn, at full length or raised on an elbow, kneeling or sitting with their legs clasped, eyes closed or narrowed to filter the rays of the descending sun, one sucking a blade of grass, others smoking cigarettes, Peter Sengall, who was hoping to be an actor, with the woollen arms of his white jersey dramatically tied round his neck.

At about six-thirty Peter said he had lines to learn and Fred Bannerman, who was obviously keen to be reunited with his Triumph Twin, offered to drive him to where he lived with his over-indulgent mother. Peter was on the effeminate side, but made up for his attitudinising with his gentleness.

Helen Lestair also had to go: her mother would not be worried, like Peter's, but angry if she stayed out too long. And the two Topps took their leave, Sheila graciously and Timmy with an excessive number of rude noises: Sheila said she had another engagement, which Fred pretended to take to mean the matrimonial kind and called the new man in question unlucky – a doubly provocative assumption.

Jenny Holton, William Douglas-Holt and Danny Ware lingered.

'Don't go,' Cath pleaded.

And when Jack and Mary came to collect the trays etcetera, wearing plimsolls and carrying rackets, another set was played. They swapped partners so that nobody was left out, Jack with Jenny and then with his daughter, Mary with William and then Danny. The older Allens were nice to play with or play against, they had won golden opinions also in that respect from Cath's gang, because they were simultaneously enthusiastic and uncompetitive. Besides, Jack's game was tweaky, not to say sneaky, and Mary could keep a baseline rally going until defeated by a better shot or by her own laughter.

Some time after seven that set finished, and although the court was only illuminated by the colours of sunset, and dusk began to darken the shadows, a final foursome was proposed and agreed. Danny said he would play with Cath against William and Jenny, a promising match, since Danny was the strongest player and Cath the weakest, and the other two were both competent.

It was great fun for Cath, who could be embarrassed by her feebleness on court and had not played much during the afternoon, although, somewhat masochistically, she loved tennis. Unselfishness had also led to her claims that she preferred to laze and watch her friends perspiring. But Danny had chosen to play with her of his own free will, and he had always been her favourite partner. He made up for her errors, he compensated for the points she lost, and never showed a sign of disappointment or impatience when her shots failed to reach the net, let alone go over it, or she skied balls into the Brussels sprouts.

'Well done, Danny!... Thanks, Danny,' she cried, and he smiled back at her and said, 'We're winning' or 'It's just a game.'

She had always admired his strength, it was a byword within the gang, and he had a reliable character to match. When he stood at the net, leaning forward with legs apart, tensed and ready to compensate for one of her dolly-drop serves, she felt proud that the friend of her childhood, her lifelong companion, was growing into such a fine all-rounder, clever with machines, competent in all he did and was asked to do.

Her thoughts did not take the direction that would have been the case today, sixty-odd years later. She had not been under pressure almost since the day she was born to connect everyone and everything with sex, as has become the rule in our new world. Granted, she and Jenny and Helen talked mostly of boys, Jenny had a secret crush on the under-gardener employed by her father, and Helen, who was the most adventurous of the trio, always got herself into amorous entanglements at parties. But they were all late developers, chaste, shy, nearly as Victorian as their mothers, and Cath was the least sensual, anyway for the time being. Love was a mirage for her, marriage was over the horizon, and she placed her relations with the opposite sex firmly on the basis of friendship.

Nonetheless, the twilight scene on the tennis court and the almost ghostly figures of the players in their white apparel, and the human voices mingling with those of birds, schools of swifts shrieking and swooping on early nocturnal insects, an owl towit-towooing in a nearby coppice, was undeniably romantic.

Cath never could keep her mind on any of her sporting activities, and now she wondered what the future held in store for herself, for all of them. Was there going to be a war? What would war mean? It was unthinkable.

At last William and Jenny were victorious, and they trooped out of the court and through the garden, two by two.

Danny and Cath walked together, and he said he had decided to enrol in a twelve-month crash course in engineering at a technical college in Manchester.

'How will your father manage without you?' she asked – Danny had previously attended a technical college in Bristol.

'Somehow – he thinks he can – and I don't go for a few weeks. The point is that farming's getting more and more mechanical, and I won't be wasting time or money by following this course in a centre of excellence.'

'When will you be home?'

'Oh – for Christmas – but I'll see you before I leave. Will you come harvesting one afternoon? Dad and Mum would be pleased.'

'I'd love to. Oh well – good luck, Danny,' she added and patted him on the back as they re-entered the Grange.

The invitation to New House Farm, where the Wares lived in succession to numerous forebears, arrived a week later. Mrs Ware rang Mary Allen and asked all three Allens to tea, and Cath to come early so that she could join the other young people who would be helping with the harvest. Mary said yes, thank you, and Cath bicycled over at three o'clock on what was another azure afternoon.

She went straight to the so-called Big Field behind contrarily old New House – she could hear the corncutter's engine and the shouts of people and the barking of dogs. The corncutter was a machine with a wide blade sticking out to one side; the blade scythed through the stalks of corn, which were then shaken together by another apparatus, tied with stout string, and shot out on to the stubble. So that these bundles of corn did not lie on the ground for too long, and run the risk of rain which would cause the grain to germinate and ultimately rot, three bundles at a time had to be picked up and stacked together in a vertical pyramidal group, forming a stook. Once stooked, the corn was relatively safe, for rain would run straight down the stalks, and, when dry, was collected and thrashed. The resultant grains of corn were stowed in bags for onward transmission to the miller, and the straw stored in barns and ricks for use as rough feed for livestock, also for bedding.

Cath was immediately spotted by Danny. He strode towards her, smiling and sweating with his hair tousled, the sleeves of his shirt rolled up and showing his muscular forearms. She called to him, seeing how busy he was, 'Don't bother about me!' She indicated Jenny and William Douglas-Holt, who were already hard at work, and called again: 'I'll stick with them, Danny!'

Other members of the gang were lending a hand, Peter Sengall stripped to the waist and with a spotted handker-chief knotted round his neck, and, over in the distance, Sheila Topps in a huge straw hat rearranging stooks that were falling apart.

The driver of the corncutter was a stranger who hired out his services. Danny and the Wares' farm labourer Tom, and Peter and Jenny and William, were engaged in a sort of race to get the sheaves of corn stooked as soon as they were dis-gorged by the machine. Three quarters of the corn had been cut, and already the pigeons and smaller birds were flutter-ing round the verges of the Big Field, gleaning the grain that had as it were fallen by the wayside. The dogs chased them, the New House collies, also terriers of unknown own-ership. Every so often a rabbit bolted from the corn, was shouted at, caught and killed by the dogs, and claimed by Tom or Danny in order to provide a meal for someone.

Cath and Jenny each lifted one sheaf while William was lifting two. They laughed and complained that the corn scratched their wrists, and William accused them of being a pair of cissies. The stubble pierced the girls' bare ankles, and they squeaked and asked each other when tea would be served. But the work was familiar to Cath, she had done it year on year; and no one could ignore the beauty of the weather and the picturesque sight of the stooks casting their shadows on the golden stubble.

The corncutter departed to cut another farm's corn when the Big Field was finished. The stooking was complete, Tom had other agricultural duties, Danny led the way to the farmhouse, Cath and Jenny wheeled their bicycles, and Peter, William and Sheila walked – Sheila had given them a lift to New House, again in her parents' Lanchester.

After being shown a few of the sights of the farmyard – pigs in sties, Danny's ferret – the visitors were ushered through the back door into the old-style kitchen with dresser and range, then greeted by Mrs Ware, a plump comfortable woman in late middle age. She was the mother of two, a daughter, Margaret, a qualified nurse, now aged thirty-three, who had emigrated to Australia, married, bred several children and never came home, and the afterthought Danny, aged eighteen. She now had welcoming smiles for Danny's friends, she smiled on all things connected with Danny, but scolded him tenderly for using the back door: 'Father's waiting to meet our guests in the parlour.'

Tea for the young people was arrayed on the kitchen table. When Mrs Ware led them through to the sitting-room, her parlour, smelling of damp and furniture polish, they shook the meaty hand of Mr Ware, who wore collar and tie and a three-piece suit. Both Wares were in their best clothes in honour of Jack and Mary Allen, and the parlour table was covered with an embroidered cloth and laid for four.

The front door bell tinkled. Cath had always loved the New House bell, a real bell hanging in the kitchen, worked by a wire attached to the bell-pull in the front porch. The Allens were admitted and warmly welcomed by Mr Ware. Jack shook hands with both the senior Wares, Mary shook the hand of Mr Ware and kissed his wife, and more greetings were swapped with the young people, who Danny eventually succeeded in shepherding back to the kitchen. Mrs Ware followed in order to 'infuse' the tea, as she put it, in a silver pot for the parlour and a big brown metal one for the 'children'.

The edibles were lavish, according to custom. Cut bread and butter and unusual jam and jelly, respectively ginger and medlar, egg sandwiches, lettuce sandwiches, flapjacks, rich fruit cake and iced chocolate sponge. The boys ate hungrily, the girls with abandonment and regret. Peter had put on a checked shirt – 'Canadian lumberjack' he explained – but was teased by William for the neckerchief he had affected out of doors. Jenny teased Sheila for the size of her hat, and William teased Cath for having no muscles to speak of. Jenny and Cath tried to speak to each other in French. Peter and Sheila agreed that William and Jenny ought to be in high chairs with dummies shutting their mouths. Cath was provoked into calling William Douglas-Holt Douglas William Holt. And Danny passed the plates and kept on replenishing teacups. In between times he answered questions about the seamier side of life on a farm, for instance the castration of piglets and pregnancy testing for cows.

On a more serious note, Peter asked Danny: 'What are we going to have to do if the situation gets any worse?'

Danny replied: 'Perhaps it won't get worse, and we'll be able to carry on with our lives.'

'What are the odds?'

Danny shrugged his shoulders, and William piped up: 'I'm thinking of going into the army anyway.'

Then the snatch of conversation was cut short by sounds

of movement in the parlour. The Allens were leaving – Jack had told Cath that he could not stay long at New House, he was chairing some committee meeting. The party was over, Danny had farm work to do for his father, Sheila had to return the family car. Goodbyes and thanks circulated, and everybody seemed to leave in a rush.

Danny detained Cath in the hallway and looked at her strangely, maybe because the area was not well lit, and said: 'I won't be seeing you again before Christmas – Christmas or New Year's Eve with luck.'

'Of course I'll see you then.'

'Okay,' he said. 'Bye-bye, Cath.'

'Bye-bye – have a good time.'

She hurried out and mounted her bicycle. She had been taken aback and even frightened by the way he looked at her. It reminded her of that drunken man at a party who had said after a similar disturbing stare: 'Bloody virgins!'

But as she bicycled away she blushed hotly and wished she had been nicer and given Danny a kiss or something.

The news was bad, and Jack Allen took shorter walks so as not to miss any broadcast on the wireless, and Mary's face lost its colour and she scuttled about as if she were being hunted.

'What is it, Ma – please tell me!'

'There may be another war – it's too awful.'

'But why? Wars aren't possible any more.'

'Don't let's talk about it. Don't you worry about it, darling.'

'I so want to go to France.'

'Yes, I know.'

'Jenny and Helen are determined to go.'

'Yes, darling.'

Cath talked to her friends on the telephone. Two percent

of the time they talked was devoted to the crisis in Europe, eight percent to what the young men they knew would do if war should break out, and ninety percent to the Paris question, the trouble with parents, and other girlish concerns. They were not political, too young to vote, had no interest in current affairs, no knowledge of the world, and could not begin to imagine total war. They had led sheltered lives, and trusted the older generation to take care of them.

And they seemed to be right. The crisis subsided, and the three girls spent that winter in the apartment of the Latille family in the Boulevard de Montparnasse, cultivating themselves.

Cath returned to Shelford Grange bearing a load of Parisian Christmas presents. She was happy to be reunited with her family, including her grandmother, Mary's mother, who always stayed for Christmas and the New Year, and with the staff and cottage people. An additional pleasure was that she received an urgent summons from Sheila Topps to sing carols in Upper Shelford on Christmas Eve.

'We're all joining in, Jenny and Helen have just said yes, and the boys too, they'll be there, you must come, you will, won't you?'

Cath, while she was away, whenever she spared a thought for the past, had regretted her parting from Danny – it was like a loose end that needed attention. In Upper Shelford she would have a chance to repair damage she might have done or, not to exaggerate, compensate for her clumsiness. She was also keen to show off to everyone the social polish she had acquired in France.

But the party of singers was much more numerous than Cath expected, and Danny arrived late. They waved at each other, and not much more. He left in a hurry for no doubt some agricultural reason and only said to her: 'Don't forget

New Year's Eve' while she was telling half a dozen carol singers about her life in Paris.

Another disappointment was that she had shied away from seeking him out during walks from one dwelling to the next. She had been embarrassed or inhibited, and he had not hurried to find her. His reference to New Year's Eve was to the party the Wares traditionally threw at New House Farm. She was annoyed with herself for failing at Upper Shelford, but at least would have another chance to set the record straight at New House.

Things again went wrong. It happened under the mistletoe, or, more accurately, had not happened. At nearly midnight at New House the members of the gang started kissing under a twig of home-grown mistletoe attached to an upstairs banister and hanging in the hall, actually not far from where Cath had behaved in a silly hot-making fashion last summer. Mr Ware was the culprit, he was responsible for the mistletoe, and he began the kissing of some of his female guests, older ladies, strangers, as well as Jenny Holton. Then William Douglas-Holt seized Sheila Topps and gave her a smacker, and Timmy Topps did likewise to Helen Lestair after an undignified scuffle.

Jenny made the fun, if it was fun, more furious by seizing hold of Danny and saying: 'I've been kissed by the father, so I'm damn well kissing the son.' When she had done the deed she called to Cath: 'Come on, I've got him, help yourself!' – all amidst increasingly loud laughter from the onlookers.

Danny was laughing too, standing there passively and looking at her, looking at her once more too intently for comfort, and she had blushed scarlet and shaken her head and taken refuge in the parlour, where she sat on a stool beside her Granny.

24

She recovered herself. When the clock struck twelve she made a point of linking arms with her gang, with Peter Sengall and William Douglas-Holt, and after Auld Lang Syne announced that she hated horse-play under mistletoe and elsewhere – she was sorry but if that was the game she would have to be counted out.

But she was confused. She did not know what was wrong with her. It was unlike her to spoil sport, to object or draw the line or disapprove; and it was not as if she was repelled by Danny. A spanner of some sort had fallen into the perfectly regulated mechanism of her constitution. She had lost the power to giggle. She wanted to be alone, and when her Pa and Ma were leaving New House she accepted their offer of a lift home although Jenny and Helen were staying on.

To make matters worse she omitted to bid Danny goodbye. He was involved with other people when she should have done so, he was too busy, she argued inwardly, and she would thank him on another day, as she had thanked Mr and Mrs Ware.

But at Shelford Grange that night, and in the first few days of 1939, she continued to worry. In fact her worries increased. She felt alternately cross with Danny for somehow upsetting her, for putting her in the wrong, for ruining her idea of herself as a capable young woman with a smooth French veneer, and for accentuating her insecurity and general sense of inferiority; and at almost the same time guilty of an injustice, for Danny had done nothing nastier than to look at her – and, she recalled, a cat can look at a queen.

The obvious solution of her problem escaped her. She had had crushes but never been in love. She expected to fall in love one day, but she knew only the exclusive letter of the facts of life, nothing of the spirit or even the practicalities. What was beyond argument to her way of thinking, or her ignorance, was that when she fell in love it would not be with Danny or any of the friends with whom she had romped since infancy. Her preferred answer to all her questions was that she must be sickening for something.

A further collapse of her confidence, which was proving to be more of a house of cards than she had imagined it was, occurred when Danny rang her up.

She was ridiculously apologetic. She heard herself twittering apologies. Without knowing it, she had been afraid that she might have offended him, that he might have decided it was not worth being friends with her any more, and relief made her sillier than usual, thanking him for the New Year's Eve do, thanking him for nothing and giggling non-stop. His voice was serious yet tolerant and he was kind enough not to interrupt her, while his quiet laughter partially justified hers.

'Would you like to come to Weston?' he was asking.

Belatedly she took it in.

'What? When?'

'Tomorrow – I've borrowed Dad's car and thought we might go and have a look around.'

'But it's winter!'

'Weston can be nice even in winter, and the weather forecast's not bad. Dad usually needs his car,' Danny added.

'Of course. Yes – well – I'd love to. Who else is coming?'

'As many as I can squeeze in. I'll ring them now. And I'll call for you tomorrow at eleven, okay?'

'Okay.'

There was more to this exchange than the words suggested. Weston-super-Mare loomed large in the mythology of the lives to date of the members of Cath's gang. A day spent there had been the chosen treat of all the children with birthdays in the summer months. Apprehensive

26

parents with others' ewe lambs as well as their own to look after had spent hours in sun or wind or rain on its muddy beach; while their charges revelled in the pullulating crowds, and stared and made new friends and enemies, and usually succeeded in cadging rides on donkeys and roundabouts. And as Cath and the others grew up they had still traipsed in promising weather, by bus or train or hitchhiking, to the scene of their happiest memories. But in winter they gave it a miss by common consent: those gentle breezes from Iceland, from over the Atlantic, could cut to the quick. Danny, however, was breaking with tradition and risking a fiasco. Weston might punish them all for expecting it to be pleasant in January; on the other hand Weston might be flattered by their attention. The plan was controversial, and if Cath had been surer of herself than she was for the moment she might have urged postponement. That she showed almost instant willingness was due to another factor. Danny had invited her to accompany him before inviting the others. His preference was further relief and even a partial cure of whatever was infecting her nervous system. She decided it was a good idea to see Weston again despite possible opposition from meteorological wet blankets, and looked forward to the outing eagerly.

The Wares' car was a battered old Wolseley. Danny arrived at Shelford Grange with Helen Lestair and William Douglas-Holt in the back seat. Cath sat in the front passenger seat, which William said had last been occupied by a pig.

They laughed a lot during the drive. They aired their favourite recollections of Weston, Danny of an old donkey called Smut, Helen of a local brand of ice cream sold in the fairground. William had liked the game of rolling a penny on to numbers into painted square compartments, and getting your money back doubled or trebled if your penny avoided all dividing lines. Cath remembered the organ grinder's music. Would the Punch and Judy operate in winter, they wondered; and what would the place be like?

It was so gloomy as to be interesting almost to an enjoyable degree. The sky was battleship grey, the beach black with its mud, and the sea a liverish opaque grey-green. The froth of waves was blown inland, the gale-force wind was bitterly salty. They sought shelter in a seafront pub that was nearly empty, draughty and chill, and drank brandy to warm the cockles, then stout, and eventually ate cheese sandwiches.

Afterwards they had some fun by leaning against the wind. They were warm now, and seemed to have Weston to themselves. They found an amusement arcade with cheery lights on and began to play the machines. There was a machine that printed letters on a strip of tin: you turned an arm to the letters you wanted to print, pulled a handle, and when a certain number of letters were indented on the tin the strip was ejected. William and Helen did jolly ones, 'Wish you were here' and 'Come on in, the water's lovely'. Then it was Cath's turn, but she could not think of anything to write, and, as William and Helen drifted across to see what the butler saw, Danny had a go. Cath was standing beside him and watched as he printed, 'D loves C'.

'Who's D?' she asked.

'Who do you think?' he countered, turning to look at her in his straight strong way.

This time she could not look away, it was as if he pinioned her with his eyes, his slight smile, his broad open countenance and thick dark hair. She felt weak at the knees and asked in a strangulated voice, 'Who's C?'

He jumped the intervening questions and said: 'Do you?'

'Oh Danny!'

'Could you?'

'I don't know, Danny!'

'Please don't walk away, please answer!'

'I don't know – I can't say.'

'It's urgent, Cath.'

'What? I don't understand. Oh Danny! Sorry, sorry!'

He let her go.

In the Wolseley on their return journey Danny said he had an announcement to make. Cath was terrified, she thought he would broadcast their conversation in the amusement arcade. Instead he announced that he had volunteered to join the Royal Air Force.

He was tactful: he dropped Cath at Shelford Grange first. He muttered something about writing, gave her a muddled kiss on her bent head, and drove the other two home. He had sensed that Cath felt she would have died if they had been alone in the car in the dark.

She could not sleep. She did not know if she was distressed or excited. Her insomnia, like everything else, was a revolutionary novelty.

At breakfast she found an envelope addressed to 'Cath' beside her place on the dining-room table.

She tried to ignore it, helped herself to coffee and wondered if she would get away with skipping the egg, bacon and fried bread – she had the opposite of her usual appetite.

Her father asked over the top of his newspaper: 'Aren't you going to open your love letter?'

Her mother scolded him, called him cheeky, told him to mind his own business, laughed it off, and with a sympathetic gesture at Cath left the room, probably for Cath's sake.

'Don't take any notice of me, darling,' Jack said.

'It's Danny,' Cath blurted out. 'He's going to join the RAF. He's letting me know when.'

'I'm afraid he's doing the right thing. I admire his patriotism. I always admired Danny – the Wares are an admirable family. I hope he comes to no harm.'

'Is it dangerous, Pa?'

'If there's war it will be.'

'But there won't be a war.'

'I hope you're right.'

'Pa, I'm meant to go back to Paris next week. You won't stop me going, will you? Will you, Pa?'

'It's not up to me, worst luck, my darling.'

She opened the letter in her bedroom.

'Dear Cath, I'll have left home by the time you read this,' it ran. 'I wrap up the course I was on and report to the Air Force next weekend. I know I'm aiming high to love you, but I always have and will, and I can't help that. If you would consider being my girl, you'd be the only girl in the world for me always. Danny.'

She wrote her reply thus: 'Dear Danny, I wish I had known you were leaving so soon. I'm sorry I did not say goodbye properly. Everything is rushing along so fast that I am not sure I shall ever catch up. Paris for a bit might be a help, if I can get there. Please don't run risks. C.'

She sent her letter to New House for onward transmission. Before she departed for France she received the following: 'Dear C, In haste – write to me at above address, a word or two from you would make a great difference to me. Thank you v. much for your last. With my love, D.'

Cath reached Paris, but this time round she might as well have stayed at home. For Danny was not at New House: her urge to flee from him was a waste of effort. And she could not get him out of her head – the Parisian experience seemed irrelevant. Moreover she began to worry about him, and to convince herself that she owed her cooperation, if not her complete collapse into his arms, to his courage and readiness to defend their homeland.

* * *

She half-confided in Jenny and Helen, who soon got the whole story out of her and fanned the flame, which was really more a spark, of passion. Cath's motives in responding in increasingly affectionate terms to Danny's ardent notes were mixed. She was flattered to have been singled out by the most mature male specimen in her gang. She felt it would be impolite not partly to do as he wished, and she recoiled from the onerous business of fending him off and issuing strict negatives. She regarded their communications sometimes as her contribution to the preparations for war, as other women rolled bandages. At other times she fancied first that she did love him in the way he loved her, and secondly, immediately afterwards, that she could not bear ever to meet him again, or, still more decidedly, be alone with him. She was more scared of than intrigued by sex.

But the letters as it were cornered her, and led to her promise that she would attend the dance at his Air Force base, which, at Easter-time, would celebrate the passing-out parade of his intake of volunteers, also his own commission as an officer and the award of his 'wings'.

She had written to her mother for permission to take this compromising step, relying on a refusal; but Mary wrote back to say she had fixed up for Cath to stay with her cousin and old friend, Mrs Somerville, who happened both to live near the base and to be going with her husband to the same dance – Mr Somerville had some connection with the Air Force.

Cath therefore bowed before fate, not knowing whether she was displeased or pleased by her mother's connivance in the matter.

At last her time in Paris came to an end. She returned to Shelford Grange and two days later travelled across southern England to Dover, where the Somervilles met her. That night the three of them in evening dress proceeded to the dance.

31

The transformation scene for Cath occurred in a hangar, where a buffet supper was served and then the band struck up. Was the magic wand a combination of his blue uniform and her long flimsy flowered gown bought in Paris? Danny was another man in his Flight Lieutenant's garb, no longer the homely farmer's boy of their yesteryears, and she had lost weight thanks to the strain of being loved, and a mixture of excitement and dread enlarged her eyes, gave them a violet tint, and caused them to shine and sparkle.

In earthier terms, love of a new kind flooded her being on the dance floor, when he held out his arms to her and she nestled into them.

They danced together for getting on for two hours. Mr Somerville insisted on dancing with Cath once, and Danny's superior officer claimed another dance. And there was a break for ices. But after each interruption they were increasingly quick to return to the dance floor and to be held by each other.

They danced not as young people do today, separately, self-centredly, without tactile or visible reference to a partner, and squirming and gesticulating African-style; nor even as people danced in the thirties, at arm's length or nearly, and with intricate footwork. Danny and Cath danced in a precocious version of the later wartime manner, as if glued together, moving rhythmically but not much, impatiently cutting through convention and simulating in the vertical position the act of sexual communion.

It was extraordinary. Perhaps they scarcely spoke because they were almost struck dumb by the change in their relationship. Cath, unselfconscious as she had been, was suddenly amazed by herself. Her shyness, her hesitation, her forebodings, her chaste maidenliness, all had been shed, kicked off like old shoes. One set of rationalisations was shoved aside to make room for another, for new explanations and justifications of her conduct.

Her yielding to and reciprocation of Danny's love was not surprising really, it was the logical conclusion of their perennial former friendship – it was their friendship with the X-factor of their time of life added, their friendship in sex's reappraisal. She had always trusted him. She had known him through and through and in every way except that which they now investigated. Nature was responsible for her simultaneous inexplicable wonderful access of strength and weakness. She felt reinforced by his reliable arm round her waist and his big hand holding hers, and equally that she was melting and that the beat of her heart measured the process of the liquefaction of the girl she had recently thought she was.

Their conversation was limited because they seemed to be in a world without time – one day, on another day, they would talk and express themselves in words.

Early on he whispered in her ear, 'You look lovely,' and she whispered back with a breathless little giggle, 'So do you.'

At another moment he whispered, 'This is the best night of my life,' and she made adequate reply with the monosyllable, 'Yes.'

But when the last dance was announced they became relatively voluble.

'I've been posted to another base up north, I'm leaving here tomorrow – or is it today? — and no one knows what's happening afterwards. Will you wait, Cath?'

She did not deign to answer so superfluous a question, but satisfied him by squeezing his hand and murmuring that she was patient.

'We're due for time off in a month. But we're the teachers now – there's such a rush to train new recruits that I've already started training them. You're not returning to France?'

'No, no – I'm going to do Domestic Science in Bath.'
'Does that mean cooking?'
'Yes.'
She giggled under her breath.
'I don't want to say goodbye.'
'No,' she agreed.
'Thank you, Cath.'
'What for? Thank you,' she countered.

The lights went out and the girls shrieked and the young men cheered and the music continued to play.

Danny kissed Cath's cheek and their lips inevitably met.

Then the lights switched on, and it was the Galop and God Save the King.

Cath Allen was not devious. She took after her parents, and now at Shelford Grange did not try to hide the changes taking place in her – she was neither secretive nor indiscreet. Long lie-ins were a thing of her past: she was down to breakfast long before her mother in order to look for a letter from Danny. She began to read the newspapers, the front pages anyway, and sometimes to ask her Pa in a voice audibly strained whether war was more or less likely. When an aeroplane flew over, she would run out of doors and open a window to gaze up at it, wondering if Danny was inside.

She treasured the little compliments she was paid by people who had not been seeing her constantly: 'You're looking bobbish, what's got into you?... What's put the roses in your cheeks?... No need to ask how you are, Bright Eyes... You're smiling through at any rate – everybody else is down in the mouth!' Again, she was not unusually vain; but she gathered praises of herself as if they were flowers, a posy for Danny or a floral tribute. More seriously than ever before she weighed up the effectiveness of her page-boy hairstyle, and she spent unaccustomed hours choosing lipsticks.

On weekday mornings she caught the bus to Bath and spent the day with Jenny and Helen at the domestic science establishment near Pulteney Bridge. The girls called themselves The Three Musquettes – they had done everything together, and shared everything, clothes, preoccupations, for ever. The others knew that Cath was in love almost before she did, and generously allowed that Danny was the biggest and best fish in their pond and that she was lucky to have landed him. Naturally they demanded a blow-by-blow account of the dance in Kent. Cath supplied an abridged edition. She loved her friends, but realised that what she and Danny felt for each other was incommunicable. When Jenny offered her a second look at the book she had found in a junk shop, *The Rites and Wrongs of Love*, her answer was sharply negative.

She received two brief notes from Danny, giving his address and pleading haste, wrote back twice and awaited a longer letter. One morning she noticed an envelope addressed to her mother and post-marked Kent. She guessed vaguely that it might be from her hostess on the night of the dance, but was rather startled when, during the evening of that day, her mother sought her out in her bedroom and said in a tense manner: 'I've heard from Kitty Somerville.'

'Oh?'

'She's taken such a shine to you. You had the greatest success with both Somervilles.'

'They were awfully nice to me.'

'She says you and Danny had a high old time at the dance.'

'What does that mean?'

'Well – dancing together all the evening.'

'I didn't know anyone else, Ma.'

'No, of course not – I thought it must have been like that – you and Danny were always such good friends.'

'No, Ma, it wasn't and it isn't quite like that.'

'Are you happy, darling?'

'Yes, terribly, sometimes.'

'I only want you to be happy, and wouldn't interfere in your private life for anything. But you will take care, won't you, and remember how young you are? And these are such uncertain times.'

'Yes, Ma.'

'I'm sorry to be a fusspot.'

'Darling Ma!'

Danny wrote fondly in due course, and correspondence carried the romance forward, and at last in May he was granted forty-eight hours of leave. But he and Cath had hardly a moment alone together. Mr Ware wished to discuss wills and testaments with his son, then they spent a day at solicitors in Bristol, then Mrs Ware invited the whole gang to supper at New House, and for the lovers it was all frustration.

On the other hand the news was getting steadily worse, the emotional temperature of the country was rising and having an effect on personal relations, consequently Cath was not altogether averse to what she mentally referred to as 'a breather'. She had studied Danny during those forty-eight hours with the eyes of love, which are contradictorily eagle-eyed as well as blind. She was persuaded that she had never looked at him before – he had been a presence, another puppy in the same basket, taken for granted, admired more as an idea than a person. Now she saw how handsome he was, tall, broad-shouldered, fresh-faced and with that regard which was at once welcoming, trusting, expectant of fair dealing yet not to be easily deceived. She appreciated his wide easy smile, the whiteness of his teeth, the honest jut to the back of his head and his round sturdy neck. She liked the way he stood as if rooted to the ground, which in fact, as scion of a line of farmers, he was. She loved the size of his warm hands.

She realised that it was not only the Air Force uniform that had seemed to her to have changed him. It was the Air Force itself, and especially his reason for enlisting in it, that was responsible for the change. It was the threat of war which forced the rapid development of Danny and of herself, and of their generation, to switch from youth to adulthood with unnatural speed – they were like plants put under glass. Cath was no philosopher, but sensitive and a woman. She had a share in her parents' wartime memories, and could not shrug off her female duty to bear in mind the future of her potential children.

In the event of war, what would become of Danny?

The mere posing of that question in subliminal form made her love him the more. She was moved by his courage and the other fine qualities he had acted on, and longed to protect him. Although she was prepared to wait for him for ever, her patience in respect of his absence in a mystery location in the north while she learned to cook in the south was wearing thin. She longed for him by day and in the night – lovers' nights with no lover to cool her blood. She wondered if she should do something, go to him instead of hanging about – she was ready to do anything if he should ask her to do it.

His longest letter arrived and she read as much as she was able to in the swaying jolting bus to Bath.

He had been thinking long and hard about the two of them, he wrote. He was in his twentieth year and the sole heir of New House Farm; his sister Margaret had already received her portion of the family treasure. He had loved Cath for as long as he could remember, he loved her best

37

and promised faithfully that he always would. She was better in every way than he was, but he could not bear to think of losing her.

He continued: 'I'm sure you know what I'm getting at, though I hardly dare to dream of that great honour for the time being. Meanwhile I would like to get things clear before we overstep any mark. Could I come and have a chat with your father when I'm next in Somerset? He may say we're too young, but age doesn't matter as it used to, now that war's certain. I wouldn't wish to be doing anything your parents disapproved of, even if my heart was broken.'

In July he came to New House Farm for a week, and on the second night of his stay he asked Cath to supper.

She had answered the letter quoted above gratefully and in the affirmative. Many other letters had been exchanged since then, and the mounting pressure of the international situation had combined with the cares of love to relegate her parents' permission to secondary importance, if not oblivion.

The weather was fine. Danny had obtained leave partly in consideration of the need to help his father with the farm work, since mainstay Tom was restless and half-inclined to join the army. Supper was at seven-thirty, and Cath bicycled over and arrived at seven. She found Danny in the dairy, where the milk cooled – and they hugged each other, and then he had to attend to the churns and it was like the old unshy days with an irresistible undercurrent of anticipation added.

They ate in the kitchen: Mrs Ware said, 'You won't mind our homely ways, will you, Cath?' The food was slices of some great pie of ham, chicken, pigeon, meat jelly, served with cold potato and lettuce salad, followed by raspberries

from the garden and cream from New House cows, ched-
dar cheese and biscuits. They drank cider cup with fruit
and herbs.

In the parlour afterwards Mr Ware filled and lit his pipe
and Mrs Ware knitted, and Cath answered final questions
about her cooking course and Danny provided details
of how to fly a fighter plane. Twilight gathered out of
doors, and Danny said that he and Cath would save the
older folk the trouble of shutting up the chickens and ducks
for the night and checking that the farm buildings were
secure. He also said that he would take Cath and her bike
back to the Grange in the van. Mr and Mrs Ware therefore
rose to their feet to bid their guest goodbye and to thank
her for coming, while she thanked them for probably the
loveliest of all the lovely evenings she had spent at New
House.

Danny and Cath walked through the dewy grass and
then the farmyard hand in hand. In the deeper shadow cast
by the Dutch barn they kissed and kissed. The open-sided
barn was stacked high with bales of recently cut and dried
hay, which scented the air. Danny led her in and helped her
up on to the bale at ground level, then to the higher one
and the one above, and so on until they had climbed to the
top, as they used to when they were younger. He shifted
some bales: they were now in a squared-off space or room
of their own. Between the bales and the corrugated iron
roof of the barn they saw the sky set with shining stars and
the paler moonlight.

But they did not waste time on the view. They embraced
vertically and soon horizontally. The stalks of hay scratched
Cath's back and Danny removed his shirt so that she could
lie on it, and when his back was scratched she removed her
skirt for his benefit. Their passion was mutual yet mute –
they needed no words in order to understand each other.
He was climactically excited and she was initiated into

some of the mechanics of love. Yet she succeeded in shaking her head at one moment, and he in resisting the temptation to force the issue.

They parted with a long last kiss in the driveway of the Grange – Danny thought the engine of the van might wake Mr and Mrs Allen.

He mumbled to Cath: 'I didn't mean to go that far.'

She reassured him by saying: 'I love you.'

She awoke the next morning feeling happy and decisive. She went downstairs and ate her breakfast and for some reason did not warn her mother that she was going to speak to her father on behalf of Danny. She only told her mother that she had had a nice time with the Wares and shut up their poultry. When Mary left the room, Cath stayed put, pretending to read the newspaper. Her father joined her and she waited until he had kissed her, helped himself and was seated in his accustomed chair.

'Pa,' she began, and changed her mind: it had come to her that what she had meant to say was fraught with possible misunderstandings and difficulties. 'Pa,' she began again, 'can I ask you a favour?'

'That depends.'

She wished he had not enunciated any condition. She wished he was not wearing the half-eye spectacles he had invested in the other day – they made him look so much sterner than usual.

'Could Danny come and talk to you some time?'

'Danny Ware?'

'Yes.'

'I couldn't tell Danny anything he doesn't know. What's it about?'

'He'll explain.'

'I hope he's not going to ask for your hand in marriage.'

'Why do you say that? Why do you hope that? Danny's a marvellous person, and most fathers would hope he was going to marry their daughters. But he's so straight he wants to ask something different – which I think is completely unnecessary.'

Jack Allen, looking shocked and stricken by her exceptional outburst, redder than ever in the face and with creased brow, stood up as if to move in her direction, apologising thus: 'But I didn't mean ... I'll see Danny any time... My darling, please...'

Cath had also stood up and was taking evasive action. She flung at him over her shoulder as she headed for the door: 'All right, all right, I'll tell him. But who and when I marry is nothing to do with you, Pa, not now, not nowadays.'

She knew her mother was picking flowers, and she ran into the garden and found her and burst into tears and sobbed on her shoulder.

When Mary had grasped roughly what had happened, she said as she escorted Cath to the summer house: 'It is quite a lot to do with me.'

They sat clasping each other on the rickety wooden seat in the summerhouse under its mantle of wisteria, and Mary explained.

'You mustn't blame your father too much,' she said. 'I've been worrying about your friendship with Danny, and I've worried your Pa. You see, I loved someone very much when I was your age, and when I lost him in the war I thought, and others thought too, that I'd never get over it. There are all these frontiers you cross when you fall in love, and if things go wrong you can't get back into the country or countries you left behind you. I've been fearful that you'd do the same and run the risk of finding you were a sort of exile from everywhere. You're so young and precious – forgive me asking a boring question: wouldn't it be a good idea to wait a little, not to commit yourself too deeply, until you know if there is or there isn't going to be a war?'

'I am committed, we are committed, Ma.'

'Can I be awfully frank?'

'Yes.'

'Are you still a virgin?'

'Yes.'

'Oh Cath! I married my Theo, our marriage lasted for seventeen weeks, then I was a widow for five years. It's not easy to get over the man you give your virginity to. Truly, Pa meant well even if he was tactless, he wouldn't hurt your feelings for the world, and he's frightened of someone else hurting you. Perhaps his mistake was not to know how serious you and Danny are about each other. He isn't as romantic as we are, men aren't, and he was thinking of things that never occur to us.'

'He was thinking Danny wasn't worthy, that's what his voice said, he was thinking we were above the Wares and they were beneath us. I hated it, Ma – they've always been our friends. And Danny's such a gentleman, he only wanted to ask if it was all right to pay court to me.'

'I know, darling, but your father's a practical man, and just supposing peace broke out, or that dear Danny got through the war, neither of us would like to see you doing the work that Mrs Ware does. We're well off at the moment, and you'll inherit from us and might be able to afford help and service and all those nice things when we're gone; but I never trust money, it might slip through our fingers, and you might be a farmer's wife and a drudge. The old Wares are good people, and Danny's remarkable and may rise far beyond his family circumstances. To wait and see, and not for long, for a year or six months, would be a great comfort for us and a drop in the ocean of time that you and Danny will have together with luck.'

'What am I to do? I won't let Pa scold Danny for behaving perfectly.'

'Why don't you talk to Danny first? I trust you both to reach the sensible right conclusion. And I'll make your Pa see the error of his ways. Just don't forget, darling, that you're everything to us and we only want the best for everyone.'

Danny was cast down by even Cath's carefully edited account of the drama at Shelford Grange. His verbal reactions seemed to turn the knife in her wound, and his occasional grim and unfamiliar demeanour frightened her.

'Wait is just what I'm not at all sure I can do,' he said. 'Have they got something against me?' he asked. He regretted having held back in the barn – 'I wouldn't have given you a baby.'

On another occasion he remarked: 'Perhaps a baby's the answer.' He wanted to make love to her, he wanted to marry her. 'Would you marry me in principle? Will you be engaged to me?' He was not interested in keeping secrets from the outside world: 'That's the point I was trying to make.' His resignation implied a criticism of her parents: 'I'll pop in before I push off to tell them I haven't raped you or eloped with you or pinched your money or disgraced your family.'

She spent three days of his leave at New House Farm. Tom had gone somewhere to try to enlist in the army, Danny had agreed to do his work and was busy non-stop, and she trailed after him, helping when she could, kissing him when she could. He kissed her back, but with the addition or subtraction of an element of reserve. They shut up the chickens, but steered clear of the Dutch barn; and she failed to remove the trace of inhibition in their lingering kisses good night. They parted without their former feelings of fulfilment, and she was preyed upon by confusion, of not knowing who to blame and how to patch up differences.

She had told her father that he was forgiven, yet she avoided her parents. She did not know whether to act as if they were right or wrong, and left messages on the breakfast table to say she had gone to New House, and returned to the Grange to find their messages by the unlocked kitchen door.

She would have, if she could have, closed her eyes and ears to the news, but the elder Wares commented on it with outright unhappiness that was catching. Mr Ware said to Cath: 'We've a lot to lose in this war' – a sentiment with which she was all too ready to agree; and Mrs Ware scolded gloomily, 'Danny always would try to calm down the old sow when she was savage, he chose to do the difficult jobs, and look at where he will be now!'

On the fourth day the supposedly fated trio of unwelcome events occurred. First, Danny informed Cath that he had made a will and that she was his heir, although she would not be much of an heiress since he had no possessions to speak of; whereupon she cried, even after he explained that a will was obligatory for so-called air crew. The next thing was that a telephone call came through from Danny's CO, recalling him to duty and cancelling a day of his leave – he would have to depart at dawn tomorrow. The third was the worst. When Danny had paid the promised visit to Shelford Grange and talked briefly to Jack Allen and said goodbye to Jack and Mary, after that and after supper at New House, as night fell and he and Cath were making the rounds of the animals, she offered herself to him, body as well as soul, and he said no. Soon, he said – his article of faith was that they would have many chances in the future – besides he was owed more leave, they would be together again in no time – but he saw the point of not rushing, hard as it was not to rush when she was so beautiful and he loved her more than he could ever say and miraculously she loved him.

They did not part until dawn flickered in the east. And they did not meet before war was declared – he could not be spared by the Air Force. A month after the declaration of war he was reported missing.

PART TWO

Cath Allen held on to hopes for her Danny for six months or so. When she lost hope she mourned him with dignity for a long time.

Some people, lacking insight and imagination, thought that her parents took Danny's death harder than she did. Jack Allen, who had looked ten years younger than his fifty-odd years, now looked ten years older, and he wore a black tie. Mary Allen's complexion turned paler and her outgoing personality was somewhat negated by a new hesitancy.

Everybody's every ill of every sort was attributed to the war; but the three main characters in the glum drama being enacted at Shelford Grange knew more precisely why they were unhappier than might have been the case. They all believed they had made mistakes. Each laboured under the burden of believing that needless damage had been done. They were good souls with bad consciences. They were too honest not to tell, at least to themselves, the truth.

Jack regretted the fact that he had entertained scruples in respect of Danny marrying Cath. Although the inferior social standing of the Wares had suggested that it would be a misalliance while Danny was alive, now that Danny was dead and a war hero, a gallant youth who had laid down his life for freedom and decency, his attitude was revealed as blimpish, undiscriminating, heartless. He had counselled a postponement of the union, and in his position his counsel was tantamount to a ban: he had refused to sanction the joy of two dutiful and obedient young people caring deeply for each other in the shadow of the valley of death. It was unforgivable. He said so to Cath even as he begged her to forgive him, and explained that he had loved her too much and he hated himself.

Mary also cried in Cath's arms. And Cath tried to assure both of them that she understood they had thought they were acting for the best. But the golden bowl of their confidence in one another was cracked. Unease took its place at their dining-room table, and brought a chill to their companionship.

Jack and Mary braced themselves to pay their respects to the Wares – Cath went to New House separately. In due course they put forward to Mr and Mrs Ware the idea of a Service of Remembrance for Danny. It was held in Shelford Church, and attended by Cath and a full congregation. After a sort of wake at Shelford Grange, Cath shed tears before her parents for the first time, she as it were cried her heart out and accused them of ruining her life, and then cried upstairs in her bedroom for hours on end, comforted in vain by her Ma.

This unfortunate episode set back the cause of reconciliation.

Jenny and Helen were helpful to Cath, but all three of them were distressed in varying degrees not only by Danny's death, also by the dissolution of their gang. Peter Sengall had gone to join the navy, Fred Bannerman and William Douglas-Holt and even Timmy Topps were in the army, and Sheila Topps was determined to be in the RAF, not because of Danny but because she had met and was flirting with a Wing Commander.

War-work was another upsetting element of the afternoons the three friends spent in Cath's bedroom, listening to swoony records. Mrs Lestair was nagging Helen to do something useful and patriotic, and was suspected of simply wanting Helen out of the house so that she could take in a male military lodger. 'I'll have to go, she's virtually given me notice,' Helen said, and wondered where on earth she would lay her head.

Jenny had a different problem. She had received a proposal of marriage in writing from William Douglas-Holt. 'Oh, he's so preposterous, he infuriates me,' she complained. 'I mean, we haven't even kissed properly. And he hasn't got two pennies to rub together, and I certainly haven't and don't propose to win his bread. He wants me to join the army, be an AT or whatever they're called, he says we'll be united by wearing uniforms of the same colour. But I won't – khaki isn't my colour. Drat the fool! It's such a red herring!'

Cath's contribution to the discussion was that until she had pulled herself together she was afraid she would be a dead loss in any job.

Additional pressure was put on the girls by measures introduced by the government. The mobilisation of manpower and woman-power was forcing them towards decisions. The evacuation of children from cities into private homes in the country was disrupting the lives of most people they knew. Some bureaucrat had paid a visit to Shelfold Grange and opined that the Allens could accommodate one adult and up to four children. Another had gone to New House Farm and made a horrid reference to Danny's empty bedroom. Mrs Lestair had obtained a medical certificate to the effect that she was not in a fit state to share her house with young persons: which, as Helen remarked wryly, was not far from the truth.

Agricultural labourers signed on for military service in spite of being in a 'reserved' occupation, and domestic servants flocked to the new factories that began to manufacture munitions. Tom Walker abandoned the Wares, and the Allens' entire staff was gradually lured away by a mixture of idealism and the higher wages obtainable elsewhere.

The solution of the three girls' problems was as it were home-made in the end. Jack Allen arranged to hand over Shelford Grange to the military to serve as a convalescent hospital for the duration, while he and Mary would live in Grange Cottage, the former dwelling of their farm manager, in the village street – actually it was a five-bedroomed house. The Allen acreage was let for a peppercorn rent to the big farmer based in Upper Shelford.

Jenny volunteered to work at New House Farm – she was so sorry for the poor old Wares; later she joined the Land Army and became a Land Girl.

The Matron-cum-manager of the hospital opening at the Grange came to inspect the premises. She was introduced to Cath and to Helen, who happened to be visiting, and, having been informed of their culinary activities, offered them the job of running the kitchen and cooking for the troops.

They accepted. Cath kept her bedroom on the attic floor and Helen moved in next door. That Cath and her parents no longer lived together was not really to do with the rift between them.

Cath Allen and Helen Lestair were contractually obliged to provide cooked breakfast, lunch, tea with cake, and supper for the inmates of The Grange Hospital, Shelford. At first the work was light, only a few soldiers recovering from fevers or broken bones were admitted, and three nurses spent most of their time gossiping in the kitchen. But after the defeat of the British Expeditionary Force in France and the glorious failure of Dunkirk, numbers multiplied and the house seemed to swell in order to accommodate everyone.

In peacetime the Grange had had nine bedrooms, four on

the attic floor, five on the first floor. There were also box rooms, linen cupboards and clothes closets. Now, when space was so much in demand, Cath and Helen agreed to share one attic bedroom, and eight nurses occupied the other four – and were fully employed in caring for the wounded, who were often far from convalescent. On the floor below, the first floor, the five bedrooms had become seven and forty beds had been squeezed in, and the old drawing-room on the ground floor could take another ten.

Cath and Helen with help from an odd-job-man called Jim and occasional soldiers began – and continued – to cook for approximately seventy people. The former kitchen became kitchens in the plural: the pantry was their bakery, the scullery specialised in soup by the gallon. The girls were extraordinarily busy, busy from dawn to dusk when the heavy work started, although later they learned to plan so as to minimise their expenditure of effort. They grew stronger, their arms acquired muscle to enable them to lift heavy utensils, they were forced to keep calm in order to cope – and their kind hearts and pity for the patients they were helping to survive, not to mention the plight of their native land, kept them going without complaint.

The front hall with its great fireplace and marble floor was where the walking wounded assembled, played ping-pong if they could, draughts or cards if not. The dining-room was large enough to seat those who could get there – trays were taken to the bed cases. There was a nurses' recreation room in Jack Allen's study. The sheds and outhouses were used for the storage of medical equipment and food, as garages, shelter for wheelchairs and bicycles, and a car-port for an ambulance.

Once every month a dance took place in the hall. Somebody had donated a radiogram to the hospital; it played a sequence of eight records automatically. The nurses and the cooks queued for baths and to wash their hair beforehand,

and Jim was besought to keep the water hotter than usual. They changed into civilian clothes and painted their faces and wore shoes with the highest heels, and danced with some of the boys and played chaste games with others. The nurses would parade in the wards, and satisfy the request for a kiss from their illest patients. Cath found it physically difficult to support partners who could scarcely stand upright, and, for the first few times, because of her memories, to allow the sentimental ones to press close to her and dance cheek to cheek. But after a year or two she had mercy and permitted such minor liberties.

Danny did not exactly fade in her consciousness, but the hospital put his death in a new perspective. It was no longer unique, and she was no longer the only bereft girlfriend or wife in the world, in the country, in Somerset or even in the Shelfords. Nearly all the men she cooked for and talked to had seen friends die, and for that matter killed enemies. Loss of life was nothing you could get too excited about in her surroundings and after listening to the news broadcasts throughout the day – most patients and nurses had special reasons for listening to them. Danny was one of innumerable heroes and victims of mad politicians, and perhaps they were all receiving their rewards in a better place. She prayed for him or meant to, but the sleep of exhaustion usually came between her and her God.

At the end of the second year of the war she as it were awoke in various senses. She rebelled inwardly against an existence of overwork and recovering from it; her body and her senses stirred again; she was titillated by the nurses' broad talk and often bawdy behaviour; and she was involved vicariously in a romance that Helen was having.

Helen, post-puberty and even pre-puberty, had been keener on men in general than either Cath or Jenny. She grew into a big-boned girl with heavy blonde hair, and developed healthy appetites. Before the war, when she was fifteen and sixteen, she was apt to get into suspect wrestling matches with Fred Bannerman or William Douglas-Holt; and when Fred possibly sought refuge from her attentions in the army, she metaphorically ground her teeth with vexation because she had planned to present him with her virginity.

She had a good sense of humour and had succeeded to some extent in laughing off her ill-treatment by her mother. With virginity, in a manner of speaking, she had a field day.

'Once upon a time,' she said, 'when we were young ladies, our chastity was a valuable item of merchandise to take to the marriage market, but now we're plain cooks, plain in every sense, our virginity's not worth tuppence, it's simply *de trop* in wartime... Where are all the dirty old men who are supposed to pay through the nose for a virgin... You remember those Kiss-Me-Quick hats at Weston-Super-Mare? I'd like one with Deflower Me written on it.'

Helen fell in love with a different soldier at every dance. Unfortunately, if they were capable of dancing their convalescence was about to end, and they were removed by the authorities before Helen could again get to grips with them. But Jim, the odd-job-man, reached retirement age, and a military replacement, Tony, took over. Tony was a lusty Cockney in his later thirties, married and the father of four, but a flirt and a Mr Fixit who was always hanging around the kitchen premises and the cooks.

Cath said he was revolting with his Brylcreemed black hair and his Woodbines staining his lips, and Helen agreed with a bit of a snigger. Helen and Tony began to tickle each other as they peeled potatoes. She admitted to Cath that they had necked behind the pigs' swill, and was obviously pleased to complain of his virility and impertinence. Telltale roses bloomed in Helen's cheeks, and one evening in the bedroom she shared with Cath she confessed that Tony had dangled a French letter in front of her face as she stirred the soup: 'I thought it was a fingerstall.'

Cath was careful not to be a killjoy, she confined her comments to saying Helen was crazy.

Inevitably Helen then broadcast the glad tidings that she felt like a woman at last, and immediately followed up with tears and laments that Tony would not leave her alone and was a sex maniac. She was in hot water with Matron, the nurses humiliated her by asking how she could, Tony called her a whore in public, and the end of the affair was his recall to duty with his regiment.

Cath would not have been averse to making a little more of a dent on the opposite sex. She now joined in the nurses' chorus that there were not enough fit men to go round and they might as well be living in a nunnery. Cath was not sure how far she would be prepared to go with a suitor; but at dances, when she tried to be slightly more than sympathetic to some partner, she realised she was out of practice, she felt clumsy and ineffective, and wished she could at least find somebody willing to let her experiment. She was roused by Helen's example to be curious rather than immune, and often she was angry both with her parents and with Danny for dying.

Christmas came again, bringing her Granny to stay with the Allens in Grange Cottage. Cath and her Gran had always been close, and one evening Cath was allowed to leave the hospital to keep her company while Jack and Mary attended a local function. They ate cold turkey and mince pies by the sitting-room fire, and the old lady asked if the young one was willing or unwilling to talk about the past.

Cath muttered something ambiguous, and Gran ploughed on as intended: 'Danny was an unusually nice boy.'

'I know,' Cath said.

'In my war, the 1914 war, all the girls of your age wore black because their fathers or husbands or boyfriends had been killed – it was too sad.'

'Were you sad, Gran?'

'Often. I was very sad that your mother had married her Theo – it would have been better for her if she hadn't been his widow.'

'Do you think so?'

'Your Pa and Ma still can't forgive themselves for putting a brake on your love of Danny just before you lost him.'

'I'm sorry...'

'You don't blame them any more, I hope?'

'I wish...'

'Of course you wish. Everybody wishes. But the water's flowed under the bridge. You're very lucky to have parents who are so scrupulous and devoted.'

'I'd love to clear it all up, Gran. But I don't see much of them these days. And whenever I try to talk to Ma we get shy and change the subject. It's stupid.'

'Would you like me to be the bearer of an olive branch?'

'Yes. Yes, please.'

'Listen, my dear child, it's not the end of the world. I mean your trouble with your parents is nothing compared with the war out there, beyond Shelford. It's one of the minor catastrophes, even if the cause of it, Danny's death, every unnecessary death of every unusually lovely boy, is major. But we live and learn – you're alive and you'll learn. Love's for lovers, and that's worth remembering. Try to be happy.'

'Yes, Gran.'

Following this talk Cath felt better, somehow released, although she was never able to recollect or exactly piece together her grandmother's words of wisdom.

*   *   *

Six months passed. Cath and her parents acted as if a full reconciliation had occurred notwithstanding the obstinate tensions between them. And Cath saw men in a different light, although they showed no sign of seeing her in that way.

The new patient created a stir in the hospital. He introduced drama into the humdrum routine of the nurses and especially the cooks, who had neither the time nor the energy to react to every twist and turn of the fighting. He arrived in a Rolls-Royce. He was called Major Ashton and had a DSO. He was a handsome blond man in his mid-thirties with a loud voice. His left leg below the knee had been amputated, he had trodden on an anti-personnel mine, but he was extraordinarily quick on his crutches. He went into the first floor ward which had been the Allens' bedroom, and, against expectations, mixed in with his fellow patients, inferior officers and other ranks, without friction. He seemed to assume command of the whole place as soon as he hopped across the threshold.

Everybody was interested in him, the soldiers because he had belonged to one of those private armies performing destructive miracles in North Africa, the nurses because he attracted and teased them and oozed masculinity and sex appeal. Cath was no exception. In fact she was more interested than most because she knew him by repute. He belonged to a well-known and wealthy Somerset family. His Christian name was Leigh, and he had come into Ashton Court and its estate when he was a schoolboy. His parents died young, he inherited from his grandfather, and his long minority had made him richer still. Cath remembered her parents talking about him, the wild exploits of his undergraduate days, the girls whose hearts he had broken. The Rolls-Royce must be his own – he must have been driven over from Ashton Court to the hospital by his chauffeur.

Cath heard tell of Leigh Ashton for a fortnight or so, but

did not see him until he gave his lecture. Lots of patients tried to provide evening entertainment of one sort or another, and Leigh Ashton responded to public demand and talked to a full house after supper one evening. He stood in front of the chimneypiece and unlit fire, supporting himself on one crutch, and refused offers of a chair, while his audience sat where they could, mainly on the floor. He spoke of his war as sportsmen speak of hunting, shooting and fishing. He was enthusiastically bloodthirsty and boyishly pitiless. His stories had a believe-it-or-not quality. He and his chums had stolen a German lorry, joined a convoy of similar lorries carrying stores into a German camp behind the lines, and blown up the whole caboodle. In another German camp he had found the Officers' Mess, walked in, thrown a grenade at one of the officers and called out, 'Catch!' The enemy always fell for that practical joke with grenades whether you said 'Catch!' in English or in German, he explained. The quietest way to kill a chap was by garrotting, he suggested, although the chap being garrotted might pass wind involuntarily.

'I'm sorry for the casualties of war,' he concluded. 'But nobody need feel sorry for me. I've had a hell of a lot of fun scrapping with Jerry. The Moaning Minnies are off-beam, frankly – that's all tea party stuff. The truth is that peace is pretty damn boring, and there's nothing like a war to relieve the boredom. Why war? I'll tell you why, because it's capital fun!'

The audience, having absorbed the shock of these unconventional but spirited sentiments, approved with laughter and cheers.

One man had a question, a Scotsman, MacWhinnie by name, nicknamed MacWhiney because he groused so much: 'I take it you're speaking from an officer's point of view?'

Major Ashton rapped out in the silence that had fallen: 'Make your point!'

'Enlisted men don't have the chance to break all the rules as your lot do.'

'Wrong – seventy-five percent of my lot were private soldiers. And you have been insubordinate. Name, rank and number?' Major Ashton demanded in formidable tones and with an alarming stare.

MacWhinnie supplied the information grudgingly.

'I'll be informing your regiment,' Major Ashton said.

Most of the young women present were thrilled by this display of military might, but Cath was frightened. Although she could agree with Helen that he was impressive, something about him made her want to run away and hide. Helen would not hear of that: she was eager to introduce herself and wanted to use Cath as go-between. They therefore joined the queue waiting for a word with the Major.

Helen said to him boldly when the time came: 'We're your cooks.'

He laughed, showing white teeth that looked sharp to Cath, and inquired: 'Do I have two all to myself?'

'You do, and we're overworked and underpaid. I'm Helen, and this is Cath, who knows everything about you.'

'Look,' he said to Helen, 'you've embarrassed your colleague,' drawing attention to Cath's furious blush, and then he made matters worse by asking her: 'Well, what is it you know?'

'Nothing.' She had to giggle. 'I just live nearby and know your name.'

'What's yours?'

At least he was more gentle with her than he had been with MacWhinnie.

'Allen, my parents are Jack and Mary Allen, and we lived in this house until the war started. Now my parents live in the Cottage, but I've kept my room upstairs – Helen and I share.'

'Do you know where I live?'

'Roughly.'

'Would you like to see it?'

'Yes.'

Helen chimed in: 'I certainly would.'

'I'll organise an expedition.'

'Thanks, thank you,' the girls chorused as he turned to talk to somebody else.

Helen was sure she loved him following this conversation, and she and the nurses disregarded Cath's stated wish that they would all stop discussing Leigh Ashton.

Yet she herself mentioned his name to her Ma and Pa, and her Pa said: 'I wondered if you'd come across him. He's going to be invalided out of the army because of losing his leg, and he's shown interest in joining our Home Guard. He'll be a wonderful addition to the troop. In the desert he was a kind of Lawrence of Arabia, I understand.'

Her mother referred to Ashton Court, where she had once attended a ball.

'If you get a chance to see it, do, darling – it's very stately and fascinating, though I think it's teeming with refugees at present.'

'Major Ashton must be a marvellous fellow,' her father said.

'I suppose he is,' Cath echoed weakly.

He invaded the kitchen.

He stood in the doorway and asked: 'Has my leg arrived?' He meant his new leg, his replacement leg, for which he was waiting at the hospital.

On another day he cornered Cath in the soup kitchen and insisted on tasting the brew.

On yet another day he told the girls there would be a population explosion after the war, a plague of wanted and unwanted babies and a shortage of meat, and the unwanted ones would be eaten.

Helen laughed at his sallies, but for Cath they were too aggressive and edgy. She could see he was a leader of men, but felt she was the one woman in the hospital he would never lead. She wondered if sour grapes had anything to do with her shrinking from his physical presence and mental and moral aura. He was too grand or arrogant or both for the likes of her, she believed, and maybe she was a little put out by the emphasis he unintentionally laid on her inferiority complex. She supposed that it was Helen who magnetised him, Helen who now kept her warpaint on in the kitchen for his benefit and displayed her willingness without shame. She nonetheless sensed that he was paying attention to or assessing herself, and that she was not wrong to dread him, although, on the other hand, she had to admit he was less disturbing than he had been.

One very hot Saturday morning in July he issued an invitation. He asked the girls if they would like a swim that afternoon. Helen said yes, please; he said his ward nurse, Julia, was joining in; Cath said yes, but where; and he reminded her that curiosity killed the cat.

At two-thirty the Rolls arrived, and the party, which now included a second nurse, Marian, piled in, the Major in the front seat beside his chauffeur Dixon, and his four guests behind, two on the back seat, two on the collapsible seats. They drove for about twenty minutes, the girls speculating as to where they were being taken, giggling about their swimsuits and shrieking. The car stopped in a field, beside a high wire fence with a gate in it which Dixon unlocked, and they all trooped along a path between brambles. The undergrowth stopped and, as they stood on some gravelly stuff, they saw before them a huge, deep, roughly circular stone quarry, a bowl holding crystal-clear spring water.

It was on Ashton land. The stone had not been mined for years. Apparently the water rose from deep in the earth, was pure and fit to drink, always the same temperature winter and summer, that is medium cold, and flowed out into a stream and on to a river. And the swimming was private, reserved for Ashtons and their friends.

When they were all in swimming gear, Leigh, as he insisted on being called, pointed to a slope leading to the water, and the four girls hobbled down on their bare feet and with their towels and immersed themselves in different ways, Helen, for instance, attempting a dive, the nurses flopping in and Cath slowly sinking. It was wonderful, they shouted to the figure leaning on his crutch up above, it was bliss, they shouted, and urged him to join them. His stump of a leg was not raw or particularly unsightly, and the nurses said the water would do it good.

'In a moment,' he shouted back.

The moment elapsed, the girls were swimming and splashing about, when Helen gave a cry and pointed, and they turned and saw Leigh standing not on the slope but right at the edge of the sheer precipice, probably seventy-five feet above the water. What was he doing, what was he going to do, what on earth was he thinking of, they screamed – and please, please would he step back!

'Watch!' he retorted, and balanced on his whole leg, chucked his single crutch forwards, jumped after it so far as he could, and with a great wild yodel dropped down into the water.

He seemed to take hours to surface. The spectators screamed and swam as if to rescue him, while one of the nurses cried that it was suicide. He reappeared laughing. They all laughed after the scolding was done. He explained that he had performed the feat ever since he was a boy, and there was nothing to it. They had a jolly swim together, and his floating crutch was retrieved. Then they spread their towels on a patch of grass at the top and sunbathed.

The nurse Julia asked what he planned to do when he was demobilised. Become a squire and till his land, he said. Marry, the nurse Marian queried.

'Sure,' he replied, lying back lazily with his eyes closed.

'One of us?' Marian pursued.

'All of you at once,' he replied.

'Shall we play eeny-meeny-miney-mo?' Helen wished to know.

'No,' he said. 'No challenges – I'm looking for a strong quiet young wife who never challenges me.'

'Well, here she is,' Helen volunteered. 'And I can cook.'

He laughed at that, and Cath's temporary admiration of him was replaced by discomfort again.

The Rolls-Royce with Dixon driving began to turn up at the hospital regularly in the early afternoon. Leigh Ashton was taking soldiers for outings, for a swim or to see sights.

'What do you use for petrol?' Helen asked him.

'Dixon uses the rations of my other cars,' he replied coolly. 'The Rolls is Dixon's toy. I can't stick it, I feel I'm posing as the Viceroy of Somerset when I'm propped up in the back seat, but Dixon wouldn't know what to do with himself if I took it away from him.'

One day somebody knocked on the door of the kitchen, startling the cooks since no one else bothered to do so.

The soldier nicknamed Half-pint, because he was short and had been a jockey in Civvy Street, entered and inquired: 'Would you do me a favour, miss?'

The girls had learnt to be cagey: what did he have in mind?

'It's the Major's birthday tomorrow. Would you do us a

bit of a birthday cake? Here's the money we've raised to pay for it.'

On another day Leigh Ashton swung into the kitchen and said to Cath: 'You picked some nice parents.'

As had happened before she did not understand him, she felt she was being slow in the uptake, and looked blank and, she was afraid, stupid.

'I met your father and mother at a Home Guard do yesterday. They're good eggs. They picked a nice baby too.'

Cath was not sure if he was paying her a compliment or teasing or insulting her.

Jenny Holton was visiting her friends in the kitchen one morning when Leigh Ashton put in an appearance. Cath and Helen introduced her, and she burst out typically: 'Golly, you're the king of the castle!'

He took it well, saying: 'I've been called a lot of things in my time, but not that.'

'Oh, well, sorry. But I know you've killed most of our enemies, and I hear you've tamed the savage soldiers in here. And you are Ashton of Ashton Court, after all.'

He laughed and said: 'I'm more of a courtier than a king when I mix with the kitchen staff.'

Helen assumed a mock-severe tone of voice and demanded: 'What or who are you after today?'

'Two hours of your time and a little willingness.'

Helen and Jenny giggled saucily.

'I'm offering a tour of my ancestral seat. What about it, girls?' He addressed Jenny: 'Wouldn't you like to see where I first made my mark on the world?'

'I'd rather see your house than your seat.'

More laughter led to acceptance of his invitation. Jenny had the day off, the cooks were free on most afternoons, and all three were interested in Ashton Court. Cath knew she would feel, and be, safe with the other two.

But when the Rolls waited on the gravel sweep, and the

foursome was assembling in the hall, two telephone calls came through. Mrs Ware rang Jenny from New House Farm to say the bullocks had escaped and were rampaging towards the cornfields, and then Mrs Lestair's housekeeper rang to tell Helen that her mother was having a nasty turn. Leigh Ashton kindly offered to drop Jenny and Helen where they were clearly needed. Cath could not have wriggled out of being alone with him, unless she had been impolite.

They walked round the outside of the Victorian Gothic pile. He drew her attention to various architectural and horticultural features. He said it was on the gloomy side, but was evidently proud of it. She privately thought it was terrifying.

They went indoors. The hall reached up to the top of the house. They looked into two huge formal reception rooms, where the shutters were closed and Leigh had to switch on bare bulbs dangling from ceiling hooks that had supported crystal chandeliers. Nearly all the rest of the building was occupied by refugees, he explained, although not a soul was about and there was not a sound to be heard. He said be would show her the State Bedrooms.

She followed him up the bare wooden staircase, their footsteps echoing almost vulgarly. She was sweating and her legs seemed to be boneless. The first bedroom he showed her was all four-poster and red brocade, and he could only find the switch for one bedside lamp. The next was bathed in dim golden light, filtered by blinds. It was large, twenties-style, and had a double bed with a fur coverlet.

He held out his hand to her and said, 'Come in, Cath,' as she hesitated in the doorway; and the low intense tone of his voice confirmed her premonitions that sooner or later, and her fears that now, he would take possession of her.

66

'Your hand's cold and damp,' he said. 'Don't be afraid, I won't eat you.'

She managed a strangulated giggle.

'I believe I was conceived in this room,' he said. 'Cath, will you make me a son here?'

'Oh Leigh...' she squeaked, thinking: what a ghastly question, what an embarrassing courtship!

He gripped her hand painfully tight and said: 'You're everything I want. I know women and you're the one for me. Believe me! My bark's worse than my bite. You'll be my queen. Please don't turn me down.'

'Leigh,' she began, but changed her mind and continued anti-climactically, 'is there a lavatory?'

He pointed at and led her towards a door. They did not speak, it was all too tense for anything like foreplay. She locked the door and regretted it: she was even afraid she had been both offensive and that her response to the call of nature was suggestive.

He had removed the fur coverlet and taken off his tweed jacket – he wore civilian clothes while he convalesced. He stood beside the bed and was holding the top sheet and blankets as if about to lift them so that she could get in.

'Shall I, Cath?'

'Leigh...' she swallowed and gritted her teeth. 'Draw the curtains!'

His impetuosity was checked.

'Are you a virgin?'

'Yes – I'm sorry.'

'Well, I'm proud – thank you, my dear. It's all the better for me. But we'll need a towel.'

She had to fetch it, because of his leg, and the errand was the opposite of aphrodisiacal so far as she was concerned.

He hurt her quite badly, and she shed tears when he had finished, tears mainly of apologetic irrepressible longing for Danny Ware.

Leigh wished to do it again.

'Can I? You might enjoy yourself more.'

He therefore did and she did not.

As they dressed she asked: 'What happens if I have a baby?'

He replied: 'You should be giving me an answer instead of posing a question. Will you marry me, Cath?'

'Oh – good gracious! – Leigh, I haven't thought – I can't say, I can't!'

'Don't worry. Take your time. But I'll make an honest woman of you if you're bearing my child, depend upon it!'

She cried again in the Rolls, staring out of the window.

Helen was late back at the hospital that day. Her mother had had a mild heart attack, which, for all its mildness, would mean that her only child would have to dance attendance and consequently cause problems for Cath in the kitchen.

'You'll be working twice as hard.'

'Julia and Marian will probably turn to and help me,' Cath said.

They continued to talk in the dark in their shared bedroom.

At length Helen inquired how Cath had coped with Leigh.

Cath confessed and Helen made no secret of her envy.

'Lucky bitch! You were getting between the sheets with a glamorous hero while I was putting my horrid old mother to bed.'

Cath expressed a few of her reservations.

Helen said: 'What do you mean, unromantic? He's romance personified. He's fourteen years older than you are, you can't blame him for not wasting his time. But he's handsome and rolling in money and dripping with medals;

how much more romantic do you want your ideal lover to be?'

The next day, and the days after that, Cath had no time to dwell on her problems. When Leigh limped into the kitchen she shooed him out. But a fortnight after their sexual conjunction she became convinced that she was hatching a pregnancy and would have to marry the child's father: single parenthood was not an option for a girl in her circumstances in those years, and she would not dream of breaking the laws against abortion. If she was going to be engaged and then married in a hurry, she felt she must prepare – warn – her parents. She was far from logical in working out her plans, since emerging from the scene of her defeat at Ashton Court she had existed as if in a bubble of panic and exhaustion. She simply longed for her mother, the past notwithstanding.

They met by arrangement at Grange Cottage in the afternoon, when Cath's Pa would be out.

They went into the sitting-room and Mary shut the door and Cath said: 'Leigh Ashton wants me to marry him.'

Her Ma stood still, then tumbled a handkerchief out of the sleeve of her cardigan, began to cry, not just to shed a few tears but to blub with heaving shoulders, and reached the sofa and slumped down on it.

'What's the matter?' Cath, because such crying was unexpected, almost the opposite of what she had expected, asked between concern and anger: 'What have you got to cry about? What's wrong?'

'Oh my darling, I've been so miserable, your Pa and I have been so unhappy, ever since poor Danny died. We shouldn't have interfered, we should have minded our own business. We were very wrong, and it was the first thing that ever came between us – and we do love you so, you're our ewe lamb and our best beloved – and I haven't been able to bear it, and your Pa's the same, although we couldn't say so, we just had to carry on as if nothing had changed. Oh Cath, do forgive me! If you were happily married, perhaps you could forgive us. I'm sorry, darling, the idea of my daughter receiving an offer that dreams are made of has been too much for me. I'm crying with relief and joy – too silly – please tell me now, tell me everything!'

It was exactly what Cath could not do. If her Ma had asked a cautious question or two, she might have answered truthfully. But she would have had to try to be discreet, since otherwise, supposing she had said the marriage would be the shot-gun type, how would her parents have stood for it? As things were, owing to her Ma's jump to conclusions, her linkage of Leigh with Danny and her own emotions, Cath was reluctant to disappoint her even with half-truths and a semi-clean breast of the whole disastrous state of affairs – or, more accurately, of the affair.

'I haven't said yes,' she confined herself to revealing.
'Is that wise, my love?'
'I'll tell him next week.'
'Has he agreed to wait?'
'Oh yes.'
'I think he's worthy of you, I believe he is, everybody speaks so well of him.'
'Yes.'
'And he seems to be the most popular person in the hospital.'
'He probably is.'
'Have you been to Ashton Court?'
'I have.'
'Is it as splendid as I remember?'
'I suppose so, but terribly dark.'
'You'll make it light and bright. Are you frightened of all the responsibilities?'

'Not really, Ma.'

'Is anything worrying you, darling?'

'Yes.'

'Oh dear, what?'

'I'm just so tired, I've so much to do with Helen away for a lot of every day.'

'Can I help? You know how I've longed to help. Won't you let me? I could come in tomorrow morning at ten-thirty, say.'

'Oh Ma!'

'Please!'

'Well, I'm too tired to argue. Thank you very much. I'll have to go back to work now. Everything's fine, Ma – no worries. Helen's aiming to be freer next week, and my future will be settled – we'll all be able to relax. Tell Pa, will you?'

She ran away, figuratively if not physically. Their conversation had been such a strain that she could not bring herself to reconsider it. She could not imagine how it could have been better, or, for that matter, worse. She had foreseen her own cry on her mother's shoulder, not vice versa. The only filial compensation was that her parents at least would be pleased when she was Mrs Ashton, and the mistress of Ashton Court.

The following morning not only her mother turned up in the kitchen, her father came too. And he looked better than he had since the war started, redder in the face, smiling more broadly. They were both smiling in a delighted sort of way.

Could they have a word in private?

She led them into the store room, formerly where Jack Allen kept his guns and fishing rods. She wished he had not barged in, but was braced to receive his congratulations. She could not be cross with either of them for caring for her.

He kissed her tenderly and said: 'What an excitement! We're so proud of you, but we're not counting any chickens yet. What wonderful news all the same – I can't stop myself patting you on the back.'

'Thank you, Pa. That's sweet of you. But I've got pots boiling over and must get back for them.'

'Cath, your father didn't come along just to wish you well. He has something else to say.'

'Oh?'

'My darling, Leigh called on us yesterday evening and, without any sort of commitment, we gave him our blessing.'

'Oh Pa!'

'He's a gentleman, my darling. He himself said that none of us could speak for you.'

'Leigh never told me. It doesn't matter. I'm glad you're pleased.'

'We've waited and prayed for you to be happy again. Haven't we, Mary? The possibility you'd be provided for means such a lot.'

'I simply must go, Pa – forgive me!'

'Of course, my darling.'

Her father kissed her goodbye. Her mother set about peeling potatoes, as requested. A little later she discovered she was not pregnant.

At first she was sorry, then relieved, and finally more worried even than she had been.

That afternoon, before she could sort out the implications of the new development, Leigh Ashton again invaded her kitchen. She had been feeling unwell, worn out, sweaty after cooking the midday meal and clearing up, despite assistance from her Ma, and apprehensive almost beyond bearing; at the sight of him, so confident, so complacent and proprietorial, she thought she was going to be sick on the spot.

'Is it the day of reckoning?' he boomed at her.

'Please leave me alone.'

'I've met your charming mother. Your father invited me into the Cottage here. He and I had been saving the country at a meeting of the Home Guard.'

'You should have told me.'

'What? There's no harm done. I didn't consume much of their whisky.'

'Please, Leigh!'

'Are you ill?'

He looked at her sharply with a hopeful glint in his eye.

'No ... Yes – but it's nothing to do with you.'

'Well, you've chosen the right place to be ill in. Shall I send one of the nurses to take your temperature?'

'Leave me – do as I say for a change.'

'I'm sorry, sweetie. I've been missing you. Take care of yourself, won't you?'

At last and at least he obeyed her.

She drank a teaspoonful of cooking brandy and reached some decisions. She went along to the nurses' rest-room and asked for a volunteer to supervise the distribution of tea, which she had prepared, and possibly to do dinner, serve up the soup and share out the spam and salad. Julia and Marian obliged. She then rang Helen Lestair at home and said she was about to bicycle over and should reach Grindleys in an hour or so.

She was delayed in the middle of her bike ride by bursting into tears. She cried on the side of the road for ten minutes and as a result felt better.

Helen met her in the roadway. They asked each other in unison: 'What's wrong?' Helen looked as bad as Cath was sure she did, they both said they were in trouble, they talked of telepathy, for Helen had been on the point of bicycling to the hospital to talk to Cath when Cath rang, and they agreed that they wanted Jenny to be in on their outpourings and deliberations.

Helen knew that Jenny was having a half-day off. She re-entered Grindleys and telephoned to fix a meeting place with Jenny, Bluebell Copse, a small wood on Allen land but on the edge of the Wares' farm – the gang had played there when they were children. Mrs Lestair was luckily absent, keeping an appointment with her cardiologist.

Helen locked the house, and the two girls bicycled side by side through the empty rustic lanes in the summer sunshine.

At one point Helen remarked: 'This is a bit different from biking to have fun at New House before the war,' and Cath was choked by the lump in her throat.

They leant their bikes against trees and sat and lay on the ground in a clearing.

Since Cath was clearly more upset than Helen, who was fuming rather than sad, she spoke her piece first. Having brought Jenny up to date, she turned to the recent past, the events of earlier in the day, and to the future.

'My parents are dead set on my marrying Leigh,' she said. 'They stopped me marrying Danny, or as good as, and now they're trying to rub out that mistake by insisting on marriage to Leigh Ashton. They don't know him, they hardly know him, but think they do because he went and sucked up to them behind my back, and because he's a daredevil with medals etcetera. I do love them, and I know it's really not their fault, but I wish they weren't involved and I hadn't involved them. Oh God, I've been so stupid! I can't count the things I wish I hadn't done. Not being pregnant solves one problem but creates others. How am I to tell my Ma and Pa that I'm not marrying Leigh because I don't love him, yet I did let him make love to me without loving him, and might have married him without love if I'd been pregnant? How am I to make myself sound so horrible? They trust me – they're Victorians, they don't understand that the war's forced us to loosen up – they'll think me a whore or something, when I've lived like a nun and would still be a virgin if Leigh wasn't what he is and hadn't bullied me. I've ruined my reputation in their eyes, and am teetering on the edge of disgracing the name of Allen and shaming them, yet I can't, I can't marry Leigh because they would like me to – arranged marriages belong to the dark ages.'

How was Leigh going to take her marching orders, Jenny inquired.

'Badly,' Cath guessed. 'He's used to getting his own way, I agree he's a splendid fellow but he's spoilt, and he may well be angry with me, which I dread, or more likely he just won't take no for an answer, which is the next horror on my horizon. He made me do something I didn't mean or want to do once, and I'm frightened he'll make me marry him against my will this time round. He's always frightened me – I feel like a rabbit caught in the headlights of a car when he looks at me, and I'm terrified of losing my head and saying yes instead of no. I'd like to run away now. I long to be somewhere else or someone else. So sorry to be such a misery! Please, Helen, what's happened to you?'

Helen said after sympathy had made Cath cry harder than ever: 'My story's short and bitter. Mum's selling Grindleys. Admittedly it's too big for a woman with a wonky ticker. She's moving into a flat in Bath where there's no room for me or for storing my things, but she expects me to continue to keep an eye on her, cook for her, slave for her, as well as doing my hospital job. Well, I give up. It's goodbye Somerset and hullo London for me. I won't be my Mum's bonded slave any longer – she doesn't deserve me, frankly. Cath, why don't you and I call it a day down here and head for rack and ruin in town?'

Practically, it might be possible, even easy. Jenny had two Land Girl friends who were pining to swap exposure to the elements and the smell of manure for jobs indoors. Helen had an uncle with a house in Bayswater, an empty basement flat, and an important post in the War Office. He, her Uncle Toby, had come down to see his ailing sister, Helen's mother, the other day, and appreciated Helen's situation and offered her a better life in London. In other words Cath and Helen could probably hand over their kitchen work to two other willing girls, leave the hospital without letting anyone down, share the Bayswater flat and obtain work in the Civil Service.

Negatively, they could also escape unwelcome love and maternal selfishness, the straitjackets imposed upon them by older generations for mixed motives, and hot stoves and the dullness of their daily round in the middle of nowhere.

Bombs were preferable, they said with a hint of the laughter that acted like the sunbeams reaching them through the leafy trees. They were prepared to put up with a lot in order to wipe the slate clean and start again, they suggested. Helen was at once more precise and more basic. Although she was a cook she had not yet found the way to a decent man's heart. There were more men in London, even in Bayswater, than in the whole of Somerset – one must have her name on him, as bullets are supposed to be inscribed with the names of those they kill. Cath said that Leigh was a better bet for mothers than their daughters. When cross-examined about love in the afternoon at Ashton Court, she explained that she might have been a dugout full of enemy forces, that was how she was made to feel.

The sun sank lower over Bluebell Copse, and the tasks of

disappointing people that lay ahead of Cath and Helen again seemed to cast apprehensive shadows.

But Jenny re-emphasised the alternatives to Bayswater, Cath, by staying put, would be ten miles distant from Ashton Court, and Leigh Ashton was noted for his determination. The risk was that she would never be rid of him; and her parents would be always on his side. Helen likewise: she would never be free if she continued to live within striking distance of her mother – Mrs Lestair in Bath would be altogether too close for comfort.

The others advanced the excuse – for doing nothing – that if they were in London and Jenny in Shelford they would lose track of one another.

Jenny responded thus: 'I've news for both of you – I've nicer news than yours. William Douglas-Holt's getting leave, and he'll spend it with me. You know we've been going steady ever since the war started. Well, I can't be mean to him any longer. We can't short-change the loving boys who are ready to give their lives for us. I suppose we're engaged. But it doesn't signify. If we marry, or even if we don't, I might move to wherever was close to him. You'd do the same. You will do the same any day now. We must be grown up about following our separate stars. Our friendship won't change, we hope.'

They hugged one another in the clearing. Cath and Helen were happy for Jenny, and Jenny promised that a Mr Right awaited each of the other two in Bayswater.

As an afterthought Cath asked Jenny: 'Why did my Pa say he was glad Leigh would provide for me? Aren't we a rich family? I live on my wages, but I thought there were pots of money in the bank.'

'Your Pa lent or gave some to the Wares when Danny died, and I'm sure the Wares lost it, they're too old and old-fashioned to run the farm,' Jenny replied. 'Mrs Ware told me they could never repay your Pa's generosity.'

Cath funked it for forty-eight hours: Helen was stuck at Grindleys and not putting pressure on her to do anything drastic.

But then Helen returned to the hospital, having said goodbye to her mother for the time being and made arrangements for herself and Cath to move into Uncle Toby's basement on such-and-such a date and to have interviews with employment officers in Whitehall on the following day.

Consequently Cath told Leigh to come back to the kitchen at two-thirty. He had looked in as usual, expressed pleasure that Helen was back in harness and now Cath would not be so tired, suggested another afternoon at Ashton Court when Helen's back was turned, alternatively a swim or a little carriage exercise. Cath said no, no, no, and yes, all right, two-thirty.

She was ill with anxiety before the appointment, and her knees knocked together when he appeared in the doorway, filling the kitchen doorway, beaming, over-confident, as it happened, yet somehow impregnable.

He swung forwards on his crutch as if to embrace or at least be close to her, but she checked him, turned away, and pointed to one of the tall stools beside the kitchen table.

'No – wait, please – sit down – I'll shut the door.'

'Are you going to cook me something special?'

She ignored his question. She struggled to remember what she intended to say. She kept on thinking that she must be the first person in the world to cross and deny him.

She stood on the other side of the table, where the wooden spoons were laid out, almost symbolically, she fancied, and said in a quavering voice: 'I'm not having your baby.'

'Oh,' he commented, and repeated, 'Oh,' in a more sympathetic tone. 'Did you have a miscarriage, my poor girl?'

'There was no baby to miscarry.'

'That's a pity. Are you sad?'

She moved the wooden spoons. She was not pleased to be called his poor girl. 'It wasn't like that,' she said.

'Oh well, we'll try again.'

'No.'

'What? What do you mean?'

'I'm leaving here. Helen and I are going to London.'

'London? London's no place to be in the middle of a total war. I don't want you going to London when you're safe as possible in this hospital. No, my dear, London doesn't figure in my grand design.'

'Nor do I – nor am I going to figure in it.'

'Cath, I've asked you to marry me.'

'I know. But I didn't say yes. And now I'm saying no. Thank you, and I'm sorry.'

'Is this something to do with working overtime? Is it because you're not pregnant?'

'It could be both. But I know my mind and I won't change it.'

'Are your parents aware that you're rejecting me?'

'I'm not rejecting you, I never accepted you, I'm only giving you my answer.'

'People in my situation are always supposed to ask "Is there somebody else?" But I won't bother you with any more questions. I'm obviously not much good at courtship. The best I can do now is to promise that I could and would love you with all my heart and faithfully if you'd give me time and a second chance.'

'I believe you, Leigh. And you must try to believe me when I say that I can't make you the same promise.'

'What are you going to do in London?'

'Be a Civil Servant – not be a cook.'

'I'm expecting to get my leg and my discharge from the army in the next few days.'

'What will you do?'

'Be a country bumpkin, look for a little woman. Incidentally, you don't need to feel shy with me while we're still living under the same roof. I won't trouble you again. You've played fair, and I'd like to be your friend. Good luck, sweetie! I'll leave you in peace.'

Later the same day, after tea and before supper, Cath walked down to Grange Cottage.

Her mother greeted her with the question, 'Are you well?'

In the sitting-room, after she had kissed her father, she noticed that he looked poorly, both her parents looked pale and constrained, and she said: 'Ma asked if I was well, and I'm asking you ditto. Is something the matter?'

'What's your answer first?' he questioned.

'I'm fine – but I've got difficult things to tell you. What about you?'

'Perhaps we know some of the difficult things already. We saw Leigh Ashton two hours ago.'

'Oh no,' she groaned.

'He didn't come here. He didn't seek us out. He passed us in his big car and gave us a lift home. He said you weren't getting married.'

'He shouldn't have talked to you before I have.'

'Is it true, Cath?'

'Yes.'

Mary Allen had swimming eyes when she exclaimed unhappily: 'Oh my darling!'

'It's not a tragedy, Ma. There's nothing to cry about so far as I'm concerned. I quite agree that Leigh's wonderful, a wonderful soldier, but he's too much of a handful for me, he'd squash me and crush me flat.'

Jack Allen chipped in: 'My dear, you must be exaggerating.'

'No, Pa – I refuse to go into details – you'll have to take my word for it – but I'm not exaggerating, I'm doing the exact opposite. He saw me as a sort of fixture and fitting, or a rug to warm up Ashton Court and for him to tread on. He didn't mean to be nasty, I'm not even saying he's a bully, he was nicer than ever before when I told him there was nothing doing, but the effort of having to stand up for myself against his heavy hand and power and force, has absolutely shattered me. To have to battle to survive, so as not to become his shadow and slave, that's what I can't do. I never did love him, and I never would.'

'But why...? Why then...?' her mother gulped inconclusively, and her father finished the sentences thus: 'Why did you lead us to believe you were more or less engaged? Forgive us for wondering, my darling.'

'That was my mistake.'

'What? Leigh seemed to believe it too.'

'Don't, Pa!'

'I only wondered.'

'Very well, I will explain. I thought I was pregnant or might be.'

'You mean you were sleeping with Leigh?'

'Oh Pa! Yes, you could call it that, but it wasn't.'

'Although you didn't love him?'

'I knew this would happen – I dreaded coming to talk to you because I knew you wouldn't understand and I couldn't explain fully – and I'm not saying another word, I won't, because they only complicate the issue – and I didn't need to start on these stupid confessions – I could have just fled to London without saying goodbye to you or anything – but I felt I owed you the truth or part of it – please let's say no more on the subject, nothing, nothing, not a word more!'

She cried, she sobbed on her mother's shoulder, they wept together and mingled their tears, clasped in each other's arms.

Jack Allen voiced yet another question in a thick unnatural voice: 'London, Cath? What's London got to do with it?'

The emotional temperature in the cramped sitting-room of Grange Cottage rose disastrously higher.

Cath, between sobs, revealed her plan to decamp with Helen. She was going where nobody could get at her or reproach her.

Jack Allen pleaded: 'Not London, please – I'll never feel easy if you're being blitzed in London – please, darling!'

Mary Allen intervened: 'Pa didn't mean to reproach you. We love you so – and Leigh would have been a brilliant match, and taken care of you.'

Cath sprang up and began to stride about, crying and haranguing her parents.

'I haven't done anything dishonourable. It only happened once, it was my first time – and I'm twenty-one, and I didn't even want to do it. But Leigh behaved honourably by his standards – he always has, though he'd prefer me to change my mind if I gave him the chance – everybody would, because I'm being a fool to refuse to be lucky and rich. That's why I'm running away. Don't worry about London, Pa – I'd be in much greater danger down here. And I'll come to see you, I'll visit you often. What's certain is that we can't lead one another's lives – it was awful before, when I didn't do what I did want to do because you were against it, and it was pretty awful this time, when I did do, or tried to do, what I knew you'd think was good and right and clever.'

She knelt on the floor by her father's chair, by her father's knees, and, reaching up, threw her arms round his neck and continued: 'Danny dying was such a bad blow for all of us. It's taken so long for us to sort of get over his death. But, honestly, because I know better than you in this one case, none of us would ever get over the mistake of my marrying Leigh Ashton. He'd be the death of me, Pa, the death of me inside, at heart, even though he spent his whole life protecting me in principle and fighting my battles. I'm so sorry to disappoint you.'

She hugged him. The quiet room was full of partly stifled sniffs and gulps. At length Jack Allen spoke in his throaty voice.

'Shall we have a drink?'

'Yes, Pa, please.'

Cath sat back on her haunches; he handed her the brightly coloured silk handkerchief he always wore in the top pocket of his jackets; she said it was too beautiful to use for mopping, and he shook his head and left the room; and her Ma came across and bent down and half-embraced her and half-pulled her to her feet.

'Oh dear oh dear,' Mary Allen said, smiling, and Cath agreed to the extent of exclaiming ruefully, 'What a to-do!'

Mary then said: 'There's a little more to your Pa's attitude to Leigh, and mine for that matter, than you know. When Danny died, your Pa made a financial commitment to the Wares – we were so stricken with guilt for robbing you and Danny of your happiness that he compensated by doing Danny's father and mother a great favour. I don't know exactly what it was, I still can't quite understand, but it means that we may become poorer. Darling, I'm afraid your inheritance is not going to be what it would have been. Your Pa didn't like Leigh for his money, but he did hope Leigh would look after you in the material way as he was no longer able to.'

PART THREE

Jack and Mary Allen resigned themselves to Cath's removal to London. They tried not to fuss, or fuss her, about bombs and white slavers. They were spoken to by Helen Lestair, and spoke to Helen's uncle, Toby Desney; and were reassured by both with regard to Cath's prospects. That Cath had a job at the War Office to go to, menial as it probably was, and would again be working alongside Helen, encouraged them, and they could take pride in both girls' resolve not to leave the hospital in the lurch, but to wait for the new cooks to arrive.

Cath had no second thoughts. Although Leigh, on the day following his rejection, received his tin leg and walked out on it, he was only bound for Ashton Court, where something could easily go wrong with the real or the false limb and bring him back to the hospital and no doubt its kitchen. She was impatient to be beyond the range of his attentions, which he might well pay her if they were under the same roof, notwithstanding his stated intention. She was optimistic that life would be easy, would be lovely again, if she could just get to London without any more trouble over love of one kind or another.

Nevertheless, in spite of her decisions and her opinions, she felt herself drawn to Grange Cottage in this interim period. She was magnetised either by her parents or by her conscience. They thanked her humbly for bothering to call in, they were careful to exert no influence. She retained her conviction that they had accidentally succeeded in fouling up her relationships with Danny and with Leigh, yet could not bear to think they were unhappy, and that she was now the cause of their unhappiness. They smiled and laughed with her in a brave way that wrung her heart.

No more intimate exchanges took place. Communication on a deep level was by pats and squeezes, or a subtly extended kiss on the cheek. But all goodbyes were dramatic in the years of war. Moreover Cath and her parents were parting in an adult rather than a schoolgirl sense for the first time. She received presents of a brooch from her Ma and a small cheque from her Pa. The way that she and her mother embraced was sufficiently eloquent, and she managed to reduce her father to tears again by thanking for the cheque and adding: 'I believe you gave money to the Wares for my sake – thank you for that, too – and I'm sorry if it's gone wrong.'

In the train with Helen, who again expressed her hopes of romance, Cath wondered if she would ever dare to get embroiled with another man.

London in November was wet and windy. The days were dark and night fell early and lasted for longer than twelve hours. No electric light was permitted to show from windows, and street lamps were blacked out. Mournful air raid sirens wailed repeatedly, bombs exploded and guns fired, and the spent particles, shells and bullets pattered down to earth from heaven. Some people were visibly sad, others frightened, all harassed, and the air was scented with smoke and destruction.

Cath revelled in it. Against expectations, after a couple of weeks she realised she was loving London, Bayswater particularly, Uncle Toby's basement and her own little part of the War Office in a back street of Pimlico. Uncle Toby was not like his sister, Helen's mother, he was a plump jolly superannuated good-time-Charlie, a widower, a diner-outer and generous to the girls. He charged no rent for the flat, and took his tenants to choice restaurants where food rationing seemed not to apply. They paid their share of residential dues, and earned more money for doing far less than they had at the hospital. They had money to spend, and, having immediately noticed and blushed on account of their hoyden hair-styles and rustic garments, they frequented beauty salons and dress shops. They went to cinemas together and Saturday matinees, and everything was a novelty and a treat for Cath, whereas, in another unexpected development, Helen was overcome with furious feelings of having missed out on all the metropolitan fun.

The flat had two small bedrooms, and a south-facing sitting-room which caught a few rays of any sun that shone. They ate in as a rule, and once cooked a meal upstairs for Uncle Toby. The question that dominated most evenings was whether or not they should take shelter for the night in Queensway Underground Station, or remain in the flat and perhaps lose their lives in the next air raid in comfort and with dignity. Air raids were terrifying in one way in the lower ground floor of an old brick house, and terrifying in another way in a deeper rat-hole in the company of hundreds of strangers. When the bombs dropped close, both girls trembled in their separate rooms and wished they were joining in the sing-song in the Tube, and if they were in the Tube they wished they were at home, in their new home, and not having to pretend to be brave.

Every weekday morning they hurried to catch their Circle Line train from Queensway to Westminster. The work they did was sub-secretarial: in different offices in different buildings they were given papers to file, or orders to extract files from monstrous storage halls and bring them here or take them there. The task generally considered more important that they were allotted was to make tea and distribute it at eleven a.m. and again at four-thirty p.m.

The conduct of the war was not much discussed by themselves and their lowly fellow-employees of the War Office. All the girls had other things on their minds, but were pleased to know the Allies were doing better and not too many nice boys were being killed.

Members of the opposite sex worth serious consideration were conspicuous by their absence from the offices where Cath and Helen worked. The staff was composed of elderly Civil Servants and women and rare pairs of trousers worn by males unfit for military or other types of service.

The amorous atmospheres in London and in the hospital differed. In the hospital men abounded, but they all were or would be invalided out of the armed forces, they had been wounded more or less severely and were on their way back to Civvy Street, and were therefore in no hurry to form links that might prove permanent with anything in a skirt. London, on the other hand, was packed with able-bodied personnel on leave who in a day or two might be face to face with death, and meanwhile were mad keen to have a touch of female sympathy, affection and flesh.

It was unsettling for good girls, very much so for those like Helen. Modesty had become another casualty of the war. Not only prostitutes were kept busy in the doorways of unlit shops at night. In cinemas it was often hard to watch the film because of the number of patrons changing seats; and peculiar noises from the back rows were apt to interfere with sound tracks. In several of the bunks on the platforms of Tube stations a blanket or a khaki overcoat often covered two bodies, not one.

The advent of more and more Americans made matters worse or better, depending on how you looked at it. They were clean-cut, well-dressed, rich and far from home and homely commitments and responsibilities. Helen, who insisted on claiming that she was about to die of sex-starvation, said that for her they represented square meals or gourmet dinners. She repeatedly threatened to respond positively to the propositions of men in one uniform or another issued verbally or physically in the street, in the crush of queues or rush-hour trains, in cinemas, shops, parks, everywhere.

One evening in December she collected Cath for their journey home in an obviously transformed state. Her blue eyes sparkled, her cheeks were pink, she had a spring in her step and told Cath to buck up. Her story was that she had met Mr Right or rather Colonel Right. She had been detailed to deliver files to Colonel Weikleman, who turned out to be a glamorous thirty-year-old American with an extremely friendly disposition. He took the files and her hand, asked to be called Aaron, invited her to dinner and to show him round the town that very evening. Their rendezvous was the Dorchester Hotel at eight, and he hoped they could go dancing in due course.

'He seems to be a quick worker,' Cath commented.

'That's what suits me,' Helen replied.

Aaron and Helen were lovers before the next day dawned: 'Aaron agrees with me that in a war there's no time to be lost,' she told Cath. Their affair was consummated in the sitting-room of Uncle Toby's flat, and future carnal exchanges took place either in the flat after Cath was asleep in her bed or sheltering in the Underground, or in Aaron's office or his car – she was not allowed into his military quarters. They spent most evenings together, dining, dancing and the rest of it, and Helen was ever more deeply in love and happier.

She gave Cath accounts that were not too indiscreet.

Aaron was unmarried, a professional soldier, eager to finish his desk assignment and be back on active service, and consequently, despite his inclinations, unwilling to make promises he might not be able to keep: 'I don't care,' Helen said, 'I don't love him for the ring he could put on my finger.' What she did love him for was his strong masculinity, energy, forcefulness and sexual accomplishment: 'He's a gent in bed,' she said, and Cath knew what she was driving at.

But Cath was unmoved by Helen's eulogies, apart from preferring to listen to them than to complaints. Aaron in Helen's description was reminiscent of Leigh Ashton; and when Cath was introduced to him she shrank from his loud deep voice and crushing handshake for a similar reason. Again, she could see he was a good man, a dutiful and quite responsible person, while also seeing that he never would have been good for her. Virility figured low in her list of priorities, perhaps because she was not very sensual or, as Helen was now in a position to suggest, she had not yet been fully aroused.

Because Cath was happy too, not to mention her generous and unselfish nature, she bore no grudges and only hoped that none of the sorrows of war were in store for her friend. She had a love of her own in the shape of London, and enjoyed every minute of being free there even though often frightened. To be an anonymous member of the crowd, somebody and a nobody at the same time, suited her, although she did not know why and was not introspective enough to inquire or worry. She observed the passing scene with interest and amusement, and was never bored. She did not turn her back on her rural past, was not one of those women who combine new loves with hating the old loves, but she realised her latent urban leanings, and inhaled the scent of soot with gratification when the bombers had stayed away, and strolled and window-shopped tirelessly in Oxford Street and Bond Street, and slept like a top through most enemy action and invariably woke to excitement.

Talking on the telephone to her parents was like trying to communicate with the inhabitants of a distant planet. The fond tones of her voice might, with luck, reach across the abyss that had opened between them. Jenny Holton and William Douglas-Holt came to stay for a few days – they slept in the single bed in Helen's room while she was snatching a brief holiday in a hotel with Aaron. Sheila Topps also spent an evening with Cath between travel from one posting to another. These reunions were pleasant in the hectic wartime sense. Yet Cath was relieved to be virtually on her own again, or, as fantasy might put it, alone with London.

She was happy in her so-called work. In the phraseology of the day, it was a piece of cake, yet simultaneously and satis-factorily a valid contribution to the war effort – somebody else would have had to do it if she were to make herself, or be made, scarce. She served a noticeably good cup of tea, and carried files from one place to another with grace and charm.

When Christmas was coming she volunteered to remain at her post for the four days of the holiday. She was one of twenty or thirty members of staff to do so – the office had to be manned – and she received assurances from her Pa and Ma that they would be looking after her grandmother, they would join in the celebrations at the hospital, and they admired her spirit. She was still afraid of venturing into Ashton country, she would be safer in one sense in Bayswater, and, as Helen was planning to be with Aaron in some love-nest, she – Cath – would have sufficient company in the office.

The office party occurred on the twenty-third of December. It was a modest drinking of healths in gin and ersatz orange for an hour at the end of the working day – everybody wanted to get home as soon as possible. Fellow-workers, known and unknown, toasted Cath, and vice versa. Roy Fincham was amongst those who did so, wishing her a happy Christmas and New Year, and she followed suit.

He was Mr Fincham to her, because he was a minor executive, sharing an office with several colleagues, whereas she was a relative dogsbody on low pay. He was only about her age, a thickset youth with a hank of dark brown hair falling over one side of his forehead and eyebrows that met in the middle. She did not know why he was in a reserved occupation, and was inclined to despise him for not being in the army; also, although she would hardly have admitted it to herself, for speaking Cockney in a rather high tenor voice. She had carried files to or from him once or twice, and the only word he had ever addressed to her personally was 'Ta'.

Now, when they had exhausted wishes and he still lingered before her, he surprised her by asking: 'Have you got family in town?'

'No,' she said dismissively, averting her eyes and hoping not to be trapped.

'It's half-day Christmas,' he said, reminding her that the office would be closed completely from midday on Christmas Day until Boxing Day morning.

'I know.'

'I've been thinking – you'd be most welcome to take Christmas tea with me and my Mum – I'd fetch you down to where we live and escort you back. But you say no if you'd rather not.'

'Thank you. I'm afraid –'

'Say no more – just a notion. We're out Ruislip way, it's quite a ride in the Tube. Well, happy days!'

He lifted his glass to her, raised his small bright blue eyes to meet hers for the first time and, momentarily, smiled without any sort of ill feeling and turned away.

Cath called him back. She was pleased and touched that he had exerted no pressure: it was a case of giving because of not being asked to give.

'Mr Fincham –'

'It's Roy,' he said, not smartly, not like a smart alec, not flirtatiously, rather as a matter of fact, and hanging his head.

'Thanks for asking me. Yes, I'll come to tea. But you won't need to fetch me.'

'I would prefer to. Please, miss. Would three-thirty be convenient?'

'Yes. I'm Cath. But the office closes at twelve – you won't want to go home and come straight back – do let me find my own way. Incidentally, are trains running on Christmas Day?'

'They are – and please not to worry – I'll be at your place at three-thirty – and that will be my pleasure.'

She gave him her address and telephone number, and he nodded, smiling with his head averted, but the thought crossed her mind that he already knew where she lived.

She regretted it. She was surprised that she did not regret it more, although she was a little worried that he seemed to know her address and might be one of those fixated pests. But she was inclined to trust him, and disinclined to take him seriously. Perhaps he was simply being as kind as her second thoughts at the party had persuaded her that he was.

At the appointed time he rang her doorbell. She had not seen him at the office that morning, she had eaten her Christmas lunch alone, she was definitely pleased to have an afternoon plan and company, and shook his outstretched hand willingly in spite of being taken aback by the formal greeting.

They walked to Queensway Station, caught a train to South Ruislip, walked for a quarter of an hour, and reached a detached double-fronted Victorian house beyond a white-painted garden gate and neat front garden. The journey was longer than it had seemed to Cath to be: she had been pouring out the story of her upbringing and former life at Shelford – Roy was an interested listener and she felt as if she was shedding a load by sharing her past with him.

His home was another surprise, it was so pretty and snug, and a cut above expectations. Roy explained that it had been built to order for his grandfather, and had quite a bit of land round the back. The front door was opened by Mrs Fincham before they reached it. Her poise and dignity, her well-arranged grey hair, and her immediately warm smile and welcome – all was again surprising, not least because she was much more socially polished than her son.

Cath and she exchanged the wishes of the season, and the visitor was ushered through a tiled hallway into a parlour, where a dated sofa and chairs covered in red plush stood round a cheery coal fire. There were Victorian watercolours on the walls, and an aspidistra and a small decorated Christmas tree on tables, and soon a portly cat called Winston swaggered in and Roy went out to fetch first a teatray, then an iced Christmas cake, then plates of crumpets and sandwiches, and finally the teapot under its cosy.

Conversation was not difficult. The ladies discussed weather, rationing, shops, food, Roy joined in with office gossip, and Cath described carol-singing in Shelford. When Cath said nothing more to eat, she was bursting, Roy spirited away the tea things and set up a card table and a Monopoly board. They played Monopoly for an hour or so, and at seven o'clock Cath said it was high time she left.

Mrs Fincham, who had no noticeable accent, escorted her to the front door and helped her on with her overcoat, saying: 'You've done us a good turn, you've made it a memorable Christmas, thank you so much for coming, and I wish you and all of us a peaceful New Year.'

In the train Roy talked to Cath about the peculiar collections he had made when he was a boy, of farthings, for instance, and by her front door he told her in a rush that he had been sure his Mum would like her.

It had not been an exciting visit, Cath admitted to herself. But she counted the blessings of the mistakes that had not been made: Roy had never got personal, neither Fincham had attempted to kiss her, she had not been embarrassed by a Christmas gift, the Finchams had not threatened her with an invitation to come again soon. Mrs Fincham had not referred to Roy's feelings for her, if any, and nobody had trespassed on her privacy.

Helen Lestair brought back a plump country chicken from her trip to the Yorkshire Dales with Aaron, but in London she was out every evening in her lover's arms and at last begged Cath to cook and eat it without delay.

Cath agreed and thought of repaying Roy Fincham for tea on Christmas Day by asking him to help her do the eating. It was a bit soon, but she was sure he would not imagine she had designs on him – he was too honourable and humble. She felt they could be or already were friends, and he was also a male rarity in that she would actually enjoy a chicken dinner in his undemanding company.

Roy was his usual amenable self. He said yes, good, excellent, thank you, as if no time at all had elapsed since the tea party. He did ask if he could come to the basement flat at seven rather than at seven-thirty; but she banished the idea that he was seeking to prolong their evening unduly.

Her entertaining was successful, she believed. The chicken was delicious, Roy had two helpings, the chatting was easy and pleasant, and he said a few things that stuck in her mind. His Mum was the daughter of a teacher, he revealed; that was why she 'spoke so nice', like Cath did. His grandfather built the house in South Ruislip with his own hands, roughly speaking; he and Roy's father had been in construction, and the latter, Rex by name, had died in an accident on site in the year before the war. 'My Dad and Grandad never could get their English straight, and I'm similar – Mum can't abide the way I talk.' But both his parents were mad on education – as a result, he got his start in life by studying to be an accountant, then landed his wartime job in the Civil Service.

He said that Cath's sitting-room was elegant – 'not like our dear old dump'. But he liked funny places and things with a bit of age about them, as well as what was up to date.

He was always ready to yield to her conversationally, and he let her tell him why she had come to London, about Leigh Ashton and even about Danny, and was grateful to him for not making any class-conscious, judgmental or trite comments. He did not mention amorous experiences of his own, and she suspected he had had none although he was twenty-four years old; yet he contributed to the creation of an intersexual bond between them, even if of a Platonic kind. He was at once physically awkward, shy, reticent, and not at all shrinking or feeble – and he rang honest and true.

At nine-thirty he prepared to leave – 'Otherwise I'll be late on the job.'

What job, she wanted to know.

'Oh nothing much,' he replied.

'Late home, late in giving your mother a hand, is that what you meant?'

'Oh no,' he laughed. 'I do fire-watching.'

'What's that?'

'We spend nights out on the tiles – no, that's our joke – we take turns on the roofs of buildings in case Jerry drops incendiary bombs.'

'Isn't that dangerous?'

'Not much.'

He laughed again, perhaps ironically.

'How often do you do it?'

'Four nights a week.'

'After a full day's work? When do you sleep?'

'We're only on for a four-hour stint. It's nothing, really. I shouldn't have let on.'

'Have you always done it?'

'Since the war started.'

'What happened at Christmas?'

'I was on, Christmas Day – we ate Mum's mince pies half the night.'

'But you had me to tea on Christmas Day, and did the journey back and forth to Ruislip four times.'

'That was fun and games, that made up for having to be on duty at half-past nine sharp.'

'I think it was very gallant of you.'

He laughed at the idea that he was gallant.

'Thank you, Cath. It's been a real nice time.'

'No, thank you for eating so much.'

They went to Sunday services in St Paul's and in Westminster Abbey together, to see a weepie film starring Ronald Colman, and to Kew Gardens. Cath invited Roy to accompany her on the outings she and Helen had planned before Helen was otherwise occupied. She did not like to visit public places alone, and he seemed to be always available and to enjoy showing her round. She returned to South Ruislip for lunch on another Sunday.

One evening, as she was leaving the basement flat with Roy in tow, they met Helen. Cath was instantly embarrassed, then ashamed of being so on account of her friend.

She said to Helen: 'I wasn't expecting you.'

'I'm only popping in,' Helen replied. 'Aren't you going to introduce us?'

'Oh yes, this is Roy, Roy Fincham, and Helen's my flat-mate.'

'How do you do?' Helen said.

'Fine, thanks. Yourself?'

'Oh? Oh yes – I'm fine too. Excuse me, I'm rushing. Bye!'

They had been going to the West End for something to eat and to squeeze into any cinema that was not full up. But Cath had lost her appetite, and she hated the gangsters in the film they were watching. She asked Roy if he would mind leaving, walking out – she wanted to go home. They caught a bus, in which she sat in silence, and parted at the top of the stops leading down to her flat.

'Will I see you tomorrow, Cath?' he inquired.

'Of course,' she replied crisply, and by way of an after-thought she added: 'Thanks, Roy.'

She felt as if she had been caught out, that was the trouble. What had been private was public, owing to the encounter with Helen, and publicity changed its character. She had been caught cheating, not playing fair with Roy, whom she was not prepared to drag into her superior world, and who deserved better than to be used and kept in his inferior place. The purity of their friendship – of hers, that is to say – was shown to have its squalid side.

But it was all too complicated for her to analyse. She would carry on as best she could, that is as usual.

At her next meeting with Helen she was asked: 'What on earth do you see in that Roy?'

'He's very kind to me,' she replied with a hint of de-fiance.

'Is it a love affair?'

'Certainly not!'

'Well – take care!'

'Oh Helen!'

In Cath's interior dialogue Roy was defended more comprehensively. He was an unusually sensitive man: he had known better than to nag her with boring questions when she cut their evening short. He was unselfish: she had never seen a sign of the cloven hoof of selfishness in his dealings either with his mother or with herself. He was patriotic and public-spirited to do fire-watching night after night. And he was not without charm, although he did not wear his charm on his sleeve. He was confidential and trusting. He had the ultimate virtue in female eyes, dependability – Cath was unusual in not being attracted to vice. He had a sweet smile and nice white teeth, and his eyes were almost butterfly blue when he ventured to reveal them. His lank forelock was not much to write home about, on the other hand his hair was brown rather than mouse and there was a lot of it. His clothes looked as if they had been through the mangle, but at least they proved he had none of the male vanity that is woman's undoing.

The fact remained that she could not contemplate the possibility of mixing Roy with her Pa and Ma, or of showing him or showing him off to Shelford.

Helen rang Cath on their office extension, and said: 'Be in tonight!'

Cath made her repeat it, and replied that she had no plan to go out.

'What's happened, Helen?'

'I'll be with you at six. Till then!'

She was engaged to marry Aaron Weikleman.

'Call me Weikleman,' she cried on entering the flat. 'I'm

going to have the most hideous name in the world, Helen Weikleman, and I'm over the moon. It's madness and I love it!'

They had decided they could wait no longer, she explained. She wanted to be Weikleman, come what may, the Second Front in Europe and Aaron's involvement in the last battle of the war notwithstanding. Marriage would be advantageous in the meanwhile, Helen continued. Aaron could have leave to be with his wife, provided the wife was living not too far from wherever his unit was based. The obvious place in which they could cohabit matrimonially, she said, wrinkling her brow by way of apology, was the flat, her Uncle Toby's flat, and without delay. While Cath signified her agreement and willingness to remove herself from the premises, Helen, in between refrains of gratitude, said she had squared Uncle Toby, who had found an almost rent-free flatlet for Cath in the home of one of his friends.

All was arranged that very evening. Cath viewed the flatlet in the Nasmyths' house within walking distance of Uncle Toby's, packed her bags, rang her parents to explain her change of address, and moved out the next morning and into her new home later in the day.

It was nicer than the basement flat. It was on the third attic floor of the Nasmyths' home in London. Its sitting-room faced south and its slip of a bedroom east, and was sunny and airy and well-furnished. But it was nearer bombs. And the Nasmyths, although friendly, had a house in Shropshire and spent long weekends and school holidays there, leaving Cath alone.

Helen's wedding was an excitement in spite of only being witnessed by a handful of people: Mrs Lestair refused to attend, and none of the Somerset crowd could come, especially at such short notice. But after it Cath felt flat, and lonely in her eyrie above the empty rooms downstairs, and

102

nervous when the air raid sirens wailed. Moreover comparisons troubled her. They had insinuated themselves into her consciousness via Helen's love and marriage, and particularly by Helen's altered priorities, and replacement of her lifelong best friend in the scheme of things by her brand new foreign husband. Cath suffered, or began to, from reflecting that she had had no love like that in her life for ages, never really, and time was hurrying by.

She had nobody even to confide in now. She contacted Roy in the office and asked him to a housewarming party for two. He hesitated as he never had before: she was both irritated and saddened by his hesitation.

They were in the passage outside his office, and Cath wished they had not been in such a public place.

'Well, if you can't manage this evening, what about tomorrow?' she asked. 'I thought you'd like to see the flat, and I could feed you, I suppose.'

'I'll be in hospital, Cath,' he replied: 'and you can guess where I'll be sorry I'm not.'

'What?'

'I'm having an operation – nothing much.'

'You never told me. What sort of operation?'

'On my foot, on the foot that's kept me out of the army.'

'Are you in pain? Why?'

'I've thought about it a long time.'

'Sorry, Roy – are you paying for this operation so you can join the army?'

'Could be, with luck. We'll have to wait and see.'

'But the war may be over soon, and you're doing warwork here.'

'Lots of people could do my job, Cath. I haven't liked being out of uniform.'

'And you do fire-watching.'

He laughed and said: 'That sounds like Mum.'

'When do you go into hospital?'

'Tomorrow morning. I'll be out the next day, and back at work after the weekend.'

'I hope all's well, Roy.'

'Will you ask me to supper again?'

Cath was concerned. She was tempted to ring the house in South Ruislip, but resisted so as not to create a misleading impression. The restrictive questions she put to herself were, first, did she care what happened to Roy because there was nobody better around for her to care for, and, secondly, how much did she really care for him considering all the impossible differences between them? The dilemma preyed on her mind and increased the emotional pressure in the next few days without news.

But on Monday morning she hurried to Roy's office and was relieved not only to see him sitting at his desk, also to be reminded that they were not more than friends. He promised he was okay, and thanked her for showing interest. She invited him to supper on the Tuesday and he accepted in his somewhat jarring way: 'Rather!' Then his telephone rang, and she beat a retreat.

But she could not help worrying. He had not stood up to talk to her as he usually did, and had not looked as okay as all that. She decided to collect him from his office when she was ready to go home on the Tuesday evening, instead of letting him hang about until seven o'clock, the hour at which they had arranged to meet. She was glad to have done so, since he startled her by using crutches and wearing a slipper on his foot that bulged with bandages; and he was the more grateful, having just heard that his Central Line train service was disrupted by the previous night's air raid and he would have to find transport to South Ruislip before it was too late.

They took a taxi to her new home, which happened to be

empty as the Nasmyths were in the country; and Roy dragged himself up to her flat. She revived him with gin and orange, and soon served a high tea with scrambled dried egg and other wartime delicacies. At about seven-thirty the air raid sirens warned of the trouble in store for Cath and her guest.

Roy could not disagree with Cath's opinion that he was not fit to get to Queensway Station and down the escalators or stairs to where people sheltered from bombs. Again they agreed that they could not shelter in another part of the house and perhaps be found there by the Nasmyths. In other words they were stuck in the attic with only a flimsy old roof between themselves and the explosions they could suddenly hear. And the lights flickered and failed.

Roy made a joke of it. He had described his operation thus: 'They cut my toenails and snipped off a bit extra.' Now he begged her not to stand on the place where his toes would have been. But Cath was frightened of every-thing, being in the dark, in the dark alone with Roy, in the dark alone with Roy in an air raid, waiting to be maimed or done to death in all probability. She found a candle, but her hand shook so much that she kept on extinguishing matches.

'Shall I have a go?' he asked.

'You're so brave,' she returned almost resentfully.

'I'm not brave inside.'

'Here are the matches,' she said.

A bomb landed unpleasantly close. She screamed and then apologised. He said: 'I'm all for you screaming, it proves you're alive.' There was the sound of fire-engines clanging their bells. Silence reigned in the flat while Cath drew deep breaths and she and Roy listened. They were still seated at the card table in the sitting-room, spread with its chequered cloth and bearing the candle on one of their side-plates.

105

'I'll leave you as soon as it's All-Clear,' Roy volunteered.

'What's the time?' she asked inconsequentially.

'Half after eight. Sorry, Cath, you wouldn't be in this fix if I wasn't here.'

'Oh do shut up! Thank goodness you are here. I'm sorry to be such a coward.'

'Well, I think it's all over even if we haven't had the All-Clear, and I should be moving on. I haven't heard a thing since we had the big one.'

'Not even my teeth chattering?'

'That's better. That's more like you. I'll be gone, and you can scamper along to the Tube.'

'No, Roy, please, I'm not having you taking risks for me, and I couldn't bear to be out in the street while it's still dangerous.'

A bomb landed and shook the house.

Cath repeated her scream with groan added, and said in a voice that trembled: 'Stay with me, stay the night.'

An hour and a half might have been for ever; but the time eventually passed. Bombs fell at intervals during it, some nearer than others, all too close, and anti-aircraft shrapnel pattered down on the roof, breaking slates. Ambulances as well as fire-engines were heard, and then the sinister buzzing of high-flying aeroplanes.

People get used to anything, they say. The saying was inapplicable to Cath Allen and Roy Fincham under fire in semi-darkness. But there were intermissions, breaks brought about more by boredom than by changes in their situation, when they chatted less fearfully than before and more inti-mately than they ever had.

Roy wished and managed to ring his Mum, and, when he had finished, said to Cath: 'I'm no mother's boy, not what they call a mother's boy, I stay with Mum because she doesn't want to sell the house and it's too big for her. It saves me money besides, and I respect her and love her dearly. I was always shy with girls, that's the truth.'

'You're not shy with me,' Cath said tactfully, although she was well aware of the shyness between them, which would have been intrusive even as she spoke if they could have seen each other distinctly.

He giggled and retreated into one of his ambiguous Cockneyisms: 'Not half!'

In another break she tried to describe Leigh Ashton.

'He must be like a great man. He may be a great man, for all I know. He dominates everyone and everything, but he doesn't really connect with ordinary normal people. He wouldn't be a hero to his wife – she'd be ground to dust beneath his feet, but he wouldn't let anybody else harm her.'

'Are you glad he didn't catch you?' Roy inquired.

'Not half,' she mimicked him.

'Same here,' he commented.

Round about ten-thirty he asked the question that inaugurated a change in their relations: 'I couldn't trouble you for an aspirin, could I?'

He admitted under pressure that he was in some pain, he had not had his foot up, he needed to lie flat. She fetched aspirin, she tried in vain to fit him in on the floor of her sitting-room, she wrung her hands and said that his pain was pretty well the last, or the worst, straw for her. She then supported him into her bedroom, where there was even less floor space, and persuaded him, begged, bullied, commanded him, to lie on her bed. She took off his shoe and his slipper, made him remove his jacket and tie, covered him with her eiderdown, and wished she could boil water on her electric cooker in order to bring him a cup of tea.

She brushed aside his gratitude. She was near to crying

in the dark. When he asked where she was to sit or rest, she snapped that she would be in the sitting-room.

But there were only wood-seated kitchen-type chairs in the sitting-room, and she had no sooner perched herself on one than flashes of light penetrated the black-out curtain followed by deafening explosions mixed with the tinkle of shattered panes of the glass in her sash window.

She fled back to the bedroom and clung to Roy. She was half on and half off the bed. They were both talking at once: 'I can't... So sorry... You climb in... No harm done!' She lay beside him and he put his arm round her shoulders. They heard odd thumps, perhaps of masonry collapsing not too far away, also a commotion of police and other service vehicles, of people shouting and running out in the streets, and they smelt smoke. Roy disentangled from Cath and went to investigate, while she covered her ears with the pillow. He returned, said he could see the fire far down the Bayswater Road, clambered back on to the bed and again enfolded her in his arms, stroking the back of her head and her shoulders.

The All-Clear finally sounded. Neither of them moved. In time their breathing altered in unison.

At length she whispered: 'Shouldn't we get into the bed?'

'You must,' he replied.

After a pause she asked: 'Won't you?'

'Not like this, Cath,' he said; 'not thanks to Jerry scaring us. It means too much to me, see? Maybe you haven't twigged that you're the one I love. But you don't need to pay attention. You don't need ever to see me or speak to me again, Cath – I promise that, I swear on your head I won't ever get in your way or darken your doorstep – and swearing on your head's serious business for me. But now I've started I might as well say the lot. I fell for you at first sight. I'm yours for life if you want me. If you'd consent to be my wife I wouldn't ask for any more luck, not on this planet. If not, I'll stay single and I'll be content, so you'll be able to forget me. I've not much to offer, I know – you deserve more, Cath. There! What a speech! No. I'm not listening to any answer, not while you're worked up, not because you're kind. You think carefully, double carefully. No kindness, either. One more word, thanks for being you.'

The lights came on at midnight. They had lain close, but not talking much, and exchanging no caresses. They now got up and had a midnight feast of biscuits and tea, and began to giggle a little over their ordeal. Roy had a shot at packing newspapers and cardboard into the empty windowpanes, and cut himself on the glass and was called 'Jonah'. She changed into her nightdress and got back into bed, under the covers, and he resumed his former position, fully dressed under the eiderdown. When they kissed good night or good morning, he avoided her lips.

At six o'clock he kissed and left her. He was determined to get back to South Ruislip to shave and wash and change his clothes before the working day. And at nine o'clock Cath was at her desk and thankful she had not run into Roy while reaching it – shortage of sleep was not considered a good excuse for absenteeism in those days.

She and Helen met to eat their sandwiches together in the lunch hour. Cath had trouble eating hers, and when she explained why Helen said: 'No wonder!'

They had walked into St James's Park and sat on the ground under one of the plane trees, leaning back against its great dappled trunk and watching the waterfowl on the lake.

Cath began by agreeing that Roy Fincham was not the most suitable match in the whole world. Then she emphasised some of his less obvious attractions. He had never shown her anything but a smiling face; he had never once

109

put pressure on her; he was a solid citizen, and was proving his patriotism by means of his operation and his aim of serving in the armed forces; he had no chip on his shoulder, and she could vouch for his virility even though the night they had spent in or on the same bed had been white.

'What did he do in Civvy Street?' Helen asked.

'He was in an accountancy business. He's clever with figures and won prizes for maths at school. He's not terribly ambitious, but he is keen to get on and improve himself. He's not lazy.'

'Would you have to live in South Ruislip with his mother?'

'That's crossing far too many bridges. I haven't said yes to anything yet. Don't frighten me! Roy was so careful not to frighten me when he made his declaration, he almost won my heart there and then by saying he'd never worry me if I chose to say no. Anyway, his mother's the least of the problems, she's a lovely person.'

'Are they religious?'

'Roy is, he goes to Communion on Sundays, but he didn't tell me that, his mother mentioned it in passing.'

'Why don't you marry him? It'd make a change at least, I mean a change from Leigh Ashton and from Shelford Grange. And there's always divorce to fall back on.'

'Oh, I couldn't ever divorce him, I couldn't bear to hurt him so much.'

Later, in the evening, Cath rang and spoke to Jenny Holton, who, in response to her confidences, made the point that good sons were supposed to become good husbands.

'Would my parents take that view?' Cath inquired or rather whimpered apprehensively.

'Does the class thing worry you yourself?'

'No, not at all when I got used to the way Roy talks, not when he shows how nice he is, not if we could spend the rest of our lives on a desert island. But it won't be easy with friends to start with. And my Pa and Ma are so apt to misunderstand me and my love-life.'

'Can't you just have an affair and call it a day or a night?'

'No – he wouldn't – he won't – he says he loves me for life, Jenny, and I believe him – it's an all or nothing predicament, and I don't know what to do.'

'Sleep on it!'

'Yes, I will – or I won't – thank you, dear Jenny.'

But Cath did not immediately retire to bed in her flat in the Nasmyths' house. She was afraid of another air raid and that she was keeping Roy on tenterhooks. She felt herself being torn in different directions. Her clearest thought or sensation was that she missed him. She tenderly washed once more the carpet on which he had spilt his blood in order to keep her draught-free.

At last exhaustion overwhelmed her, and she went to bed and to sleep for hours. She awoke to, or was perhaps woken by, the memory of her Granny telling her 'Love's for lovers'. Her understanding of it seemed to cause her heart to swell and her spirits to rise.

She reached the office early and wrote the following note to Roy: 'Please come to my flat as soon as you can after work. Only reply to this if you're not able to come. C.' She asked a messenger boy she trusted to deliver it into the hand of Roy Fincham.

She survived the working day and excused herself half an hour before it was due to end. She bought some stuff to eat on the way home, then waited for Roy in the downstairs hall. She was impatient but not nervous. She was sure of herself and sure of him.

They told each other they were happier than ever before in their lives. They were happier still as every day passed. They met in the evenings, they spent most of their weekends together. They walked hand-in-hand through the spring weather, laughing at nothing, daring the war to make them sad. They ate together, they spent hours in bed, they pined when they were apart. But no decisions bigger than the one to love and be loved were taken.

Roy did not spend another night in Cath's flat, he always caught the last tube to South Ruislip. She had ruled that she could not keep him away from his mother until she was ready to talk to her and to give her definite and possibly welcome news. And Cath was not ready, and explained that she was in an even more complicated position than her attitude to his mother suggested. She not only preferred to remain his girlfriend rather than his fiancée in maternal and mundane eyes for the time being, she also could not discuss matters with his mother before she had discussed them with her own.

That she dreaded the introduction of Roy into her family was not a secret between them. An element of her joy was that he guessed at her secrets before she shared them with him, and that however they came into his keeping he never used them to embarrass her in any way. He had no vain illusions as to how he would be regarded by Cath's parents, but did hope that in time they would get to know him better and might forgive him for loving their daughter and trespassing so far above his station in life. However, they had now been lovers for getting on for a month, and they both increasingly felt that action had to be taken before nature chose to force the issue.

One evening Cath rose above her remaining inhibitions and presented Roy with the proof of her surrender or her conquest. They were not in intimate circumstances, they were not even alone, they were walking along the Bayswater Road after seeing a film at the Marble Arch Odeon, and the pavement teemed with people. They had their arms round each other, and she matched her footsteps with his limp.

112

She said: 'Couldn't we make it legal without anyone else being involved? Just in case, because I long to bind you to me and be bound to you, couldn't we tie the knot in a Register Office, and be married later on in church?'

He hugged her tighter, expressed pleasure and excitement, and asked: 'Are you pregnant, Cath?'

'I don't know. But you told me you were mine, and now I want to be yours in every sense.'

'Oh Cathy, my Cath, you're so lovely to me! But I can't make any of our dreams come true, not until I've spoken to your people – I'd feel a sneak and a thief, a sneak-thief, and that I'd not done things right and proper.'

She had to agree. She sighed and agreed. And later, when passion had exhausted itself and heads were cooler, they decided that the best plan would be for her to go down to Grange Cottage for the weekend, travelling on the Saturday, and that he should follow on Sunday. If he set off from South Ruislip at dawn he ought to reach Upper Shelford round about noon, she would fetch him by car, they would have lunch with her parents, Roy could talk to her Pa, and the couple who might be engaged by then would travel back to London through the rest of the day.

She arranged things accordingly, and reached Grange Cottage at six o'clock on the Saturday in question, having been driven from Upper Shelford by the local taxi.

She had not seen her Ma and Pa for three and a half months. Their reunion was bound to be emotional. But Cath in her overwrought state could not stifle her sobs or stop tears rolling down her cheeks – she was so shocked by how much her parents had aged in the interval. It was as if they were blanched; they looked anaemic. Her Pa filled his pipe with trembling hands, and her Ma never removed her spectacles. They both said in answer to her queries that they had been too busy with the Home Guard and the WI and so on, and that they found the war a constant strain. When they commented on her good looks, she dissolved again.

But love is supposed to cast out fear, and in time she braced herself for their interrogation.

Mary Allen asked: 'Are you happy, darling?' – a reference especially perhaps to Cath's tearfulness.

Very, Cath claimed.

'We're so intrigued by your friend who's coming down to see us tomorrow. What's his name?'

Cath gave it and added: 'You don't know his family, Ma.'

Her Pa said: 'He must be very fond of you to take a day-trip to Shelford and back to London for a bite of lunch.'

She replied: 'He works in the War Office too, and we've become close friends.'

'How close is close?'

'That depends, Pa.'

Mary intervened: 'Can you tell us more about him, Cath?'

Cath gulped and ran through a catalogue of Roy's virtues, and his fire-watching and how brave and cool he was in air raids and crises in general.

'Why isn't he in the services?' Jack asked.

Cath had to go through the rigmarole of the whys and wherefores of Roy's foot and the operation.

'What's wrong with his foot?'

'Nothing, Pa, now, we hope. But he wasn't passed A1 for military service before he had the operation. You'll have to ask him to show you his foot if you're so interested. He had a problem toe or two. He may be A1 as a result of the op.'

Mary weighed in again: 'Where did you say he and his mother live?'

'In South Ruislip in a pretty house with a garden.'

'I'm afraid I don't know where South Ruislip is.'

'It's up north – I don't know where it is geographically – but it's easy to get to on the Tube.'

Jack said: 'Nothing like a farm, and no farmers, in those suburbs, I imagine.'

'I'm afraid not, Pa.'

'Ah well – I expect he's a charming chap if you think such a lot of him.'

'He is – and he's not – I'm worried that you'll find him not like the friends I used to have. He's the exact opposite of Leigh Ashton – and he never went to public school. Can't we leave it at that until you've seen for yourselves?'

'Of course, darling,' Mary hurried to say in soothing accents, and Jack chimed in: 'You should know what Nosey Parkers we are, but we don't mean any harm.'

The rest of their evening together was constrained, although they pretended it was like old times. They all regretted their earlier conversation. Jack felt he had been clumsy, Mary that she should have kept Jack quiet and talked to Cath alone, and Cath that she had not needed to be so brusque. Their kisses good night were mainly apologetic.

Cath slept badly. Her loyalties seemed to tie her thoughts into knots. She knew that if she had described Roy and his courtship in detail she might have won her parents over, and if she were to do so in the morning Roy would probably secure their blessing; but to excuse the man she loved would be to accuse him – she would have to draw attention to his class, his accent, his unimpressive appearance, as if they were defects, faults, and to claim that what he had overcome in order to win her hand and her heart were not so much her own uncertainties as his drawbacks. She could not do it. She could not bring herself to utter a word against the man who would die to defend her against the slightest calumny.

On the other hand it was cruel of her not to help her parents more. The filial duty to cut the emotional cord had been fraught with difficulty in her case. That she was an only child, affectionate and biddable, and her Pa and Ma had always been loving and good to her, prolonged the agony – for such gentle people to hurt and be hurt for a change was agonising. But history as well as her new allegiance combined to compel Cath in the hurtful direction.

She got through the next morning somehow, although every friend of hers in the hospital, every old and young retainer in the Shelford cottages, passed tactless remarks about her unmarried and childless state. She duly borrowed the family Rover and fell into the arms of Roy at Upper Shelford Station, notwithstanding his shiny dark suit and his presentation of himself which she had never bothered about before.

Lunch, for Cath, was pain. Her parents' valiant struggle to be polite and pleasant caused her to wince inwardly. Roy's conversational efforts made her soul ache and cast a cloud over the future. He was too respectful, addressed Mary Allen as Madam until she instructed him otherwise, had to ask Cath for guidance in respect of the cutlery he should use, called the cottage a house and showed surprise when Jack Allen told him the family home was actually four times bigger, and expressed a hope that Mr and Mrs Allen would one day come for a meal with him and his mother in their humble abode.

After lunch Cath whispered to her mother, and the ladies withdrew.

In the sitting-room Cath said: 'I love him, Ma, I love him more than you can understand yet, I expect, but you will love him too.'

Her mother mumbled yes, and they embraced and waited.

When the men emerged Roy spoke to Mary Allen thus: 'Your husband has just given me permission to ask your girl to be Mrs Fincham. Cath's my life, my whole life, that's the long and short of it, and I can't say more. But if we marry – all right, when we marry – and ever afterwards, if I could help you or Mr Allen anyhow, any time, at all costs, I will.'

Then the four of them had to hurry into the Rover, which Jack drove to Upper Shelford, where they were to catch their train back to London.

Jack and Mary shook hands with Roy and kissed Cath goodbye. Wishes for a safe journey, all sorts of good wishes were exchanged. But the maternal cheek that Cath kissed was wet and salty, and she thought her father would never let her go.

In the train Roy asked Cath: 'Did I embarrass you?'

'Not at all,' she replied.

'I must have made mistakes.'

'You didn't.'

'Did I say the wrong thing?'

'No. What you did and said was right for me.'

'I know I wasn't dressed correctly. I should have worn a tweed jacket, like your Dad, but I haven't got one. You never told me what to wear.'

'I want you to be yourself, I don't want you to be like anybody else.'

'That promise I made –you know, about helping out – was it cheeky? Would your Dad think I was being cheeky?'

'No – how could he? – and it doesn't matter. Your promise was beautiful.'

'I wouldn't offend your people for the world. They were good to me, considering.'

'You're my people now,' Cath assured him.

Later he said: 'There was one thing missing today. I never popped the question. Will you marry me, Cath? Sorry I can't get down on my knees.'

'Please,' she replied.

Later she slept with her head on his shoulder, and woke to a strange new sense of peace and strength. She had not cried on the station platform. She had shrugged away the negative aspects of the last twenty-four hours, and was exclusively happy to be alone with Roy again. She looked ahead to the future with a certainty that had nothing to do with complacence.

They parted reluctantly; but Roy wanted to carry the good news to his Mum without delay.

The next day Cath received, via Roy, a letter from Mrs Fincham, saying every possible nice thing and signed Annie.

The day after that the post brought Cath a letter from Jack Allen which ran: 'My dearest, more congratulations! You deserve great joy, and I hope and pray you will be granted it with the man of your choice. Roy Fincham impressed me, and there is no doubt that he has behaved impeccably over your engagement. He is also lucky, a useful attribute! Forgive me for striking one cautionary note. You will remember, probably even better than we do, the awful bloomers we made in respect of poor Danny Ware and then Leigh Ashton. We were and are truly sorry, as you know, and I am not going to fall into the same booby-trap. My most tentative worry relates to Roy's admirable desire to be a soldier. The war is at last veering towards victory for us, but harsh fighting is bound to be in the offing. The foot trouble may still stop Roy from joining up, but if he should attain his objective I fear for him and for you and possibly for little ones. I wonder if he would consider sticking to his present honourable occupation, or, if not, whether you both would delay just until Roy could return to remunerative work in the accountancy line. The fact is, dearest, my finances are not as good as they ought to be, and, should anything bad happen to your husband in the front line, they might not stretch to supporting you and your children in an independent manner. Whatever you decide to do will be for the best, I'm sure. With my fondest love as always, Pa.'

Several days elapsed, and Cath rang Grange Cottage on an evening when she knew the Home Guard drilled.

'Hullo, Ma,' she said.

'Cath? Oh Cath, I've been longing to talk to you, but telephoning is so difficult nowadays. Are you well?'

'Yes, Ma. Are you?'

'Yes, yes – and I'm glad you're happy, darling. I saw what a decent person your Roy is, and I believe he'll be kind to you.'

'Thank you, Ma. You know Pa wrote to me?'

'Oh yes. I hope he didn't distress you?'

'No, not a bit. Will you tell him a couple of things from me, and thank him for all his trouble and anxiety on my behalf? I couldn't postpone anything this time round, even though Pa suggests postponement for a much better reason than before, when I didn't marry Danny. I can't because, for one thing, Roy won't be able to join the army and therefore is and will be able to support me and mine, and, for another, because I'm having a baby, Ma.'

EPILOGUE

The war ended, but as yet Jack and Mary Allen had not surrendered their daughter unconditionally to Roy Fincham.

It was not obvious. Roy either did not notice it or pretended not to. But Cath was all too aware of her parents' hesitations, their holding back, in the presence of her husband. It was not out-and-out snobbery, she realised. It was perhaps a case of oil and water not mixing. What inhibited her, and stopped her from telling them to stop, was the intuitive certainty that they were motivated by their love of herself, nothing else, by their thinking she was too good for Roy, and their fear that the unconventional marriage could not last.

There had been unavoidable causes of friction. The wedding was in South Ruislip rather than at Shelford: Roy's relations could not get to Somerset and back to London within the time scale, and Cath dreaded the possibility of having to cope with Leigh Ashton. Again, she gave birth to her baby in London, near Roy, rather than under the parental umbrella. John Fincham's christening was another bone of contention: she, Roy, the baby and four god-parents could not manage the journey. Then the senior Allens were not altogether approving of Cath, and in due course of Cath and their grandson, taking residence in the Fincham house in South Ruislip, and sharing it not only with Roy but also with Roy's mother.

But these events and circumstances were not her fault. They were brought about by the force of practicality, and because she was observing her matrimonial vows. She was nonetheless nagged by regrets, especially by regretting that the person she loved best was being treated unjustly by her beloved Pa and Ma.

Her married life had been perfect otherwise. She had given birth to John without undue difficulty, and he was beautiful and doted on. She was on leave from the War Office, and could concentrate on her very own family matters. Roy had been approached by the firm of accountants that had employed him pre-war, and offered a job, a chance to complete his studies, and in principle a partnership as soon as peace broke out. Meanwhile, he hurried home on weekday evenings in order to play with John, and at weekends he would hardly let mother and son out of his sight.

Now, with the ending of the war, Annie Fincham announced that she was going to move out of the old house and into a new modern one with her widowed sister. Cath tried to persuade her to stay on, but in vain, and Roy had a different announcement to make. He proposed that they should sell in South Ruislip and buy a small snug house closer to the centre and more convenient for his work. Cath was excited by the prospect, and counted the latest addition to her blessings, not the least of which was Roy's apparently blissful ignorance of the reservations of his in-laws.

One evening Mary Allen rang up and said she was worried about Jack, who was not quite ill but not well, distressed and refusing to say what was wrong.

'It's to do with money,' she said. 'I know he'd love to see you and talk to you, darling, although he hasn't asked me to ask you. Would you come down for a night? We'd both love to see you, and Johnny too.'

Cath mentioned a Saturday night.

'Oh,' Mary commented. 'For once, darling, would Roy spare you?'

Cath agreed reluctantly. She was upset both by the news of her Pa and by her agreement.

She told Roy, who raised no objection.

But he sensed her reluctance to exclude him from the visit, he might have sensed everything, and he worried her by saying: 'Sorry, Cath – I wonder if your parents are ever going to forgive me?'

She arrived at Grange Cottage in an uncharacteristically grumpy mood with her loyalties disturbingly divided. The time was five-thirty. She had taken a taxi from Upper Shelford.

Her Pa's appearance caused her exclusive concern. He had shrunk, was bowed as if carrying a heavy burden, looked like a prematurely senile man. He was fidgety and fretful, and his emotions were clearly closer to the surface.

The second shock was that her Ma looked not much better.

They were touchingly grateful for the company of Cath, and shed a tear or two over John. A late cup of tea was brewed, and while Cath was drinking it her mother told her that Mr Ware, Danny's father, was extremely ill. He had had a stroke and his speech was affected, she said. Her father changed the subject by grumbling: 'I do wish you wouldn't dwell on it.'

Mary Allen then asked Cath in a meaningful manner if she might be permitted to bath Johnny before he was put to bed. Cath saw the point, that she had received her cue to talk to her father alone, gave permission, and gathered her forces for the task ahead.

'Pa, what's wrong?'

'Don't ask, darling.'

'I must. Is it to do with money? Is it to do with the Wares?'

He lowered his head into his hands, looked up tearfully and said: 'We're ruined, Cath. I've ruined the family.'

'You can't have. How is that possible?'

'It's easy. It was easy. I was too polite and stupid to look after my interests.'

'Tell me what happened?'

'I don't want your mother to be worried. She'll be worried soon enough without you spilling the beans.'

'I think she's more worried not to be told than she would be by anything we could tell her. Are you talking about what you did for the Wares?'

'They ran through their money. They managed to lose a fortune on farming even in the war. The old boy had no idea, he wasn't a crook, just a simpleton, and my guarantee of his debts had loopholes. I should have known what was going on, or taken better advice. He was paying out thousands on his mortgages and loans. But I couldn't reclaim a penny even if he was fit and well. And he's not entirely to blame. I borrowed money myself and lost it. Oh Cath, I'm ashamed, and so very sorry.'

'Poor Pa, I'm sorry for you. In terms I'd be able to understand, what will happen?'

'I'll be bankrupt. I sold our land long ago, and the cottages. The Grange and this place will be up for sale as soon as possible. We're living on tick. Your dear mother would never accept money from me, but she has a little of her own. I don't know, Cath. I'm all at sea.'

'I'll discuss it with Roy.'

'Oh no! I definitely don't want to have Roy butting in.'

'It wounds me, Pa, when you say and think of my Roy in that sort of way. And it's not right from lots of angles, but specially because Roy's almost an accountant and has a wonderful head for figures – he's been offered a top job that proves it.'

'But he's not like us, and we can't believe that he's really like you, darling Cath. Forgive me for not having money for you to fall back on if you and he should come to grief.'

'Pa, listen! You wouldn't have been so kind to the Wares if it hadn't been for me, for me and Danny, so you must let me help. I love you and always have and will, but I can't bear it when you speak of my husband so distrustfully. Pardon me for reminding you that you were wrong twice before about my men. Please don't – you're not to – make another mistake by alienating me. I'm not flattering myself, but I believe you'd regret it more than the money. The truth is I keep no secrets from Roy, we tell each other everything, and I have more faith in him than in anybody. I'm going to talk about your troubles openly with Ma, and we'll try to comfort you, and then I'll ask Roy for his assistance.'

Three weeks later Roy asked Cath to fix up another visit to Grange Cottage. He had been thinking over her parents' plight and would like to put forward a plan to ameliorate it.

Cath expressed her doubts by inquiring: 'Will they take it amiss?'

'No.'

'Are you sure?'

'Yes.'

'What is it?'

'Wait and see.'

'Shouldn't you let me in on it?'

'Perhaps, but I'm not going to – and I keep my word.'

'I hope they won't be beastly.'

'No chance of that.'

She obeyed him as she had promised, rather wishing she had done as her father wished.

In the train on the Saturday afternoon she should have been in high spirits. They had exchanged contracts on the instant sale of the South Ruislip house, which was bought for twice its residential value by a builder with an eye on its large garden, and on the purchase of an unassuming comfy mews house in the Bayswater-Ladbroke area. Her nervousness was not allayed by the memory of her parents' inhospitable reaction to the suggestion that she together with Roy would like to spend the night.

They reached Grange Cottage, and over the customary cup of tea Roy rushed in with a clearly unwelcome interrogation of Jack Allen. He apologised, he acknowledged that it must be painful, but if Mr Allen could stand it, and provide the information, he hoped he had a positive solution of the problem. Mary kept on glancing at Cath and raising her eyes heavenward during the question-and-answer session, and Cath felt her toes curling.

Finally Ray said: 'Okay! My guesses weren't far wrong, and my plan would fill the bill. You'll have to cough up, Mr Allen, no doubt about it – everything's a-goner. But Cath and I have sold my home for much more money than we need, and after setting aside a good whack for my Mum, and the deposit on the house we're moving into, we'll pay the difference between what you've got and what's wanted, so no bankruptcy, and we'll buy Grange Cottage from you, so you and Mrs A. will be able to stay on here and have pennies to rub together. And by-the-bye, if Cath's agreeable, we'll put Grange Cottage in John's name – you two will be your grandson's tenants. I'll arrange matters with your solicitor, Mr Allen, if that suits.'

When the hubbub of astonishment, polite rejection, eager acceptance, and gratitude had died down, and handshakes and kisses were done, Jack Allen retired to his study and reappeared with a small framed picture in his hands.

It was the miniature portrait by an unknown hand of the Allen forebear who had been one of Wellington's generals. General Allen was a moustachioed fierce-looking man, and no oil painting, as they say, but the picture was brightened up by his chestful of medals and glowed effectively. Jack Allen loved it and had always kept it on his desk at Shelford Grange and again at Grange Cottage; he was also convinced it was the work of a fine artist and would prove to be valuable one day. Now he made a short speech, expressing his opinion that it was the best thing he possessed, and ended it by saying the time had come to pass it on to the next generation.

Cath protested that he should not deprive himself, she could not accept such a gift: 'Please go on enjoying it yourself, Pa.'

He laughed and replied: 'I wasn't thinking of giving it to you, my darling. I'm trying to be sensible for a change, and believe I ought to hand it over to John.'

'Oh well,' Cath said, 'if you must – John makes a little more sense, but only a little – I'd still like it to be yours.'

'No – and no again – I am giving it away, and I'm not giving it to John. I want Roy to have it. There you are, Roy – it's my olive branch, and my penance, and I'm giving it to you because I trust you to bequeath it to your son and our grandson and to keep it in the family.'

The next stage of the evening was the happiest time ever spent by the Allens and Finchams together. In spite of arguments about Roy's proposed benefaction, the Allens' negatives getting worn down by Roy and Cath's positives, supper was celebratory, and marked by the lowering of barriers.

After supper Cath excused herself to attend to John, and in the relative quiet upstairs she appreciated the full force of Roy's surprise. It had taken her breath away as well as almost stunning her Pa and Ma. It was even more generous than they knew. He was purchasing their peace of mind with all his money – or all his and Cath's. He was right, she grudged nothing, but she marvelled first at the cleverness of his gesture, for he was at once presenting her parents with the money they needed and investing the same money for herself and his son, and he was making a gesture of great confidence in himself and his ability to win bread and feed his dependants.

The aftermath of the emotional feast of relief would be shyness, she foresaw. Her Pa and Ma had indeed forgiven Roy; but they were bound to be shy to be so beholden to him, at least for some months or years. But they would get over it eventually, they would love Roy as predicted, they could not help loving such a fine man.

She was proud of her husband, and even entertained a modest moment's pride in herself. She knew she was not a brainy person, and that her aims were modest in a worldly context, although sky high by her measurements. She had never wanted anything except to love a man with all her heart, and bear and bring up his children to be decent citizens. And although she was also cautious, and willing to take the rough with the smooth if she had to, she dared to hope that she had achieved her object.

Later, when the grown-ups had said good night, and in the Finchams' room John slept in his carry-cot beside their bed, Cath rewarded Roy in her own sweet way.

THE FIRST NAIL

PART ONE

Turville Place frightened me when I was a boy. It was, and may still be for all I know, the big house in the hamlet of Ashe Turville in Gloucestershire. We lived a couple of miles from Ashe Turville, and caught trains from the station there, which only merited the name of a 'Halt' in those days – it boasted no more than one platform and a shed. Our road to Ashe Turville Halt passed under an extended arch of trees, a stretch of darkness in summer, in all seasons darkened by the evergreen foliage bulging over the park wall of Turville Place. The wall was not particularly high, the wrought iron gates at the entrance to the drive were not closed; yet the jungle of greenery looked damp, impenetrable, sinister and forbidding.

What was Turville Place, I asked. The answer, a house, was mystifying and not much comfort. Who lived in a house that was a place? Mrs Wiley, once the cook of old Mrs Morfe, now took care of it for Mrs Morfe's son Alexander, who worked in France. Probably, in other words, a witch, I concluded.

One day I was taken to a tea party at Turville Place. It must have been a children's do for a charity that Mrs Wiley supported. The outside of the Victorian Gothic house in the gloaming was a shock, but inside there were wonderful fake mushrooms to eat, made of meringue and chocolate powder, and then jelly in oranges and lemons.

The years I have referred to were the early thirties. When I was old enough to register, if not to comprehend, snatches

135

of my parents' conversation, I overheard them saying that Mrs Wiley had died and Alexander Morfe had not bothered to attend her funeral. They described Alexander Morfe in unmistakeably disparaging terms. He was an only child and had not been kind to his mother. He was a playboy and gigolo, they said, who mucked about in France and never came home. He was a second generation 'counterjumper' – his father had made money in furniture, selling furniture, and jumped over the counter of his shop to play at being gentry in Turville Place, which he built.

Something was also said about the need to find another caretaker for Turville Place, and that maybe it was just as well that Alexander was not choosing the woman to reside in his house and be at his mercy.

I lost my father in 1939, the first year of the war, but that is another story.

In 1944 or thereabouts my mother announced at breakfast that she had invited Alexander Morfe to tea.

By then I had finished with school and was waiting to be called up into the army. Her announcement surprised me because hospitality had not been the strong suit of her widowhood, in fact she had lived reclusively. That she was entertaining an old friend or making a new one was good news, especially as I would soon be deserting her, but I had completely forgotten who Alexander Morfe was.

She reminded me a trifle sharply. He was our neighbour. He owned Turville Place and was spending time there for a change. He used to live in France, but had been busy with war-work at some ministry in London. Now he had got rid of the caretaker and was doing badly needed repairs.

I asked idly: 'Didn't Father hate him?'

'Of course not. Your father didn't hate anybody. What an extraordinary idea! I can't think where you got hold of it.'

'Isn't he the "counter-jumper"?'

'What? No. That's not a nice thing to say. He's a charm-ing gentleman, and he doesn't know anybody down here. I hadn't seen him for donkey's years, but I met him in the village yesterday.'

'Is he married?'

'No – so far as I know. Anyway he's coming to tea, and I think you should put in an appearance.'

'All right.'

'No, darling – you will help me to entertain him, won't you?'

'Okay.'

I regret to confess that I displayed the typical gracious-ness of youth by turning up late for that tea party. I entered our front hall via the swing-door, silently but without any intention of spying, and saw a disturbing scene, although nothing indiscreet by normal standards was in train.

My mother was probably considered, and had considered herself, older than would be the case nowadays. She had mourned her happy marriage as if the romantic side of life were a closed book to her. She retired from the competition, renounced vanity, wore no make-up, and concentrated on her offspring and her good works.

But she had suddenly undergone a change. She had changed without my permission, and in honour of a male intruder, our guest. She sat in Father's chair at the head of the refectory table at which we ate our meals, and the westering sun shone in on her prettiness, which I had never consciously noticed before. She had applied a touch of lipstick and done something becoming to her eyes. And the changes that struck me as unnecessary, even as disloyal, did not stop at cosmetics. She was laughing and reaching forward to touch, or at least in the direction of, the arm of Alexander Morfe. She had never laughed quite like that in my experience, and was not in the habit of rallying

137

members of the opposite sex with coquettish pats and pushes.

I felt that it was almost disgraceful in my puritanical innocence, and, either because she sensed my attitude or for another reason, she blushed as she introduced me to Mr Morfe.

He stood up politely to shake hands. He was tall, six feet tall, and dressed strikingly. He wore cream-coloured slacks, a blue blazer with what seemed to be an excess of crested brass buttons, a chequered shirt in vivid colours and a diagonally striped tie forming an outsize knot.

His countenance came next in my peculiar boyish order of priorities. For what one male opinion of another male's looks is worth, I thought him handsome. I could see he was middle-aged, but he did not look old. His figure was slender and lithe, and he exuded fitness. His thick greying tousled thatch of hair, his bright blue eyes, his smile that showed tight white teeth, and his clear complexion with a hint of summer tan, impressed me despite my automatic bristling.

Charm, like talent, has become a dirty word in our egalitarian era. But I had to agree with my mother years ago, and I have additional reasons to claim that he belonged to the ineradicable elite of the charming. He greeted me, he greeted the world, with an open expression, outgoing, receptive, and his voice was deep and sounded somehow lazy.

We sat down to tea. He amused us with tales of the builders working at Turville Place. Apparently they were so spoilt by being the only men available in wartime, and usually so old, that they deigned to ply their trade for no more than an hour or two a day, and otherwise were searching for their spectacles.

He said he could not remember why he was doing up his country seat. He was doing it up in order to stop it falling down. The war was as good as won – he had been a Whitehall warrior for four and a half years, and was now retired or, literally, put out to grass. His new job was to squander money on Turville Place so as not to let the devil make work for idle hands. But, in rural terms, the house was a sow's ear if ever there was one.

As for Gloucestershire, it seemed to him the land of the sod, agriculturally speaking. He had shaken the dust of Gloucestershire from his feet when he was a raw youth, and could not believe he would spend his declining years with Gloucestershire mud on his gumboots. He felt as if he had been exiled to Ashe Turville. But maybe he would meet a country maiden with straw in her hair, and settle for becoming a turnip.

My mother, unnecessarily in my opinion, urged him not to turn his back on poor little Ashe Turville in a hurry. He bowed his head by way of response and said he had learnt the lesson that one must always yield to the ladies.

Alexander Morfe did not exclude me from his fun or even from his flirting, although there is no blanket wetter than a sulky teenager. He glanced at me, and smiled and winked. And his eyes meeting mine as it were dragged me into the magic circle of his verve and vitality. When he finally addressed me, asking the questions that young people are almost honour bound to resent, I was willing to volunteer that I was nearly eighteen and waiting for the summons from my regiment.

'With luck you won't have to fight,' he assured me. 'But if you do, get a blighty as quick as you can.'

What was that, what was a 'blighty'?

'London was called Blighty once upon a time,' he explained, 'and a "blighty" was a wound that didn't kill you and a ticket home. I got one in the last war – there's still shrapnel in my leg to prove it. A friend of mine got the best. He enlisted in 1914, trained for a few weeks, went to France, fought for an hour, won a DSO, was bayoneted in the buttock and sent home. He became a war hero in three months flat, and never fired another shot in anger. What have you been doing while you await the call to arms?'

'Nothing much.'

My mother rushed in regrettably to qualify this answer.

'He writes stories and things, he's hoping to be a writer.'

'A writer!' Mr Morfe exclaimed. 'Fancy that! You might be the very man I've been looking for.' I was relieved when he turned to explain to my mother. 'I've toed the line for a change and along with many too many old boys written a book. Don't laugh! For better or worse I can still hold the instrument meant to be mightier than the sword. But grammar isn't my forte – I need a learned scribe to cross my Is and dot my Ts. Would your son and heir be tempted by filthy lucre to do a spot of editing?'

Again my mother put her oar in, or, to my way of thinking, her foot in it.

'I'm sure he'd be glad to help if he could, though not for money – wouldn't you, darling?'

I mumbled an affirmative.

'Oh well,' he said, as if to change the subject. 'We'll see, shall we? The army may need you more than I do. I have no deadline, and publication and publicity are definitely not on the menu.'

My mother said to him: 'I'd love to read that book of yours.'

'So would the lawyers who specialise in libel,' he replied.

Mr Morfe had a way with him, and wore flashy clothes, and had presumed to write something; but at my age I still thought of grown-ups in general as unaccountable beings, like chimpanzees or Martians, and could not take their activities too seriously. I did wonder why my mother was metaphorically all over her guest. And I did hope he would not call on me to work for him cost-free. That was the end of the story, I hoped.

Then the army delayed, it was not keen on conscripts at that stage of the war, and my mother told me that she had promised I would look in on Mr Morfe on a certain after-noon – I was to be at Turville Place at four o'clock.

I obeyed orders, as advised by Alexander Morfe himself. It must have been a weekend, a Saturday or Sunday, for there was no sign of workmen on or off his scaffolding. I bicycled through the gates and up the drive flanked by laurels and rhododendrons, and the house looked even worse, more forbidding, than it had done in my memory. The gravel sweep was weedy, the lawns overgrown, the plate-glass windows streaked with dust and paint, and the double doors beneath the portico not in use – bags of sand and cement were piled against them.

I ventured round a corner of the building, looking for another door. In the creepy silence I jumped to the conclu-sion that my mother had compounded her offences by telling me to turn up on the wrong day. The back door had a car parked nearby, which was comforting, but the court-yard lined with outhouses was again neglected. I knocked and, when there was no response, tugged at a screwdriver attached to wire which might have been an apology for a bell-pull.

The bell duly tolled in the interior and after a minute or two the door opened. He opened it. He wore down-at-heel slippers and a cardigan over an open-necked shirt. The cream flannels with knife-edge creases were replaced by shapeless corduroys. And he had a two-day growth of white stubble.

But the shock was mutual.

141

A series of expostulations indicated that he had not expected me: 'Oh ... How do you do? ... Hullo! ... My God – I asked you to pay me a visit.'

'Shall I come another day?' I suggested.

'No no!' He was emphatically against it. 'You'll have to take me as you find me – warts and all. But come in! You might as well see the other side of the medal – all part of the story. Follow me – I'll lead the way.'

It was embarrassing. What had happened to his dignity? At least my mother was not to blame.

He led via the ill-lit passages flanked by former servants' offices to a cavernous kitchen with a solid fuel cooker, a central pine table, and Windsor chairs and a sofa by the window which looked out on more laurels.

'I'm pigging it in here while the builders render the rest of the house uninhabitable,' he said. 'Have a pew! I can cook you tea – or would you prefer whisky?'

I opted for tea – he had the whisky. He insisted on spreading honey on bread for me to eat. He dealt with household chores ineptly, and made a remark to which I had no answer, that he was a dead loss without a woman.

At last he joined me in the sitting area.

'You probably want to know what's happened to me since we last met,' he said. 'You may assume I've gone to the dogs, and wish I still looked like the man who broke the bank at Monte Carlo – people of your age are usually conservative. I hate to disillusion you, but alas, somebody has to start rendering that service. It's vice versa. What you see is the genuine article, and the guest of your dear Mama was the phoney. Money isn't everything – lack of the ready isn't my problem. It's a loss in the region of the heart, not the wallet, that's brought me to what and where I am. Don't make such a sympathetic face, dear boy! There are many nice people in the world who'd believe I'm getting my deserts, and quite a few nasty ones who'd laugh their heads off if they could see me down and almost out.'

He delivered this rueful speech with a contradictory smile on his face.

But when he spoke the old toast, 'Happy days', the hand that held his glass of whisky trembled.

It was beyond me. I had thought my mother was making a minor mistake by creating a literary link between me and Alexander Morfe, now I began to think she had thrown me together with a lunatic. I hoped he was not going to stab me unexpectedly and chop me into little pieces – we were in the kitchen, I recalled. As a rule grown-ups, however weird, did not tell me their hearts were broken. Besides, he was too old for stuff like that, I decided with the sagacity of my eighteen years. Was he putting on an act for my benefit?

He and I sat by that viewless window, and I asked him some anodyne question about the progress of his building works.

Instead of calming it excited him.

'Don't let's talk about it,' he said. 'I wish Turville Place was at the bottom of the sea. My mother made a mess of her will, and left most of my inheritance to this house instead of to me – she wanted me to come and live in it. But that's ancient history – and lucky you, it's not your mess. Recently everything went haywire for me, and I wanted to get away from London, and dreamed up the idea that my old home might do me a power of good. I'd got my hot hands on my money, family money, the money my mother tried to bribe me with, and thought I might as well spend some of it on modernising Turville Place. I expected to find answers in this miserable hole – talk of wild goose chases! Now I regret signing contracts with my builders and can't wait for them to move off. The best news is that I haven't cut links with my business completely – I'm a wine merchant, or was one when there was any wine to sell. As soon as peace breaks out I'll go back to doing business in France, God willing. Sorry to ramble on.'

I referred to his book, the book that had lured me into his kitchen.

'Not written,' he replied. 'I was boasting when I said I'd written it – wishful thinking – I know what should be in the blasted book, but how to put it there, that's the problem, as you'll know soon or may know already. I have had a shot at chapter one.'

'Are you pleased with it?'

'You must be joking. I have difficulty in stringing a sentence together, let alone a chapter, and I should be shot for presuming I could ever write a whole book. But what the hell! My problems are plural, not singular, as a matter of fact. I'm in possession of a great many secrets – they used to be called the secrets of the bedroom – and the trouble is I can't exclude them from my autobiography, nor can I include them without hurting feelings and damaging lives.'

'Is your book going to be pornographic?'

'I wouldn't put it as strongly as that. I'm hoping it'll one day fall into the hands of people who can read between the lines. But, supposing the deed was done and publication day was tomorrow, I can think of a few dear friends of mine and quite a lot of third parties who would wish I was dead.'

'Couldn't you write under a pseudonym or anonymously?'

'I could. But revenge is sweet, isn't it? I have a low opinion of the majority of husbands. I'd quite like to strike a blow for all the downtrodden wives.'

'So you'll write in the first person and under your own name?'

'I don't know. It's all hypothetical. It's mostly intention, to be precise. But I'm grateful to you for listening to me, and giving me tips. The one definite part of my book at this stage of the game is its title. Shall I let you in on it?'

'Please.'

'*The Catcher Caught.*'

I mentioned my previous visit to Turville Place, and my memory of the mushrooms. The book I had come to discuss was to all intents and purposes non-existent, there was not much point in staying, like his catcher I felt caught, and longed to escape or at least make a move in the direction of my bike.

'I'll show you the dining-room where you had mushrooms for tea,' he said, and muttered: 'Mrs Wiley's cooking was about my happiest memory of Turville Place.'

I followed him with relief along more passages, through the remains of a green baize swing-door and a hall full of builders' materials into a large empty unrecognisable room. The floor was bare boards, furniture was piled under dust-sheets in the middle.

'Did your people know my mother?' Mr Morfe asked me.

I mumbled some reply, of which he took no notice.

'She thought I was God Almighty,' he said.

I tried to laugh off his remark.

He continued: 'I might have been a better son if she'd beaten me.'

Again I laughed, although I realised he was not trying to be funny.

'Shall I show you upstairs?'

'Well...' I began, but already he was heading for the staircase.

The tour of the bedroom floor was on the whirlwind side. He pointed in passing to guest rooms, his father's dressing-room, his mother's bedroom, and paused only at the room he was now sleeping in, which, unlike the others, had a bed, chest of drawers, pictures on the walls and fitted carpet.

'I had it when I was a boy,' he explained, waving a hand at photographs of school groups. 'You might call it the cradle of my innocence. But I can't remember being innocent.'

We returned to the kitchen. I had not comprehended his last few statements, and was torn between feeling inadequate and wondering what was wrong with him. But now, for the first time since my arrival, he stopped talking to himself, as it had seemed, and looked at me in his particular personal way that charmed.

'Gloucestershire's no damn good for me,' he said. 'I've had to scribble to keep myself company. Apologies again for having nothing for you to transform into deathless prose.'

We laughed together at his pleasantry.

He resumed: 'I couldn't stand old men who tried to tell me their life stories when I was your age. I'm ashamed to remember how often I snubbed my father. But you've gritted your teeth and heard me out with patience. I hope you survive and achieve fame and fortune with your writing. About mine, if I can ever get down to it, somebody's going to have to knock it into shape – and as I was saying you may be the one to do the job. I'm not threatening you. My book's a feeble knock on the lid of my coffin. You'd better forget all the hot air I've treated you to – forget and forgive, which is exactly what I'm finding it hard to do.'

We had walked together to the side door of the house.

He opened it and said: 'Thank your mother for the loan of you.'

I thanked him in return, and added a cliché about seeing him again.

'That I doubt,' he replied.

We shook hands.

He then detained me.

'Half a tick! You know what discretion is, don't you? – the better part of valour. I trust you to be discreet. Adieu!'

'Oh – goodbye,' I responded awkwardly.

'Did you enjoy your visit?' my mother wished to know.

'Yes.'

'What was Alexander Morfe like?'

'Not bad.'

'Was anyone else there?'

'No.'

'Are you sure?'

'No.'

'Well, who's looking after him?'

'Ask me another.'

'You must learn to be more communicative, darling. What did you think of Turville Place?'

'It's a wreck. He's not staying there.'

'Where is he staying then?'

'He's living there, but he isn't going to stay on.'

'Why the workmen in that case?'

'Because of his mother's will – something to do with money.'

'Does he mean to sell the house?'

'I don't know.'

'He must be selling if he isn't staying.'

'You'll have to ask him – he didn't tell me exactly.'

'I can't do that. I'm not joining the queue for his attention. You don't seem to understand what sort of man he is. When is he leaving Ashe Turville?'

'He didn't say.'

'Was he pulling your leg? Or was he ill? Did he look ill?'

'No, not ill.'

'What did he look like?'

'He hadn't shaved.'

'He wasn't funny with you, was he?'

'I don't know what you mean.'

'Did he show you his book?'

'No.'

'No? Why not? He told me that was why he wanted to see you.'

'He changed his mind. His book isn't written.'

'It sounds as if he's gone crazy.'

'He wasn't bad.'

Eventually she gave up. And the arrival of my call-up papers re-directed her thoughts and mine.

Some months passed. The war ended, I was granted longer periods of leave, and renewed proximity to Turville Place prompted me to ask my mother questions in my turn.

'You were right,' she informed me with unwonted terseness. 'He's gone.'

'Gone where?'

'He's cleared out of Turville Place. Where he's gone, I've no idea and don't like to imagine – gone to the dogs, I shouldn't be surprised.'

'Did you see him again?'

'Oh no. He had better or worse things to do.'

'But you rather liked him.'

'He was our neighbour. I was quite prepared to be civil to him. He had other ideas.'

'Such as?'

'Well – the usual – women.'

'What women?'

'You may well ask. Women arrived from nowhere to visit him. I suppose they came from an agency.'

'Servants, you mean?'

'Not in the normal sense. They looked very out of place

in the Ashe Turville Post Office, I can tell you. They were dripping with mascara and wore six-inch heels.'

'Were they tarts?'

'I suppose so. But they might have been friends of his for all I know. Such a pity! A man with his advantages shouldn't have sunk so low.'

'He was pretty nice to me.'

'He can be nice. He's charming when he wants to be. But I'm afraid he lived up to his reputation while he was down here.'

'What was his reputation?'

'There was some unpleasant gossip pre-war, when he walked out on a girl in trouble, then in France he was involved in court cases and other squalid goings-on, I gather. Women are so silly about men like that, who can only make them unhappy. But apparently he now has to pay for his pleasures. His life story seems to have begun with scandal and to be ending pathetically. I can't help feeling sorry for him.'

'What about Turville Place?'

'They say it's for sale.'

'I wonder if he'll ever write his book – it might be interesting.'

'I doubt it – he's too lazy, and reading and writing haven't been his forte. If he ever does write anything, you'd be well advised to steer clear, that's my opinion.'

'Oh well, thanks for telling me.'

'I just thought you'd be amused to hear that he's done it again – fleeing from Gloucestershire, I mean.'

I said I was, but added more for the sake of accuracy than to reproach her that he had been her friend or acquaintance, not mine.

Years and decades whirled me into middle age. One

morning a bulky envelope arrived. It contained Alexander Morfe's 'book' and a letter from a London firm of solicitors. Mr Morfe had died in France, in the city of Nice, the letter stated, and he had bequeathed the enclosed papers to me.

How can I explain that I did not bother to read them?

I was busy, busily scratching my living with my pen, and had too much reading to do and was always behind with it. The postponement of the task turned into deliberate omission. I was reluctant to find disagreeable references to my mother, who had been briefly magnetised by the name, fame and charm of Alexander Morfe. I therefore forgot to remember those forty-five quarto pages, badly typed, disfigured by crossings-out and illegible hand-written revisions, dog-eared and even stained by age, as if they had been written in the distant past, probably at Turville Place.

Sea-changes occurred again with time's assistance. The death of my dear mother made me interested in anything written, or that might be written, about her. In a strictly academic sense my speciality was and remains women, the female psyche, and I was particularly interested in the type of man loved by them in the plural. And a clear-out of my writer's full bottom drawer, in which rejected works and juvenilia were stored, dredged up Alexander Morfe's bequest.

At last I read it. A little more time elapsed and something happened, the strangest coincidence occurred, that changed my mind about it, as will emerge in the following pages. After half a century I decided to have a shot at doing what the author once suggested. His 'book' was actually notes – they would have to be expanded. They were bones for me to reassemble with the aid of literary flesh and blood. My book would be fiction, discreet fiction, an imaginary panorama of the landscape of love, my reworking of Alexander Morfe's autobiography and my representation of his personality. At his best he must have been champagne as its beneficial effects are usually described, and he was ashes such as dustmen have to deal with. He was the Pied Piper and latterly the Chief Mourner. He was mercury, or a tarnished star. I still remember his tousled greying hair and his infectious compelling smile.

He himself replaced the title he originally had in mind, and substituted three different words connected with, or deriving from, something else he said to me.

My mother and I do not figure in his typescript.

PART TWO

He always regretted the fact that his parents called him Ecky. Ecky was infantile and frivolous, whereas Alexander might have developed into a serious citizen.

His mother, Mrs Morfe, bore him too late and breast-fed him too long. And she was willing to feed him at all hours of the day and night. Her spoiling never stopped; but he soon twigged that there was a price to pay for gratification of his whims. He had to toe an emotional line, or else to withstand her reproaches and her tears.

He had a nursemaid in his early years at Turville Place, Ethel Cooke. One of his precocious humorous sallies was to draw attention to the Cooke who looked after him and Mrs Wiley, the cook down in the kitchen. Ethel was a buxom country girl and Ecky was attracted to her 'buffers', as he chose to describe her breasts. He nestled against those buffers of hers of his own volition, and kissed her for fun instead of to order.

Mrs Morfe got rid of Ethel as soon as he was house-trained. She became his nurse and constant companion from then on, and he slept in his bed or sometimes in hers in her bedroom.

Ecky never saw his father there. Mr Morfe was a businessman – he later thought the word should be spelt 'busy-nessman'. His life seemed to consist of consulting his pocket-watch and catching trains. He was smaller than his wife, and a fusspot with a small bristly moustache.

Although Mr Morfe did not cut a lot of ice in his son's

childhood, they had a few shared understandings. Ecky had inherited his father's sweet tooth: they were of one mind when it came to chocolate eclairs. They also agreed wordlessly, but by the exchange of a glance, or no doubt by trial and error, that there was not much point in challenging the edicts of the lady of the house.

One night Ecky had a bad experience or perhaps a bad dream. His mother's bedroom door was ajar and a slice of light lay on the carpet. His father out in the passage said: 'Can I come and tuck you up tonight?' and his mother replied: 'No, no, for pity's sake!' His father uttered uncharacteristically angry words; his mother stepped hurriedly into her bedroom, shut the door and must have leant against it, panting. His father rattled the door handle, but failed to gain entry. His mother made movements in the dark, a dark rendered almost more mysterious by the glow of the night-light, then lifted Ecky out of his cot and transferred him into the empty half of her own double bed. He pretended to be asleep throughout – he was afraid of getting embroiled in a row, in other people's passions. If it was a dream, he dreamed of going back to sleep. The next day he temporarily forgot the drama.

Some time after that Mr Morfe expired on his train to the City of London. Ecky knew almost nothing about it, his mother shielded him from the news and advised the servants not to gossip. He did not attend the funeral, the wake was held in a local hotel, the widow and her staff did not don mourning attire, and eventually his mother remarked that his father had gone to heaven, which sounded like another of his train journeys for business purposes.

He went to boarding school at the age of nine uncomplainingly. He had a nice home, but he was fed up with being made much of in the feminine fastness of Turville Place. He did not yearn for the company of school-fellows; it was change and novelty that attracted him, and a step in the direction of adulthood.

At his preparatory school, so-called because it was meant to prepare him for 'public' school, a typically illogical English misnomer since our 'public' schools are the private fee-paying ones, the unpleasantness was caused by the schoolmasters.

One master made a favourite of him and spoke to him of love, another hated and treated him harshly, a third gave him secret tuition in the facts of life, the PE instructor initiated him into unusual exercises, and the headmaster missed no opportunity to beat him for being saucy and lackadaisical.

Alexander Morfe, who wished to be known as Ecky no longer, took it all on the chin, or at least in his stride. None of it made sense to him. What were they all driving at? They seemed to be speaking another language – those objections to himself trotted out by the headmaster were certainly double Dutch. But he was growing accustomed to the phenomenon of his ability to rouse strong emotions.

His public school was at once different and the same. Now it was the older boys who pursued and persecuted him. What were they after? Why did he provoke peculiar laughter? Was it unpopularity?

Nature came to his rescue. He grew older and bigger, and suddenly a miracle translated his boyhood into youth. He had been a complete ignoramus, and he began to feel well-informed.

He was in receipt of the key that unlocked the door into the past, and at the same time opened up a future of infinite promise. Gradually, miraculously, he plumbed the mysteries of preceding years, the bedtime skirmish between his parents, the erratic behaviour of those schoolmasters, and the motives of the boys who had whistled at him and

157

signalled with their fingers. He was not surprised that his school reports had complained of his being half-awake. It was true, or almost true – he had been half-alive.

Luckily he was never in two minds as to which sex could and perhaps would satisfy his yearnings. Any woman served at first to populate his fantasies. But he developed into a special kind of aesthete, a lover not of the beauties of art, rather of flesh and blood, and the flesh and blood that added up to the female form divine. He was as keen a critic of the feminine physique as academics are of the objects of their erudite preoccupations. Amongst the Rubicons he began to cross was the re-evaluation of his mother's charms. He now observed unmercifully that she was a dowdy old lady with a sharp nose and a shrivelled chest.

He thought he loved women. He believed he was ready and willing to love them. Yet his romantic attitudes were not marked by unqualified sympathy for the fair sex. In his opinion his mother had been selfish and mean to his father on that night of marital discord. Retrospectively he sided with his father, and was therefore the more drawn towards membership of the ancient fraternity of sexual chauvinists.

In his seventeenth year his eye was caught by a girl in his Gloucestershire circle of contemporaries and acquaintances. She was called May Poore. At Christmas time she came with a group to sing carols and eat mince pies at Turville Place. She had rosy cheeks and wavy blonde hair and a deliciously ripe little figure. He wanted to hug, fondle, kiss and make love to her, and to be told that she loved him. But he discovered with a shock that he was living in the aftermath of the Victorian era.

His upbringing had been timeless so far as he was concerned. And he was used to getting whatever he wanted without delay. But May was the daughter of a respectable yeoman farmer and his wife, a church-going couple, who had taught her not to respond to the questioning gazes of bold boys. She blushed when he spoke to her and answered him in monosyllables. For a change he could not do – do to her, do with her – exactly as he pleased. He felt hemmed in by the conventions, rules, regulations, and other people's feelings, and public opinion.

Not knowing what was going on inside May annoyed and provoked him. Long ago they had played together at a children's party: he regretted the fact that he had pushed her and made her cry at musical chairs. They had both been included in juvenile tennis tournaments organised by the Ashe Turville vicar's wife. And two or three years ago he had spotted her in Tetbury, although she was still cocooned in puppy fat. She had been accompanied by a grown-up, possibly her elder brother, a forbidding six-footer.

How was he to get to grips with her?

Their first meeting in an adult sense occurred at a local dance, given to warm a house recently bought in the Tetbury area. This time round she caught his eye, and he was encouraged to invite her to dance. They danced twice, and again, and again. He was aroused by her proximity and scent, by the warmth of her small soft hand and the flexing musculature of her back. Occasionally they swapped a con-spiratorial glance or a smile, and he was pleased to notice her flushed cheeks – he guessed that she was sharing with him the novel thrill of yielding to animal forces. They were united ever more closely by the rhythm of the music, and after all dancing is a sort of foreplay. But she called a halt to it in response to signals from her mother. She danced with other boys, and Alexander lost interest in her – other girls were more than willing to dance with him.

Midnight approached. Then it was God Save the King. In the crowd of guests queuing to say goodbye to the host and hostess Alexander found May beside him. She was with her parents and behaving properly, but managed to look up at him with half-closed eyes and to say in an undertone: 'Don't forget me!'

It was a bit like Cinderella's slipper. It could not be called a proposition. It was chicken feed in comparison with the later developments of his love life. Yet it excited him more than most of the latter.

Alexander acted in character, the character he was assuming, and did nothing to reach May Poore or to continue from where they had left off. He was too idle to write, and there was no telephone at Turville Place. While he obeyed her instructions, for her image was engraved on his imagination, he did not care enough to force the issue. He could not be bothered to try to solve the problem of what he should do next.

He had left school and was kicking his heels. He had money, but had yet to learn how to spend it. He was sick of being told by his mother that he should apply for any old job, in the City or diplomacy or agriculture. He did not like it when she gloated over his marketable personal qualifications, his good looks, his charm: he thought she was fibbing to force him to work against his will.

He took trains from Ashe Turville Halt to London in order to meet school friends who lived there. But one was at university, another was studying law, they were both in a perpetual hurry and they made him feel a drone. On his own he lost himself geographically, he was tantalised by prostitutes, and embarrassed and even alarmed to be stared at by women who were obviously not for sale. He was then contrarily relieved to be back with his mother.

May Poore eventually helped him to remember her. She wrote a note inviting him to play tennis, and he duly bicycled over to her home. It was called The Poore House, an address attracting ridicule and criticism, not least because the family farmed several hundred acres. Alexander was introduced to Mr Poore, May's hefty father with a beetroot face, her mother, a stout housewife who also seemed to stare at him, and her brother Ben, somewhat hostile for unknown reasons, who shook his hand punitively. Their habitat was an extended Cotswold-style farmhouse.

Other youngish people arrived, and on a lawn at the back of the house they played tennis for two and a half hours before tea and two and a half after. It was serious adult stuff organised by Ben, not like the patball played long ago at the Ashe Turville vicarage: jokes were frowned upon and sex was overruled by sport. Alexander partnered May for only one set, and she praised him when he hit a good shot and excused him when he hit bad ones, and wrinkled her nose at him and was altogether adorable. But his chances to touch her when he handed her balls for serving were few and far between, she shrank from such contacts, and was obviously inhibited by the surveillance of members of her family, especially Ben, and by the interest of her female friends.

When it was time to leave she managed to say to him as he mounted his bicycle: 'I've hardly seen you at all.' And she pouted and besought him: 'Couldn't we play next time at Turville Place?'

He duly invited May and two others to tea and tennis as soon as he had had the lawn mown and the net stretched and so on. It was a jollier occasion, except for the tea presided over stiffly by Mrs Morfe. But again most of the afternoon slipped by without advancing the relationship of two of the players.

Evening threatened, dusk was in the air, and May swiped at a ball that flew up and over the netting and into the laurel bushes.

'Sorry,' she laughed, and said to Alexander: 'help me find it.'

He followed her into the bushes. She said she knew where it had fallen and, reaching the place, sank on to her knees. She extended her hand to him and said: 'Here – quick – before the others come – it must be here.' He obeyed, realising vaguely that he was participating not in an accident but a design. Their heads were close together, and she was gazing at him with a rather red face and a challenge in her blue eyes. He hesitated momentarily. She kissed him without waiting. They were cheek to cheek, and by the cleverest small movement of her head mouth to mouth. And her arms were round his neck and she was doing other amazing things to him.

'Fetch it,' she said, releasing him abruptly and pointing, as the others stumbled into view.

That was the end of all the games. The three guests said their goodbyes to Mrs Morfe and, as they had apparently promised parents, bicycled off together after also thanking Alexander.

He re-entered the house. His mother delivered herself of the following opinion: 'May Poore's a minx. Those Poores are silly people and not good enough for you, Ecky.'

'Hell's bells!' he retorted.

Yet again he subsided into passivity. It was not as if he were courting May with marital intentions, and to seek a nice girl out for sexual purposes was fraught with difficulty and risk. Alexander settled for the soft option.

But May did not. A fortnight after the second tennis party she sent him a note that ran: 'Will you be going to the hop at Lowton?'

He could decipher the cryptic message. The hop referred to was a dance for charity in the new village hall of Lowton, the dormitory suburb of the town of Marchbury on the Somerset border. The dance had been widely advertised, and the hall's modern architecture and amenities had received months of publicity. But May was unlikely to have thought of attending for charitable or architectural reasons. Moreover Lowton was a good eighteen miles from The Poore House, too far for horse-drawn or mechanised transport there and back at night. Turville Place, on the other hand, was located between her home and the scene of potential festivities. What she was suggesting was that Alexander should invite her to spend the night, or more than one night, under his roof.

It took much trouble and negotiation to bring this plan to the point at which it could be submitted to Mrs Morfe. May had to enlist the services of her uncle Jim, her father's brother, who possessed a motor that might do the nine miles from Turville Place to Lowton twice over without breaking down. She also provisionally booked an older woman, Virginia Rowley, and another man, David Vickers-Williams, to lend the group the safety associated with numbers.

Mrs Morfe was suspicious.

'Whose idea was this?' she demanded.

'That's beside the point,' Alexander replied. 'I'm asking you a favour.'

'You're asking the household to open up a bedroom each for the gentlemen, and one for the two girls – they had better share.'

'The servants have too little to do in this house, and I never have my friends here.'

'Very well – but one night only!'

Mr Poore, Jim, turned out to be middle-aged, bonhomous, and to have come down from London to be May's chauffeur and escort. Virginia was dark and in her early twenties, a forceful personality, and David Vickers-Williams was tall and fair-haired. They all arrived in time for lunch, at which Jim made himself agreeable to Mrs Morfe and promised to take care of the young people. He tinkered with his monster of a car throughout the afternoon, while Alexander took the others for a walk.

He began by walking with May, who opened the conversation thus: 'Haven't I done well?'

Alexander assented, but was feeling the strain of having to entertain his guests and might have sounded lukewarm.

'You could show more enthusiasm,' she complained.

He tried to supply the enthusiasm, wishing she had not demanded it.

She must have realised that he was not as pleased with her as she had expected him to be, and tried to remedy the situation with winning smiles and little bumps against him. But he was too spoilt to take correction with grace, and his extra-politeness showed it.

He then walked with Virginia, and was amazed and amused by her saying: 'You look like one of those who kiss girls and make them cry.'

Back at Turville Place May and Virginia went indoors accompanied by David, and Alexander was relieved to stay behind in order to chat to Jim.

He felt sufficiently comfortable with Jim – he was already using his Christian name by request – to say something about his future.

'Have you thought of wine?' Jim queried from under the bonnet of the car, referring to possible employment.

Alexander said no.

'I can see you as a wine merchant. It's not a bad life – I had a go at it when I was young – and you're never short of a drink.'

Alexander asked how, where, when.

'I'll give you a letter of introduction to a friend of mine in the trade. Say the word! You could probably start tomorrow if you were prepared to seek him out in London. He's always looking for likely lads to draw in customers of both sexes.'

Alexander accepted this offer without guaranteeing that he would take the matter any further.

Later, at five-thirty, the party-goers had high tea together, and soon after six, wearing the thickest and most weatherproof outer clothing available, they piled into the car and set off with a roar in clouds of smoke.

Luckily it was a dry night, and they got to Lowton without breaking down.

'Hop' did not do justice to the occasion. It was a celebration of the opening of the village hall, local dignitaries were present, the organisers of the charitable connection charged steep prices for tickets, and the Turville Place party were proved right to have dressed in their evening finery.

May chose to dance first with David Vickers-Williams. She told Alexander unnecessarily to dance with her friend Virginia. He did not like it. He was not jealous, he disliked the bossiness. And he did not like the way Virginia danced or, rather, jogged – she always seemed to be dancing to a different tune.

Then May danced with her uncle, and, when Alexander scowled at her for not dancing with him, she defied him by leading David on to the dance floor again

Finally he was holding her in his arms, but in such a manner as to provoke her to ask: 'What's wrong with you tonight?'

His answer was traditional: 'Nothing.'

'Why are you cross?' she persisted.

'David belongs to Virginia – can't you leave it to her to look after him?'

'Well, I don't belong to anybody,' she said. 'And I don't have to obey you yet.'

Alexander was silenced and shaken by her pert riposte, which included a matrimonial hint, but as the evening progressed they patched up their difference, forgot it more or less, and flirted as much as they dared in the crowd.

The return journey was not exactly romantic. The boys had to push the car to start the engine, and later to help Jim change a tyre in the pitch-dark middle of nowhere. They got too hot and the girls got too cold.

At Turville Place Mrs Morfe provided sandwiches and soup, and in due course instructed May and Virginia to say good night and follow her to their bedroom. Jim Poore scribbled that introductory note as promised, then Alexander led him upstairs to his room and retired into his own.

Shortly afterwards Alexander noticed Jim's snoring. It grew louder and began almost to shake part of or even the whole house. Combined with the disturbing propinquity of May it denied him any chance of sleep. In time he heard a scratch on his door and a suppressed giggle. He opened the door. May and Virginia were there in their white night-gowns.

May found his hand and whispered: 'Come into David's room. We want to say good night again.'

Alexander was unwilling. He tried to whisper back, 'My mother's got ears like a lynx,' but May was pulling him and being pulled by Virginia towards David's room.

Inside it, in the dark, May threw her arms round Alexander's neck and they kissed. Virginia was apparently kissing David as he lay in bed. It was more funny than any-thing else – giggling reduced the temperature.

Quite soon Alexander said: 'You must go back to your own room, my mother'd kill you if she found us together.'

May made them all giggle by saying: 'Uncle Jim won't find anybody, that's one thing certain.'

They parted. Alexander eventually drifted off to sleep. He woke with a great start. A white-clothed figure was by his bed, whimpering and tugging off his covers. He feared it was a ghost. He thought it was May. But Virginia clambered into bed with him and was gabbling, gibbering, in an undertone. She was saying how beautiful and wonderful he was, and she could not resist him.

He was completely surprised. Sleep and surprise reduced his protests to repetitive negatives. She did not listen. She took no notice and was crying. And her hands were everywhere and she had pulled up her nightdress.

'You do love me – I know you do, I knew it when we danced,' she cried in his ear, and she shifted so as to be underneath him.

She did the rest. He could not help himself. Then she was triumphant, and he got rid of her as soon as he could.

He knew it was a mistake. But his what-the-hell attitude took over. He slept soundly for the remainder of the night.

In the morning he managed to treat May and even Virginia as if nothing untoward had happened.

For a week or two Alexander felt queasy when he thought about Virginia Rowley. But he tried not to and to some extent succeeded.

His latest feelings for May were wary. She had earned bad marks with the sharpness of her tongue and for bringing Virginia into his life. And what was the point of David Vickers-Williams? David was to blame for not being the type that Virginia was determined to get into bed with. Alexander wished the village hall of Lowton had never been built. He was not displeased to be having a sort of breather from silly girls.

The idea of escape was gaining ground in the back of his mind. He would go crazy if he wasted much more time at Turville Place with his mother. He wanted real life and adventure, and to be beyond the reach of grasping female fingers. He decamped from Ashe Turville Halt to London, and, having signed into a cheap hotel near Paddington

Station, presented Jim Poore's reference to Mr Frank Begby, the proprietor of Continental Wines Ltd of St James's. Mr Begby offered instant employment, as Jim had suggested he would. But Alexander was now non-committal. He had not liked the way Mr Begby eyed him. He recalled Jim's suggestion that he – Alexander – would tempt female wine-bibbers into the shop, and was reluctant to become an advertisement or the cheese in a trap. Besides, trade was really beneath him, and would horrify Mrs Morfe.

For another couple of weeks he drifted through the streets of the metropolis, and realised, as he had not done before, that he was more at home than he ever had been at Ashe Turville. Anonymity suited him. And raffishness appealed to part of his personality. London had no conscience, maybe that was the link between them. London was in motion, in transit, impatient to reach the next stop or the next sensation, and thus explaining himself to himself.

His breather had to end – he had promised his mother he would return by such-and-such a date. On his last night in London he counted and recounted his cash and yielded to the overtures of one of the sirens who sang their songs from doorways in the vicinity of his hotel. She was no pristine village maiden, but generous and kind – she waived her fee although she could hardly have given more value for money – and she treated him in addition to the following words of advice.

'You're a lovely boy... You're going to be a lot of trouble to women, and the other way round, too... And men won't forgive you for having all the fun, unless they're cashing in on you somehow... Don't you marry if you can help it – you'd be giving up too much, and why should your wife have all the luck?... Don't thank me, dear – I should be paying you, that's the truth.'

In the evening of the next day Alexander took the train

home, and the morning after that he breakfasted alone at Turville Place – his mother had her breakfast upstairs. At about ten o'clock he still lingered at the dining-room table, reading the newspapers. He was disturbed by the drumming clank of an internal combustion engine, and, stepping over to the window, saw Jim Poore in his car with a load of people. He went to the front door and opened it with a welcoming smile.

May Poore was in the front passenger seat, scarlet in the face, crying and shouting at him furiously: 'How could you? How could you?'

The darkly veiled woman in the back seat must be Virginia Rowley, and the capped and goggled young man beside her, also red in the face and shouting at him, was Ben Poore, May's brother.

Jim Poore meanwhile was clambering out of his car, not an easy task – the others stayed put.

At least Jim spoke to him in a fairly normal tone of voice, not that what he said, or what was happening, made sense to Alexander.

'You're in trouble, young man. Sorry about the intrusion, but some people were determined to give you a piece of their minds.'

'What is it, what's wrong?'

'Now don't act innocent. It's the wages of sin. You've got a young lady, a friend of my family who I was responsible for, into very hot water.'

'I don't understand.'

'She's pregnant, and you'd better start thinking what you mean to do about it.'

'Oh.'

'Nobody's going to take "Oh" for an answer. And I've a personal interest in how you repair the damage you've done. I warn you, it'll be wedding bells or the lawyers – they'll have the law on you, and I'll be on their side.'

Jim returned to the car, the engine of which was turning over and adding to the noise and confusion, and drove off. Alexander saw May still mouthing the words, 'How could you?', and her brother waving a meaty fist at him.

He walked into the garden and slumped down on a garden seat. He needed to have his brain examined. Believe it or not – and he scarcely could believe it – he had ignored biology throughout. He had been a virgin; but he might as well have been a halfwit into the bargain. He had behaved as if the facts of life were a tall story.

Of course it was all over with May. She had cursed him twice over, for betraying him as well as for impregnating Virginia. He had cooked a whole flock of geese in record time, not least his future and his youth.

He could not marry Virginia, misnamed Virginia, he would not. She was a stranger, or at best a mere acquaintance, who had taken advantage of him, taken a liberty, and reappeared in her black veil to give notice that she was out to wreck his chances.

But how was he to defend himself in a court of law, say she was no virgin, prove that she had seduced him by force? His name would be dirt in Gloucestershire. He would be called a cad and coward for trying to excuse himself by blaming his poor young victim. Was she poor? He knew nothing about her. If she happened to be poor he would be shown in a worse light, as a rich philanderer indulging himself at the expense of poverty.

The notion of the thundercloud overhanging the name of Morfe reminded him of his mother. He would have to tell her he was likely to be sued, that they might both be ruined, and would definitely be exposed to public censure whatever happened.

He must do it at once, so that they would not be caught

napping, without anyone to speak up on their behalf. He could not be so irresponsible as to delay, although he longed to shelve the whole issue and creep into hiding.

He walked indoors despite the weakness of his knees, mounted the stairs and knocked on his mother's bedroom door.

She sat on a stool at her dressing-table and looked at his reflections in her triple mirror.

'My dear,' she said in a surprised tone of voice; 'good morning.'

'Not good,' he replied; 'a bad bad morning.'

'What? Who were those people in the car?'

'Jim Poore, May and her uncle Jim, and that girl Virginia who stayed the night here.'

'I didn't like her, and I don't like those Poores. What did they want?'

'Virginia's pregnant – and they're threatening blue murder.'

'Did you make her pregnant, Ecky?'

'She's a lunatic, she invaded my bedroom when I was asleep – I couldn't stop her. I'd scarcely spoken to her all evening. I won't marry her.'

'May Poore should never have wangled a girl like that into our home.'

'May's a back number, don't worry, she'll never speak to me again.'

'She will, she'll be keener than ever, jealous cat – I know her type. But you mustn't speak to her.'

'We'll have to have a lawyer.'

'No, no law – I won't have lawyers doling out injustice at a price. It'll be blackmail, marriage or money, marriage or a breach of promise case. Oh Ecky!'

'I shall emigrate.'

'Oh no – spare me that! What would you live on? We're not so well off as you seem to think.'

171

'I've been offered a job abroad.'

He explained that Mr Begby of Continental Wines Ltd had mentioned the vacant post of a kind of commercial travelling for his company in France. The job was not to be sniffed at, he insisted. He said he would do it temporarily. His absence would minimise the difficulties Virginia could cause. Anyway he refused to be exposed to the probable unpleasantness. He was sorry and all that, but was leaving immediately.

His mother, who had buried her head in her hands while he spoke, now stood up and embraced him.

'Clever Ecky,' she said in a tearful voice; 'you do whatever you think is best. I'll deal with everything, don't worry. Only, you won't leave your old mother in the lurch for ever, will you, darling Ecky? You go and enjoy yourself, but please write to me – and it won't be for ever, will it? Will it, Ecky?'

He was leaving the room and did not answer her question.

PART THREE

On the day on which Alexander Morfe heard that he was in danger of becoming a husband and father he took the first train from Ashe Turville Halt to London, then a taxi to Continental Wines Ltd, persuaded Mr Begby to give him the job abroad, travelled to Dover and crossed the Channel, and on French soil inhaled the air of freedom smelling of alien tobacco and drains.

In about twelve hours he had uprooted himself completely. He had left no forwarding address – he had none. He had mentioned Continental Wines to his mother, but she might not remember the name. Even if she should find out where he was, letters from her, or from other interested parties, would not reach him for ages. He had no luggage to speak of, and no idea when or if his exile would end. And he was not sorry.

He liked change. He was all for excitement. He had enjoyed the race to get to Mr Begby before Jim Poore could cancel his recommendation of his niece's boyfriend. He was not exactly a coward, fleeing the fury of two women scorned. He just preferred not to have to listen to predictable and shrill reproaches, and could see no reason why he should stick around in order to make nobody happier and himself unhappy.

He contacted his boss in France, the representative of Continental Wines, when he felt like it. Mr Bowles-Book, who insisted on Christian name terms without delay, Roger Bowles-Book was in his sixties, and wore tight double-breasted suits and sporty bow-ties. He had been notified of the arrival of his assistant and colleague, and welcomed Alexander with a greeting that was neither a firm English handshake nor a French-style kiss on the cheek – he held hands with Alexander while administering half an embrace with his free hand and arm. He said at once that they would do well together. He explained that he was almost ready to retire and could now do so with a clear conscience, because he was sure he would be handing over to a man after his own heart.

Alexander was sure of something similar: he and Roger seemed to be exemplars of the old adage that 'it takes one to know one'. Roger was quick to show – or show off – that he was a ladies' man in the Gallic tradition. He never failed to flirt with waitresses, he was ever ready at least to pinch female French flesh. Although he was far from inhibited by his age and thin flat hair and red nose and insecure dentures, he openly envied Alexander's attractions and licked his lips when he described the sexual favours Alexander was bound to enjoy.

Roger was more like a superannuated Artful Dodger than a wage slave, and his financial arrangements were unconventional. He explained to Alexander: 'I regard my money from CW as a modest retainer. It could be worse, but that's not to say it's good. I wouldn't call it remuneration for my services, I'd call it a means to an end, which end is the gratitude of the wine-growers for the orders I place with them. The French are a most generous race, such has been my experience for thirty-odd years. Contrary to the popular view, I have always found my friends in the wine trade in this country open-handed and unselfish. As a result I have lived like a fighting cock – no pun intended. I'm proud to claim that I've played as fair with CW as they've played with me, and still savoured the best of everything life has to offer while saving for a rainy day.'

Roger Bowles-Book had met Alexander at the Gare du Nord in Paris, and swept him off by car towards the north-eastern parts of France. The season was early summer, and Roger's view was that it would soon be too hot for comfort in the south. They progressed in a leisurely fashion from one vineyard to the next for the ensuing six months – that is, they stayed for up to a week or even a fortnight in the homes of the respective wine-growers, who were rewarded with a larger or smaller order for their merchandise depending on Roger's estimate of the value of their hospitality.

In the autumn Roger remarked that they might as well look in on the company's office in Paris. Alexander was surprised when the office turned out to be a room in a down-at-heel building in the suburbs. Roger skimmed through some of the letters, then elected to give Alexander a week off, a paid holiday – 'We've both earned a rest,' he claimed.

Needless to say that Alexander's seven days and nights in Paris were not restful. He nonetheless managed to report back to the office at the appointed time. Pinned to the door was an envelope with his name on it containing a key. He used the key to open the door and walked in. The room was empty except for a small pile of address books in the middle of the floor and a typewritten letter – the desk and chair and filing cabinet had vanished.

He read the letter. It was written not to himself by Roger, but to Roger by Mr Begby. The burden of it was that Roger had defrauded the company consistently, embezzled its funds, blackmailed its suppliers, and was sacked and would face the rigours of the law if he ever returned to England.

Alexander put two and two together and arrived at more than four. His boss must have read that letter when they arrived at the office, and no longer required the attentions of an assistant while he sold the company furniture and made his getaway. Roger had spoken of retirement, and now taken it earlier than expected. How could Alexander blame him, even if his own job might be adversely affected? He himself had followed a similar course of action not so long ago.

But he had been enjoying his job. He would enjoy it even more if he were able to do it on his own. As impulsively as he had obtained employment in the first place, he packed the letter and the address books in his suitcase and returned to the Gare du Nord, to England, to London and the headquarters of Continental Wines. He told Mr Begby what had happened and pleaded for a chance to prove that he was capable of taking over the agency despite his youth. He was beginning to know the ropes, he had Roger's address books full of names and commercial information, he promised faithfully to be honest and loyal, and would buy a car with his own money and be quite content with his present salary.

Mr Begby allowed him a trial period of six months; whereupon Alexander called at his bank to arrange for a transfer of his inherited funds to France, and caught the next train to Calais without contacting his mother.

His trial period was extended, eventually to years. He learned to speak French, and to respect the customs of the country. When his thoughts strayed in the direction of his English past, in other words rarely, he was pleased not to have received communications from Virginia Rowley or her solicitor. At length a few letters from his mother reached the Paris office of CW, but he only picked them up when he felt like it, he only answered them with postcards, and he was also pleased that she never referred to Virginia. Sometimes he did wonder if his child was alive.

To say he was happy in his work would be doubly misleading. Happiness seemed to have been left out of his composition. He had a cast-iron digestion and a steady temperament, his spirits were high rather than low, and he knew the difference between satisfaction and dissatisfaction; but if he said, or rather agreed, that he was happy, his meaning was that he was not sad. Actually he was never sad, a characteristic considered a quality by some women and a defect by others, especially by those who were out for revenge and wished to make him suffer.

As for his work, it was more women than wine. Again, it was more pleasure than pain. Alexander Morfe learned the language of love in a fraction of the time it took him to learn French; he must have set records for graduating from his own seduction by Virginia Rowley to being in possession of umpteen female scalps. But he did not consider himself a seducer. Later on, when the umpteen had multiplied, he would still say that he had never made a pass at a woman – say it under pressure and in self-defence, and be thought by other men outrageously boastful for doing so.

The basis of his claim was a technical and controversial matter. The accurate side of it was his looks and his charm. His clear blue eyes, his fresh complexion, his lithe and supple physique, and his power of concentration on pretty well every woman he came across, combined together into a powerful elixir of desirability. He was so attentive, open-minded, patient and apparently sympathetic, and he noticed so much, clothes, hair-styles, the good and bad sides of faces, the state of marriages and the yearning of hearts, that intentionally or unintentionally he posed an almost irresistible temptation to the opposite sex. Besides, his diffidence, his shy reluctance, inspired the forthright approach.

The fact beyond reason that remained, and remains in every academic study of ladies' men in general, was that he emitted an overpowering and mysterious sexual signal, similar to those which summon denizens of the animal kingdom and even insects to travel across continents, to brave hardships and risk their lives in order to mate.

Time added to his attractions; setting aside beneficial

physical changes, it lent him the sort of reputation which reassures women that they are unlikely to be spurned or embarrassed.

As he drove through the countryside of Europe he would occasionally amuse himself by recalling the various names he had been called in intimate situations: for instances, as it were in one column, Adonis, God of love, *Monsieur Toujours Prêt*, every woman's ideal, deliciously vicious, a gentleman, kind, good, sweet, now a tomcat now a kitten, a rabbit, stoat, newt, tasty morsel, toy, and, in the other column, heartless, selfish, cruel, unfaithful, a liar, cad, coward, a destroyer of defenceless women, a devil's disciple who deserved to go to hell.

The compliments and curses nullified one another, and reinforced his feeling that he had every right to be glad he was alive.

Alexander's business was unbusinesslike. He kept paperwork to a minimum, he could not be bothered with mathematical figures. He escaped awkward questions from Mr Begby in London, and niggling criticism, because he did not tax the wine-growers and therefore obtained better deals for Continental Wines than Roger Bowles-Book ever had.

Business was his convenience. It paid for visits to hostelries where he was served by female members of the staff, and vice versa. And in private houses ladies would lure him into their parlours with hints that Continental Wines would profit thereby. His professional activities followed no regular pattern. He too, like Roger, aimed to spend summer in the north and winter in the south for meteorological reasons. But the impulses of a sexual nomad took precedence over geography. The Mediterranean sun might be turning the southern provinces into a desert, yet the memory of a certain oasis there, overflowing with the nectar he preferred, and with languor and luxury, would drag him away from temperate climes and green fertility.

He did not get on too badly with the menfolk of the women who fell into his arms. He was careful enough not to provoke them to charge exorbitant prices for their wares. To deflower virgins would not encourage their fathers to sign on dotted lines. Anyway, if need be, virgins could retain their virginity without disappointing anybody. Alexander favoured country wives with hardworking spouses and children at boarding school. He sensed, although he did not go in for analysis, that female boredom and male availability were his accomplices. But he recognised jealous consorts a mile off and steered clear of them. Again, his favourites in the husband line were older than their better or worse halves, and were grateful to him in a grudging way for relieving them of another duty and putting the roses back in their wives' cheeks.

If he prided himself on anything, it was not on that for which women would no doubt have given him prizes, but on his diplomatic skills. He side-stepped trouble. He slipped through possessive fingers. He soothed savage breasts, masculine and feminine. He disappeared in the nick of time, and reappeared when all was forgiven and he was badly wanted. He had intuition and sensitivity, although sentiment was a closed book to him and he defended his freedom ruthlessly.

Sometimes Alexander's observations brought home to him the realisation that he differed from most men. Promiscuity was his province, monogamy was another country. He was not only incapable of fidelity, he never expected others to be faithful. He was not a breeder – dynasty meant nothing to him. Even in the lengthening shadow of the age of thirty he did not tire of the sexual game as Romeos of his acquaintance had done. He lived for the moment when a woman showed herself to him, offered herself, the climax of the hunt in his perception, and the object of the exercise of his individualistic roaming.

As for the accusations hurled at him by his mistresses or his victims, was there a grain of truth in them? Was his heart as cold as they swore it was? Well – he did not care. He cared not a jot that he earned money by stooping to do work that his father and grandfather had slaved and striven to rise above. He recognised no conventions, he took nothing seriously, apart from his chief preoccupation, which is ruined by laughter and frivolity. He was pleased to be an outsider in a worldly sense, but an insider in the context of love.

Alexander Morfe was human, whatever some of his jilted women might say, to the extent of feeling the need of a holiday from time to time.

One summer he had been hard at it for months in the north-east corner of the country, Lorraine to be precise. He was sick of buying wine and a great deal of bother to boot. He found himself in Nancy, and on impulse entered a church and asked the priest, who was leaving one of the confessionals, if he could possibly recommend a hotel or lodging in the country for a short visit. He had remembered that money simplified matters: so long as he or his company paid for his accommodation, retreat from emotional entanglements was easier to beat than would be the case if he were receiving hospitality in a private house. The priest answered his question by introducing him to a lady sitting in a nearby pew, Madame Vallette, Béatrice Vallette.

Alexander knew at once that he had made a mistake – she was too attractive. He did his level best to correct it. The lady was saying that her home had a simple room sometimes let to a lodger, and she would permit him with pleasure to rest there for a few days. But he would need food: she would feed him. He pretended to be anxious about the rent: it would cost very little.

He accepted her offer with an inward sigh. Although she

might spoil his holiday with her olive skin and shapely figure, she seemed to be pious, she must have been in the church to confess her sins, which he hoped were trivial, and surely the priest would not have thrown them together if there was no Monsieur Vallette to keep them apart.

They were now outside the church. She had given him directions to the Vallette farmhouse, and she asked his name. Obviously she recognised it, because he had been active in Lorraine for several years, and she hesitated. He hoped for a negative moment that her Christian morals and modesty would induce her to withdraw her offer and save them both potential tribulations. But her religious faith or inclinations opted for the opposite line. Instead of deciding not to expose herself to the wiles of a man who had led other women, including women she knew, astray, she perhaps decided that her duty was to try to reform him. At any rate she firmly fixed the time at which she would expect him to clock in.

He drove to the farm. She had returned earlier with her daughter. Her husband, Gaston, was in his fifties, twenty years older than Béatrice, heavily built, balding, authoritative yet gentle. Marie, their daughter and only child, was fifteen with huge glowing dark brown eyes.

Alexander spent four nights under their roof. They were uneventful by his standards, thankfully. And the days were jolly. He liked, admired and even envied the family. Gaston and Béatrice were a demonstrative pair, always hugging each other, and Marie had inherited their outgoing emotional gifts. She hugged each parent equally, and, on the second day of Alexander's stay, himself even more so. Poor Marie got a speechless crush on him, seized hold of his hand whenever she could, clambered all over him, straying innocently on to his lap, and begging to be admitted into his bedroom while he shaved.

He was included in the family's countrified pursuits and

expeditions. With the mother and daughter he picked mushrooms in the dawn, in dewy fields strewn with silver spiders' webs. With Gaston he cut down brambles and made bonfires. Alexander watched Béatrice and Marie make butter in the dairy, and was lent a gun by Gaston so that he could join in a large-scale organised shoot of the pigeons that pinched the farmers' crops.

Picnics in the fields were shared with the farm-workers at midday, and in the evening delicious meals were prepared and consumed in the old-fashioned kitchen with its glowing range and highly polished dresser.

On Alexander's final evening special wine was opened in his honour, and Marie clung to him and tried to force him to promise he would marry her. But the girl eventually consented to go to bed, and then Gaston was summoned to deal with some agricultural emergency.

Béatrice sat at the head of the refectory table with Alexander on her right in the candle-lit room. Her smooth skin shone and her brown eyes reflected the flames of the candles.

'Perhaps you should marry,' she said, smiling.

'Perhaps I will one day,' he replied, returning her smile.

'Perhaps it would be better for some people if you did not wait too long.'

'What people?'

'Women.'

'Oh, women!'

'No, Alexander, many women love you, they say, and you don't love them back and then they're unhappy.'

'What would you think if I did marry and didn't love my wife?'

'I'd be very sorry for her, and cross with you.'

'Well, as it is, there's nobody for you to be specially sorry for, and please don't be cross with me and spoil our friendship. I've had such a nice time in your home.'

'All right. I'm lucky, I have Gaston. But I know you can be a bad boy to women not so lucky as I am. Come back to see me, will you, Alexander? I am your friend, and I won't change.'

Of course he did not trust her; nor could he trust himself. But he pretended to believe her and behaved as if they were both trustworthy. Gaston rejoined them before too long, and in the morning of the next day the adult good-byes were formal enough, while Marie's complimentary tears were sweet.

Twelve months elapsed. He had been touring round Lorraine and was once more at Nancy. Why not, he reflected, utilising the unwise words that sprang so readily to his lips. He could do with a peaceful platonic interlude, and he drove out to the Vallette farm.

Béatrice greeted him. Gaston was absent, buying a bull in Scotland, she explained. Marie? Marie was at boarding school.

They faced each other in the doorway, pausing, pondering.

'Another time,' he muttered.

'No – come in,' she retorted.

Again he knew it was wrong, but could hardly run away, and, typically, was not sure he wanted to. The change in her was marked. She was flushed, constrained, and met his eye with difficulty, as if they were planning an unspeakable crime. After dinner she invited him to take a stroll in the balmy night air. When he hesitated again, she said in a challenging manner, 'You can do as you please,' and he followed her.

She led the way to a summerhouse, which had uphol-stered benches round the walls although it was partly open to the elements.

'Make love to me,' she commanded peremptorily.

A little light from the house reached the summerhouse, and he saw that she was standing rigidly with her back turned towards him.

'No,' he began.

She whirled round and warned: 'Don't insult me again!'

'Insult you? What do you mean?'

'I won't be the only woman in the world who's no more to you than a friend.'

That settled it – settled it for several hours of that particular night. But Alexander had arrived at the point at which he was sure of something for a change, namely that he must wriggle out of her clutches in a hurry. Her intensity and fierceness frightened him. She was another religious adulteress who brought an exciting sense of sin to the sexual act; but her insatiability was too much even for him. She had seemed to him a well-adjusted wife, and had turned into a mistress obsessed with him, suffering from satyriasis, and saying she was being driven crazy by her boring old husband.

They parted eventually, and he insisted on sleeping alone and in his bedroom. But she joined him there in the morning, and he then told her he had to leave, he had remembered he had an important engagement to keep.

She cried. She said he had stayed longer last time.

'I happened to be on holiday,' he replied. 'Now I have to work in order to eat. I'm sorry.'

'Oh yes,' she commented sarcastically, thought for a moment, and inquired: 'When will you come back?'

'Béatrice, I don't know, I can't tell you, my work may take me anywhere, the other end of France, even London – I can't give you a date when I'll be free.'

'Oh but you must. If you don't give me a time to look forward to, I shall tell Gaston that you raped me and he'll shoot you.'

'Béatrice, for heaven's sake!'

'I swear it, Alexander. You don't understand I've betrayed my husband and my God for your sake, because you're the love of my life. You understand much less of love than I do, although you've had more. Even if you don't know why, it is your turn to sacrifice for me. Tell me when you'll be back!'

He yielded, he produced his diary, he said he would try to be in her vicinity in six months, and mentioned January.

She cried again and said: 'How can I love a man like you? I hate you in so many ways, for not being worthy, for not being sincere. Believe me before it's too late, come in January or Gaston will kill you.'

'Béatrice,' he started to reproach and reason with her, but her grim white tear-stained face stopped him. He continued lamely: 'Love isn't desperate in my book. You believe me, my dear, love doesn't have to be misery and murder. I'll turn up, never fear – and here's to the next time!'

She had to laugh. She failed to get an address out of him that she could write to. She clung to him, but he tore himself out of her arms. He drove off with a cheery wave and gloomy forebodings.

Alexander duly travelled northwards in the appointed month, and the dropping temperature matched his attitude to the impending reunion. He did not keep his promises to women as a rule; the exceptional factor in the present instance was that he had no wish to be shot dead, or, what could be commercially worse, wounded and the subject of publicity. Wine-growers would not be keen to do business with the unmasked seducer of their wives.

Béatrice awaited him, although he had not named the day of his arrival. She ran out of the house and shed tears as she kissed him. His heart, in so far as he had one, sank.

187

She had now broken her promise not to change with a vengeance: she had lost weight, all her curves had become angles, and her olive complexion had turned greenish and she had dyed her hair blacker than black. As for her emotions, they were out of control, more so than before. She showed him up to his bedroom and demanded love there and then – Gaston and Marie were apparently in Nancy. Afterwards she said she had been ill without him, but, because he had proved in two ways that he cared for her, she would now get better and fatter in order to give him greater pleasure.

The redeeming feature of his forty-eight-hour visit was Marie Vallette. She was sixteen by this time, no longer a child, a young woman in the budding stage, and the richest of feasts for the eye of a gourmet of female beauty. She returned from Nancy and was shy, now running forward to kiss him, now blushing crimson because she had done so, now looking as if she would weep because her father teased her for worshipping her hero, now giggling helplessly when Alexander compared the little caterpillar she had been with the butterfly she had grown into.

Marie was the perfected version of the Béatrice who had once attracted Alexander. Did her beauty reside in the brilliant whites of her brown eyes, or her features, especially her strong moist teeth? Or was it her overall colouring, or her smooth unblemished skin? Or, more likely, did she dazzle and charm with her figure that seemed to stretch upwards like a flower to the sun, and her suppleness and grace?

Gaston Vallette clearly doted on Marie and vice versa, and Béatrice and her daughter were still close. But Gaston had aged since Alexander saw him last, probably as a result of concern for the wellbeing of his wife. He suspected nothing, he was grateful to Alexander for sparing them a couple of full days of his company, and spoke openly of how fond his womenfolk were of him, adding with unconscious irony that his visit would do Béatrice good.

So long as the four of them were together, at family meals and gatherings, there was no trouble. And Gaston took Alexander for walks, and again lent him a gun so that they could shoot pigeons together. On one evening he even referred to the deterioration of Béatrice's health, which he ascribed to the change of life and some sort of nervous breakdown. She had grown less affectionate, he confessed, and he hoped she was not ill.

But inevitable gaps in the social programme gave Béatrice chances to hiss asides at her lover, technical lover anyway. Two days were not enough, she warned repeatedly, and he was not to stare at Marie. The pretence was killing her, she hissed – and how were they to be alone?

Her own answer to the last question really scared him. She came to him in the middle of the night, stirring disagreeable memories of Virginia Rowley. Although he could make sure she would not have a baby, he was in even greater peril this time round from a jealous husband with guns. He tried to send her back to her marital bed, but she threatened to scream the house down. He gave her what she wanted and got rid of her, and spent the rest of the night cursing her and himself inwardly.

On the second night he locked the bedroom door, having told her he was going to. In the morning she was angry with him during a short walk they squeezed in before he departed. Unless he returned soon, she again swore she would tell Gaston. Unless he stayed longer next time, she would leave home and track him down and never let him out of her sight. And if he was not kind to her, she would cut her throat.

He made his escape without climactic melodrama after offering another visit in three months. Gaston was pleased, Béatrice did not show she was displeased. Marie was nowhere to be found, she must have been unaware that he was leaving so early, but he refused to wait and told the elder Vallettes to kiss her goodbye on his behalf.

Gaston stood with his arm round his wife's shoulders, smiling, waving and calling, 'Until the spring!'

Alexander breathed freely for the first time for hours.

Half a mile down the road Marie flagged his car to a stop. He began to bid her goodbye, but she wanted him to get out. He complied, although she was red in the face and agitated, and he should have smelt a rat.

'Please,' she said, sounding as well as looking irresistible, and led him towards a dilapidated hay barn.

Inside in the semi-darkness she explained that she wanted him to be her first lover, she wanted to give him the prize of herself, and to make that offering to the one she worshipped, although it would always be their secret, and she would never ever make a nuisance of herself.

She wore an overcoat, nothing else. She would not take no for an answer. He acted in character and obliged.

Every time he thought of the Vallettes, of Lorraine, of North-East France, in the ensuing twelve weeks, he called himself an idiot. He weighed up the pros and cons until he was sick of them, and, his promises notwithstanding, resolved not to walk into that probable death trap of his own volition. Let Béatrice try to find him, let Gaston do likewise: they were unlikely to succeed, and if they did he had had a lot of practice in shaking off superfluous females, and at least would be a running target for Gaston instead of a sitting duck.

The contrary upshot was that he travelled north at the appointed time. His excuse was that he had orders to place with wine-growers in fairly adjacent Moselle. The truth was that he was curious, he suffered from a version of the curiosity that killed the cat.

Besides, he was subject to the general law according to which satisfactory sex is almost never confined to a single act of communion. He dreaded Béatrice, but Marie was a different matter.

He chose to stay in a hotel on the far side of Nancy, far from the Vallettes, that is to say. He aimed to spend the night and move on in one direction or another on the following day. He sat alone in the hotel's dining-room and asked a waiter for a newspaper to read.

The paper that was produced was a local one and weeks old. He was on the point of rejecting it with a sharp word or two when he caught sight of the headline on the front page.

'Vallette guilty,' he read.

He hardly needed to read on, he could guess the gist of the story. There had been a terrible scene at the farm – it dated back to a few days after he had left. Monsieur had discovered that Madame had a lover who had seduced Mademoiselle. He had fetched a gun with which he intended to shoot the seducer, but Madame wrestled it from his hands and thus accidentally shot their daughter. Monsieur then shot his wife. It was a *crime passionnel*.

Alexander knew more than the journalist. What he had vaguely foreseen had somehow occurred. Either Marie had not been able to keep her mouth shut, and, not knowing of her mother's affair with himself, had poured a poisonous boast into that almost insanely jealous ear; or maybe there had been a telltale stain on her coat. Béatrice, who had told him she longed to scratch out the eyes of every one of his women, might have gone for a gun to shoot Marie with, or else lost her reason completely and spilled the beans to Gaston. That Béatrice had wounded Marie in the stomach struck Alexander as deliberate, punishment fitting a crime in her deranged judgment. And of course Gaston's defence, that Béatrice had turned the gun on herself, was more than

191

likely the case, although not accepted by the court. Another possibility was that Marie had shot her mother and Gaston was just taking the blame.

Marie had survived in a more or less injured state, apparently. Alexander was grateful to her for not revealing his name. Her own and her father's discretion spared them all scandalous revelations. He did not eat much dinner that night in the hotel. But his constitutional realism reasserted itself as he drove back towards the sun and the luxury of the Côte d'Azur.

PART FOUR

1914 and World War I wrong-footed Alexander Morfe.

He had thought the politicians could not be so stupid. Their war inconvenienced him – he was cognisant of, but not particularly interested in, its effect on millions of other people. An end to peace coincided with the following letter he had eventually received from his mother.

'My dear boy, I have not been well, and I wonder if you could come and be with me for a little time. Forgive me for asking you again. I have tried not to bother you for more years than I like to count. That Virginia girl has married and had her first child. You have nothing to fear from her. It has been very hard not even to know if you are dead or alive. Please come home. There are money matters that we need to discuss. With love from your old mother.'

The handwriting was spidery and each line of it dropped downwards, suggesting despondency and frailty. Alexander jumped to the conclusion that he was meant to have pity on her because she could no longer use a pen properly. But pity was not his line, and he had raised an impregnable barrier against having his emotions controlled by women. While not displeased to know that Virginia had solved their little problem and had become another man's headache, he hated the past and to be reminded of it, and he did not like to be told that he was or had been afraid of her. His unwritten answer to his mother's letter was that wild horses would not drag him back to Turville Place.

His mother was not dead yet, he reasoned. If she had

been, lawyers and bankers would have notified him. Money, her will, did need to be discussed, he could agree. Meanwhile, however, there was no rush – he refused to be rushed into turning his life upside down even temporarily.

But the war made nonsense of his logic. Mr Begby also wrote to him, explaining that his job was done for the duration – the trade in fine wines was going to be severely curtailed. Continental Wines might be able to offer work in the shop or the office, but Mr Begby expected that Alexander would wish to serve his country in some capacity.

As a result, and as his mother tactlessly put it, the prodigal returned after all.

The new reasons that influenced Alexander without exactly changing his mind were, first, that unemployment in France in wartime was not an amusing prospect. Secondly, he did not want to be thought a coward: he hoped to carry on from where he was leaving off, and would not be able to face his French friends after the war if they had fought gallantly and he had skulked and made no contribution. The third reason, arrived at reluctantly, was that since he would be in England and at a loose end for more or less time he might as well again show his face to his mother.

Turville Place was his worst experience for ages. He had wondered if he was exaggerating the horrors of his home, but he had under-estimated them. His mother had deceived him: although she had shrunk and her hair was whiter and thinner, she looked as if she had years ahead in which to pester him. She postponed the discussion of money, probably in hopes of delaying his departure. Her sycophancy revolted him, and her plots and plans to keep him out of danger were counterproductive. He could not stand the climate, or the gloomy house stinking of medicaments, or the old servants fawning on him, or the boredom, and decided without a doubt that armed conflict with a fierce enemy must be preferable.

He pined for action, whatever its difference from the sort of action he was accustomed to.

He joined the army, was sent out to France, fought at Mons and was wounded. Shrapnel had penetrated his thigh and shattered his left thigh-bone. He was taken to a field-hospital behind the lines, then to other hospitals. His leg mended, and Lady Luck proved to have been as faithful to him as ever. His personal war was brief if painful, and left him unscathed, apart from a limp that added to rather than subtracted from his sex appeal.

He remained in uniform and obtained a desk job in Whitehall. One of the main tasks allotted to him by his superior officers was to pay visits to the bereaved mothers, wives and sisters of heroes and casualties.

Those superior officers were unaware that they had as it were given a fox the key to the chicken run and ordered him to smooth the feathers of the chickens.

Alexander was good at the work, professionally speaking. With his sympathy for the majority of women, and his wide experience of their emotions, which did not scare him, he might have been made for it. Again, he himself was untouched by the sadness involved, and brought a refreshing serenity to the clichés of condolence.

He did not stay long with ladies advanced in years, or so shattered as to be blind and deaf to his implicit offers of consolation prizes. He was encouraged to spend more time where his attendance was appreciated, for instance by the utilisation of his shoulder to cry on, or of his ear in which strange confessions could be whispered. Tears were apt to wash away barriers; and Alexander's special talent was never to inhibit a woman from doing whatever came naturally.

He must have borne bad news to a few hundred females

in the tragic years of war. Sometimes an especially unhappy widow or a sister overwhelmed by sorrow would fall into his arms, or, rather, entreat him to fall into theirs. It would be on a strictly temporary basis, a single circumstantial lapse, and more than once he was cut dead by women in mourning who knew him well in the biblical sense. He was usually able to discourage repetition by showing or saying that he had nothing more to give but elusiveness.

His accumulation of women's secrets took even himself by surprise. Here was one whose late husband never consummated their marriage, he had slept on a sofa for years rather than on the nuptial couch within reach of her advances. There was another whose spouse had only claimed his marital right after getting drunk and beating her on Saturday nights. For one woman intimacy had occurred twice and saddled her with three children, twin boys who became delinquent and a daughter who hated her. Weird fancies and practices had to be indulged in order to bring men to boiling point – lavatorial routines, pain inflicted or endured. Impotence was apparently commoner than muck, and, like frigidity, a frequent consequence of the birth of offspring.

Women previously happy sustained the loss of their beloveds better than those who would be racked by regrets. They might make love to or with Alexander on the spur of bereavement for opposite reasons, the first in order to recall the embraces that were theirs no more, the second to try to compensate for not having granted their dead partners such service. Both were liable to cry their eyes out while they grieved in his arms, and one or other would occasionally wind up proceedings by slapping his face.

He was tethered to London, whereas his former amorous estate had been the whole of France. He could not escape some women – and however inconvenient their adhesiveness, they were better than his mother waiting for him in vain at Ashe Turville. As a result he was involved with, though not committed to, a couple. His health, strength and virility were still equal to twice the trouble.

He met Violet Stephens on one of his errands of mercy, as the office was pleased to call them. She lived in a terrace house in Chelsea – it was painted white and had window-boxes full of flowers. She opened the door to him and demanded in a forbidding voice: 'Yes?' She was tall with untidy brown hair and a narrow bony face.

'I'm afraid I've been detailed to bring you this telegram from the War Office,' he began, holding it out to her.

She tore it open on the doorstep, more impatiently than with dread, as if it was a boring communication of a social kind instead of probable notification of a death on active service.

She read it, looked at him, and remarked: 'They've got Bernie,' referring to her husband, Colonel Bernard Stephens.

'I'm sorry,' Alexander murmured.

She said: 'I'd like a cup of tea. Join me for a cup of tea, will you? It's teatime, isn't it?'

He followed her indoors, having translated her invitation into the secret language of sex. He sensed that she had made up her mind as women do, at a glance, that he was sexually acceptable. And because she was willing in principle, although not many principles were involved, so was he.

She poured brandy into the cups of tea, and they drank more than one cup apiece. She spoke of her late husband coolly: 'I knew he'd catch it... He liked to play at being toy soldiers... He was braver than he was clever... Poor old Bernie!' They moved from the kitchen into the sitting-room, and she wanted him to sit beside her on the sofa: 'I may need your handkerchief at short notice,' she explained. She drank more brandy without the tea and referred to her Bernie in increasingly patronising terms. 'He was never where I wanted him, he was always fighting somebody, or on manoeuvres or courses, or in hospital because he had hurt himself with his rifle or his bayonet... He had no appreciation of any of the things I was interested in, he never read a good book, he stuck to the biographies of grisly army men... I married him on the rebound, and because I knew that, unlike his predecessor in my affections, he would never have the guts to look to right or left.'

At length she did cry. Her tears of a bitter sort of pity or self-pity flowed when she said: 'He was a rotten husband.' Alexander duly supplied a handkerchief and a shoulder. She then gulped out: 'God help me for telling you all these things. You'll have to forget them. Anyway they're not true. I'm sorry! I don't even know your name.' But in spite of her verbal recognition of the fact that they were strangers she rested her head on his shoulder for longer than was necessary.

He gave her his name. She wanted to be called Violet and to call him Alexander. She had a sarcastic or ironic manner of talking: 'A nice way to meet you,' she said. Although she was now in a slightly maudlin state, she conducted their next exchanges with skill.

'Can I ask you a favour? Have you a pressing engagement this evening? I'd rather not be left alone, if you could or would keep me company. There's nobody else I can turn to,' she began.

He said he would stay with her.

'Are you married with six children?'

He said no.

'But you like women, that's easy to see.'

He said he did.

'A lot?'

'Too much.'

'I thought so. Bernie put me on a pedestal and did his damnedest to keep me there.'

'But he couldn't, I suppose?'

'I had to live my own life – he was away so much, and so shy – he blushed if I kissed him on the cheek.'

'What about now? Have you got a little friend, as they say in France?'

'Not at the moment, that's the problem. Will scrambled eggs do for supper?'

They ate early and quickly. At the end of it she seemed to be semi-paralysed by shock, sorrow, alcohol or play-acting.

'I must lie down,' she said, 'give me a hand!'

He had to manhandle her up the stairs, while she giggled and slumped against him. In the bedroom with its inhospitably narrow double bed a sea-change overcame her. She was briskly practical and savagely lustful.

When they were done, she emerged from the adjoining bathroom in a dressing-gown and demanded in peremptory tones: 'Please leave my house.'

He laughed at her.

'Be careful you don't laugh on the other side of your face. You've assaulted me, and I may report you to your commanding officer. Get out, get out!'

He repeated something she had already said, 'Poor old Bernie,' and hurried to obey her before she could hit him.

Violet Stephens, in a metaphor perhaps more typical of her husband, returned to the charge, as Alexander had expected. He found a note from her on his desk, asking or telling him to be at her house in Chelsea at nine-thirty p.m. on such-and-such an evening.

He complied. She scolded him. He had behaved disgracefully, taken advantage of her when she was crippled

.

by misery, she said; and she called him a jackal, profiting from the death of a better man than he was, and a vulture, picking on carrion.

He heard her out, and then inquired: 'Why did you ask me here so late in the evening if you only wanted to black-guard me?' – and she had to laugh and was soon sitting on his knee.

Violet had no particular attractions, physical or spiritual; it was her peculiarity, her perversity, that lured Alexander into her parlour. She was in her early forties and already convinced that it was too late for her to bear the child or children she had not wanted when she was younger. She complained of having always been lonely, but was too choosy to make platonic friends of either sex. She pretended to be a dainty arty classy lady, yet was a sexual predator and a dictator in her bedroom. She was driven towards nymphomania by usually failing to get whatever it was she required from men.

Her pillow talk was all fairy tales. She would paint a ver-bal picture of her father in glowing colours: he had been her wonderful mentor, a paragon and a saint, and a few days later claim that he had forced her as a child to share his bath and instilled in her a horror of the male physique. Sometimes she even dwelt fondly on the charms of Colonel Stephens. Sometimes she wondered aloud if she might be a lesbian, an idea unlikely to have overcome the shyness of her Bernie.

She paid Alexander only back-handed compliments: he stank of other women, he was a filthy brute. She would hold back and accuse him of having a one-track mind, and alter-natively taunt him with having run out of steam. She was exclusively self-centred: if he spoke on any subject for too long by her standards, she would yawn and close her eyes.

He compared her to the black widow spider that eats its mate, to a queen bee that makes sure the drone that fertilises her does not survive, to the human queens who emasculated their lovers or cut off their heads, and to all the females who are keen on castration. Why then, she snapped back argumentatively, did he return to the scene of his original crime, why did he recommit it? Because he was amused by trying to juggle with quicksilver, he said if he was feeling friendly, or, if he was sick and tired of her, because he had never believed in the existence of a hell of a woman such as she was.

They had their good times. She forgot to remember to mourn and could be skittish behind the drawn curtains of her house with the wreath on its front door. They did not go out – she was unwilling to parade about with a new man in front of her neighbours – and he never stayed with her for more than an hour or two. The lighter side of their association showed itself while they drank reviving cups of tea in her kitchen – she had no living-in servants, and was far from flush with money.

Alexander offered to pay for things, and it tickled her to drive up the price of her favours.

'Is that all you think I'm worth?' she asked. 'What can I do for you to earn a bit more?'

She took his money and bought undergarments to please him. She played games in bed and assumed different characters to keep boredom at bay, her own as well as his, and actually would have embarrassed him if he had not been studying her from his own version of a scientific point of view. Her widowhood was his guarantee that she was not going to turn nasty and discuss matrimony.

Once she asked him: 'How did the other women let you off scot-free?'

'I'll never marry you, Violet.'

'What do you mean? What's the answer to my question?'

'My answer is that when I heard your sort of question I made myself extremely scarce.'

'You flatter yourself if you think I'd sink so low as to be your wife.'

'Well, don't you flatter yourself by thinking I belong to you or you can bank on me.'

'How romantic you are!'

'What's romantic? I've never known the meaning of that word.'

'And I sympathise with the wretched women who were as stupid as I've been and let you into their beds.'

'Shall we call it quits?'

'Why not? You give me damn all that matters. I know nothing of your life. You're no different from my dustman.'

'Do you sleep with your dustman?'

'Oh go away, I've had enough of you.'

'*Adieu* or *au revoir*?' he inquired and headed for the exit.

No wonder that Alexander, being Alexander, should have diluted the acidic brew of his sessions with Violet by the addition of the sweetness of Rose Berowne.

He had often driven two in hand, as the chauvinists say. But he had never found himself driving – or perhaps being driven – by a pair so complementary as Violet Stephens and Rose Berowne.

Violet was nearing the end of her fruitful feminine life, Rose aged twenty-two was still near the beginning of hers. Violet was a darkish colour both physically and psychologically, Rose was golden. Violet was depressive, twisted and grim, Rose straightforward and indiscriminate in her friendliness. Sex was a torturous obsession for Violet, for Rose it was an integral part of the breath of life. And Rose had a baby daughter, Daisy, and was not short of cash.

Rose's husband Toby, Captain Berowne, was not necessarily dead. She loved him, they had not been married for long. The report which Alexander bore to her home in

North London, in a residential avenue in St John's Wood, stated only that Captain Berowne was missing. Rose was therefore enabled to give free rein to her optimism and resilience almost from the moment she read her telegram.

She, too, asked Alexander into her house after reading it. She was shaken, large lustrous tears rolled down her pink cheeks, but good manners combined with the effect he had on women to gain him admission into her sitting-room and good graces. When she boo-hooed for her Toby he provided the comfort of his warm hands and the consolation of his expert embrace. What did it mean, she sobbed. It could mean nothing bad, he assured her, wiping away tears with his handkerchief. She refused to believe that Toby was dead and gone – he was so tough, such a brave survivor, and would somehow manage not to abandon herself and his little Daisy. No, she was sure he would reappear in his own time, she was determined not to lose faith that he was alive somewhere and certainly kicking.

What did the telegram mean she should do, how she should behave, in the immediate future, she asked Alexander. She refused to go into mourning. She would continue to dress in the bright colours that suited her and Toby preferred, but should she stay indoors and not have any fun for Toby's sake?

When he said maybe, she asked him to visit her. She dreaded having to dwell on Toby's possible fate with friends, she would not see them more than she could help it, and was going to be so dull with Daisy – would he come and cheer them up sometimes? She did not have to explain anything to Alexander, as she had been instructed to call him – please would he see her through the difficult weeks ahead?

He was ready to oblige her however she wished. She cried and she smiled equally attractively. She was as healthy and natural as Violet was strained and self-conscious. He returned to her light and airy house in its garden setting, he spent odd hours there on different days, and won the heart of Daisy. Rose now chattered and laughed with him as if they were at least old acquaintances, and she thanked him with chaste kisses when they said goodbye.

She had invited him to dine one evening. When he arrived in her house she was having temporary qualms: was she right to entertain a lone gentleman in her circumstances? His answer applied to both of them: nobody should or would know that they were meeting – she must try to stop her servants' tongues wagging. Thus they became conspirators before dinner was served. After dinner had been eaten and wines had been drunk, Rose told him the story of her love of Toby and confided that the withdrawal of Toby's marital attentiveness had caused and was causing her distress. The overture leading to the third and last stage of intimacy was the kiss good night that they exchanged in the sitting-room.

They made love not as he made it with Violet, dramatically, conditionally, but instantly and simply.

They did take precautions, and they were careful not to give her servants too many chances to gossip. She would admit him into her house late at night. If the weather allowed they would go for midnight strolls, she with her face hidden by a hat or a shawl. She had had no adulterous experience and was thrilled by it: potential inhibitions were relieved by her confidence that she had no need to mourn. As for unfaithfulness, she thought Toby would understand and forgive her: after all, she said, he had been an absolute dog before they married, whereas she was a virgin. She regarded the ethical aspect of their affair with naïvety: how lovely it was to be wicked, she bubbled.

She told Alexander she loved him – Violet never did. Rose loved him and Daisy and Toby and goodness knows who else dearly. She exuded all-embracing generous love, which was charming if not as deep as Violet's feelings, whatever they might be. She would pay him positively un-English compliments while thinking aloud in attempts to understand why she had broken her marriage vows for his sake without hesitation.

'I suppose it was because you were so nice to talk to,' she mused.

'But I didn't do much talking.'

'Well, you listened to me nicely, and you understood me.'

'I'd stirred up your emotions with my telegram, perhaps that was it,' he suggested.

She was too honest to accept such an excuse.

'No, I had this strange feeling that I knew you through and through and you knew me likewise.'

She continued: 'Your face was part of my undoing. You always look carefree, and your complexion and hair are such lovely colours. But there are other handsome men in uniform knocking around, and I hadn't even noticed one since I met Toby. In my opinion there really is more to chemistry than people allow. There must be a chemical in you that's just the job for a chemical in me.'

He inquired: 'What about the action we took when we stopped talking?'

'You made it seem like the logical thing to do, and I couldn't let you go without a cuddle,' she said.

Rose and Violet had something in common, apart from himself: neither of them probed into how he spent the rest of his spare time. Their reasons, of course, were diametrically opposed: Rose had respect for the works of man and imagined he was engaged in important military business when he was not with her, whereas Violet was bitterly convinced that he had other female fish to fry, and did not want to have her low self-esteem lowered further by finding out exactly what he was up to.

Rose did say it would be special if he had premises of his own where they could meet out of range of prying eyes, but he was not leaving his bolt hole in army accommodation for any woman, and countered the idea by reminding her that he might be posted elsewhere or even abroad at short notice.

'Don't leave me,' she begged. 'I'd be such a lonely sad girl if you as well as Toby deserted me.'

He corrected her aptitude for assuming that he was hers for as long as she liked.

'I'm a bird of passage,' he warned her. 'I'm naturally undependable, and foot-loose to boot, and anyway I've taken the King's shilling and belong to His Majesty in wartime, and when peace arrives I'll be buzzing off to turn an honest penny in France.'

'But you love me a little, don't you? I love you such a lot.'

'Don't forget Toby!'

'I love you both. I do! But what will I do when Toby comes home?'

'You'll have to remember not to call him Alexander.'

She giggled and said not for the first or last time: 'Am I wrong to be happy?'

'Don't ask me – happy-go-lucky has always been my motto.'

One evening he reached St John's Wood before Daisy had gone to bed, and played with her in the sitting-room. He let her pretend to give him tea and cake in her dolly's cups, and he pretended to be drinking thirstily and eating hungrily. After Daisy's nurse arrived to cart her upstairs despite her howls of protest, Rose remarked: 'I couldn't help thinking we were like a family.'

She was not her usual cheery self for the rest of that evening, and eventually she too cried as she made the contrary confession: 'I'm afraid the war's ending.'

Another similarity between Alexander's two mistresses had emerged. Down in Chelsea, Violet was threatening either to murder him or commit suicide if he tried to slide out of their relationship when, and because, there was no more war or reason for him to remain in London and at her disposal.

He was relieved to hear that his mother was seriously ill. He really had nothing against her – spoiling him could not be called a crime. His relief derived from the opportunity to extricate himself from his two love affairs, which were losing the charm of transience. He obtained compassionate leave and dropped lines of explanation on office paper to Violet and Rose.

Turville Place was like a morgue already. The November days were wet, the nights interminable. Starchy nurses, unfitted by their age and weight to alleviate his vigil, had been engaged. His mother was on the point of death, but her brain was unaffected and she had now neither the energy nor apparently the wish to spare him home truths.

She said during various visits to her bedside: 'Fancy you being here, Ecky – I must be dying... They tell me you spend your life chasing women – what good is that?... I hope you're better to your women than you have been to your mother... No one in your father's family or in mine was mad on women – you must be a changeling, Ecky, and that's why you've been bad to me ... I've got money, but what did you ever do to deserve it?... You'll have to wait to benefit, as I waited for you... It's high time you settled down in your ancestral home ... Will you love me when it's too late, Ecky?'

Mrs Morfe's death coincided with the signing of the Armistice, and Alexander saw a connection between the two events. From his selfish viewpoint he had been rid of two irritants, although he would not have liked anyone to know that he bracketed his mother with a war that had killed and maimed millions.

However, the reading of Mrs Morfe's will irritated him all over again. She had left her entire fortune in a tight trust, the Turville Place Trust, the object of which was to maintain the house in a fit state for him to live in for fifteen-odd years. Not until he was into his fifties would he get the money.

The meaning of the words she had muttered on her deathbed was clarified. She was trying to force him to settle down. She was trying to separate him from wild French women. She had done it again, attempted to control him, just as she had with her spoiling. 'Will you love me?' she had asked. His answer was a negative with hateful implications.

He had money of his own, but not enough to pay his way unless he earned more. He had looked forward to inheriting the family funds and having money to burn. Instead of finding himself a rich man, and the richer for having no responsibilities, he was saddled with a large property, trustees in charge of what was his by rights, a shortage of cash and no likelihood of obtaining the sort of job he liked in his rural confinement.

No, he could not love his mother, but, on the other hand and at least, he could no longer forget her. What was he to do? And what entertainment was on offer in darkest Gloucestershire?

He was granted an extension of leave by the army and after three months was demobilised. But peace was not peaceful for him: he was either too busy with lawyers or too restless, frustrated, and unable to see light at the end of his damp, muddy, tree-infested tunnel.

At noon on a windy early spring day a vehicle between a bus and a pantechnicon rolled up to the front door of

Turville Place. Alexander opened the door and stepped out, and the driver, a burly blond young fellow wearing khaki trousers and an open-necked shirt, dismounted from the cab.

'Alexander Morfe?' the stranger inquired with noticeable disrespect. He added, when Alexander had confirmed his identity: 'I'm Toby Berowne.'

Alexander recovered from his surprise sufficiently to say: 'I'll be blowed! How nice to meet you! I hope you're all right after your wartime disappearance. Do come in.'

Toby Berowne relaxed; he could not help smiling at Alexander's courteous welcome, and replied: 'I suppose we might as well do this thing politely.'

'Will you have a drink?'

'No, thanks,' Toby said. 'The point is I've brought you the woman who was my wife.'

'Is Rose here? I'd love to see her. Won't she come in?'

'You can have her permanently. I was faithful and she wasn't, and I'm not interested in soiled goods. You pinched her and you can keep her. All right?'

'It's generous of you.'

'Generous? I didn't expect you to call it that. She's in the van with Daisy and the nurse – they're all yours.'

'Thank you very much. Of course you'll have them back if or when you want them. Rose was always so fond of you.'

'Well, she can be fond of you now. She's not a bad bargain, she can pay for herself and she's pretty. I'll keep tabs on Daisy, who also seems to like you better than she likes me.'

'I'm sorry.'

'Let's blame the war.'

A few loose ends were tied up. Three women in tears and lots of luggage were deposited on the gravel sweep. Toby and Alexander shook hands, and Toby kissed Rose and Daisy goodbye. The van drove off.

A month later Alexander caught the London train at Ashe Turville Halt, and then took a taxi to Violet Stephens' house in Chelsea.

Violet would not unchain her door, and asked what he had to say for himself through the crack.

'I've come to tell you I'm getting married,' he said.

She screamed. She let him in and tried to scratch his face. She bit at his hands and slapped and beat him. She called him names, a cad, a cruel cad, she used the language of the gutter as he manoeuvred her into the sitting-room. She sobbed and fought as he undressed her and she pinched him as she undid his buttons.

When she was in a more receptive mood he gave her adequate reasons why he had retired to Turville Place, had not communicated with her, had not had time for even short visits to London, and was marrying a woman with a child, two homeless casualties of the disruptions of war.

'How old is she?' Violet asked.

He told her.

'Is she pretty?'

In a way, he replied.

'Do you love her?'

'God knows.'

'But do you want to marry her?'

'How can I avoid it?'

Violet sort of forgave him in return for his face-saving promise that he would see her as soon as he could, which she cannot have believed.

PART FIVE

Alexander Morfe had posed an unanswered question to Violet Stevens: how could he avoid marriage to Rose Berowne?

The facts were that the latter was in his house; she was still another man's wife – they were therefore living in sin; her daughter Daisy's involvement compounded that sin; and he was about to be cited in her divorce case; and she was a Christian, racked by guilt, conventional, obsessed by what other people thought of her, and might go crazy unless he vowed to marry her as soon as possible and to love her until death came to the rescue.

But how was he to make another promise he knew he could not keep? Rose was too nice for him to be nasty to her, she was not like Violet. He would be the most unreliable of husbands, and she would be the most miserable of wives. The prostitute who pointed out to him the primrose path of his philandering had urged him to stay single; but how could he tell Rose that he was going to ditch her in order to follow the stale advice of a whore?

In short he was impaled on the horns of a dilemma, and cursed himself for not believing the comfortable words he had dished out to Rose, to the effect that her missing husband was not necessarily dead.

But, and despite the other buts, they had their moments of happy cohabitation. They slept in separate bedrooms so as not to shock the servants, and behaved with a degree of discretion. They nonetheless shook down even if neither of them settled. She dried her eyes for the sake of Daisy and to present Alexander with a more attractive picture of his potential legal consort. She tried her best not to be a bore about the future, and spoke coherently of the recent past.

She related that Alexander had walked out of her life, when his mother was dying, a few days before Toby walked in. Finding her husband on her doorstep had been a terrific shock – she had been flabbergasted, and had upset him rather by saying, 'You might have warned me.'

'I was awfully pleased to see him actually,' she continued. 'Well, he is my husband, or was, and poor Toby, he'd got lost somehow because he was set to work on a Prussian pig farm in the back of beyond. The first of all my problems was such a silly one. I'd forgotten that he wasn't as tall as you, and I kept on looking over his head. Then his kisses felt funny. Oh, I did wish he was my naughty one, I couldn't help wishing it while we were celebrating and drinking champagne. I'm so sorry he dumped us on you, Alex – but I never was any good at secrets. Do you think you'll ever be able to make the best of such a bad job?'

'Did you tell Toby outright that I was your lover?'

'No, certainly not, I'm not so silly as that! He found out for himself.'

'You didn't call him by my name?'

'No! Honestly, Alex, I'm not a fool.'

'But that's what I like about you, your foolishness. Go on, tell me! My imagination's jumping to unpleasant conclusions. Was it sex that gave the game away?'

'Yes and no. We both knew it was different.'

'Why no?'

'You won't be cross, will you? It was Daisy. She wanted her father to play at tea parties, and she said he didn't play as nicely as you.'

'Oh well, there's always a price to pay for compliments.

216

You used to think Toby would understand and forgive you.'

'I know. But you men have no common sense. Toby wouldn't say what he expected me to do for love when he wasn't doing it. I mean you're only young once, and it wasn't my fault that he volunteered to go and fight people. We had arguments, and he wasn't my dear old Toby any more, he didn't love me for myself, he loved me for being his, whether or not I was happy. I hated him lovingly – if you know what I mean – and he hated me even when he was making love to me. Then he hired that van and drove it round to our home and told us to get in – I was afraid he might drive us over a cliff. But he had your name and address. Wasn't it lucky that you were in?'

'Or unlucky.'

'Don't tease me. You are teasing, aren't you? I cried the whole way because I was sure you were the next person he was going to fight and kill. But you were so clever and polite that he couldn't do a thing apart from driving back to London. And you were kind to take us in, otherwise we would have been waifs and strays – so kind and sweet.'

'You're making the same mistake, Rose.'

'What do you mean?'

'I'm no more kind and sweet than Toby was understanding.'

'Whatever you are I love you, Alex.'

He shrugged his shoulders and murmured under his breath, 'Hard cheese!' – which she chose to think laughable.

The law as usual dragged its feet, and allowed Alexander time to be indecisive. He agreed with Rose that her divorce was taking too long, and inwardly thanked heaven for the delay; and he justified his hypocrisy by references to peace and keeping it.

He had never before lived with anybody at such close quarters, or on the same basis, as he did with Rose, Daisy, the Berowne nursemaid and the Turville Place staff. Living with his parents had been temporary; living with other women had been short term; what he was now serving was in theory a life sentence. He was not so slow as the lawyers, which was perhaps a blessing in disguise: fairly soon he realised that he might not be able to bear it, and then that it was unbearable. He therefore wrote to Mr Begby to inquire if Continental Wines was going to reopen its agency in France.

He did not tell Rose. She would not understand his explanation that he was a sprinter, not a runner of marathons. He hesitated to say that routine was bread and water to him, and co-existence his idea of hell. The former virtues of Rose he translated into vices – it was unfair in every context except the context of love: her jollity grated on his access of melancholia, her optimism deepened his pessimistic estimates of the possibility of escape, her sturdiness reminded him of a gaoler, and her motherly inclinations alarmed him. He took extra care not to let her get pregnant. After winning Daisy's heart he had not much use for the child. He had nothing to do, and he no longer wanted to do anything with Rose and Daisy.

They had friends to stay, Rose's closest friends and contemporaries: he was intolerant of them. He failed to see the point of sociability without sex, and was too old for the games they liked to play, tennis, dead-end flirting. He would quite have liked to seduce one or two, but refrained in order not to complicate issues, and thus added frustration to his catalogue of woes.

Rose began to call him a bear with a sore head. She would tell him that Toby had still not found a replacement for herself, no doubt hoping to inspire Alexander to be more loving and proprietorial. She had to confer with her ex-husband about Daisy, and discussed their conversations and plans with Alexander in a transparent attempt to make him jealous.

She went further by asking: 'Toby's taking a train to Reading, and Nursie will hand over Daisy there, and I wondered if you'd mind if I joined in – I'd only see Toby on the station platform?'

'Go ahead,' Alexander replied.

Again she asked: 'Could I meet Toby at a boarding school near Bagshot where we're thinking of sending Daisy?'

'Certainly,' he said.

Then she pleaded that Toby should be allowed to collect Daisy from Turville Place.

'Why not?' he agreed.

On a later occasion she wondered if Toby could possibly spend the night, because he was bringing Daisy back from London one evening and to return immediately in the dark would be more than his eyesight or health could stand – his constitution had suffered a lot from his hardships in the war.

'Of course,' Alexander said, and played the perfect host on the night in question, and they all got on well together.

Rose was encouraged to say the following: 'I love Toby and always will, but I'm in love with you, Alex. You do see, don't you? I'm wedded to you, although you can't marry me yet, and that makes it easy for me to be friends with Toby. He wasn't ever a bad man. He's really a hero. I was the monkey, we were the naughty monkeys, and he might have been much worse than he has been. Also, he's lonely now, stuck in that house of ours quite alone. I'd like to invite him down for a weekend. I have invited him in principle, but I won't run off with him, I promise.'

'Okay,' he said.

Toby came to stay on the Friday. He and Rose took Daisy out for the day on the Saturday. He left on Sunday, late afternoon, and in the evening Alexander accused Rose of having had sexual intercourse with her ex while they were together in Toby's bedroom and she was ostensibly checking that he had packed everything.

She denied it. She could hardly deny that Alexander was well-versed in all the post-coital signs, but she cried and called him a horrible suspicious old bully.

At length and at last she defied him: 'If I had let Toby love me, why shouldn't I? I'm not married to you, remember! And you've been asking for it. I can't go on like this, feeling like a kept woman, giving you everything for nothing in return. You've changed so, Alex, you're miles away from me for most of the time. Well, I may not be able to stand it for much longer. I may refuse to be faithful and get put in the dock by you for doing no wrong.'

A month later she confessed she was having a baby.

He engaged a suitable vehicle, forcefully evicted the two Berownes and, with a minimum of explanation, had them, their nurse and their effects, conveyed back to St John's Wood.

He had been fairly sure that the child was not his. But his doubt did not deter him from freeing himself from encumbrances. He was not stumbling into the mantrap of anything in nappies. As for Rose, he had had the best of her.

He left his home later in the day on which, so far as he was concerned, he consigned her to oblivion. He had written a letter to the trustees of the Turville Place Trust to say he would be living abroad for the foreseeable future, and asking them to pension off all servants, apart from a caretaker. He had made the necessary arrangements with Continental Wines, and called in at the shop in St James's Street to sign a contract, then caught the cross-Channel train.

From then on it should have been the same pre-war story with a happier ending. It was to some extent, and for a long time. He was not poor, and in a new car he motored far and wide, enjoying mostly good weather, good food, good wine, and women who were not too good. He had no ties or trammels, no social commitments to sap his substance, he was Don Juan on wheels, a moving target that dodged bullets and brickbats, a predator that hovered above the humdrum world and swooped to seize his prey.

His prey did not die of it. He was not, even metaphorically, a killer of ladies. He was neither irascible nor violent, nor one of those men who feed on female souls. His touch was light. His technique was to give as well as to receive pleasure. His looks still broke down outer defences. Additional barriers were negotiated with the aid of his humour, banter, and ability to switch small talk into intimate conversation with some suggestiveness thrown in. His statistics proved that many women were willing to accept his advances without attaching any more strings to them than he did. Those who rebuffed him were apt to have second thoughts, and caved in eagerly when he returned to the charge. He feared and ran a mile from none but the ones who failed to see that his romanticism was mere mimicry, and claimed that he was the other half of themselves and they were fated to live and die together.

He had a sensitive nose for trouble. As a rule he steered clear of soulful monogamists, and took care not to offend true love and incorruptible virtue. Logical husbands seldom complained of his visitations, which put their wives in penitential and amenable moods. Yet now, and as time wore on, he did begin to find it an increasing strain to be always quick on his feet either physically or in a diplomatic sense. There were occasions when he had to run as fast as his older legs would carry him in order not to be shot or beaten up; and after hours of entertaining a husband he would wonder if the reward of the wife was adequate compensation. Moreover time was upsetting his calculations. The women who had played games with his youth had turned into pneumatic matrons preoccupied by pointless nostalgia, while girls of the desirable sort were not in such a hurry to grant him favours as their mothers had been, or had never heard of him and were unmoved by his reputation, or expected him to be a sugar daddy.

He had recourse to love that he paid for. Less expenditure of effort was involved; a word and a coin provided him with companionship for a night; and the perils were not so daunting.

Yet here again, even in the more or less squalid havens where innumerable womanisers of a certain age had sought refuge, novel emotions burrowed into the back of his mind. He was told or reminded that prostitutes lead terribly dangerous lives, and are usually injured in one way or another, including mortally, by their customers. He had to be sorry for them, if unwontedly. And then he was haunted by memories of the women he had abandoned in tears and often in terror because, thanks to him, they would be called to account and punished by someone in authority. When he suffered a pang of guilt he was concerned in case his constitution was finally about to let him down.

Prostitutes also shamed him with their outspoken good will. They would say that they had heard on the grapevine what he was ready to pay for. They would repeat his instructions as if he had ordered a meal or a new suit. He could relax, they said – they would show him no affection, and service him without any of the normal refinements, as required.

Was he abnormal?

He toyed with the idea of alternative life styles. His mother, by belatedly cracking the whip at him, had defeated her own object. Nothing would drag him back to Turville

Place, he would not be bribed to kowtow to her. Gloucestershire combined with Rose Berowne and her family had been a great mistake. He would have to wait until he could lay hands on his inheritance, wait and see. The difficulty was that his constant travelling, and the repetitiousness of buying bottles of wine, were starting to pall; and he was not sure whether or not the same applied to his vocation.

He spent more time alone. He had always needed recuperative intervals of solitude; but the feeling crept up on him that France was too small in spite of its size, and that wherever he went women lay in wait for him, and he would be recognised by men, many of whom were out for his blood. Sometimes he retired early to his room in an out-of-the-way hostelry, and, waking in the night, would sit by the window, gaze out at the moonlit landscape, and risk a glance over his shoulder.

He had not been born so unsentimental as he had become. His mother's worship of himself, and the webs other women had tried to weave around him and entangle him in, had blocked his personal spring of sympathy. He had or might have loved May Poore; but Virginia Rowley introduced him to the sporting side of the relations of the sexes, and he had agreed to be hunted and to join in the hunt. Love got lost in the pleasures of the chase, and nothing counted except competing and capture. His amorous history was not very different from the mating habits of animals, although less legitimate since it was not even dynastic.

He had no regrets, he did not wish to be anybody else, he drew no cool conclusions, but wondered what was going to happen next.

One night he had a strange dream. He had slept and woken, smoked a cigarette by his window, gone back to bed and dropped off again. He was with a woman, but chastely, watching her, observing her. He had never before seen a woman so elegant and attractive. Again, it was more than attractiveness: she had a quality that plucked at an unused fibre of his being, causing a sensation of being powerless to resist her. He longed simultaneously to be hers and to possess and protect her. She was of indeterminate age, fair-haired, he thought, and extremely well-dressed. She was clearly a lady in the sense that she was above and beyond other women, and she mocked his classlessness and made him admire her the more for not being common or ordinary. The sweetness of her showed in her eyes and her smile, in her grace – she was like an angel with warm flesh and bones of the correct proportions. Gradually, sadly, she faded from his view, but before she disappeared in the mists of fancy she seemed to look straight at him and to beckon him with a tremulous movement of her lips and an appeal in her eyes.

He awoke with reluctance. Where had she come from, how could his imagination have created her? He had not merely never met a woman like that, he did not believe one could exist. He faced the compromises undoubtedly in store for him with dissatisfaction. He realised that she had accidentally or by design cast aspersions on the whole of his past – worthless and spoilt were the words he put into her mouth. If only, he said to himself. And he added to his heartaches by not being able to recall or recreate his vision.

Life went on, and old Mr Begby of Continental Wines travelled to France partly to see him. He brought a youth along, explained that he was about to retire, hoped that Alexander would take over in St James's Street, and that his great-nephew Timothy Begby, the youth in a suit that seemed several sizes too large, would look after the French side of the business. Alexander consented – it was perhaps the very push he had been waiting for.

He spent a couple of months initiating Timothy into the work he had done, the professional work, and at last returned to England. He rented a flat in an Edwardian purpose-built block in Arlington Street, on the western side of St James's Street and conveniently placed for the shop. He enjoyed being a shopkeeper for a change, he liked to imagine he was following in his grandfather's footsteps, and spent longer hours in the business premises than were contractually necessary. He was loath to have time on his hands: for reasons not consciously connected with his dream, he was not keen on leisure which would tempt him to get embroiled in another stupid love affair.

He worked mainly in an office behind the front sales area. On a cool sunny spring afternoon an assistant knocked on his door and asked him to talk to a customer. He responded to the summons and thought he recognised the back of the lady outlined by sunshine streaming through the shop window.

She wore a waisted black overcoat with a fur collar – he noticed nothing much else. Her stance, grace, poise, stillness were probably reminiscent. He stopped, hesitated – when did he last hesitate to speak to a woman? It was the strangeness of the scene, of her outline, that made him pause and catch his breath.

'Can I help you?' he asked.

She turned and smiled at him. She was extremely pretty. But he could not be sure she was the woman he had dreamed of. Her manner was simultaneously energetic and melting.

'Oh yes, thank you,' she replied; 'I'm here to make an inquiry on behalf of my husband. Would it be possible for you to take wine down to the country for my husband to taste before ordering? I should explain that he's disabled, also that he's bought wine from your shop for many years.'

'That would be perfectly possible,' he said. 'When would suit you?'

'I have another query. My husband wondered if a weekend would be as convenient for you as for us.'

'That's very considerate. A weekend would suit me. Which weekend did you have in mind? Would next weekend suit you?'

Yes, she said. Ideal, she said. And she produced from her bag with a gloved hand, first Continental Wines' latest list with items marked, secondly her husband's visiting card, and thirdly a local map.

'Shall we expect you at six o'clockish on the Friday evening?' she wound up. 'We eat at eight, and change for dinner.'

Alexander bowed her out of the shop and retreated to his office. Her husband was Sir Laurence Doward, Bart, an hereditary baronet living at Doward Towers in Somerset, and his wife, according to *Who's Who*, was Sybil Helen, daughter of people called Delpen and formerly wife of Maurice Maybine. Lady Doward's first marriage had ended in divorce, she had remarried ten years ago, and apparently borne no children. Sir Laurence had been a top Civil Servant and was sixty-six years of age, whereas his wife could not be much more than thirty-five.

The difference in the Dowards' ages was surprising and not a bad omen in Alexander's eyes. Why had she married a man thirty years older than she was? And how disabled was he, and for how long had he been disabled? The bias of his speculations was involuntary.

On the Friday afternoon he drove towards Somerset. The weather was almost balmy: it was one of those compensatory pleas for forgiveness that the English climate occasionally offers. Doward Towers did not live up to its name: it was a square white-painted villa of indeterminate age with a pair of semi-circular protrusions on its right and left corners – the 'towers', imaginatively speaking – and stood fifty yards from a country lane at the end of a short driveway.

A maid in uniform admitted him and led him along a dark passage. A door at the end was open and Sir Laurence sat in his wheelchair in the embrasure, obstructing his wife, who stood behind him. He addressed Alexander as Mr Morfe with the extra politeness that snobs reserve for trades-people. His handshake was limp and he was hatchet-faced, ashen-coloured, and wispily bald.

The contrast between Sir Laurence and his lady suggested not so much beauty and the beast as death and life. Sybil Doward smiled at Alexander conspiratorially inasmuch as she was imploring him to be nice to her husband. Her ungloved hand in his was firm and warm, and she did not withdraw it in a hurry.

An awkward hour ensued. Sir Laurence was obviously ill and not averse from sharing his pain with others. His whipping boy, who was submissively female, was his wife, but he was also pleased to embarrass his guest or try to.

'You have come a long way for little, I fear, because I lack the wealth to pay your prices,' he said, addressing Alexander. 'No doubt you granted me a favour to please my wife, and to get a buckshee meal or two. She has deigned to mix us a martini, for you have arrived by luck or good management at the sacred hour of the cocktail. I used to be a great wine-bibber, but now my wife drinks more than me. Don't you, my dear? She would drink anything she could lay her hands on, although I hope to teach her to value the finer wines and vintages. Sybil, pick out two of Mr Morfe's samples for us to taste with our dinner, a white with a touch of acid, which should remind you of your husband, and a full-bodied red, which might bear a resemblance to our handsome visitor. We have no nubile opposite number for you,

Mr Morfe – there will just be the three of us to entertain one another. I apologise in advance for the dullness of your visit, but in my case the spirit is willing though the flesh is weak when it comes to the social niceties, and my wife thinks she has better things to do than to arrange weekend parties for my pleasure. However, perhaps it will cheer you up to know that I have to go to bed earlier than you and Sybil will need to.'

Setting aside the peculiar implications of his reference to bedtime, the truth soon emerged as to why Alexander had been invited for a weekend instead of for an hour or two in business hours. He was expected to help Sir Laurence up and down stairs and into and out of his wheelchair, and in general supply services usually provided by the gardener who was allowed his days of rest.

Sir Laurence had a disintegrating spine; he had had it for a good or bad few years, he explained. He could only manage social life in short spells, in between doses of painkilling drugs. At about six-thirty on the Friday evening he had to be helped up the stairs to change, at eight he had to be helped down, and at nine he bade Alexander good night. He was capable of walking short distances with crutches, and could change his clothes and get himself into bed.

At nine-thirty Sybil Doward joined Alexander in the sitting-room. He had been increasingly impressed by her beauty, charm, tact and good humour. Now she offered him something more to drink, but he refused, saying it would be coals to Newcastle considering his job; and she laughingly contradicted her husband's claims that she was a tippler – 'I don't even drink to counteract his teasing.'

She thanked Alexander for being kind to Laurence, and he thanked her for admitting a shopkeeper into her home.

'But you're not really a shopkeeper, are you?'

'I seem to have become one. What did you mean?'

'Well, Laurence used to know the Poores, and my first husband had to travel on business in France, particularly in Lorraine. Your home is in Gloucestershire, I think.'

'Correct – or nearly so.'

'And you cut a swathe through the female population of France.'

'I like your agricultural way of putting it.'

'Oh, we're very agricultural here. Our social life is agricultural or nothing, consequently mainly nothing. It's a treat to have a visitor from outer space – London, that's to say. And I don't hold with all the conventions, I don't understand half of them. How long did you live in France?'

'Ages.'

'Why did you come back?'

'Events – and everybody thought I should settle down.'

'Women thought it, I suppose.'

'Exactly.'

'Were they right?'

'Their case is not proven to date.'

'Have you never married?'

'No.'

'I hope you'll pardon my curiosity.'

'I don't expect it to kill anyone.'

'Why I'm curious is that I can't help feeling we've had similar experiences.'

'Yes.'

'Do you agree?'

'Oddly enough it has occurred to me that we might have known each other in a previous life. But what were you going to say?'

'My first marriage didn't last long, and then it became all too clear that I should settle down. When I married Laurence he was different, and he depended on me, and offered me security.'

'No children?'

'Oh no.'

'Now it must be difficult for you.'

'I'm luckier than I might have been. Laurence protects me. All his teasing is bluff, because he's at a disadvantage and his judgment's affected by the drugs he has to take. It doesn't bother me unduly.'

'Is he your protection against men?'

'Yes. And he's quite understanding. I have holidays – breaks – often.'

'Where do you go?'

'We have a small flat in Bayswater. Do you spend time in Gloucestershire?'

'I haven't been there for years. The last time I was at Turville Place I had a ready-made family dumped on my doorstep, and it taught me to keep on my toes and duck and dive.'

'What happened to the ready-made family?'

'I dumped them on the jealous husband who'd dumped them on me. French farce flourished in the war years, and especially when prisoners-of-war were repatriated.'

'Will you write your memoirs, like Casanova?'

'Did he write his? Did he publish his memoirs while he was still alive?'

'I think so.'

'He deserved a medal for bravery. Will you write yours?'

'Never! I try to forgive and forget, and to live for the day and the future.'

They parted with a handshake that was not altogether a formality.

In the morning he and his hostess walked and talked together, and again in the afternoon. Sir Laurence had to be helped downstairs before lunch and up afterwards, and the wine tasting happened in the 'sacred hour', between six and seven on the Saturday evening. Dinner was a threesome once more, and Laurence, as he asked to be addressed, joined the other two for lunch on Sunday, after which Alexander took his leave.

Laurence Doward's pleasure seemed to be to nag Sybil and to drop improper hints about her to Alexander. He invariably complained of the food: 'What is this muck we're meant to eat?... I wish you'd take some lessons in cookery, my dear, and turn your well-manicured hand to producing edible food.' He criticised her clothes: she was 'dressed for Piccadilly' in the daytime, and wearing 'old faithful' in the evening. He contradicted her and challenged her opinions, and made matters worse by then saying: 'Poor Sybil, I give you such a hard time, don't I, ducky? But I'm a devil, of course, and you're an angel.'

He inquired of Alexander at lunch on Saturday: 'I hope you enjoyed Sybil last night,' and excused his double meaning by adding: 'She can be good company.' Another question was: 'Did you have a rewarding walk with Sybil? I'm sorry the ground is still rather wet to lie on.'

He combined both strains of his teasing thus: 'I am the last of the Dowards. Sybil and I failed to have issue. Gentlemen in my unfortunate situation have been known to bribe a lusty lad from the village to come to the rescue. But I'm afraid it's too late for me and especially for her to contemplate such a proceeding, and, although you have a cooperative disposition, Alexander, I wouldn't like to offer you so onerous a task.'

Sybil objected to none of Laurence's jibes. She and Alexander, following her lead, sat dumbly, like guilty children for all their innocence, while he lashed at them with his wicked tongue. Yet the looks they exchanged, conveying patience under pressure and mutual support, served to draw them closer, whether or not that was what Laurence

Doward wanted for physical or emotional reasons of his own.

At last, again at nine o'clockish, they were alone in the sitting-room.

'How can you stand it?' Alexander burst out.

'He isn't usually so disagreeable.'

'Doesn't he appreciate that you hold all the best cards?'

'Oh yes. That's a lot of the trouble. And your presence has made him silly this weekend.'

'Why's that? I've done him no wrong, I've been his guest as well as yours.'

She flashed a blue glance at him, smiling.

She said: 'He's heard of your prowess with women.'

'I can't help that. I came here to sell wine.'

'Couldn't you help it?'

'One has to bow to the ladies.'

'Is that a boast?'

'I'm not proud of my life or of myself.'

'What's the matter with yourself?'

'The consensus is that I have no heart.'

'Are you asking me to take your pulse?'

'I don't like to ask you for anything, I'm being careful not to presume.'

'You don't need to be as careful as that.'

'People say I've no feelings and no conscience, and perhaps they're right.'

'Or wrong.'

'Yes. Who knows? I don't think any of my women have known me properly, nobody has. But you're clever, Sybil, you're far and away cleverer than me. I don't really want to retire and settle down, but I would love to settle the question of whether or not I could care for someone in the accepted sense.'

'Have you a candidate in view?'

'Probably no, maybe yes.'

'Your situation doesn't exactly surprise me,' she said.

'What do you know about men who don't care? You must have suffered from too much caring by too many men.'

'I was thinking along different lines.'

'For instance?'

'I've been cared for more than I've cared. That's the similarity between us I mentioned last night.'

'Similarity or affinity.'

'Oh – affinity – what a big word!'

'Yes,' he agreed.

She interrupted their talk to offer him something to drink. He asked for water – they both drank water as if to cool down their interior temperatures. But they soon resumed their conversation, which had lasted on and off for twenty-four hours and resembled verbal acts of love. The time flew by, not least because they knew it was limited, and some clock in the house struck eleven before they expected it.

'I'll have to go,' she said.

'Please wait a moment,' he begged her. 'I shouldn't tell you – it's premature and I have no right – but I want you to know how much I admire you. I've never in all my wanderings met anybody like you, so sympathetic – and I've never told other women what I'm trying to say. I'm sure you've a friend who knows you better than I do, and tells you the same things more eloquently than I can.'

'No,' she said.

He continued: 'I'm sorry, I haven't time to be cautious, and you must have realised by now that I wish I was your special friend and as close to you as it's possible to be. But affinity's irreversible, and passion ruins many a loving friendship, and returning affection long-term is an obstacle race and exhausting. I respect you too much to want to multiply your difficulties. And although I hope I could and would care for you, I'm not sure – I might disappoint both of us, or myself if I didn't disappoint you. There's something else to be said. I owe you in a sense to Laurence, and my days of stabbing husbands in the back were meant to be done. All I ask is that I could see you sometimes, here or in London, on your terms.'

'You're quite eloquent,' she said.

'I've been called many names, but eloquent's a new one. You've raised my game.'

'I think you're eloquent and wise.'

'Wise is another new name for me.'

'Thank you for compliments I shall treasure. I'm sorry too, because I can't stay with you longer. But haven't we struck a bargain of sorts?'

'We have – and the best kind of bargain, not based upon illusions or promises, and costing neither of us anything to date. Shall we shake hands on it?'

'Well, yes – a handshake should be safe,' she suggested.

They laughed and they parted.

On Sunday after lunch, as he was getting into his car, and almost under the eye of her husband, she thrust an envelope into his hand.

He drove away and stopped half a mile down the road to open the envelope and read her brief note.

It ran: 'Tuesday seven-thirty.'

The card written on bore the address: Flat 5 Sussex Mansions, Sussex Crescent, London W.2.

PART SIX

Alexander Morfe's courtship of Sybil Doward was short by most standards, if not by his.

His first sight of her and the feelings it aroused had not misled him, and the preliminaries at Doward Towers greatly increased his gratification at Sussex Crescent.

Who had courted and seduced whom remained a moot point. Their tacit agreement was that intuition had served them well, and their flesh proved it.

Each of them brought a wealth of experience and inventiveness, of wholeheartedness and enthusiasm, to the arts of the bedroom. Her reserve, as is so often the case with refined femininity, was cast off along with her garments. Her inhibitions, if she had any, likewise, and her passion took his breath away. On her side, she was encouraged by his responsiveness and energy.

Rationing sharpened their appetites. He had to leave her flat before neighbours would notice the lateness of the hour. She had to return to Somerset on the Thursday of that week. Moreover they both had business to attend to in the daytime, and she was never sure she could come to London in the next week, and he was told not to telephone her at Doward Towers or write to her. They snatched at each other's company, and at their loving, in her flat in Bayswater or in his in Mayfair.

Adultery was not a restraining factor: secrecy is aphrodisiacal. On the other hand the eternal triangle, so regular in shape, began to show its amorous irregularities. Ailing

237

and impotent Laurence Doward often seemed to Alexander to be playing a part in his intimate exchanges with Sybil, for how he had treated his wife before she arrived in London, and how he would treat her when she returned to Somerset, had bearings on her attitude to love. Two members of the triangular association discussed the third, who did not discuss them, at least openly, until the outsider was almost inside. There was never any question of Sybil leaving Laurence for Alexander, and in fact the intermissions in the love affair, ruled and regulated by Laurence's illness, lent extra intensity to every adulterous hour. Nevertheless, perhaps because Alexander felt he should be more possessive than he was, he objected with the force of hypocrisy to himself and Sybil being dangled like puppets on Laurence's string.

He had never been jealous, he had complete confidence that his mistresses would not opt for another's man's ministrations. And Sybil knew him well enough not to subject him to any of those half-baked tests of love and theoretical stimulants: he would have simply walked away. Anyway, she with a husband was hardly in a position to be jealous of her lover, who had no wife.

Besides, one element of their mutual understanding was that they were veterans of the war of the sexes. They were far from being fools of love, they shared the knowledge that each knew what he and she was doing, did it from choice, and would not run any of the common or garden risks of ruining everything. She dressed well for him, she showed herself in a light as complimentary to her lover as possible. She was aware of the damage that could be done by a word out of turn, a hair out of place, make-up missing, nakedness unrestrained, or an excess of sweating over a hot stove. He likewise: love put him on his best behaviour in her presence – dirty fingernails and bad manners never won worthwhile lady, and he was not a boor any more than she was a slut.

238

Their love endured for a year, for another year and other years. They marvelled and ceased to count. They were no longer young, judging by teenage Romeos and Juliets. But their constitutions were equally unaffected by the passage of time, and her beauty in full bloom and his less slender though still fine physique had novel charms. And late love, love that could be the last, has a poignancy of its own. Alexander was not drawn to poignant relationships; pity, let alone self-pity, did not enter into his brisk kind of con- sciousness. All the same he sometimes clung to Sybil not merely with sexual intent. At moments they both clung together, when the future refused to be excluded from their consideration. He might have to kiss away a sudden salt tear on her cheek, she might have to reassure him with the strength of her embrace. They had each other, that was the wonderful thing, but life was not to be trusted. The news, not their news but world news, which was beside the point of love and joy and themselves, was bad. Was it possible that the world would again prefer to make war?

Laurence Doward's wine sometimes ran out, notwithstand- ing how little of it he was able to drink at a sitting; and sometimes Sybil was stuck at Doward Towers for longer than usual; and Alexander realised that he ought to go to Somerset not just for commercial reasons, also to pay his respects to the person he was cuckolding.

The Dowards' marriage was possibly the only subject that Alexander and Sybil could not discuss with open minds. She would reveal that she was often made miserable by Laurence, and he would rage against the man who legally possessed the only parts that he did not possess of the woman they shared. But she drew a veil over where the services she rendered Laurence began and ended, and he never liked to ask embarrassing questions, for instance did

Laurence know that he was her lover, and were some of Laurence's conversational innuendoes as pimp-like as they sounded. Again, Sybil refrained from rubbing it in that Alexander was actually the saviour of her marital union, and Alexander omitted to tell her that he was quite glad that, thanks to Laurence, he could either rest from the labours of love or go in for a little of the sexual variety which is as good as a holiday.

The weekend that Alexander spent at Doward Towers in the spring of 1939 was exceptionally hard going, especially for somebody unaccustomed to facing up to trouble. To start with, Laurence's invitation struck a depressing note. He wrote that as there was bound to be a war, which would probably last for years, he intended to lay down as much wine as his means allowed and his cellar could hold.

Laurence had not died on cue in earlier years. This latest letter of his accentuated the fact that his health had not deteriorated noticeably much since he and Alexander were acquainted. It also implied that he intended to live and drink his fill throughout the war in question however long it lasted, and therefore disappointed Alexander in spite of their interdependence.

He again arrived at the sacred hour on the Friday. Laurence thought he looked tired, and said that a martini and some country air would buck him up. He also tried to introduce Alexander to Sybil, 'You know my wife, of course' – which must have been a deliberate mistake. He compounded it by adding: 'But you and she probably meet in London, and you may have a high old time for all I know.'

Then at dinner he harped on the war and how horrible it was going to be. He described his participation in the 1914 fighting in gory terms, as if with the intention of putting them off their food. The coming one would be total, he warned, it would interfere with private life as previously

240

known, and to prepare for it he meant to pull in his horns and sell the flat in London.

'I hope you won't mind, my precious. There'll be no more bright lights for you, or for Alexander, for that matter. Poor Sybil will have to make do with me – we'll grow old together, won't we, sweetie? Oh dear, Darby and Joan – what a come-down – but maybe I'll drop dead and you'll be the merriest of widows.'

When Alexander had half-carried Laurence upstairs, and Sybil had got him into bed, the two lovers in these loveless surroundings argued about whether or not the injured party knew every detail of their affair. Alexander wanted to know if Laurence was complaisant at Sybil's instigation. Later, upstairs, she stole along to his bedroom; but sex is never at its best when ulterior motives are involved. She was apologetic, she apologised for having a spiky curmudgeon of a husband, and he was sorry, too, and tried in vain to convince her that the war would probably never happen. They parted sooner than they had on similar nocturnal occasions.

The next morning a young man called on the Dowards before lunch. He was the son of neighbours, called Archie Thyne, nineteen years of age, handsome and bubbling with vitality, and wearing the blue uniform of a Pilot Officer of the Royal Air Force. He was passably respectful of Laurence, and polite in a rushed way to Alexander, but puppy-like with Sybil, hugging her and proudly drawing her attention to the stripe of his commission as a fully-fledged officer. They were clearly old friends, the generation gap notwithstanding, and she laughed with him and congratulated him repeatedly.

Laurence asked: 'Is this a proclamation that Archibald Thyne is going to war?'

'It can't be avoided,' Archie replied without hesitation. 'And I thought it might be a good wheeze to get into the action on the ground floor.'

241

A bottle of champagne was opened in his honour. Archie did not stay long after toasts were drunk all round. His visit reinforced the threats overhanging the future of the lovers. But his youth and vigour, and especially his forthright attitude to Sybil, mainly reminded Alexander of himself at the same age, and she was contrarily cheered up.

In the summer Alexander volunteered to contribute to the war effort, but was turned away on the grounds of his old war wound and his age by the military, and had to make do with spare-time posts in civil organisations dealing with fire prevention, air raid precautions, first aid and amateur policing; while Sybil in Somerset was inescapably involved in the activities of the Women's Institute and other patriotic bodies. As a result he was sometimes otherwise engaged when he might have been with her, and she was less often in London.

Yet the evenings they did spend together were exceptionally sweet, and under pressure of events they occasionally dispensed with discretion and slept together. He was apt to buy something good to eat at Fortnum and Mason and to bring it to Sussex Crescent together with a bottle of his best wine. After loving, after dining, and if the weather permitted, they would stroll out of doors on those last peaceful evenings and cross the Bayswater Road and promenade under the plane trees in Hyde Park. It was safe there in those days, and the prostitutes plying their wares helped to ensure its safety. The noise of the traffic receded, and sounds of the voices and the laughter of other lovers replaced it. Often they wandered into and through moonlit spaces, or paused to enjoy the moonshine, which they both considered their element.

Alexander and Sybil could be said to complement each other. He supplied the earthy materialistic side of their relationship, and she the sentiment. If they were soulmates, as she had claimed they were, he looked after the mating and she mixed in the soul. But durable love cannot be explained in a few slick sentences. At any level it may be indescribable and inexpressible in words. More than likely the tantalising truth is that the deeper the love the more it is defined by the secrets it keeps.

Alexander stuck to Sybil not for any of the reasons supportive of monogamy. He had made no promises, and he recognised no obligations, was not honour bound, or dutiful, or conscientious – he was a free man, although psychologists might say he was in the toils of his freedom. Realistically, he was faithful to her, more faithful than he had ever been before, because she delighted him. She gave him without fail, over and above the gift of her body, the thrill, the pins and needles, the seemingly unique treasure, of what he thought of as delight.

He was not a great one for saying 'I love you' and 'I hope to die in your arms', but he did say: 'I could watch you for ever, it's that turn of your head, it's the way you read a letter, nobody else has ever delighted me as you do.'

And she would ask: 'But what do you mean? What was I doing that was different from what everyone else does?'

'I don't know, I suppose it's what lots of men see in their women, the individual bit that isn't ten a penny and plucks at heart strings and won't let them go. But I'll tell you something you probably won't believe, which is that you're up there with all the other heroines. You may not have made history exactly, and thank God you're caviare to the general, but men who really know what's what, who can judge women and their charms by the most exacting standards, would all give you a prize. Those funny little ways of yours have hooked me good and proper.'

Walking in Hyde Park in the semi-darkness, Sybil was

rendered the more emotional by the looming prospect of war.

'You're so stoical,' she would say, 'I feel feeble and hopeless sometimes.'

Live for the day, he advised.

'Aren't you ever frightened?' she asked.

'I'm a cold fish,' he replied.

'Not always,' she corrected him.

She had a presentiment that the war was going to do very bad things to them, to her, as well as to the rest of the world.

'I can't imagine how you and I will ever see each other. And undiluted Laurence will poison me to death. He keeps on talking about selling the flat.'

She had not arrived at these bridges yet, he reminded her, so there was no need to cross them.

'But I love you,' she protested. 'I love you more than you love me, or anyway in a more recognisable form, and I can't see how I'll live without you.'

'You will, and we'll meet somehow.'

'What I love about you is your reliability,' she said and quickly qualified the sentence. 'I mean that I love the loan of your reliability, because I'm well aware of your reputation for being fickle. But I've been lucky, you've never let me down, and that's what every woman wants, just that, provided it's not on offer from a boring old creature of habit. You're not moody. You're not nervy. You don't compete with me, as Laurence does, you don't tease, like Laurence, you're not a bully or a drunkard or stingy or chippy, you don't let me down and do come up to scratch. You may have been a devil to some women, but you've been the opposite to me, if it's possible for an angel to be such a billy goat.'

One night, late, as he was leaving Sussex Crescent, when the moon shone straight into her flat, she stopped him turning on a light and produced an object wrapped in tissue paper and said: 'It's for you.'

Her present was a mug bearing the inscription, which he succeeded in reading by moonlight: 'Forget me not'.

He thanked her. He stifled the cynical thought that women were always determined to be remembered. She was shedding tears when she kissed him good night. The following day war was declared.

Their next meeting carried on from where the previous one left off, although three months had elapsed in between: she greeted him in tears.

She was distressed. It took time for her to reach the point at which she began to reveal the reason why. It had been so long, she sobbed, it had been dreadful. And the flat was definitely for sale, and the war was a nightmare, and everything was horrid. Worst of all, Laurence was dying. Yes, he had deteriorated suddenly, he was living on knock-out painkillers, he was incredibly demanding, and he could not be left alone.

'Isn't he alone now, while you're here?' Alexander inquired.

'I've got a local girl with nursing experience to be with him until I go back tomorrow.'

'Should I be saying I'm sorry?'

'But I can't leave him, don't you understand?'

'He's been ill before.'

'Not like this – I tell you he's dying.'

'Well, when is he going to die?'

'I don't know. Nobody knows. But you're missing the point. I won't be able to see you any more.'

'When or if he dies we will, supposing we want to.'

'Oh, oh, how can you be so detached? You can be so chilling and cruel sometimes, Alexandre,' she said, using

245

the French version of his name as she did in their passionate exchanges. 'Don't be unkind to me, please, I get enough unkindness at home, and I've been so wretched to think we're finished and the war's getting worse.'

'Well, keep calm – Laurence's illness may not last as long as you fear – anything may happen – let's make the most of this evening. Besides, the first rule of war is don't waste time.'

'No,' she said. 'I mean yes, you're right. Yes, you're absolutely right. Thank you, darling.'

She dried her eyes. The hours of love they made were to compensate for her absences past and future. Early in the morning they prepared to part.

He suggested a weekend visit to Doward Towers, but she said she could not bear to introduce him into a house of sickness, where she was run off her feet and would have no chances to be nice to him. She said their years of loving each other had been wonderful in spite of the frustrations. He said she had meant more to him than any other woman. When he left the house, he crossed the road and looked back at the window of her flat, and they waved to each other and blew kisses.

Time passed. He consoled himself according to his custom. But after three or four weeks he wrote her a letter. Since Laurence Doward had not been pronounced dead in any newspaper, Alexander wondered how things were for Sybil, and gave a brief account of his less controversial doings. She eventually replied that Laurence lingered on, nothing had changed, and she was worn out but just about okay.

He wrote to her again. He dropped her lines when he had nothing better to do. One night he was walking home through Bayswater and made a detour via Sussex Crescent. Looking up at the window from which she had waved goodbye to him, he was shocked to think he saw a glimmer of light through the blackout curtain. He walked up the steps to the front door of the block of flats and lit a match in order to see the panel of bell-pushes with names alongside. The slot beside her bell, which had held the name Doward, was blank. When he reached his own flat he rang her telephone number, but it was out of commission. The next day he wrote her a rueful account of this incident.

He was not really missing her. He had Continental Wines to keep going and his war-work, not counting his form of recreation. He wrote for a change, because he had never written much to women, and because he was curious and hoped to have news of her and to see her handwriting.

Eight months after they parted, eight months and four days, as he was later to remember precisely, he read in the death column of *The Times* the name Doward. Laurence had finally expired, he assumed, and read on as follows: 'Sybil Mary, beloved wife of Sir Laurence Doward Bt, owing to enemy action. Funeral private. No flowers.'

It was the greatest shock of his whole life. It was the biggest surprise. And it was a mystery: why should the Germans bomb Doward Towers? What enemies did Sybil ever have?

He wrote a letter of condolence to Laurence, but received no answer. His mourning was more like puzzlement. He turned over every possibility in his mind without being any the wiser. Because they had loved each other so covertly, there was no one he could ask for further information.

Some time after the appearance of Sybil's name in the death column, the wrong column from the point of view of Alexander who could recall only her vitality, he was once more in Bayswater and he went to pay a sort of memorial visit to the block of flats where she had lived and they had made so much love.

It was a pile of rubble.

Not long after this still more confusing discovery,

247

Alexander received a packet of letters with a covering note from Laurence Doward.

He had been hit terribly hard by Sybil's death, Laurence wrote, but had regained such health and strength as he had enjoyed before his bereavement, and was now able to respond to kind correspondence.

'Thank you for your sympathy,' he continued. 'I herewith return your letters to Sybil. You and she were clearly closer than I knew, and I thought you might be interested in the other letters enclosed, written by another man who loved her. I believe you met him, Archie Thyne, who was killed in action a few days after Sybil died, which might or might not have been a coincidence. A sad world, I fear. Sincerely.'

Truths like the drops of water used in the Chinese torture fell on the head of Alexander Morfe. Truths like the cumulative doses administered by poisoners rotted his being. He had been straightforwardly lustful and promiscuous, he considered himself a straightforward man, and he was ushered into a hall of mirrors. He felt he was losing his grip of reality and his confidence.

Laurence Doward wrote that he had not been specially ill before Sybil's death: that would mean Sybil had lied to Alexander in order to escape him. She had said repeatedly that she could not leave Doward Towers because Laurence was dying: was that a complete lie, or was Laurence lying in order to persuade Alexander that she was a liar and preferred a younger lover than he – Alexander – was?

Sybil had told him that the flat in Bayswater was being or had been sold, and certainly the name Doward had been removed from beside her bell-push by the front door of the block. But he had seen a light in her window, and she was a casualty of enemy action, and the building with her flat in it had been demolished by a bomb: could these three facts be connected?

He glanced through the packet of letters hurriedly, as if with eyes partly averted. But he could not miss the envelopes bearing her London address in stranger's writing. And the dates in the postmarks referred to the months during which she had convinced Alexander that she could not abandon Laurence for a day or a night. She had refused to be seen by Alexander in Bayswater so that she could see Archie Thyne there.

She had done to him what he had done to innumerable women. All was fair in love and war, he had preached. Sybil had been in love in a war and acted accordingly. But he had joined the unlucky ones, for whom war was not fair, for whom love was cruelty and deceit. He had become a paid-up member of the club of cuckolds, of those other men he had pillaged and degraded.

How could she? He racked his brain for memories of Archie Thyne. He might have been reminded of himself by that bubbling boy in the fancy dress of his officer's RAF uniform, but how could Sybil love him? How could she value puppy love higher than his attentions for which women had vied for more than thirty years, also higher than her own integrity?

He ventured to read a few of Archie's letters. They were not like his, which took everything for granted and bore an unflattering resemblance to office memos. They were offers of the writer's body and soul. They were not only romantic, they were romanticism in action, a dedication of his life to the recipient, and his death too if she should spurn him or if he should lose her love.

Archie was not circumspect or diplomatic. He cursed Laurence Doward for exploiting her, for his barbed teasing. He was jealous of Laurence, he wanted him to die or to kill him. He loathed Laurence for being her husband, and having had carnal knowledge of her however long ago. He wrote of marrying her, that was his ideal and aspiration, although she was at least twenty years older than he was.

Two notes paper-clipped together touched even Alexander, or at least caused him some sort of pang. The first asked or almost ordered Laurence to include the second in any grave or memorial to Sybil. It was an impossible request both physically, because nothing like a grave was feasible in the circumstances, and emotionally, considering the content of the second note. It ran: 'You were beautiful, you were mine, and your death kills me.'

Alexander took the trouble to ask the RAF for details of Archie's end. Laurence was not far wrong in this context. Archie had made too sure of blowing up and shooting down a German bomber bearing bombs similar to the one that had dropped on Sybil. His last act was heroic or reckless, and revenge that might have been sweet.

Just as once Alexander had seen similarities between Archie and his young self, so now he recognised the differences. Archie gave Sybil exactly what he had not given and could not give her: that is, his heart, his heart entire. Objectivity forced Alexander to own up that Archie's gift surpassed his own. But subjectivity was horribly wounded by the comparison.

He had heard of old lions being seen off by young contenders for the top job in a pride. He knew age had to give way to youth at some stage. He was aware that everyone's days in every context were numbered. But he was not old. He had never been ill and felt, and was still being assured by professional girls, that he was in his prime. None of what had apparently happened fitted his image of himself, or could be reconciled with his memories of Sybil. Again, he could imagine the possibly irresistible pressures on women to love or allow themselves to be loved by ardent warriors about to risk life and limb on the battlefield; but

Sybil could be firm, as he had discovered. She loved him, she had loved him – would she have thrown him over even for Archie blackmailing her with threats that he was fated to die? And why did she have to lie?

But the answer to the last question was easy and uncomfortable: she was right in thinking he would not have liked to be informed that he belonged to yesterday.

Changes occurred in Alexander Morfe, the first changes since puberty, unwonted and unwanted.

He had been the man blessed with a short memory, who forgot fights and slights, who was oblivious of the pain and sorrow he caused, who did not worry or care – and he could not get over Sybil or Sybil's defection.

He was born with a talent, or rather the power, to seduce women. He did not have to try, he never thought about it – women as it were fell into his lap or he fell into theirs, that was the beginning and end of his story, up to the point of Sybil. Now, to start with, and to contradict his character completely, her behaviour rankled. It was not anger, he was not given to anger, it was as if his every thought and feeling rasped against what she had done. In terms of noise, she was the steak knife and he was the china plate, and the discordant screech of one grating against the other set his teeth – and mind – on edge.

He had never before been jealous. Why should he be jealous when he was awarded the first place in his women's affections, if temporarily? But Sybil had ruled that he came second or even third, after that sado-masochist Laurence Doward. Alexander's memory was encyclopaedic in respect of sex: his studies of female expressions of love were at once his reference books and his souvenirs. Had Sybil done this or that to Archie, he wondered. He mentally thumbed through his last night with her in Sussex Crescent: those pleasures were divided in half by the idea that Archie Thyne might have enjoyed them too. They were more than divided, they were transmogrified into an ache and then a pain.

He did his daily duties, and his nightly ones as the bombs fell around him. But the outer life he had always led, the active physical life, was no longer what it had been. A new life, another inner life, preoccupied him, and he could not shut it out. Sybil obsessed him unhealthily: she had put a sort of curse on him with her mug that said 'Forget Me Not'. He rescued casualties and corpses from buildings absentmindedly, he sold wine bemusedly, and was not surprised when he was medically ill.

He had to have an operation on his prostate gland. It was another blow to his confidence, which impotence did nothing to restore. He sought out prostitutes he knew, but their surprise at his ineffectiveness was counterproductive, and their sympathy was not Sybil's. He steered clear of women, which was like volunteering to become somebody else after being Alexander Morfe for more than half a century.

He was bewildered, and his new inclination was to be sad rather than glad. He grew anti-social and sought solitude in which to remember Sybil and concentrate on her as he failed to do when he had the chance. He regretted not having photographs of her. Sometimes he could see her vividly, especially in exclusive reveries, the line of her hair, the sweetness of her smile, and a certain expression on her face when she was ready for love, but more often she eluded him. He lost sight of her – it made him think that he himself was responsible for losing her, for the loss of her life, since he had not paid sufficient attention to her soul. How could he have taken her adieu coolly? How he must have hurt her with his mad nonchalance and prodigality!

Alone at night, alone in bed, when he decided yet again that everything was his fault, he was stricken with pains in his chest. Perhaps he was going to have a heart attack: but he was not afraid, he was not afraid to die nowadays, on the contrary he was pleased for roundabout reasons. He seemed to have a heart after all, and, belatedly, pointlessly maybe, he could at least love Sybil as she had always deserved.

The war redeemed itself in his eyes: it had killed the woman he loved best, whether or not she would have found his truer love acceptable, but it was also granting him the opportunity to exhaust himself in rendering essential services. He saw sights sadder than he himself could claim to be, and in dangerous circumstances worried about nothing so much as the end of the war and having nothing more to do. He did not love Sybil any the less, but he began to resent the fact that she was not and never would be by his side either as mistress or dearest friend.

Peace loomed up, and the notion of writing a book occurred to him. He was encouraged by the amateur's wishful thinking that it would not be difficult, and the dilettante's that he could tear it off in his spare time. It would be a celebration of Sybil, and would plug the moral that she had dragged him back from the edge of the abyss of his selfishness. But he rejected a working title that had seemed to paraphrase his story, *The Catcher Caught*. He settled for another, more accurately descriptive of his last thought about love and summing-up of its consequences: *The First Nail* – nail in his coffin, that is.

EPILOGUE

Alexander Morfe confessed to treating scores of women more or less badly and without remorse. But he was not quite the Don Juan of myth and fable. He was not consigned to the fires of hell to my knowledge. Although, in his autobiographical notes, he claimed he had been to some extent redeemed by loving Sybil Doward and suffering on her account, he contradicted his redemption by eventually opting for title *The First Nail*, a reference to his own coffin rather than to hers. When I went to tea with him at Turville Place in my green youth, I can see, looking back, nothing like a man expiating sins and making peace with the world: he was self-centred and seething for all his charm.

His notes boiled down to an essay in immorality and resentment, and I could not be bothered to add to the modern preponderance of immoral books. In literature at least, no morals equal no art, no interest and not much fun. I therefore neglected Alexander's typescript for years, until I obtained by chance the missing piece of the jigsaw puzzle of his story – and in a sense of mine.

I obtained it in hospital: the relevant coincidences are inexplicably strange. I was there for minor surgery for a night, and heard tell of Alexander's demise in another hospital in another country. I happened to have unearthed and taken with me the packet containing his notes, on the cover of which I had written with a thick pen his name, Morfe. A nurse noticed it and asked if it had anything to do with Alexander Morfe. Yes, I said, why? A colleague of hers, her best friend, had looked after Alexander Morfe in his last two or three years and still talked about him often.

When did he die, and how, and what did her friend say?

She provided me with the following information. The name of my nurse's friend was Molly. She – Molly – completed her training and signed up with an agency: she was keen to do private work. She accepted an assignment to nurse Alexander, who was living in Nice in the South of France. His residence was a two-bedroom flat in a smart block, and its sitting-room had a picture window and a balcony overlooking the *Promenade des Anglais* and the blue sea. The date was the late fifties, he was seventy and a bit, and physically a wreck but not actually ill. Needless to say he soon charmed Molly, and she stayed with him for three years.

He was well-to-do, he had inherited money and sold a family house in England. He could have afforded a more enjoyable existence; but he was a virtual recluse, despite suffering from a mixture of loneliness and pride. He would not compromise, he shunned the other expats and their representatives, and only left his flat to go along to the daily open-air market and buy food and flowers.

Exceptions to the above related to his health. He was friends with an English doctor, whom he called in several times a week. He thought his doctor was a quack and a fool, and would only admit that he was better than nothing. He spent his money on every kind of aid to survival, while denying that he had the slightest wish to survive.

He lashed out on the luxury of Molly largely for companionship. She was expected to fit in with his routine, the walk to the *Marché des Fleurs*, the stroll along the *Promenade* in the evenings. Occasionally she persuaded him to take her to a restaurant. As a rule they would sit together for hours on the balcony, admiring the perfect curve of the *Baie des Anges* – 'So feminine,' he called it – and she would bring him his medicines at the appointed times.

Molly was pretty and young, and would not have stayed put even in Nice with any old man. She would not have renounced her contemporaries and devoted her life to a valetudinarian at almost his last gasp. But she felt needed; she had slipped into a strange intimacy with her patient almost at first sight; she had no difficulty in handling his body for medical purposes; and she was intrigued by his frank reminiscences. He spoke fluently and graphically, without boasting, rather as if the hero of the love affairs he described had been someone else, and perhaps aroused Molly's competitive instincts. When she tucked him up in bed she would kiss him good night.

After six months or so, as dusk fell in the sitting-room where he had been regaling her with an account of one of his conquests, she asked: 'Do you miss love very much?'

Yes, he replied, and asked in his turn: 'Are you missing it?'

She must have made a face expressive of both yes and no, and he said: 'What a shame! As things are, we'd only manage to spoil a beautiful friendship.'

A few days later he gave her an envelope containing a cheque for a large sum of money and a note bearing the words, 'In lieu and with love'.

But in the second of Molly's three years with Alexander his mind began to give way. The form taken by the loss of his grip of reality was that he imagined himself in sexual situations. At home, in the privacy of his flat, she could ask him not to use disgusting words and laugh him out of his orgasmic dreams, but on the *Promenade des Anglais* his expletives and groans could be embarrassing.

She wished she was back in England. She wanted to get away even more when his fancies – or were they memories? – turned nasty. He would curse these non-existent women who had invaded his brain, and copulate with them imaginatively in sordid places and in the coarsest fashion. He named women whom he was sure he had forced to submit to his will. He often claimed he had raped women who deserved it, and got what he wanted by twisting fingers back and squeezing breasts.

Not only was his parade of the horrors of love or hate difficult to live with, pure invention though Molly chose to think a lot of it; but the fundamental selfishness of the person he either was or had been came to the fore in his real day-to-day life. He was no longer amenable. He was uncooperative and tricky. He tested Molly's patience and goodwill, and gave her extra trouble. He was worse than inconsiderate – she had to admit to herself that he was deliberately cruel.

His health was deteriorating: she counted the possible number of days before it collapsed fatally. She could not stand very much more of his unkindness, the harsh commands and complaints, the verbal malice and once or twice the attempts to injure her physically. She had been wrong about him in the early days, there was nothing charming in his ungrateful and vengeful attitude to women. He was an outstanding example of the chauvinist beast, and she had scant pity for the fact that he was now at bay.

However, some days before he died he talked of – or to, according to his recent custom – a certain Sybil. It was extraordinary by all accounts – his changing so much, so suddenly, although by no other means than the tone of his voice. He could not move, or see properly, or hear, but he spoke to Sybil in such heartfelt, ungrudging, tender, caressing, and softly melodious accents that Molly at once forgave him and realised why he had been lovable and beloved.

THE LAST STRAW

Heredity cannot be relied upon. In nature, and perhaps even in science although it is heresy to say so in our scientific age, there are no sure things. Beautiful people seldom produce beautiful children. Brains are not always inherited. An ugly husband and a stupid wife may well be the parents of a handsome genius.

Rupert Deverel was a personable man, blessed with intelligence and all the worldly advantages. Amy, his wife, was a lovely lively girl, full of idealism and hope. Unfortunately their first child, a boy they called William, died in his forty-eighth hour of life. It was a hard blow, and not surprising that they never really got over it. Rupert took to drink, and Amy continued to wear mourning clothes throughout her second pregnancy. The birth of their daughter Ada was not and could not be celebrated since it left the mother mortally ill. Poor Amy soon expired, Rupert then succeeded in drinking himself into the grave they had wished to share, their baby Ada was appropriated by her aunt, Amy's sister, and nobody expected her to survive for long.

Her heredity encouraged the general pessimism about her chances. Her father had proved to be a broken reed, and Amy was almost blamed not only for dying and deserting the infant, but also for not curbing Rupert's dipsomania, which had finally made an orphan of Ada. Moreover the latter showed every sign of having been cursed with her parents' feebleness. She seemed to be teetering between this world and the next. She suffered from chronic croup, she

263

coughed continually, breathed with difficulty, and was always going, going, if not gone.

She had something else against her. Her Aunt May was ten years older than Amy, and had been married to Edward Ames for a dozen years. The Ameses had children of their own, two hulking boys aged eleven and ten, and did not have a lot of energy to spare for the little invalid. Their home in Harrow, Middlesex, was not seething with servants; Edward Ames was a wage slave who commuted to the City of London on weekdays; money was tight; and Ada was sometimes referred to in the privacy of the Ames' bedroom as 'our cross'.

However May was a good sort and did not neglect her responsibilities. She prayed that Addy would grow stronger, and she and her husband strove to look on the bright side of the unbargained-for addition to their family. After a year or eighteen months they were rewarded for their kindness in one way, even if May's prayer was not answered. It turned out that Rupert Deverel had more money than his in-laws were aware of, and that Rupert's father was rich and growing richer. Old Mr Deverel, a Scottish lawyer who dabbled in the property market, began to take more interest in his grand-daughter, and offered a virtual blank cheque to help to pay the expenses of her upbringing.

The immediate consequence was a new and with luck a healthier home for Addy and the Ameses. They moved up in the world, that is to Harrow-on-the-Hill, where the air was supposed to be purer and more invigorating, and into a larger house with room for a full-time nanny. Addy stopped coughing and started to grow. Her Aunt May was able to write letters to Mr Archibald Deverel of Beltran Castle, Aberdeenshire, that mingled slightly less gloom with her gratitude.

Yet the baby still gave the impression of being a by-product of tragedy. No one told her she was an orphan; no one was meant to make pitying noises over her cot; and the word 'poor' was taboo. Nevertheless she laughed rarely, and then somehow under her breath. Her huge eyes seemed to emit the colour blue, but not interest or amusement or mischief or even hunger. She cried almost as often as she had coughed, and in a particularly heart-rending way, as if she were suppressing even deeper sorrow. She was dark-haired, and her hair had an enviable soft curl to it. In spite of her prettiness and daintiness, her personality cast a considerable blight; and her personality had apparently commandeered most of her strength.

A few years passed. The Ames boys were day-boys at Harrow School, and spent holidays and spare time playing games of one sort or another. Their mother was therefore able to be more with her niece, who in her fourth year was or should be reaching the age of reason. Instead of answering Addy's questions about her parents by saying they were in heaven, and adding in assurances that they were happy there, she tried to tell the truth even though it might lower still further the child's spirits.

'Your Mummy, who was my sister, went to heaven because she was very ill,' May Ames said.

'When was she ill?'

'Soon after you were born.'

'Did it hurt?'

'No, darling.'

'If you're ill, do you always go to heaven?'

'Oh no, you have to be very very ill to go.'

'Can I go to be with my Mummy if I'm ill like that?'

'No, Addy, you have to be very very good and much older than you are to be in heaven. And your Mummy would want you to be good and happy here, I'm sure. The best way you could please your Mummy and all of us would be to laugh and be a happy little girl.'

Such conversations were rather a strain for May: Addy's

265

responses were at once problematic and alarming, and her non-committal attitude caused doubt and worry. Yet, despite her fear that she might be making mistakes, May felt she had to be honest – she could not fob Addy off with euphemisms. Perhaps thus she began to create a connection of trust between them: they both found it funny that the letters of her mother's Christian name, Amy, were shuffled to produce her Aunt May's name.

But the circumstances of her orphanhood were now discussed by the orphan herself.

'What happened to my Daddy, Aunt?'

'He was ill too.'

'Like my Mummy?'

'His illness was different.'

'Is he in heaven?'

'I hope he is.'

'Aren't you sure?'

'I don't know, Addy – none of us knows much about heaven. It's a surprise for everyone.'

'When we die?'

'Yes.'

'You were sure Mummy's in heaven.'

'Was I? Well, she was so sensitive and sweet that I can't believe she could be anywhere else.'

'Wasn't Daddy sweet?'

'Oh Addy, you're tying me in knots. Please don't! I can't answer all your questions. You'll understand everything better when you're grown up.'

'Will I?'

That Addy was clever was proved beyond doubt by her precocious aptitude for putting two and two together.

One day, a year or more after the heavenly dialogues, she asked: 'Aunt May, when was my Mummy so ill?'

'Before she died, dear.'

'Was it when I was born?'

'Not exactly, no.'

'Was she ill because of me?'

'Addy, I can't tell you why anybody's ill. God settles these things. We're all in the hands of God.'

As on previous occasions, Addy gave no sign of satisfaction or dissatisfaction with such information as her aunt would and could supply. But she was tactful and considerate enough not to force the issue.

Nevertheless, a stranger exchange occurred at a later date.

'Did my Mummy want to die?'

'Of course not, darling. She loved you so much, she longed to look after you and be with you always. She would have cut herself in half for your sake.'

'Did she cut herself in half?'

'No no, that's just a figure of speech, I meant she wanted to bring you up more than anything else.'

'Did Daddy die when she did?'

'No, not quite.'

'Did he want to?'

'What?'

'Want to die?'

'No, I don't think so.'

'Why didn't he want to look after me and bring me up?'

'I never said that, Addy. You're asking me another question I can't answer. But you mustn't be too sad to have lost your Mummy and Daddy. Lots of children lose their parents, and every single person loses theirs in time, when they all get old. I'll lose mine, and Uncle Edward will lose his, and then we'll all be in the same boat. And meanwhile we'll be trying our hardest to fill the gap for you, and be as nice to you as your Mummy and Daddy would have been.'

'I know,' the girl said thoughtfully, and after some moments of cogitation continued: 'Thank you, Aunt May.'

The end of such interrogations coincided with the

relatively rapid growth and development of Addy Deverel. She put on inch after inch in height, and became a gangling beauty of skeletal slimness in spite of eating voraciously as if to compensate for the years in which she could scarcely look food in the face. Her withdrawn quality notwithstanding, she excelled at her lessons in her first schools, and was never anti-social at home, although quiet and reserved.

When she was ten she crossed her own Rubicon, on the bank of which she had been teetering ever since she was born. It was not puberty, except puberty of a psychological kind – it was an unexpected move in the direction of adulthood, which left childishness behind. Her relations were immediately aware of it, everybody noticed it, inexplicable as it was, and apparently incomprehensible to Addy herself.

The outward change in her was that she ceased to be glum. She evinced a marked and infectious gaiety of the girlish kind. She introduced her personal beams of sunlight into the Ames home and household, and her school reports suggested that she had become much more amenable and popular. She clearly dwelt no longer on premature death and bereavement, on what could not be changed. She withdrew from nothing and nobody, shyness was shed as if it had been a skin, an unassuming boldness was the new order, and introversion was swapped for its opposite.

Her Aunt May benefited in particular from a niece who had become her close friend. Addy was helpful, Addy was demonstrative, Addy was different, and made no secret of her appreciation of having been virtually adopted by the Ames family. In place of the dry thanks that she had volunteered formerly, now there were hugs and kisses all round.

'Dear girl, what on earth brought it about?' her aunt inquired.

Addy parried that question with one of her own, a jokey ironical one.

'Was I a monster?'

'No, dear – you did your best, I've no doubt – but you had things weighing on your mind, and you had to come to terms with them.'

'Well, I can never repay you for not telling me never to darken your door.'

'What an idea! And I've got my reward already. You've turned into the daughter I wished for and never had. How proud your mother would be of you!'

Addy's age kept pace with the century. She had come into the world in 1900, in the month of August and under the sign of Leo, and was eighteen when the first World War, World War I, ended in 1918. By then she had grown into a tall statuesque young woman with arresting looks and an elegant figure.

She had not relapsed. She had not, as it were, wriggled back into her cocoon. Puberty in the normal sense had not affected her character adversely, and, again to her Aunt May's surprise and relief, she had circumvented the usual female teenage phase of surliness.

Her war was not too terrible. Her Uncle Edward was unfit for military service and did his war-work in a government department. The Ames boys got through safely: Jim was a prisoner-of-war for most of the four years, and Tony received a minor wound in 1915 and was invalided out of the army.

Addy's steady courage eased the strain on the Ames family throughout, and her sympathy was a boon to her friends who had lost loved ones. Members of the older generation, who were recipients of her letters of condolence or her cheering visits, reported to her aunt and uncle that she was a remarkable and even an inspiring person.

Death had not spared her altogether. Setting aside the

servicemen killed in battle who were known to her or related to her friends, she could not help noticing all the black mourning clothes and the black armbands on sleeves. Besides, her Deverel grandfather had died. He had been no more than a name to her, he was also her last grandparent – the parents of her mother and her aunt had expired years before. Addy, at eighteen, was fully cognisant of the mortal condition attached to existence; but now her reaction to that fact of life was simultaneously neither broken-hearted nor heartless.

Unintentionally, although she had solved problems for herself, and was the solution of problems for others, she posed a troublesome question for the Ameses. Could they leave Addy to find her social feet in their suburban circle, or should they turn her into a debutante, try to have her presented at Court, and launch her into a higher society by means, for instance, of organising a gathering of gilded youth?

They were not snobs. They were modest self-effacing people. They were also realists. If Addy had been their own genealogical girl, they would have kept her at home, encouraged her to find some congenial employment, hoped that she would soon agree to marry a reliable boy with prospects. But Addy was not only not that sort of daughter, or even that sort of girl, and a further great difference between her and the one that they might have had was that she was an heiress. At intervals over the next ten years Ada was due to inherit huge instalments of capital and property, bequeathed to her by Grandfather Deverel. Should her aunt and uncle restrain her from meeting her peers, folk as wealthy as she would be? Would a local boy, however reliable, be equipped to live like a prince, or be ready and willing to act as consort to a princess and as second fiddle in their matrimonial establishment?

Edward and May Ames took advice from Addy's trustees.

The consequence was that they rented a house in Mayfair and contacted Lady de Casselis, a middle-aged widow and a professional agent, who arranged Addy's presentation to the King and Queen, and a ball in her honour at a smart hotel, and innumerable invitations to a variety of similar functions. Before the season began, while they remained in their Harrow home, they regretted their decision. They were sick of spending and probably wasting so much money, and exhausted by scanning lists of strangers.

But Ada's mounting excitement carried them metaphorically up to their temporary residence in Sussex Square, Bayswater. Her enthusiasm and energy buoyed them through confabulations with Lady de Casselis and fittings for clothes. At Buckingham Palace they were proud to see their charge, who could have been a waif and stray, arrayed in virginal white, in her finery, standing out from the hundred and more other girls. At the Ames-Deverel ball, both of them shed tears as they watched Addy and their elder son and her first cousin Jim dancing together to inaugurate proceedings.

Uncle Edward was soon too tired to act as Ada's chaperon, escort, protector and chauffeur – he had to get to his office early in the morning. May Ames made allies of other ladies in her position, but was really kept going by vicarious satisfaction with Ada's successes and by Ada's confidences.

Addy seemed to be the leader of her gang of girls with a few boys thrown in. Their doings, their jokes and pranks, were quite amusing, but dull stuff in comparison with her introduction to love.

It was all most unusual – May Ames was not sophisticated, nor was she a woman too dense to spot compliments. Addy was in receipt of two proposals in the first month of her participation in the marriage market. Then suitors were queuing for her warm, white, sensitive, long-fingered hand.

What was perhaps even less usual was that she let her Aunt May in on the romance of it all, apparently omitting nothing. The younger woman's trust in her elder was flattering, and there was more than enough excitement to be shared between the two of them. What else was unmistakeably out of the ordinary was Addy's assurance and common sense, and absolute refusal to lose either her head or, in a hurry, her heart.

The first couple of proposals caused much merriment in the house in Sussex Square. Sir Ninian Forbes-Waugh was a superannuated Scottish baronet, bald as a billiard ball and bursting out of his kilt, who begged every girl who might have been his grand-daughter to be his wife – he was a perennial hazard of debutante dances and popped the question to Addy almost as he introduced himself. A few weeks later she was asked to marry Jeremy Arbuthnot, a man of roughly the right age, good-looking, smooth-talking, well-connected, with a country seat in Devonshire. She took Jeremy more seriously than Sir Ninian; but then her aunt discovered that he was a gambler on his uppers looking for a fortune to stave off bankruptcy, and Addy rejected him when her friends produced evidence that for some time past it had been mostly money he was after.

The faces in the queue of her other rejects belonged to noblemen and commoners, rich and poor, desirables and duds by normal matrimonial criteria. Some claimed they loved her romantically and some betrayed the fact that they had an eye on the main chance; some were arrogantly stooping to conquer and some were humble supplicants for her favour; and the rest seemed to be half the unwed male population of the British Isles.

She remained adamant in spite of being called cold, frigid, cruel, a flirt, a head-hunter, a gilded bitch, and, for a joke by members of her gang, 'the girl who couldn't say yes'.

272

Her aunt backed her up. Why rush, she repeated. Take your time, she urged.

But as the summer season advanced towards the concluding festivity of Goodwood Races, Mr Wrong emerged from the crowd. Addy recognised him, she knew from the moment they met that she could love him and should not, and her aunt was tactfully in agreement with the negative proposition. He was called Michael Trane. He was ten years older than she was, and, although fiercely individualistic and determinedly unconventional, the complete stereotype of Don Juan. He was beautiful, he had black curly hair, aquiline features, good teeth and a suntan. He had been everywhere, he was widely travelled and an intrepid explorer, and done everything, he had been in the Secret Service in the war, ridden in the Grand National. He was clever, he had written highly praised travel books, he was an adulterer much in demand, he was unhappy, he was desperate, he cried out for consolation, and he was feckless and fun.

'I don't know if I can resist him, Aunt,' Addy said.

'He'll let you down, dear.'

'He says that himself. He wants me to marry him and keep him in order. He thinks I could stop him letting everybody down.'

'Not a very appealing prospect when you think about it.'

'Exactly.'

'You don't need to be needed in that way, Addy.'

'I don't, do I?'

'What about postponement? Time always tells.'

'But I might lose him.'

'Well, if you do you'll be meant to.'

'I know it.'

There was an alternative to Michael Trane. Rufus Forester was an alternative not least in that he was Michael's exact opposite in a number of ways. He was a giant whereas

273

Michael was a physical lightweight. His face was granite-like whereas Michael's was precious stones. He was twenty-nine, approximately Michael's age, but his contributions to the common weal made Michael's look like mere showing off. He had won a DSO and an MC for conspicuous gallantry in the war, whereas Michael was undecorated for the feats he said he had performed. He was the scion of an old Northumberland family, he tilled the family acres, was a Justice of the Peace and a company director, whereas Michael appeared to have come from nothing and to be going nowhere, except perhaps abroad on another wild goose chase.

The greatest difference between them from Ada's point of view was that Michael pressed his suit, as they say, besought her, bullied her, took liberties and much too much for granted, whereas Rufus showed that he liked and more than liked her for lots of reasons, but said nothing of note, was careful not to get personal, did not declare himself or ask any of the questions she had been led by other men to expect.

Rufus was the favourite of her Aunt May.

'He's always so courteous,' she said. 'He's a real gentleman. You could trust him. And he'd be a wonderful father.'

'But he doesn't want me, Michael does.'

'Do you want him, do you want Rufus?'

'I don't know.'

'I expect he also knows it.'

'Oh dear!'

The Ameses' tenancy of their London house came to an end and they returned to Harrow-on-the-Hill. Rufus began to write Ada letters and send her postcards either from Forest Court, near a place called Fowick in Northumberland, or from Scottish addresses – he was attending agricultural shows in Scotland and cramming in some shooting and fishing; but Michael came to call on her unannounced. His visit was like the rest of their relationship, exciting and a disappointment.

They were pleased to see each other. She was flattered but wary. He had arrived in the afternoon, and when tea was finished he asked her to show him the local sights. It was getting dark and drizzling, and she could not think of sights he would not jeer at, but she agreed to a short walk. Out of doors he began by proposing yet again, he continued by kissing her roughly in a street full of people, and in a dark alley he spoke of further dalliance. In the end she checked him by laughing at him.

'You're mad,' she declared.

He switched from praising to blaming her, and from masterful domination to self-pity and despair.

'You're the mad one, you stubborn girl,' he said. 'Thousands of women would fall over themselves to grab the chance I'm offering you. I'm not perfect, but you'd never have a dull moment with me, that I could guarantee. Well, I'm fed up, and not only with your cucumber sandwiches and iced buns. I guessed you'd be stupid, so it's goodbye, it's *adieu*, Addy, because I'm off to Brazil tomorrow morning. I haven't found Eldorado here, I'll be looking for it there – no, that's a joke. You've added another disaster to my biography, and I'm half-hoping it'll be the last and I'll meet my Maker in the rain forest.'

She told him not to be silly; he told her he had better things to do in London than to get soaked to the skin for the sake of an unappreciative miss in Harrow.

She said *au revoir* and tried to plant a final friendly kiss on his cheek, but he flung away, calling her Judas.

She walked home alone and in tears.

Her Aunt May comforted her. Girl friends invited her to stay in country houses. In November her uncle and aunt received a letter from Rufus Forester. Rufus was hoping the whole Ames family, four plus Addy, would spend Christmas

275

at Forest Court. Mrs Forester, Joanna Forester, his mother, wrote a note to May Ames to say she would be staying with her son for the relevant period and was so much looking forward to meeting his other guests.

The Ameses accepted. Rufus wrote letters of thankful anticipation to Addy, who answered them cautiously but without delay. She and the others travelled north and arrived on Christmas Eve. She was folded in Joanna Forester's arms by way of a greeting, and Forest Court seemed to embrace her likewise. She never doubted for a single second that she loved Rufus' widowed mother and his home: the first was good sense and charity personified, and the second was a repository of the architectural charms, the solidity and the security that she realised she had always been looking for.

Christmas Day was happy and hectic. They exchanged presents after breakfast, attended Matins, entertained neighbours before lunch and Forester relations to tea, went for walks, played games, and all helped to prepare and serve supper to the servants. For Addy it was only marred by the present given her by Rufus, a thimble bearing the Forester coat of arms, a cheap trinket, far inferior to his lavish gifts for the Ames family, and troubling her on several scores. Her present for him, a leather-bound book of border ballads, was obviously far too expensive in comparison; it could suggest that she was doing the courting, just as his had suggested he was doing no such thing; their minds had not met in the context; and a new worry and sadness affected her increasingly.

After supper she followed him bearing unopened bottles of wine into the pantry. He also carried bottles of wine, and he said they belonged in the cellar, opened a door, switched on a light and descended a stone staircase. They were in the cellar together and she remarked that it was a bit frightening. If she had meant the cellar was frightening, he misunderstood her.

'You mustn't be frightened, you needn't be, I promise, but I am,' he said, kneeling on the flagstones as he laid the bottles in their proper places.

'I can't believe you could be frightened,' she murmured.

'More now than ever before in my life. My present wasn't my present, Addy. I'd very much like to give you something else, but I don't know what you'd think of it. And I haven't dared to speak to you all day.'

'Don't be afraid, Rufus.'

'It's my heart, it's yours anyway and always will be, it's my whole heart for ever, it's my everything. Don't you be frightened, I shan't die on the spot if you turn me down.'

Her answer was to kiss him and raise him to his feet, and to offer him her heart in return for his.

He then handed over the diamond engagement ring which he had intended to give her earlier in the day, and they rejoined the party, her hand in his great strong one.

Ada Deverel was married to Rufus Forester in the little church in the village of Fowick. The reception was at Forest Court and the honeymoon was spent at Beltran Castle, her property across the border in Scotland. She was extremely pleased with and proud of her husband. She was only sorry that she was not able to show him off to more of her friends – it was too far for most to travel to Northumberland, and accommodation would have been a problem. Michael Trane had made no sign of life since they parted on that damp evening at Harrow.

Nine months later she bore Rufus a son, Conrad. Three years later, in 1923, a second son, Guy, arrived. In 1925 she gave birth to a daughter, Evangeline, always called Eve. In 1928 Ian was born and in 1930 another girl, Faith.

Having children was easy for her. First of all she was a very affectionate wife and her husband was an heroic lover.

Secondly she was blessed with the requisite physique and constitution, she never felt better than when she was pregnant. Above all she was maternal, she wanted her children, also to counteract the loneliness of her own childhood by surrounding herself with a family that belonged to her and vice versa. Besides, she presided over, she created, a household that was the admiration and often the envy of all who knew it. Harmony and happiness were the keynotes, the roles of everybody dovetailed, the children were obedient and good, and the inner glow of the old house seemed to defeat even the gloom of Northumbrian winters.

Addy had help, of course. Rufus was not typical of men in his position, and of his stamp and age, in that era. He was pleased to be her slave, and nothing was too much trouble, too menial, grubby, boring, unimportant, for his tireless energy. And then she had the loan of other willing hands. Forest Court and the Forester estate were run on feudal lines. Feudal is nowadays a term of abuse, it jars on the ears of the arrogant and ignorant who consider themselves modern. In fact prejudice alone fails to recognise that a so-called feudal system, ruled by responsibility and benevolence, has never been bettered.

The Foresters for several generations had been efficient and successful agriculturalists. The estate had funds with which to oil every wheel even before Addy shared her wealth with her husband. Rufus' employees might be servants in the bureaucratic sense, but they were his friends, old, new, and more or less close. He worked with them, he worked for them in that he was ever ready to use estate money to supplement pensions or pay for extra medical care or send a gifted child to a private school or advance a loan; and their social lives intermingled.

Addy fitted into this scheme of things without hesitation. She was not used to it. The Ameses' design for living had been more modest and economical. Her Aunt May had a treasure who did cleaning for a couple of hours each week-day; otherwise she cooked and washed socks. And Addy's paternal grandfather was lowly stock and had made his money the hard way. But her nature was ladylike, and her character aristocratic in the true meaning of that adjective: in other words she gave herself no airs and graces, she let her actions speak for themselves, and took every possible precaution not to embarrass or upset anybody, while setting high standards and expecting others to follow suit.

She satisfied Rufus' employees by satisfying him. She was a positive example of the old adage that the woman in charge can make or break a home. She was much loved, and the love she received she seemed to give back in the form of the brightness of her blue eyes, the sheen on her curly dark brown locks, her laughter by which she was always traceable, and her imperturbability in the face of adult crises and those affecting her children.

That is not to say she was insensitive: on the contrary, her responsiveness to every sort of stimulus was intense. But she was brave, and she had Rufus' courage to prop her up if need be.

Her family, her Forest Court extended family but her husband and children in particular, and perhaps her children especially, absorbed her. She doted on them. At the same time she was not indiscriminate or unaware. She was too clever to be soppy. She exemplified another truism – or is it a witticism? – for her love was not blind.

Conrad was a strange fascinating boy, Guy was like a big warm puppy, Eve was pretty, Ian was rather a mystery, and Faith a roly-poly. She was so lucky to have them, they were all wonderful, and their differences added to the pleasures of their company. She thanked God for them and prayed that they would be delivered from evil.

Conrad was moody. When he loved her it was lovely, when he did not love her it was awful. He lived in two worlds, the real one and another world of his imagination. He was thick with animals – that is, they apparently understood one another. He was an escapist as soon as he could crawl away on his own. He would toddle to the farmyard when grown-ups' backs were turned. One day he was lost and found by his mother in the old bull's pen – he was looking up at Bully and patting his nose. Five farmworkers had to rescue the child, and then his father rebuked him.

'You worried us all, Conrad. Bully might have trampled on you or tossed you on his horns. Please don't do it again.'

'Bully likes me,' Conrad replied. 'And Bully's kind.'

'All the same he might hurt you without meaning to. And he can be cross.'

'He wouldn't.'

'Why do you say that, Conrad? How do you know? You must be careful.'

'Somebody told me.'

'What? Somebody told you to climb into Bully's pen?'

'Yes.'

'Who told you?'

'Jesus.'

Conrad was extraordinarily quick to learn his first lessons. Addy was his teacher, and when he discovered he could read he hugged and squeezed and kissed her in a passion of excitement and gratitude. She was often bowled over, sometimes almost literally, by his impulsive embraces. But then for reasons of his own he would relapse into silence, turn his head away when people spoke to him, take interest in anything and have no energy, and sit slumped by himself in dark corners.

'What's wrong, darling? What is it? Have I hurt your feelings? Has someone hurt you? Don't you feel well? Shall I take you to the doctor?'

His anxious mother's questions went unanswered.

She consulted her Aunt May on the telephone.

She described Conrad's moods and asked: 'Was I as bad as he is when he's withdrawn? Was I like that?'

'So far as I can remember you were worse,' her aunt replied, and they both laughed.

'Have you forgiven me?' Ada inquired.

'Oh yes – long ago – but is your Conrad forgiven?'

'I think there's nothing to forgive. He doesn't seem able to help himself. He isn't trying to be a nuisance. I wasn't when I was so ungracious, Aunt – you do know, don't you? And his black moods are pretty much redeemed by the other sort. When he smiles again it's like the sun coming out from behind clouds. It's dazzling. He lives life so intensely, Aunty – I can't convey his emotional intensity in words.'

'He's stolen your heart, dear.'

'He has. So has my Guy in a different way. But Conrad's such a man already, although he's only a little manikin. He's inherited his father's strength and big personality.'

Father and first-born son were firm friends. While Rufus was in the house in the hours of daylight, and not in his study or eating a meal, he usually had Conrad on his shoulders. When the boy was six years old, on summer evenings they would go out together to stalk and shoot rabbits; or Rufus might take his twelve bore instead of the rifle, and they would wait in the beech wood behind the house for pigeons to fly in to roost. In the six months before Conrad left home to go to school down south, Rufus constructed for him – with Conrad's help, as he put it – the hammock that caused delight, amazement, horror and concern.

Rufus was given to outbreaks of physical exuberance. He walked to Edinburgh and back without much warning, some fifty miles. He repaired a wall at Castle Beltran with granite slabs that nobody else could lift. He had performed notable feats before the war, winning a race on foot from

London to Brighton, and swimming across the Solent for a bet.

Addy once asked him if his medals were awarded for his immunity to danger and exhaustion: 'I hate to think of the risks you must have run, and how nearly we might never have met.'

But he explained that he could not bring himself to talk of those horrific days of carnage, and would only say that he had been lucky.

'Lucky to be alive,' she persisted, 'or lucky to have rows of medals?'

'Both,' he replied.

'Thank goodness,' she commented. 'Thank goodness you survived to be my Rufus, and thank goodness you're not a coward. But promise me not to go in for any mad capers, please. Promise me, Rufus!'

He laughed at that sheepishly, and she knew him well enough not to pursue the subject: she just shook her head at him and loved him for not telling her a fib.

The idea of the hammock originated in Conrad's longing for a house in a tree. Rufus developed it into an even more exciting project. They would create and sling an outsize hammock between the crowns of a couple of the highest beech trees in the wood, and then be able to swing about up there, sixty-odd feet above ground and amongst the rooks' nests.

Hundreds of yards of rope were delivered to the farm – Rufus was keen for Addy not to see things that would worry her until the hammock was complete. On an evening without a breath of wind he climbed to the top of one tall tree with rope tied round his waist. He fastened an end of the rope to the trunk, climbed down and up another tree, fastening the same rope to that tree. By means of clambering upside down along the rope, he stretched a second one from tree to tree. Over a period of weeks and months, on selected still days, he created a cat's cradle of rope between the trees, impossible to fall through, braced by ropes to keep it steady. Finally, with the aid of his bailiff, who tied Conrad securely to his father piggy-back, he climbed up and into the hammock and gave the signal that Addy could be summoned from the house.

She nearly fainted. But Conrad's screams of joy, combined with Rufus' assurance that they were in no danger, mollified her. Rufus dropped a long rope, instructed her to put two bottles of lemonade in a carrier bag, and, when she had done so, hauled up the refreshments. She had to laugh, and to congratulate Rufus and tell Conrad what a brave boy he was. The hammock was considered a great success in the annals of family history.

The day of Conrad's departure for his boarding school approached. He did not allow apprehensiveness to get the better of him. He was determined not to let anyone think his gloomy moods were anything to do with fear, and kept cheerful. He was unaccountably busy, bustling about and going missing for hours at a stretch. Addy was worried that he might be planning to run away from home, and asked Rufus to make sure that all was as it should be.

Rufus reported back to her that Conrad had been saying goodbye to each and every one of the livestock on the farm. The shepherd had seen him with the sheep on the hill, and the cowherd with the bullocks and the milking herd in the water meadows. One morning Rufus hurried Addy out and into the farmyard, where apparently Conrad had been talking to the ducks and geese. They were looking for him and, rounding the corner of a barn, saw him by the big iron-barred gate into Bully's pen. Bully staggered towards the gate, breathing hard and showing the whites of his eyes, and the boy reached in and stroked his wet nose with the ring in it.

His parents revealed themselves. They did not mock

Conrad's fond farewells, instead they praised him for being kind to the animals. Privately they were relieved on two counts: he was safe and well, and he had not been motivated by sentimentality – he explained to them that he had not bothered to say 'See you at Christmas time' to the turkeys.

His goodbye to his mother was tearful. Conrad's tearfulness was violent and desperate, in line with a certain streak in his nature. Addy was at once sympathetic and bracing.

'You may not believe it, my darling, but you're fortunate to be going to a good school. And you've got the train journey with your father to look forward to, and lunch in London – not many boys have those privileges. Don't forget that we'll be waiting with open arms to welcome you home in not many weeks – remember how much luckier you are than our young turkeys. Aren't we all lucky to have one another and to be alive? I think you and me and our family are the luckiest people in the whole world.'

She was able eventually to dry his eyes, and he went off with Rufus, standing straight and laughing at some joke.

Then she cried.

By this time Addy had other children to worry about. Guy Forester was five, Eve was three, and Ian on the way.

Guy was lost without his elder brother. He was large for his age, and, when he had pleaded to be sent to school with Conrad, his parents were inclined to agree that he could probably have held his own at work and even in games, far too young though he was for the schooling in question.

He was golden-haired and pink-cheeked, and the picture of health. He smiled at life, and life seemed unable to stop itself smiling back at him. He was a joker, and his ironical sallies were precocious inasmuch as he could elucidate the double meanings.

'Not half' was one of his favourite expressions. When he was told that iodine applied to a graze did not sting much, 'Not half it doesn't,' he replied. He would say that rain was lovely weather for ducks. The following was his answer to the question of what he would like to eat next: 'Puppy dogs' tails.'

Guy hero-worshipped Conrad, who, in turn, was tolerant of his brother's junior status and amused by his jokes. Guy was Conrad's shadow, and puffed and blew in order to keep up with the other's quicksilver activities. Why they occasionally came to blows was not known, possibly even by themselves, although their parents suspected that Guy might sometimes blunder provocatively into Conrad's sessions of solitude.

The only person who benefited from Conrad's absence was Eve. She, in her turn, hero-worshipped Guy, and now she liked to think she had him to herself. Her still infantile form of love was to be continually convulsed with laughter in Guy's company. He called her Evangeline, brat, silly filly, Miss-take, and her response was to split her sides as if at wit beyond compare. He was no doubt flattered by the evidence of his effect on her funny bone, but he was also patient, indulgent, and protective of his baby sister.

Rufus and Addy were not exactly hero and heroine to their children: he was more like God Almighty and she was a sort of goddess, accessible, demonstrative, warm and comforting, yet the arbiter of their fates – and everybody else's for that matter. Rufus was so tall that he appeared to his children to have his head in the clouds literally, and was often an absentee Daddy. On the other hand he built the hammock, and could excite them to a frenzy by sometimes playing hide-and-seek or fox-and-hounds – he would be the fox and they hunted him by following the paper trail he left behind. The nanny who presided over the nursery was a calming influence, and perhaps less of a strain to be with

285

than powerful parents; but Addy was a more than devoted mother, she was dedicated, and never far from her offspring, anyway in spirit.

The family moved north to Beltran Castle in the autumn and for Easter. 'Castle' was a presumptuous name for the house built by Addy's grandfather: it was modelled on Balmoral, but much smaller, and bore a greater resemblance to all the bungalows and cottages scattered across the country that shared the address of the royal residence. In a lodge at the bottom of the short drive a caretaker with other interests and responsibilities lived with his wife, who cooked for the Foresters as required. Mr McCabe had been the employee of old Mr Deverel and was equally snobbish. He called himself the Farm Manager, a title he did not deserve since no farm was attached to the property; but he would justify it by reference to his right, granted verbally long ago or acquired by usage, to run a few sheep on the lower slopes of the several thousand barren Beltran acres of Grampian hillside.

In August and September Rufus sometimes invited a friend or two to try to shoot a grouse on the heathery uplands, or they would fish in the two or three miniature lochs or dewponds, where the water was always too cold to swim in. Addy and the children would drive to vantage points with huge views reaching right to the North Sea, bringing picnics for lunch or tea. The air was good for all, but the heather scratched young legs and such expeditions were apt to end in tears. At Easter there was usually deep snow on the hilltops, and they tobogganed and skated, and came home to roaring fires of sweet-scented pine logs and, at teatime, hot drop-scones spread with melting butter.

Rufus was not on holiday at Beltran. He had repairs and maintenance of the house to see to, and the backlog of gardening work done or undone by Mr McCabe. He had to burn the heather in a controlled way and by agreement with neighbours. He would rush back to Forest Court to deal with a crisis or attend an essential meeting. Recreation was confined to a minimum so far as he was concerned. But he loved Beltran nonetheless, for Addy's sake, and for the relatively carefree type of fun they had there. Sometimes there was a bonus when a herd of red deer strayed on to the Beltran land, and he was expected by those who conserved the species locally to cull a superfluous stag if he could.

Conrad and even Guy were included in most of the events of one stalking day: it must have been either before Conrad went to school or during a late summer holiday. Their eager anticipation met with no disillusionment. All children and every normal man are hunters, and modern political denials of that fact, and the theory that foxes are sweethearts and lamb chops grow on trees and human beings are herbivores at heart, will probably tempt nature to take corrective action. The excitement at the Castle was carried to extremes by the boys. First thing in the morning a local free-lance gamekeeper arrived, together with a youth leading a shaggy hill pony. With luck, the pony would soon be bringing the dead stag down from the hills. The gamekeeper, Mr Fraser, a beetle-browed man wearing suitable headgear, a tweed deerstalker, also hairy plus-fours, carried by means of shoulder straps a rifle in a canvas case and a large telescope in a leather one.

The weather was not too bad, grey but dry, and after breakfast everybody went out to watch Rufus take a few practice shots with the rifle: an envelope was drawing-pinned to the trunk of a tree for him to aim at. He fired four times, made four separate holes in the envelope, and was applauded and congratulated. A sandwich lunch with thermoses and bottles was packed in panniers straddling the pony's broad back, and the shooting party set off on the long climb uphill. Before long Conrad was riding on the pony and Guy was perched on his father's shoulders; and later the youth gave Guy a lift.

After a couple of hours, about midday, they reached a peak and the boys, the lad and the pony rested or hid amongst jagged rocky outcrops, while Rufus crawled after Mr Fraser some yards farther and into the open. The telescope was withdrawn from its case, and first the gamekeeper and then Rufus studied the panorama of high ground and, again in turn, spotted the herd of deer. It was far away, a mile or so distant, but could be stalked effectively from a certain angle: there was cover for the stalkers and the wind would not waft their scent towards the deer. The lad, Jimmy by name, was given instructions and left in charge of the boys and the pony.

Getting on for half an hour passed much too slowly for Conrad and Guy. But at last Jimmy indicated that they were to follow him and keep quiet. They crawled to where their father and Mr Fraser had lain, and, after considerable finger-pointing and hushing on Jimmy's part, saw the herd. But just as they focused on it the deer trotted off, and Conrad cried out with disappointment: 'They're going!' At the same moment they heard the crack of the rifle and Jimmy scolded: 'Now, now, watch yon stag!' It – he – was standing still, being passed and left behind by the other deer. Guy piped up: 'What's it doing?' And as if by way of answer the stag's legs crumpled and he fell on his side on the ground.

'Did Dad shoot it? Is it dead?' the boys chorused.

'Ay, stone daid,' Jimmy pronounced in his own way.

'How do you know it is?'

'Because he fell daid.'

'Can we go and see it now?'

'Ay – there's your faither waving.'

Rufus hurried back towards the boys and they stumbled along in his direction. Their meeting was celebratory. Jimmy

288

with pony and lunch, and Mr Fraser reunited with his rifle, joined them, and they shared the picnic in another sheltered location beside a tumbling tinkling burn.

Afterwards they went to fetch the stag, which was lifted on to the pony's saddle and strapped there. Conrad knew why the red deer of Scotland had to be culled, and his feelings for the stag shot with a single bullet by his father were neither regretful nor mixed. Guy, on the other hand, was sorry the stag's eyes were still open, and squeamish when he saw it had been gutted. But at home, in front of their mother and Eve, they both basked in reflected glory and were so happily exhausted that they fell asleep over tea.

Shooting the stag, the antlers of which were mounted and hung in the hall of Beltran Castle, was another of the feats from which all Rufus' children in due course derived inspiration. If winter evenings at Beltran seemed to drag, he could sometimes be persuaded to tell tales of his wild prewar exploits. He would describe what it had felt like to go over Niagara Falls in an outsize barrel, the shock of hitting the water, the increasing shortage of air, and how cramped and cold he had been. And his account of the night he had spent alone in a house that was meant to be haunted thrilled most of all, in spite of the nightmares it was responsible for. Conrad and Guy, Eve to a lesser extent, and later on the two unborn siblings, aspired to be as adventurous and dauntless as their father.

On such an evening Addy as it were played truant from her unremitting cares and responsibilities, and viewed the scene objectively, from a stranger's point of view. The firelight played on the faces of her family. Her dear Rufus, now heading for middle age, his hair greying over his ears, looked powerful, a solid citizen, straight as a die and infinitely competent. He had given her almost everything she wanted, he still gave her his physical self, and she could dream of no better father for her children. Conrad was a small Rufus with imagination added and a more sophisticated intelligence and nervous system: he could well turn into a heartbreaker. Guy was so handsome, clever and strong that he often worried his mother: would jealous fate permit him to grow up? The flames and shadows of the fire were reflected in his wide-apart, wide-open eyes, and the gold of his hair was like a halo. Eve, pressed against Guy, was another golden child; but Conrad was the most interesting. She herself, she realised in an unwonted instant of self-consciousness, was part of the picture of a somewhat exceptional family. She remembered, without either dismissing them or taking them too seriously, the compliments showered upon all the Foresters by their friends and guests. At present she was large with child, but she had regained her slender figure after bearing three, and was hopeful of once more having the pleasure of fitting into her pretty clothes. Although she had ceased to bother unduly about her appearance, maternal love had not blinded her altogether to the tributes she often read in the faces of a variety of men.

At bedtime, after Rufus had gone to sleep, she counted her blessings and swore by all that was holy that she took nothing for granted. She thanked God for more favours than she could count, and also promised not to squander a moment of her wonderful life on futile apprehensiveness.

In the fullness of time she produced another boy, Ian, and in 1930 she bore her fifth and last child, Faith. Some internal complication meant that she could have no more children. She was not sorry. She loved her two littlest ones very much. But Ian was nothing like Conrad and Guy had been at the same age, he was a sombre unsmiling infant with sadly questioning eyes; and for that matter Faith was quite the opposite of fairy-like Eve – she was greedy and soon fatter than healthy puppies are.

*   *   *

290

There was a chink in the armour of Rufus Forester's competence. At first Addy thought it was nothing to bother about: she was not materialistic, did not understand money, did not care whether she was rich or poor, and was confident that she could earn her daily bread, along with other young women and even with responsible wives. But she foresaw that she might be the mother of many. It dawned on her that her children would not have their maternal grandmother, her mother, to look after them if she – Addy – had to work in an office or travel abroad on business, or were to fall ill. She grasped another fact, that their paternal grandmother, Rufus' mother, was too old and arthritic to step into the breach if she should be otherwise engaged or incapacitated. She therefore came back to the conclusion, first, that, rich as she apparently was, she was dependent on Rufus for providing a delightful life-style for the family and ultimately for feeding it, and secondly that he seemed not to be so good with money as he was in every other context, and might plunge them all into debt and penury.

He had introduced her to his family's solicitor before they were married. The solicitor was called Samuel Hillage, and Rufus introduced him to Addy thus: 'Sam's looked after my finances for the last twenty years, and his father looked after my father, and now he's willing to save us a lot of trouble by taking charge of yours, too.' She had made grateful noises without meaning them. She disliked the lawyer's little brown eyes: he was reassuringly rubicund and dressed like a country gentleman, but his eyes were too small and his regard was restless. But Rufus became her lord and master, and she yielded to his every suggestion without demur.

A few years passed. The Foresters and the Hillages, Sam and Vera, mingled socially. Rufus and Addy dined a couple of times at Hillage View, Sam's family home, recently enlarged, and repaid the entertainment. One morning Sam called unannounced at Forest Court and talked privately to Ada – Rufus happened to be in London.

Sam wanted her signature. He explained that Rufus had bought a cottage for an old retainer, Alf by name, a simpleton who had done odd jobs on the farm, and that, as Forester funds were on the low side temporarily, he would like to have permission to use some of her money to pay for it.

'Oh yes,' she said. 'Yes, I see. How much does the cottage cost?'

'Three hundred and fifty pounds.'

'Isn't that quite expensive, as prices go? Would Alf really need such an expensive place to live in?'

'Probably not. I haven't had the pleasure of meeting Alf, nor have I set eyes on the cottage, to tell the truth. Rufus simply gave me the instruction and told me to get on with it. You know how generous he is. I'm always warning him that if he isn't careful he'll be in need of charity instead of splashing it out.'

'Well, I'd hate to curb his charitable impulses. Would Rufus have to know that I've paid his bill?'

'I could do my best not to worry him. I called in today because a little bird informed me he'd be absent.'

'How bad are his finances? I thought he was well off.'

'He is at the right time of year, when he receives his dividends and sells his crops and livestock. Large sums of money come into the Forester coffers, but sometimes, alas, even larger sums go out.'

'There's no alternative to my meddling in his business, is there? The last thing I want to do is to seem to him to be interfering.'

'My firm could advance the money, but that would have to be at a regrettably high rate of interest. It would cost Rufus a lot more to borrow from us than to receive a contribution from your good self.'

'Where do I sign?'

'Here, on the bottom line, as they say. This paper will authorise me to sell sufficient securities belonging to you to pay for Alf's cottage.'

'You'll only take three hundred and fifty pounds, is that right?'

'Quite right. And I'm sorry to be a bore with legal papers and stuff. You might decide at some stage to give me a blanket authority to balance the books on your behalf.'

'Would Rufus be supervising everything? How often does he go through the books?'

'Whenever he has time. But of course he is more and more in demand to sit on boards and the bench and goodness knows what else, because word of his honesty has got around. My aim is to spare him trouble, and the same already applies to you and could apply even more.'

'Thank you, Sam.'

'Let me know if you'd like to talk further about unifying the two accounts, his and yours.'

'Thank you again.'

The conversation left her feeling uncomfortable. In rare spare moments, usually when one of the children had woken her at night, she would lengthen the list of the anxieties it introduced into the back of her mind. Would Rufus find her out and be displeased? Was she right to have gone behind her husband's back? How could Rufus spend money he did not possess? Was she mean to hesitate to transfer her wealth altogether into his keeping? If she were to do so, would he safeguard her children's birthrights? How could she harbour a scintilla of distrust of her darling honest husband?

She passed the cottage in question in her car. Actually it was less grand than she expected, but it measured up to her expectations in that it showed every sign of neglect, the garden undug, the paintwork peeling.

She was pleased to think that Rufus had not over-housed Alf; but then she glanced into the window of an estate agency in Fowick and noticed that cottages similar to Alf's were advertised for no more than two hundred pounds.

Her reaction was to say to herself: 'I knew he was paying too much.' But her next idea was inescapable: had she been cheated by Sam Hillage? Suddenly, as in a kaleidoscope, her ideas changed into suspicions and formed a most disturbing pattern. She was in a trap, she saw it – she had foolishly stepped in and did not see how she could step out. To tell all to Rufus would be to confess that she had practised a sort of deception in collusion with Sam, she had almost certainly let herself be robbed, she was pretty sure the robber was Rufus' friend and the steward of his fortune and his children's inheritance, and that her hero and champion was more than likely a willing victim and a gull.

She could not do it, and she hated Sam Hillage for having taken advantage of his knowledge that she was too fond of her husband at once to reveal his silliness and the identity of the villain of the piece.

Yet she had to do something before it was too late, and Sam had pinched the lot, and maybe moved from Hillage View into Forest Court.

For several months she seethed with frustration; avoided Sam if she could; pleaded a headache when the Foresters were due to dine with the Hillages; noticed with a sinking heart that Sam's surname rhymed with pillage; and prayed for an opportunity of some sort that she could seize.

A friend of both generations of Foresters, Rufus' mother and Rufus himself, and a more recent friend of Addy, Sir Theodore Edmunds, a big noise in the City of London, a bachelor of obvious distinction in his fifties, came to stay at Forest Court. It was autumn, and Theo Edmunds was paying his annual visit on his way to Scotland. He said he loved the air of Northumberland, and to catch up with

Forester news and to see his godson Guy; but Addy was aware that, in addition, he had a soft spot for herself. On a day on which Rufus had to drive to Beltran Castle for some pressing reason, she offered to keep Theo company on one of his long walks into the hills. She wondered if she would be swapping one danger for another, but felt under pressure to be bold.

After an hour or so of walking and small talk they stopped to rest by the lonely wayside.

'How pleasant to be sitting here in this beautiful landscape with you,' Theo remarked in a light-hearted tone of voice, then amended what he had said. 'Perhaps I should put it the other way round – how pleasant to be sitting here with beautiful you in this landscape.'

She laughed and thanked him for the compliment.

'Not a meaningless compliment, my dear,' he corrected her.

She laughed again and launched into possibly deeper water.

'Theo, can I confide in you? I'm sorry, you must have people confiding in you till you're sick of it, and I may be wrecking your holiday, but can I ask your advice?'

'Of course. I'd like nothing more than to advise you. You should know that.'

She told him the whole story.

He heard her out – he was still a good listener in spite of being so much listened to – at any rate he listened to her.

His response was to say: 'I'm afraid I can't involve myself in catching another thief posing as a solicitor. The spirit's willing, but the flesh balks at the time it would take and the dreadful distance between where you live and I live.'

'I understand that. But Theo, my question is rather what should I do, if you can think of any answer to it.'

'Well, I do have the answer, but I'm shy of proposing it.'

She hesitated, blushing and wishing he had not spoken of

proposals, then said: 'Tell me – I trust you not to embarrass either of us.'

'My answer's another question: would you like me to be in charge of your financial affairs?'

'Oh Theo, do you mean it? How could you when you're so busy?'

'I could, I would, and I'd love to. The advantages would be that you'd have a good excuse to sack your solicitor, and you might be able to persuade Rufus to do the same thing and follow you into my fold. But we'd have to communicate more than we do at present, and you might decide that was a disadvantage. I'm speaking in discreet terms, and my advice is that you should think my offer over carefully. There is another matter to consider, to wit my ability to keep your money intact, but perhaps I can claim that I would stand a better chance of succeeding in that respect than Mr Hillage.'

'My decision's taken. Please, please, Theo – all I have is yours, all I have in the bank!'

She blushed again at her own choice of words.

'Have you considered my feelings for you?'

'What?'

'I've been your great admirer since we met. Only seeing you approximately once a year has been a sadness for me, yet I can assure you that my thoughts visit you much more often. I've never married, I've never wished to, my work has been my wife, and if you were unmarried I'd probably stop myself asking for your hand. My bachelordom is confirmed, which is not to say I'm anything but heterosexual. Nevertheless... Nevertheless, dearest Ada, you mustn't run away with the idea that I'm conferring a favour on you, it's the other way round. The highest ambition of my personal life has been, and is, to be of service to you and to be regarded as a closer friend of yours. Money isn't everything, but to look after yours, to look after you in that sense, would mean more to me than I can or should say. No, please, wait a moment! I'm not threatening you, I won't bully you, I promise never knowingly to make a nuisance of myself or even refer to this confession of mine, and never to harm your Rufus or any member of the Forester family. But I couldn't steal into your good financial graces under false pretences, and I'd understand if you were now to rule that my devotion would be out of place, and inhibiting and even boring, in what is usually a business relationship.'

'Oh Theo... Have you finished?'

'I'm afraid I've said too much.'

'No. I'm honoured. Thank you, thank you. Will you forgive me for being unworthy, and for having so little to offer you in return?'

'My dear, I'm easily old enough to have been your father, even if my affection for you isn't exactly paternal.'

'Well, your terms are acceptable to me – isn't that how you seal a deal in the City?'

'It'll do. But here's another way of putting it – you've made me very happy.'

She leant across and hugged him. Then she pulled him to his feet and they walked on, discussing practicalities.

That evening, when Rufus returned, she said at once that Theo had sweetly lowered himself so far as to offer to manage her finances and she was over the moon about it.

Rufus could not and did not fail to see the point: he kept on telling her how fortunate she was, and, when Theo extended his offer to include the Forester finances, he accepted it immediately.

Sam Hillage took the news fairly well. Since he could not possibly claim to be as clever with money as Sir Theodore Edmunds, he made a virtue of necessity, recollecting that he would still be paid to fight Rufus' legal battles. However, Addy occasionally caught a glance in her direction that was on the nasty, or at least reproachful, side.

Theo, later on, mentioned that Sam Hillage's accounts were a perfect example of inexactitude; but his tact was Sam's salvation, just as it made all well between himself and his new clients.

When Conrad was at boarding school, and was joined there by Guy with unnecessary haste, or so it seemed to his mother, and Eve had lessons to do, and Ian and Faith had their very own fish to fry in the nursery, Addy underwent a change. It was not the change of life for she was only thirty, nor was it that she could make no more babies: she did not know what it was, except that it had never happened to her before, and that it summoned a small cloud into the blue sky of her marriage.

She did not complain. She did not show that anything was wrong. She would have insisted that 'wrong' was not the word to describe her odd quarters of an hour of wondering what to do next and whether or not she wanted to do it. She loved her husband, she adored her children, she was replete with worldly goods; she had Theo Edmunds who loved her truly, friends galore and no known enemies; she thought she was healthy and knew she attracted men – her luck was boundless, if dangerously so, and she was determined to enjoy it to the full.

She was never impatient with Rufus. She never told him things, for instance that she felt herself changing, that he would not begin to understand. She was unwilling to be told that a longer walk on the hills would chase away the blues, or possibly a weekend in Edinburgh might be the ticket. Admittedly she knew she was cleverer than he was, but she was not the first wife to be privy to such a secret nor would she be the last; and she respected and admired Rufus nonetheless, as well as loving him. In fact she loved him all the more to make up for her transient whims that verged on disloyalty.

In so far as she could analyse herself, and pin down what it was that unsettled her, she at length decided that the culprit was truth. She had begun to see her circumstances truly, stripped bare, minus her youthful fancies, without the glamour and excitement of her successes by worldly standards. The orphan she had been was transformed into the lady of the manor with an enviable spouse and five fine children, and her life had been lapped in love. But the truth was that her Aunt May and the other Ameses were sweet and stodgy: Addy refused to believe her mother, May's younger sister, had been so ordinary and dim. A more daring truth to tell, or toy with, was that Rufus' dutiful daily round, which, together with his family life, fulfilled him completely, was not quite the answer to the question of the rest of her own life – she pined mildly for something more than to be his helpmeet and exist in his shadow.

A further disturbing realisation was that part of Northumberland and part of Aberdeenshire, even taken together, began to seem too small for her – she felt as if she needed more room, different air to breathe, another home in another place, London probably, where she could associate with people who were less parochial and earthy.

Finally, of course, she recognised the truth that her thoughts were thoroughly ungrateful, and therefore tried the harder to suppress them.

Into this dark phase she was going through an unexpected light shone for better or worse. Michael Trane rang her up. He had come home, he announced, and then accused her of not sounding particularly pleased. He would like to see her: could she offer him a bed for a few nights, a single bed? He was speaking from York, he could be with her later in the day: 'Okay – see you at six o'clock,' he said.

She was not pleased. Her alarm concentrated her mind. She did not want to have her loyalties divided further by Michael. She absolutely could not spend time in London, perhaps without Rufus, if Michael was going to batter on her bedroom door. She had not forgotten him, but had recently forgotten to remember how distracting he could be. She trusted herself, but did not trust him to leave her in peace. And after all, peace was her top priority.

She prepared Michael's bedroom. Rufus knew him slightly and was looking forward to renewing their acquaintanceship. Michael rolled up, physically untouched by the decade that had elapsed since he had said '*Adieu*, Addy' at Harrow. He was still slim and bronzed, and his curly hair looked black by electric light. He surprised her, as usual, but by behaving well.

They were not alone until the afternoon of the day after the next day: Rufus and the children had monopolised Michael. The weather was fine, and they slipped out for a walk after Michael had said he would have to leave Forest Court in the morning.

He wasted no time to cut through the conventions as they followed the path uphill she had taken with Theo Edmunds.

'You've grown into a beauty,' he said.

She laughed a little more breathlessly than she had with Theo, and said: 'You haven't changed.'

'What on earth makes you think that? It's ten years, Addy – and don't judge by externals.'

'Well, how have you changed? Have you left a wife in South America?'

'No, children possibly – no wife. I should have married you. Now we might have had five babies and a happy home.'

'I'm not convinced that it would have been happy, Michael. Would you have graced it with your presence?'

'Good thinking, Addy. But you might have reformed me.'

'I didn't have to reform Rufus. He did the reforming, he's responsible for the happiness of my home and my life.'

'That's a pretty speech. Your Rufus is a better man than I am. He's the salt of the earth – and I'm not being sarcastic. You stick with him and you won't come to much harm.'

'I mean to. But I was afraid you'd jeer at us. You used to say that marriage was for bores, and naughty things like that.'

'You don't need to be afraid of me, Addy. I promise I won't ever try to put you and Rufus asunder. And I'll bow out if I worry you. There – do you understand me? Do you see how much I've changed?'

'Yes. Why? What changed you? Was it only time?'

'A bit of everything, time, too many women, getting sick of it and of myself, and loneliness. I spent a lot of time more or less alone in lonely places, not for any excellent reason, not for fun or sport like Rufus, and I've nowt to show for wasting my substance, apart from a desire for friendship and a brand new set of standards. Will you be my friend, Addy?'

'Is that a loaded question?'

'Don't be suspicious – you used to be so trusting.'

'Once bitten.'

'Oh yes, all right, let me explain. I'm about to start a new job – in a bank, believe it or not – South American desk – and I want to settle down. I'd like to marry, but that may be asking too much of myself. On the other hand I love women and understand them and can be great friends with them so long as it's platonic. I wouldn't expect much – we could write and speak on the telephone, and perhaps you'd let me stay and be included in your family circle. This is a funny sort of proposition, isn't it? That's my story. What about yours, Addy? And what are you thinking?'

'You will have read my story since you've been our guest.'

'I could complement Rufus, you know – he and I are chalk and cheese, and variety's the spice of life, remember.'

'But I don't want two husbands, Michael.'

'Listen, I'm trying not to say anything rude, but Rufus is quite heavy going, and sooner or later you'll need light relief. Motherhood's fine and dandy, but to some extent it's temporary. Plan for your future, Addy. Be nice to me, Addy. Can't we have a shot at it?'

'You're still an upsetting person, Michael. You walk in and out of my life as you please, and I'm taking all your talk with large pinches of salt.'

'What I'm asking you boils down to very little. There's something in you that tempts me to bare my soul, which is probably a mistake. It's your mysterious serenity – because you keep your secrets I feel I must blurt out mine. I'll just pay you one compliment, if I may. You're a wise girl not to describe your happy marriage in too much detail. Girls less wise than you are pick their marriages to bits for the sake of friends and psychoanalysts, and then they can't stick the bits together again.'

'My marriage isn't fragile. I don't funk friendships with men, real friendships. You can think me your friend if you like, while you'll be on approval for me. Would that suit you?'

'Thanks,' he said.

Their walk, or the rest of it, was enjoyable for Addy. Michael might lack the virtues of Theo Edmunds, but he supplied a subliminal demand in her for a touch of romance. The playfulness between their former selves revived, and their adult solemnities dissolved in giggles.

That evening, at Forest Court, Michael chatted to and charmed Rufus, and received encouragement when he said how delighted he was to be back on friendly terms not only with Addy, but also with her family.

In the weeks that followed Addy received communications from Michael as well as from Theo. The first were fun, postcards, jokes, letters, and telephone calls from his bank with offers to sell her South American gold mines, whereas Theo's sharpened her interest in serious business and contained welcome assurances. Gradually it came to her attention that she had either recovered her poise or was developing a new extended form of happiness. She and her Rufus were still one, but others figured in the picture of her happy days. Eternal triangle there was none: rather, three men provided her with service of different kinds and degrees, and her children were reasons to live and laugh for, and in an outer circle were all the dear people and the rest of the world.

Winter descended on Forest Court, and the long nights and the east winds contributed to the following conversation between the Foresters.

'Rufus?'

'Yes, my love?'

It was after dinner. Rufus had been nodding over his newspaper, Addy had been doing some needlework, and the fire was burning low and the wind howled in the chimney.

'Should we have a house in London?' she asked.

'Do you want one?'

'Well ... do you?'

'I'm not keen on London, as you know. I never was – I'm a bumpkin born and bred.'

'Well ... yes.'

'What's the big idea, Addy?'

'My idea is to talk over things like geography, where we live in relation to the children's schools, and how far we or the children are starting to have to travel, for instance at half-terms, and the future, when our children will all want to meet their friends in London. We do live in the back of beyond, which is perfect, but maybe we should branch out.'

'Isn't it a bit soon to think of Conrad becoming a man about town?'

'Time flies.'

303

'Would you like to be in London?'

'We could escape the worst weather sometimes, if we had a bolt-hole in the south. And we could see our friends. It's difficult to invite them to travel up here in the depths of winter.'

'I definitely don't want to hide you away from your friends, and I'm sorry I can't be company for you when I'm out and about so much.'

'I cannot find fault with you, Rufus darling, try as I may. But now Theo Edmunds has become my good friend as well as yours, and we're all business partners in a way, it would make sense for us to see him more often than once a year. And I would like to keep up with Michael Trane, after he's been abroad for so long and at last seems to be on the straight and narrow. Besides, there are Aunt May and my cousins, and my girlfriends, who I've almost lost touch with. I'm setting out a few extra reasons, apart from the main ones affecting our children.'

'Dear girl, thank you for consulting me. No doubt Theo would agree that you could well afford to buy somewhere nice in London. I'm not raising any objections. You've convinced me over the years that you know best.'

'Oh Rufus! Doesn't it worry you that you spoil me?'

'Not at all. The point is, you don't get spoilt.'

How marvellous were the days of the early 1930s for Addy Forester! The gods smiled on her, and the sun shone. Her blessings were hard to count, there were so many, but she did constantly try to count them. Happiness had transfigured itself in her case into joy, into ecstasy.

Her house in London was in Walkers Row in Chelsea. It was big for a bolt-hole, it had gardens front and back, and five bedrooms, and a basement flat for a cook and her handyman of a husband to live in.

'Is there enough money to pay for it all, Theo?'

'Yes. I'll see that there is. The house is a bargain from my point of view. And the Foresters' finances are on the up and up, I'm pleased to report.'

She spent time in Walkers Row with and without Rufus, and mostly without children, but was never short of visitors. One of the marvels was that she had made a name for herself, and become popular, in her absence. Those who had ventured north and stayed at Forest Court had relayed golden opinions of her appearance, charm, intelligence, and her remarkable brood, and now they brought their friends to meet her, and their friends invited her into their homes, where she met more appreciative people, and the social snowball gathered pace and increased in size. Rufus was appreciated, too, for his heroism in the last war, and for having unearthed such a jewel in Addy, whose advantages included a hefty fortune; but female socialites agreed that he was a discouraging man to have to sit next to at dinner parties, benevolent though his monosyllables were.

Addy was possessed of two prerequisites for success in society of even more importance than charm etcetera. She was tireless, and her digestion could cope with surpluses of rich food. She was able to look as if she floated ethereally through a season of elaborate lunches and dinners, late nights and early starts on jaunts and excursions, while a majority of other women flagged and wilted, spent days in bed in darkened rooms or else in Harley Street.

She also had the gift of enjoyment. She refused no invitation if she was free to accept. She could discriminate between good and bad people, but kept her critical faculties in check. She was never bored, she was even interested in the phenomenon of boredom. The world of fashion was new, exciting, and never less than fun in her eyes. Soon she realised that she could enjoy it even more if she was in charge of the entertainment and picking and choosing her company. She began to give select luncheon and dinner parties, and to win further plaudits as a hostess.

She did not reign alone over her court. Rufus was the king of the revels when he was in town, or at least her consort. She missed no chance to show that she was as proud of him as he obviously was of her. She invited his old comrades-in-arms to meet him, and sprinkled his friends amongst hers at parties they gave together.

'Did you hate it, darling?' she would ask after their guests had gone.

'No, I was glad to see old Dick again – he's a capital fellow.'

Or she would ask: 'Are you homesick, sweetheart?'

And he would either answer, 'I'm all right,' or, 'A little.'

'Why not go home, poor darling unselfish Rufus?' she would urge. 'I'm sure you've got terribly important engagements up north, and you've just been kind to join in my silly fun and games. Would you like me to come home with you? You know you only have to say the word. But please don't think me naughty for spending so much time in London – I never forget that you and the children are my first and last priority. When I'm fed up with high society, you'll wish I wasn't always hanging round your neck.'

On average she spent approximately ten days a month at Walkers Row. It was more in winter, and much less during the children's holidays. Rufus was with her for about two or three days a month. In his absence, other men acted almost as host at his wife's festivities, and, in a sort of rotation, as her escort – Theo, for instance, and Michael Trane in his new incarnation as somebody punctual and sober.

Addy, unwontedly and fleetingly, reflected that she might be carrying essential feminine adaptability too far. Exceptional moments of self-examination suggested that she might be turning into – by some process of late development – a human chameleon. Even worse, she was finding surely unworthy fulfilment in being not all things, but quite a lot of things, to quite a lot of men. She was as usual a traditional spouse to Rufus; with Theo she was at best like a daughter, but frequently, she feared, like a woman fawning on a sugar daddy; with Michael she impersonated a femme fatale; and with her boys she was heroine, playmate and nursemaid – everything rolled into one.

'Oh, dearest Theo, should I pay this bill?' she would plead. 'Will you look after this income tax demand? Where would I be without you?'

Somehow her relations with Michael had taken a strange twist: she had become the arbiter of his love life.

He brought to her, he laid at her feet, accounts of the ladies, and the females who were not ladylike, whom he was pursuing or pursued by: they were a variety of those corpses cats are inclined to carry home.

'How am I to shake off so-and-so?' he asked Addy. 'She's big and strong and she's suffocating me, she'll drag me to the altar dead or alive, and when I tell her I hate her she splits her sides. She thinks I'm a comic cut, and I curse the day I tickled her for the first time.'

Again he begged her: 'Lady such-and-such is playing hard to get – how am I to bring her to heel?'

'Isn't she married, Michael?'

'There is an apology for a husband lurking about, I believe.'

'Why on earth can't you fall in love with a spinster and do the decent thing?'

'That's rich, coming from you. But I suppose it's to be expected from a little rich girl. You know damn well why I can't find Miss Right – it's because I've already found her, and she happens to be a missis with knobs on.'

'Well, I wish and hope and pray you'll stop being a hopeless fool, and rearrange your emotions in a practical manner.'

'You'd lose me if I did.'

'I want you to be happy.'

'Oh, I'm happy enough to be your willing slave and obey your orders. Answer my questions about Lady such-and-such!'

Addy's throne was not merely a three-legged stool, supported in an emotional sense by Rufus, Theo and Michael: it was stabilised by between three and five other supporters, namely Conrad, Guy and Ian, and to some extent by Eve and Faith. She was never so dazzled by the bright lights as to lose sight of her best beloveds.

Perhaps the hardest internal struggle of her whole life was not to make favourites of any of her children, but she never felt she was winning it. Her first-born undid her intentions and efforts. Conrad vanquished her. He bowled her over without meaning to, effortlessly, innocently – and partly by having no awareness of his attractions. Addy's love of him was extreme although strictly maternal: she was in awe of this godlike young man she had created with a little help from Rufus, but she could also judge him objectively, by comparisons and high standards.

He was nudging his teens, and moving to public school, where he would stay until he was nearly grown up. But he was already as tall as she was, slender yet athletic and strong, and his features showed an adult bone formation. He was not exactly easy-going. His schoolmasters, after praising his work and his character, usually added that he was moody. He would rag with Guy, they would chase each other and wrestle and laugh till they cried; at other times Conrad was not to be persuaded to fool about, and would be somehow beyond the reach of even his parents. He was a precocious moralist, ready to air his views of what was right and wrong and dish out stars and black marks to his siblings: what saved him from being a prig was his mixture of integrity, sincerity, open-mindedness and humility.

He had always pined for a dog of his own, and at length Rufus and Addy relented and, at the start of a long summer holidays, bought him one of the puppies of the accidental litter of a collie belonging to the Home Farm shepherd. Conrad called the puppy Max. He and Max became inseparable – Conrad said he would sleep with Max in a barn if he was not allowed to have the dog in his bedroom at night. Conrad immediately exerted authority over Max without ever being heard to speak crossly or roughly to, let alone beat him. Max turned into a small graceful lurcher-type, and he seemed to understand Conrad as well as vice versa. Max knew when to play, hunt or lie quietly and close to his master.

They hunted as a team. Conrad was appointed by Rufus to try to control the plague of rabbits that nibbled away both at the Home Farm and at the grazing for sheep at Beltran Castle. The boy had had a ferret for some years, it was called Whizz and lived in a hutch in the farmyard, was a keen ratter and rabbiter, and was used by the farmworkers when Conrad was at school. The method for rabbiting was to cover the rabbit holes in a warren with nets, then to put Whizz down a hole and wait for a rabbit to run out, into a net, and be killed with a blow to the back of the neck. Conrad was an expert at delivering such a blow by the time he was eight years old. But Max introduced a novel element into the operation. Conrad would no longer net the rabbit holes, he would leave it to Max to deal with escaping rabbits.

One afternoon he invited Rufus and Addy to come and see how quick and clever Max had become. Addy was duly impressed – Max moved like lightning and killed rabbits with an invisible bite, and responded to every word and whisper uttered by Conrad. Rufus was congratulatory and grateful; and she tried to follow suit, but was a trifle alarmed by the excitement evinced by both the dog and her darling son. Conrad's eyes flashed fire, and she suspected that he would have been capable of killing the rabbits with his teeth if Max had not done so.

The hint of latent savagery in Conrad's make-up did not detract from his charm. Often nowadays, at Forest Court and at Beltran, she would watch from a window as he and Max set out on a day's adventure. He might have Whizz in a travelling box slung across his back, or the gun his father permitted him to borrow on occasions, or possibly his camera with the telescopic lens. He wore an open-necked shirt in summer, and in winter an old tweed jacket that had belonged to Rufus and reached to his knees, and a tweed cap on his head. He walked boldly, looking around him sharp-eyed like some proud beast of prey, and was light on his feet, as if ready to spring. He was a figure of romance with his faithful dog at his heels. He was fiercely masculine and untameable by women.

But did she love Guy more?

She showed them off in London, her marvellous boys: she found it difficult to hang on to her modesty when it came to her children. She cajoled them into helping her to entertain her guests, Conrad with his dark and dashing cast of countenance, Guy the golden, beaming on all and sundry, both displaying intelligence and a modicum of social grace. She hoped it was not cruel of her to introduce them to the mothers of dumb sons with acne and hostile attitudes.

Guy was her antidote to Conrad, she often thought. When Conrad was withdrawn and remote, she was apt to turn to Guy for a reciprocal kiss and to be squeezed for a joke in his strong arms. If life was a puzzle and a strain for Conrad, for Guy it was potty. He knew how to do things, mend fuses, mend china, he knew where everything was. He was even more successful than Conrad academically, he

310

won prizes that Addy could find no room for in the crowded shelves of her children's trophies. And he was kinder, generally speaking. While Conrad sought to solve the problems of this world and the next in the company of Max, and would then ignore his three youngest siblings or else tease Eve, and frighten Ian by telling him ghost stories at night, and reduce Faith to tears by remarking that she was fatter than ever, Guy would permit the little threesome to follow him about, and amuse them somehow. Guy was good nature personified, setting aside his battles with his elder brother; Conrad's form of kindness was stunning self-sacrifice, for instance his ten-mile run to and from Fowick in order to buy stamps for his mother, having overheard her saying regretfully to someone that she had none.

All the children were athletic, but they played games for sport, for amusement, to master a difficult discipline rather than competitively and to beat an opponent. They particularly liked to play against adults and strangers, whose methods and techniques differed from those of the family, and could be instructive. One consequence was that Addy felt freer to invite an increasing number of her London friends to stay at Forest Court. To the hardier type she offered a visit to Beltran, cramped quarters included. Such visits were nearly always successful, largely thanks to the children, she was pleased to think – and perhaps rightly. Visitors were taken over by one or other of them, or by all at once, and were lured by friendly overtures, or led by beguilingly warm little hands, to tennis court or croquet lawn, to ping-pong table or card table.

And the Forester children were not completely normal in one respect: they were not boring. They told no rambling shaggy dog stories, they never cried, they laughed at pain, and were exemplary losers. Moreover they were exceptionally healthy – no chesty coughs, no running noses. They delighted Addy's guests. Not only Theo Edmunds and

Michael Trane, but jaded sophisticates of both sexes and all ages were ready and willing to come out and play.

For Addy, the only crack in the crystalline bowl of her happiness was caused by time hurrying by. Her personal life could not be improved upon, it had everything to recommend it, or perhaps more accurately it had a bit of everything.

The sun does not always shine on Northumberland and Aberdeenshire, but in her 1930s it seemed to. The days were packed with treats. Now it was a discovery made by one of the children – a book read and loved, an ability developed. Now there was an expedition to see a sight or swim in the sea, or to make hay on the farm or stook the sheaves of corn, or to take the London train, or even to go back to school and return for the holidays. Sometimes they all piled into a farm wagon and went to call on neighbours; but they had more fun at home, and still more when the visitors arrived.

Scenes were etched in Addy's memory. A sunny afternoon at Forest Court was unforgettable: she looked down on it from her bedroom window – Rufus and Conrad playing a doubles match against Michael Trane and Guy on the lawn that served as tennis court, Theo and Eve playing croquet with Aunt May Ames, Ian being bowled at by Edward Ames, and Faith waddling about, stealing balls and getting chased by one player after another. The cries and the laughter reaching through the waves of heat up to the first floor window were like celebratory music.

Conrad took snapshots of especially happy occasions, and Addy pasted them in her family albums. Elaborate picnics in the English and Scottish hills figured: ladies fresh from Mayfair on all fours blowing on the bonfire that would not light, peers of the realm eating burnt sausages in their fingers. There was a series showing respectable men in their underpants and the Forester boys daring one another to jump into the freezing water of one of the Highland lochs. Posed groups photographed by Conrad also found their way into Addy's books – her children inevitably having much made of them by the guests, Guy being kissed on the top of his head by some female, Eve embraced by an ancient male, Ian arm-in-arm with a man in a tartan Glengarry, Faith on a friendly lap. Some of these photographs of groups included the photographer, looking somewhat strained: he had bought a delayed-action gadget which gave him thirty seconds to scuttle from behind his camera.

Confirmation that all was well reached Addy from numerous sources. Rufus invented playful pet names for her, 'commanding officer', or, what was more acceptable, 'guiding light'. The senior Ameses congratulated her on having transformed her bad beginning into such a happy ending – an ongoing end, they clarified quickly. And guests in their thank-you letters raved at unusual length over their experience in the bosom of the Forester family. Theo Edmunds told her she was no longer nobody, she was somebody, and warned her against envy and wagging tongues. Michael Trane said she was his spiritual home, and that one of his reasons for not marrying was that he dreaded having children who were not a patch on hers.

The latter compliment was not timed to perfection. Addy was nagged by a couple of worries when it was paid her. The lesser one was that Ian was so much slower than the other children. He greeted her efforts to teach him to read and write with an impenetrable and possibly obstinate thickheadedness. He could not concentrate, and did not care how 'cat' was spelled. He insisted on signing his name either Nia or Ani. He only wanted to know what the older boys were doing. And she was nonplussed by his dark blue eyes and strangely uncommunicative personality.

Her other worry was Conrad at fifteen years of age. He seemed to have turned against her: at least she thought so,

313

although Rufus saw nothing wrong and diagnosed puberty. In subtle ways he was not as nice to her, as trusting and confidential, as he had been, she realised or feared. The first climax of this sorry state of affairs occurred during summer holidays and the visit of two extended families heading for Scotland. The parents were friends of Rufus and Addy and between them they brought along two sons and four daughters, all approximate contemporaries of Conrad and Guy. The crowd of guests caused complications of a housekeeping kind, but eventually the youths occupied the last spare room and the girls were consigned to mattresses in the store room with the ping-pong table in it below stairs.

At supper Addy was embarrassed by the faces Conrad pulled, his speciality of funny or ugly faces, which reduced the girls to silly and apparently uncontrollable giggles. Some time after the young people had left the table, shrieks and cries were heard in the garden. Rufus investigated and returned to say they were playing French and English by moonlight – it was a balmy evening and he thought they would come to no harm. But the shrieks grew more raucous and excitable, and at length the grown-ups agreed to call a halt to the game. Down on the tennis court lawn, where the net had been removed, the children chorused pleas to be allowed to play a little longer.

Addy said no to Conrad, while the other parents gave out similar rulings.

He retorted, not looking at her and in a disrespectful and cutting undertone: 'You spoilsport!'

She did not answer back, she was too startled. In the days that followed she and Conrad were shy with each other – or did she imagine his sulky shyness? Was she in the wrong? She hoped she had not been jealous of his flirting with those girls – she had not been consciously so. She felt bruised in the region of the heart, and prayed that their differences were temporary.

314

At the end of the same holidays a most unusual event worried the majority of Foresters: Addy was unwell. She was at Walkers Row with Eve, who had been keeping appointments with an orthodontist. Needless to say she had no London doctor, but she heard of one, consulted him and soon found herself in hospital minus her appendix. Rufus and the other children rushed to be with her, but for a few days she only felt equal to seeing her husband. The complete family was due to visit her one afternoon – Conrad did not turn up. She excused him, said he must have got lost, and persuaded Rufus not to be cross and not to be too anxious, concealing her own anxiety and disappointment. Although the condition attached to the visit was that it should be short, it was cut shorter by Rufus wishing to inform the police that his son was missing.

Half an hour elapsed, and Conrad was shown into her hospital room. He had brought a huge bunch of white roses. He was redder in the face than she had ever seen him, and he laid the roses on her bed. She reached out her arms and embraced him, saying: 'Oh thank you, thank you for coming, thank you for the flowers,' while he said or muttered that he hated her being in pain. She was tearful, and he probably was, but they both blinked back their tears.

'How lovely to have you all to myself,' she began. 'Listen, darling, just ring through to Walkers Row and hand me the telephone – I'll tell your father you're safe and sound.'

'Sorry I didn't stick with the others. Tell Dad I'm sorry, will you? I'll explain when I see him.'

When she got through to Rufus, she described the wonderful flowers that Conrad had been so kind as to give her.

She rang off, and Conrad, still looking red and rather unhappy, said: 'But your room's full of flowers, Mother.'

'Lots of people have been kind, but your roses are special for me – and they must have cost you so much.'

They talked about her operation, she laughing it off, he frowning sceptically when she assured him it had not been very painful, and seeming to have something else on his mind.

At length he blurted out, gazing straight at her: 'Mother, I haven't been nice lately.'

How brave, she thought, how brave of him at his age to apologise without flinching!

She said with a smile: 'Oh darling, I'm prepared to take the rough with the smooth, not that you've really been rough. I think I can understand our misunderstandings and I hope you can, too.'

'I didn't like you being ill.'

'That may be my cue to apologise.'

'No,' he said. 'No,' he repeated, and added with his first smile: 'Roses speak, don't they?'

'Yes,' she agreed, 'they do.'

Addy convalesced at Walkers Row for a fortnight. The older children departed for their various schools, and Rufus at her request returned to Forest Court. Faith stayed behind to keep her company.

One fine Saturday afternoon Michael Trane took Addy and Faith to the Zoo. The plump little girl, who was passive as a rule, ran ahead of them, shiny-eyed and glowing with enthusiasm. It was infectious – Addy said she was suddenly back to normal, and how much she was enjoying herself.

By the Penguins Pool she remarked: 'To be as lucky as I am sometimes makes me feel guilty.'

Michael's response was to regard her with unwonted solemnity and warn: 'Dear girl, never tempt providence.'

When did she notice it first?

Rufus often retailed bits of news in the papers, but she

316

had not listened. She had better things to think about, and news was never new. Wars had been waged somewhere or other ever since men were men.

Rufus had been a soldier in the last war: no wonder he took an interest in sabre-rattling, armaments, munitions and things like that. He spoke to her of politics; but she understood politics even less than she understood money. Rufus and Theo and Michael not only all loved her, but all bored her sometimes with their political chit-chat. She would leave the room if possible when they started arguing. She had no time to waste on abstruse hypotheses. She banned politics from the table-talk at her parties.

In 1937 Conrad was seventeen, and at school he wanted to join the Officer Training Corps, Royal Air Force Section. His headmaster had written to Rufus, who showed the letter to Addy when the post arrived mid-morning at Forest Court.

'He can't,' she said. 'Does it mean flying? Flying's so dangerous.'

Rufus explained.

'He may be thinking of signing on with the Air Force when he's old enough. He said something of the sort in the holidays.'

'Not to me.'

'Well, no. He was considering your feelings, I expect. But everybody joins the OTC at school – it used to be compulsory. The only difference in Conrad's case is the Air Force bit. And flying isn't involved – he'll study the theory without doing any practice – he's too young to have a licence to fly.'

'Why join the Air Force? He can't make a career in the Air Force. I never dreamt he'd want to go into the armed services.'

'It's the war, Addy.'

'What?'

'He's thinking there may well be another war.'

'Oh Rufus!'

'It's not a certainty, thank God!'

'War with Germany again?'

'Some people believe so.'

'Do you?'

'Not if I can help it.'

'I've been an ostrich. Tell me how serious it is.'

'None of us know.'

'I've got to take Ian and Faith to their gym class. Can we talk later?'

'Of course. Don't fret too much, my dear!'

'Don't you, either!'

For the rest of the day he was out and she was rushing round, and they had the Fowick vicar and his wife to dinner.

After their guests had left they returned to the sitting-room and Addy said: 'We can't stop him.'

'No,' Rufus agreed.

They were carrying on from where they had left off, and did not need to name names.

'He's patriotic, isn't he?' she said.

'Very. So are the others.'

'Shall I write and praise him for what he's doing?'

'He'd be pleased. I could add a line or two to your letter. These young people who are preparing and prepared for the worst are admirable. We've reason to be proud.'

'Might it blow over?'

'Yes – yes and no.'

'At what age are boys called up to fight for their country?'

'Pretty young – I'm not sure.'

'You are. Is it nineteen?'

'Or younger.'

'He's seventeen.'

'Not that young.'

'Guy's fourteen and a half.'

'Yes.'

'You won't have to fight, will you, darling?'

'I think I'm too old, and food from farms would be much in demand.'

'Is there anything we could or should do?'

'Run away, you mean?'

'Certainly not!'

'Exactly.'

'I'm proud, Rufus. I'm proud of him and of you, you especially.'

'Ditto.'

'And we must keep happy.'

'Don't cry, Addy!'

'I'm not. But I am tired. And the same applies to you. Let's go to bed.'

'You're the best wife I've ever had.'

'That's good. That's better. Come along.'

In the Christmas holidays of 1938 Conrad told his parents that he was hoping to join the RAF, not go to university as had been the family plan.

They gave their blessing. At least he was seizing his chance to be properly trained in peacetime. The alternative, postponement, could send him into battle in a hurry and without self-preservative skills.

He wrote to them from the camps and colleges he was sent to, letters full of zest describing drill, physical exercises, lectures and boot-polishing procedures, and his impatience to be airborne. He came home on leave, looking fit and manly in his blue uniform, and in due course wearing his wings and his Pilot Officer's thin blue stripe. He loved flying. Characteristically, he was passionate about it. He tried to explain that in the air, above clouds, alone in a plane above the world, he felt more at ease with himself and people in general than ever before. He spoke haltingly of the beauty of his experience of flight, and of the spiritual side of the job he and his comrades-in-arms were doing. But in spite of his mother's encouragement he was loath to commit the sin of sounding pretentious, and he was too tactful to suggest that, at least for the moment, the RAF meant more to him than his family. He did his best to hide his sigh of relief when he waved goodbye to Forest Court.

War was declared on the third of September. Conrad saw no action to speak of for ten months, until the following June. In that period, before his battle began, he wrote two letters to his parents and one to his mother.

The first one ran: 'I'm too cowardly to say this to your faces, but feel I must write to thank both of you for giving me a perfect home and upbringing. Try as I will, I cannot think of a single complaint to level against either of you.

'Sorry if the above seems a bit dry and brief – these days sentiment has to be kept to a minimum, and there's no time to spare. You will read between the lines, won't you?

'I'm sorry about something else. Comparisons of the dangers faced by soldiers, sailors and airmen are particularly odious. Besides, everyone's in danger in a war like ours, more's the pity. I'm not yet in a position to say how dangerous my job may or may not turn out to be, because I haven't fired a shot for any warlike reason or been shot at, but I promise you I didn't choose to go into the RAF lightly or recklessly or without considering the concerns of my nearest and dearest. Please always remember that I love flying for better or for worse, and that somehow or other the sky's become my element, where I'm happy and – strangely enough – most at peace. Nevertheless, apologies for perhaps, and unintentionally, adding to your worries.'

The second letter, dated April 1940, took Rufus and Addy by surprise.

'I've met a marvellous girl and asked her to marry me,'

Conrad wrote, and qualified his dramatic opening sentence thus: 'Not to exaggerate or think wishfully, she and I have an understanding, as Victorian understatement used to put it. She's called Peggy Saunders, and is pretty, and good, and clever, and a WAAF – she works in the Admin block on this aerodrome. Have no fear, Mother! Her background is as beautiful as she is – old Yorkshire squirearchical. Her parents are still married, her father's serving King and country, he's in the army, and she volunteered to join the Air Force. She's nothing like the girls I used to flirt with. She is my first true love, and I'm prepared to say she will be my last. Furthermore, wonder of wonders, she has assured me that she reciprocates. Alas, no nuptials yet – I cannot, I should not, and am determined to resist temptation. Notwithstanding all the arguments to the contrary, I know it would be better for her not to commit herself to me, come what may in wartime – and I leave the possible difficulties of wifehood to a fighter pilot to your imagination. Lots of the boys here, my comrades-in-arms, and most of the girls for that matter, are agreed that matrimony is one risk too many, at least until horizons recede a bit. But the question has been popped – Peggy and I are engaged – please forgive me for not seeking your blessing before I put ring-number-one on her finger. She longs to meet you as much as I long to show her off to all the family. I'm certain you will love her, and not only for my sake, and that I do not need to beg you to be kind to her always. At present we're hoping to be able to get away together for enough days for me to meet her people and for her to come to Forest Court. It could be next week or the week after that – not much belligerence about for the time being. When I'm with Peggy and with you, my cup really will overflow.'

They arrived at Forest Court as promised on one of April's sunniest afternoons. They had driven north from Peggy's home in Yorkshire, and wore civilian clothes – his checked shirt was open at the neck, the cotton of her frock had a pattern of flowers. She was prettier than Conrad had boasted, a beautiful blonde girl with steady far-apart blue eyes, and together they looked like the archetypes of young love, or like youth in its strength and confidence standing firm against pain, sorrow, age and defeat.

Addy swallowed the lump in her throat, and Rufus lived up to his reputation for bravery. Individually and together they congratulated Conrad and made all the promises he wished for. Rufus hugged Peggy whenever he had the chance, and Addy at last insisted on stealing her from her fiancé and the others for a few minutes.

In Rufus' business room they spoke to each other as women do, realistically and despite the difference of their ages.

Addy said: 'Loving a man in wartime can't be easy.'

'It's lovelier than anything I've ever dreamed of,' Peggy replied, 'and terrible.'

'You and he were made for each other.'

'Thank you for thinking so.'

'I'm exclusively happy for both of you. We mustn't cross bridges before we have to.'

'I try to remember that.'

'He's outstanding. Goodness knows what mountains he could climb when the war's over.'

'I'm not worthy, although I belong to him body and soul.'

'He belongs to you.'

'I'll never let him down.'

'You know you're a member of my family now, now and for ever.'

'Thank you for everything, Conrad and everything.'

'Telephone me or write to me if or when you feel like it.'

'I'd like to give you the number of my offices.'

'Let's live for the day.'

'Yes.'

'Come on, I don't want to be selfish, I won't keep you from Conrad – or should I say I'll hand him over to you?'

They kissed goodbye.

The following month, in May, Germany invaded France and the Low Countries, and the remnants of the British Expeditionary Force were rescued from the beaches at Dunkirk by a fleet of big and little boats manned by professional and amateur sailors.

The so-called 'Phoney War' was over. Germany made clear its intention to cross the English Channel and take possession of our island as soon as it gained control of the relevant airspace. The RAF denied it that control – the Battle of Britain had begun.

Conrad was in the front line. He telephoned Forest Court once, to say he was fine, and flying between eight and ten sorties every twenty-four hours. Eve took the call – everybody else was out at the time. He told her that the aim of his very own personal war was to get enough sleep, and he sent loads of love.

Addy then received his letter scrawled in pencil on cheap lined paper torn out of a notebook.

'In haste,' she read: 'I'm being run off my feet by Fritz. But I have no secrets from you, and must confess that I'm having a hell of a good time. It's probably wicked to say that I like to kill my neighbour, even if that neighbour happens to be my enemy, but I do like it, I'm quite intoxicated by the distilled brew of life simplified into "Kill or be killed". Dog-fights are my pleasure so long as dogs are not involved. And they always remind me of hunting with dear old Max – no wonder the chase used to be reserved for kings.

'Don't worry too much – I am convinced that our national cause is okay, and I'm happy in my work, not to mention Peggy and the rest of my lucky breaks.

'In case of accidents, darling Mother, whatever arrangements you decide to make will be completely suitable, I know.'

Addy took up residence at Walkers Row as soon as London was bombed. She wished to share the danger to which Conrad was exposed. There she received the news from Rufus that their eldest son was lost.

She traced Peggy, who had been granted compassionate leave and was with her mother, and they swapped condolences; then she caught the next train to the north.

She was worried about Rufus, and her four children. Despite what she had said to Peggy those few weeks ago, she herself had crossed the bridge of present circumstances as soon as Conrad decided to join the Air Force: her husband had never been apprehensive. She was nonetheless surprised by the extent of her tranquillity. Of course, in a strictly limited sense, she had nothing more to fear.

Rufus looked more like seventy than fifty. Eve and Faith cried when they saw their mother. Guy and Ian were at their schools and had not yet been informed. Rufus spoke to Guy's headmaster and Addy to Ian's: both headmasters were sad to say that they had experience of how to break bad news. They explained that they could not summon boys to speak on the telephone without telling them why – it had proved to be a mistake to leave things to lurid boyish imaginations; again, it seemed to be beneficial to keep boys at school, with their friends and their routine, until the holidays, although if they pined for home they could be immediately released.

Guy and Ian betrayed little emotion to their parents, and opted to stay at school in the meanwhile. Addy told each in turn that he was doing the right thing, and promised the loveliest holidays.

Life went on at Forest Court almost as before. There

could be no funeral: a memorial service was planned. Decisions in respect of property and the farm had to be taken. Cows must be milked, roofs must be mended. The girls had to be ferried to their day-schools and back again. And people fell ill, Faith had earache, the cowman went down with flu.

The differences were, first and foremost, a world without Conrad. As for the rest, which Addy nerved herself to deal with, they were, in the order of their importance: comforting Rufus; answering innumerable letters, and writing often to Guy, Ian and Aunt May Ames; hours on the telephone – her longest conversations with Theo and Michael Trane; and infusing with sincerity repetitions of the clichés of bereavement. She now had more right to encourage other parents mourning their children, also to boost the morale of the wounded servicemen at the local hospital where she did menial tasks.

A letter from Conrad's Commanding Officer, and the medal for gallantry awarded posthumously and the citation, meant more to Rufus than to Addy – they told her nothing she did not already know. Apparently he had been the star pilot of his squadron, had shot down a record number of the opposition, and proved himself a fine leader of men. On the day of his death, in the afternoon, during his fourth engagement since dawn, he bagged two of the fighters escorting enemy bombers. Then his Spitfire was hit and he was possibly wounded. Instead of trying to bale out, he succeeded in crashing his plane into one of the bombers loaded with bombs to be dropped on London.

Addy was surprised again by her resistance to the temptation to succumb and collapse. She shed no tears in public or even in her husband's company. Resolutely she stuck to her line that she was grateful to have been close to Conrad for twenty years. She ate her dinner and did not weaken. And she listened to, and kissed and patted and cheered her loved ones and anybody else needing a shoulder to cry on.

The oddest manifestation of her grief was a sudden involuntary cessation of activity, a sort of trance, momentary, although she feared it might occur and prolong itself while she was driving a car, not exactly sad, more blank. She would stop whatever she was doing, she would stand still. Her eyes were fixed and sightless – some people snapped their fingers at her. Perhaps it was a fit, the epileptic kind called *petit mal*: but she consulted no doctor, she knew it was to do with Conrad, and wondered if her soul was slipping away to search for his in another dimension. A more down-to-earth suspicion was that her constitution was taking a break and drawing attention to her exhaustion.

Pulling Rufus through, at least in principle, called for continuous effort. His taciturnity made hard work of conversation: he almost refused to speak of Conrad, and he never spoke on any general subject. He was as good and kind as ever, and supportive too in his large clumsy physical way, but he would only discuss practicalities and plans, and his monosyllables were heard more and more often. He sometimes thanked her or apologised inarticulately – for comforting him, for not providing her with sufficient comfort – but he seemed to be incapable of checking his relapses into oppressive silence. She had to act virtually as interpreter between him and the children: and persuading him to remake his will was a marathon of tact.

Theo Edmunds was more than ever her right hand man. He helped to force the issue of the Foresters' wills. He played truant from his war-work on committees and boards in order to pay flying visits to Forest Court. He solved her problems, motivated Rufus temporarily, reassured their children, and distributed largesse to the staff. Three months after Conrad's death he began to urge her to spend at least a few days at Walkers Row. He reasoned that a change would be as good for her as a holiday, and she could come south while the boys were at school, bring a daughter or two with her, distribute sympathy and sense to her equally bereft friends, and build up the strength she needed to cope with poor Rufus' melancholia and all her other responsibilities.

She argued with him weakly. They would soon be going to Beltran Castle: but, Theo reminded her, life there was more tiring for her than Forest Court. She could not abandon Rufus: but he might profit from not being cosseted. She did not want to drag the girls from their lessons: in that case let them look after their father. She yielded – Theo had known what she wanted better than she had, and he broached the matter to Rufus.

In London she duly met and ministered to her friends, and was reunited with Michael. She had to admit to herself that his notes and telephone calls had not been exactly what she required of him. She had yearned to be again within the personalised haven of their flesh and blood friendship. Propinquity meant more than remote control, although her urge to attach herself to his aura was chaste, she assured herself. He would be too much of a handful for her to manage in a fully loving context, she had known it always. Moreover, now, she could not behave disgracefully by Conrad's sky-high standards, or punish her husband for being sorrowful.

They spent two of her five London evenings together, she and her Michael. They dined first in her house, secondly in his – discretion was essential. She could be sad with him as with no one else. She reminisced with him freely, and not in fear that she would cry. She felt womanly with him rather than wifely or motherly. As more serious adulterers than she had discovered, she returned to the matrimonial fold refreshed and relaxed, also ready to persuade her family to be grateful for the past and to rejoice in the present.

She saw Michael on and off during further visits to London. He was sometimes otherwise occupied or abroad; but he tried to be available and, at once, to provide the services she valued and to keep his balance on the tightrope of their romance.

Shortly after the first anniversary of Conrad's death they spent an evening in Michael's house. When they had eaten they adjourned to his sitting-room and sat together on the sufficiently spacious sofa. There had been no air raid, none as yet, and the silence out of doors seemed to have caused unaccustomed pauses in their conversation.

Michael ended one such pause by asking: 'How long have I been your vassal?'

'You're not my vassal,' Addy replied, laughing. 'I don't want you to be my vassal or to think of yourself like that. I never have forgotten or will forget how indebted I am to you for having been my faithful friend through thick and thin.'

'A pretty speech,' he said.

'Oh, I don't speechify, Michael. Why are you saying these things to me? Is something wrong?'

'You haven't answered my question.'

'What was it? I've forgotten since you've gone back to teasing me.'

'How long, Addy?'

'I don't remember.'

'To hell with it! I'm not whining – you're my own fault. Besides, you did me a good turn, at least one good turn. When I came back from Brazil, I had to keep my nose to the grindstone, and remake a life for myself in this country, and you stopped me marrying any old trouble and strife, who would have been bound to bear me a shoeful of babies.'

'I never meant to stop you doing anything. I've often begged you to live your own life. But you'd better tell me more. What about wartime? Are you going to reproach me for what I've done to you in the last two years?'

He stood up, fetched the bottle of the wine they had been drinking and refilled their glasses.

'A *femme fatale* is the woman a man feels obliged to protect,' he remarked.

'Oh dear! Am I fatal, dear Michael?'

He remained on his feet, he was standing by the fireplace, one elbow resting on the mantelpiece. He had kept his figure and hung on to his top-quality curly black hair. At present his countenance was showing his intolerant devilish expression. He was the exact opposite of Rufus Forester.

Addy continued: 'I must have been a burden to you in these last months, too dependent and fragile.'

'Oh for heaven's sake!' He came and slumped down beside her. 'Yes, I'm wrong, and I thought you were wrong this evening, and now everything's wrong.' He took hold of her hand and kissed it. 'You can't be blamed for making me love you. It was my choice to wait on you. I suppose I thought you'd be willing sooner or later.'

'How could I, Michael? I thought we'd cleared that hurdle when I was a girl, when we were children. Now it's too late – and please don't accuse me of fishing for compliments. We can't change our friendship into a different thing.'

'Have you never heard of trial and error? Have some more wine and fall into my arms.'

'Must I be responsible for you? I didn't realise that you've been feeling responsible for me and hard done by. Rufus protects me – it wouldn't be protective of you to persuade me to betray him.'

'You're out of date, Addy. Wars aren't moral. Is Rufus the only man you've known?'

'Don't, Michael.'

'I can show you another world.'

'But I can't.'

'I'm afraid I'm insisting on one kiss, a proper one, an improper one – you owe it to me. Close your eyes and count your blessings – not many women get kisses from me cost-free.'

'Michael, this is ridiculous.'

'Do as I say.'

'Oh well!'

She failed to be impervious. For a moment in the middle, inwardly, she asked herself that most dangerous of all questions, 'Why not?' But at last she laughed and he let her go, muttering, 'Who's teasing now?'

He pleased her more by saying: 'You're a good kisser, that's a fact.' But he stood up again and said sternly: 'Changes, Addy, changes are in the offing.'

'I hope not because of our kiss.'

'Not exactly.'

'It was nice but not a hanging matter. I won't ever forget it.'

'Thanks, Addy. You remain my ideal, but reality's caught up with me.'

'What do you mean?'

'A woman wants to be Mrs Trane.'

'Oh?'

'I'm growing too old to live alone and look after myself.'

'How old is she?'

'Twenty-five.'

'Do you love her?'

'I could – not as I love you.'

'Are you serious about her? Will you be kind to her? Will she be kind to you?'

'Yes, yes and yes.'

'How wonderful!'

'If the kiss had had other consequences, I still couldn't have carried on, seeing you four or five times a year.'

'Of course you couldn't. I'm happy for you, Michael,

really. I've never liked to poke my nose into your private life, but I've often wondered how it was and if it was satisfactory. I couldn't order you to go away and come back with a wife. Will we still be friends?'

'Always.'

'She might have other ideas.'

'She knows about you.'

'Don't talk about me too much.'

They laughed, and Michael said: 'You're a brick, Addy. I knew you'd be unselfish and sweet, but you've been more unselfish and sweeter than I could have imagined.'

'Ask me to your wedding!'

'I won't be married if you're not there.'

She cried. She hid her face and her tears flowed between her fingers. He embraced her and she leant her head on his shoulder.

'Sorry, Addy, sorry,' he kept on mumbling. 'I didn't mean to hurt you, I'm sorry.'

At length she said to him: 'You don't understand. It's not you. It's nothing to do with you. Your news is the best news for me. I haven't been myself all evening – you were right to think I was wrong.'

'What are you talking about?'

'Guy's going to be a soldier.'

He was killed in Sicily in 1943.

Guy was sixteen at the time of Conrad's death. He was a golden boy. He was a young giant with golden hair and a golden complexion, and a character to match. He was as strong in the upper storey as he was physically, he won prizes for work and in peacetime would have been put in for scholarships. He was an all-rounder, a precociously fast bowler and a centurion with his bat, and an alarmingly good rugger player.

He and his elder brother complimented each other. Conrad was romantic, Guy sceptical. Conrad had wit, Guy a sense of the ridiculous. Conrad was the straight man to Guy's comic clowning. Conrad read Walter Scott for the heroism, Guy P.G. Wodehouse for a laugh. Conrad was intolerant and did not suffer fools gladly, Guy was tickled by the pomposity of power and the absurdity of revolutions, and found folly entertaining. On days out in Fowick they were apt to separate to see different films showing in the two cinemas, Conrad a soulful weepie, Guy some swashbuckling rot. Conrad was always attracted to blondes like his Peggy, whereas Guy's dish was a dark lady.

Guy's decision to remain at school following Conrad's death surprised Addy. She applauded it, she could imagine that he had deferred to his headmaster, who was no doubt considering parental sensibilities, and she was glad to have a little time in which to prepare for the homecoming of the two schoolboys; but she would have expected Guy to be less dumb on the telephone and to rush to take his place by her side. She was not hurt that he had kept his distance. She understood her children too well not to forgive them. But then again the letter he wrote was stiff and short.

The holidays, Guy's next holidays, began badly from his mother's point of view. He was more chilly and stand-offish than sympathetic. On the first day at Forest Court he gave the impression that he was avoiding her. On the second she invited him to walk with her into the hills: he agreed ungraciously. Yet no sooner were they out of earshot and out of sight than he stumbled against her or seemed to, and threw his great arms round her shoulders, and said things in his loud harsh deep and recently broken voice that sounded like retching.

'Isn't it awful?... What are we to do?... I can't bear it for you, Mother... How can you be so brave? Poor Dad, poor Dad!'

Physically she was almost floored by having to support him; psychologically, by the force of his passion, likewise.

She comforted him. At length they were able to resume their walk. On the windy tops they reminisced about Conrad's happy hikes with Max, and referred to his love of hunting on land and in the air.

Guy confided that Conrad had also told him how he enjoyed the ultimate competition of war.

Addy remarked: 'He wasn't a coward and he wasn't a hypocrite, and I can't think of anything better to say about anyone.'

Guy agreed, if vaguely, and asked: 'What's Peggy like?'

'Lovely,' she replied, and described her.

'Could I meet her?'

'When it would be less painful. She can't face Forest Court yet.'

'Would they have been all right together?'

'She loved him very much. I believe there was enough love between them to have smoothed out the rough patches. He wasn't child's play, I will admit that, but he always rewarded patience.'

Later on Guy said: 'They shouldn't have killed Conrad.'

His voice was uncharacteristically grim, and startled her.

'Nobody should do the dreadful things that everybody does in wars,' she replied pacifically.

'Well – they shouldn't have,' he repeated.

'No – but that's the cry in all the countries. You won't take his death too personally, will you, darling?'

'How else are you supposed to take it?'

'I meant, don't think it's up to you to be revenged.'

'No,' he commented ambiguously.

Later he asked in a sadder intonation: 'Where do we go from here?'

'For your father's sake, and for Ian's and the girls, and most of all for Conrad's, I'd love things to be as normal and nice as possible. Wouldn't you? Couldn't we aim for a nice time?'

'Yes,' he now confined himself to saying.

Addy left it at that, although afterwards she wondered why she had ignored some of his hints and implications. She was so pleased to have broken down the barrier between them, and forged a new alliance with him, that she omitted to shoulder an extra burden of care. He was hers again, and his sweetness to her and the family and the Forest Court and Beltran people was largely instrumental in making her wish come true and recreating a normality of a poignant kind.

In the ensuing months, fourteen months, to be precise, Guy grew still more in every sense. Rufus sought his advice, Addy leant on him, and Eve was his shadow. He devised treats, played games, taught Faith to play tennis, cracked jokes and kept order. At school he was the captain of everything. Christmas at Beltran was nowhere near as gloomy as had been generally feared, thanks to Guy.

During the year that followed, Addy was aware of an emotion creeping up on her that could be called joy. Maybe it was only a sort of relief – maybe it was shameful, it was definitely contrary. But she could not arrest or disown it, and lacked the willpower to wipe smiles off her face. Besides, mourning had to be minimal in wartime, and especially for a mother of four. She believed Conrad would not have objected, and would have been the less likely to, considering that part of the joyousness derived from second thoughts about the glory of his life and his death.

She could rationalise it, she had not been driven dotty. Apart from Conrad, Rufus was on the mend. He was reforming into the rock on which she had built so much. And Guy was Guy, and the younger children were getting on as well as any parent dares to hope. Theo had not failed her in emergency, he had been one lifeline in her most grievous days, and unwed Michael, despite his chronic undependability, had been the other.

Her surge of vitality, her rebound, or whatever it was, even withstood Guy's announcement that he was joining up. Of course he would volunteer, not wait for an official summons to serve his country. Of course he was keen to strike his blow against the enemy. She had had the inevitable in the back of her mind ever since war was declared. She said yes, not no, and 'Well done!'

But too soon she saw it differently. The war showed no sign of ending – Guy would not only be wearing a smart uniform, he would have to fight. And he had sprung the news of his military intention on her, on his parents, without discussion or warning, probably because he was hell-bent on dangerous exploits and did not want to cause distress in advance or to have to argue any point.

Rufus calmed her down. He told her to let the future look after itself, and to support Guy. She did so, she succeeded in doing so. She was glad to be able to take a genuine interest in Guy's schedule.

Then she went to London and to dine with Michael.

Her tears were inexplicable – that is, she could not explain them to Michael. The lead-up was emotional owing to his proposition, almost his ultimatum, the kiss that weakened although strength survived it, and then his announcement that he intended to marry and to lower the curtain on their old relationship. Naturally he assumed that he was to blame for making her cry; and that she could not convince him otherwise made her cry the harder. She could not go into the shortcomings of her beloved Rufus, or her unconventional manner of mourning Conrad. She cried for the misunderstanding, Michael's, and the way that the world in general had seemed to her bleaker reveries to misunderstand everything.

She said she cried for Guy. It was not the whole truth;

but it was true enough, credible, and once she started she could not stop. For her premonitions cut through all the euphemisms of cheerfulness – yes, the war was just and had to be fought by idealistic boys and girls, yes, winning it was essential, and Guy would see to that: she was nonetheless afraid he would die. She cried in the end for that unspeakable reason – to say it would definitely tempt providence – and released all the unshed tears dammed for ages by the unselfishness of her character.

When she had dried her eyes, Michael invited her to stay the night, and she amused both of them by telling him not to be trying.

She returned home, and at some moment that was stressful on account of Guy she reproached his father thus: 'Why on earth did I go and marry a hero?'

Rufus turned the tables with his reply: 'If you'd married a lily-livered husband, you'd still have given birth to champions and heroes who were taking after you.'

Guy duly enlisted and was posted to the North African theatre of conflict. Then he was assigned to duties he could not describe in his rare letters, except to say that he would probably be incommunicado for a while.

One day Addy felt she should warn Eve that Guy must be in considerable danger.

'I know,' she replied proudly.

How did she know?

'Guy was dead keen to get into one of those daredevil outfits. He wanted to be in on the killing war.'

'I never knew he was bloodthirsty.'

'Oh yes. But he wouldn't show you his ferocious side.'

'He wasn't ferocious, darling Eve, not really. He was the gentlest of giants.'

'You've forgotten how he and Conrad fought.'

'That was just rough play.'

'No, it wasn't. He often said he'd kill Conrad, he wanted

to kill him often. But it was awfully strange, because he loved Conrad. And when Conrad was killed he started to count the days until he could pay back.'

'Oh darling!'

'Don't worry, Mother. Guy's superhuman. Nobody'll get the better of him.'

'That's right, my sweet. But we must pray for him all the same. And a little bit of us has to be prepared.'

'I'm preparing for him to be famous and covered in medals.'

'What a lovely picture!'

Addy was unwilling to undermine Eve's confidence. Moreover, the future might rule that Eve was right. But Eve's revelations were a reminder of Guy's grimness on that walk with his mother.

A note from Guy virtually settled the matter so far as she was concerned. He wrote: 'Darling Mother, I'm having a whale of a time. What I'm at means much more to me than routine active service. Thanks for everything.' It was too like Conrad's last letter, and for her it ushered in a short period of waiting.

The story of his death that reached her was that he had led an advance party into Sicily. Their activities had made the invasion of the island by the Allied army, coming over from North Africa, less costly in terms of casualties. He had saved uncountable lives by the sacrifice of his own. He deserved his medals, it was generally agreed.

Michael Trane came to stay at Forest Court as soon after hearing the sad news as he decently could. He brought his wife – Addy had insisted that he should. She was called Helen, and had a job in the Whitehall war machine.

Addy was grateful to Michael for his sympathy, and between them they glossed over the evidence that their friendship was not and would never again be what it had been. She was quick to demonstrate to Helen that there was no cause for anxiety, probably superfluously, since the latter appeared to be confident that her relative youth gave her every advantage. Helen was not boastful, however; she recognised and respected tragedy, and was soon won over by Addy's attentiveness and indomitable bearing.

At the end of the Tranes' visit, when Helen was alone with her hostess, she asked how it was possible for Addy to show such poise and dignity.

'It's vanity, my dear,' Addy replied. 'I'm flattered to have become a member of an extremely select club. The members don't always know one another personally, but I think we all feel we're linked together and the better for it. The subscription's high, but unavoidable. We're the mothers who have contributed the lives of two precious young sons to the war effort.'

Eve was just coming up to seventeen in 1943, Ian was fifteen and Faith thirteen.

Eve was Addy's most pressing problem as a result of Guy's death. The girl had been described as his shadow by the family in happier times: now she became a shadow of herself, and existed amongst the shades of her brothers, especially the younger one. She did not cry. She was silent and listless. She scarcely ate. And she would not talk about Guy, except in mystical pronouncements.

She said: 'He was my soul, so now I'm soulless.' Instead of listening to comfortable words or trying to comfort anybody, she said: 'Heaven's not going to suit Guy. They won't be happy in heaven, Conrad and Guy – they liked to be up and doing, not lazing round. They must be miserable, and that's why I'll never be happy.' She claimed to be able to see Guy in the sky from the hilltops.

The verbal lifelines offered by her parents were ignored or rejected. Rufus spoke to her patiently but in character:

the boys had done their duty, he explained, and paid the price for acting like gallant English gentlemen. Eve would have none of it, and mocked his logic. Conrad and Guy also owed duty to those who loved them, she retorted – they had not been dutiful in that sense. And why did gallant Englishmen have to die, why could not gallant Germans have done the dying?

Addy's line was also characteristic. She spoke against bitterness. To be bitter was a form of cutting off your nose to spite your face. It did no good, it made matters worse, it would not have pleased her brothers, it was the opposite of what Jesus recommended.

Eve retorted: 'Did Jesus have brothers and sisters who were killed? Well, my heart's never going to heal. I care too much to just forgive and forget – I don't know how you can talk of forgetting so soon.'

Addy was ashamed to own to herself that Eve was poisoning the pleasure of her home life. True, she had liked to escape to Walkers Row occasionally, for a change, for amusement, but her heart was always left at Forest Court in the safe keeping of her family. Now she was more at ease washing floors and carrying trays at the hospital than she was, and could depend on being, at Forest Court. And she could not altogether pardon Eve for piling difficulty on difficulty. She therefore felt guilty on two counts, for fleeing her nearest and dearest, and for failing to forgive her daughter in the way that she urged her daughter to forgive.

Eve was determined not to heal, and thus rubbed salt into Addy's wounds.

But Addy did not complain with any force. Her kindness and maternal instincts apart, she suffered in a silence that was not like her for another reason. She was afraid she had not paid as much attention to Eve as to Conrad and Guy, and she was in no doubt she had not given enough of herself to the two little ones, who were not little any longer.

The united emotions of all Foresters in peacetime, when the children were young and surely the sun shone on every day even in Northumberland, had been straightforward, without twists or grey areas, as she remembered. The general reaction to Conrad's death had seemed to Addy to be overwhelmingly simple. Yet Guy's death had wheeled out a monster of emotional proportions that resembled a Russian doll.

Addy was having to open one doll after another, each representing her relations with her three surviving children. Eve was less nice to her than she was to her father. She obviously blamed Addy, who blamed herself. And if she blamed herself for not having been a really good mother to Eve, she blamed herself still more for having been unintentionally bad to Ian and Faith. Belatedly, in the case of Eve, who was more troubled than the other two, she tried to compensate by not saying anything sharp or corrective, and by attempting to soothe and divert.

She also recalled that Michael had noticed Eve. She reinterpreted those glances of his, unpurified by his age, his marriage, the presence of his wife, and the company of Addy. She saw Eve with new eyes, that she had graduated into womanhood, was good-looking and had a beautiful slender physique.

She switched her conversational strategy from death to life, and from past to future, Eve's future. She dropped hints that the girl was about to win the love of many men, and must not throw herself away on a feckless or cruel suitor. Eve was dismissive of the references to her looks, and shocked and reproachful that her mother should toy with the idea that she could love any man other than Guy, anyway for ages.

Addy tried another tack – it was just about a year after Guy's death. There was going to be a dance in the Church Hall at Fowick to celebrate the Allied landings in Normandy, and she had been asked to help to bring along a party of convalescent soldiers from the hospital where she worked. Would Eve like to join in – she could chat to Rufus, who had agreed to come, and they could all leave early? Eve said yes, ungraciously.

At the dance Addy was kept busy by the soldiers in wheelchairs and on crutches, and Rufus was monopolised by local worthies and members of his Home Guard company. The Hall was crammed with people, since a few lorry-loads of soldiery from the camp at Alnwick were present, and the elder Foresters immediately lost sight of Eve. Two hours later, at eleven sharp, the coach-type of ambulance arrived to ferry patients back to the hospital, together with their attendants, including the three Foresters. Addy found Eve on the dance floor and said it was time to go. Eve, who was dancing with a lieutenant in battle dress, did not show willing; and her partner, whose first name was Tony, she muttered sulkily, had a car and would drive her home. Addy accepted his offer – she was in a rush, and pleased that Eve seemed to have found something she wanted to do at last.

Eight hours later mother and daughter were reunited with tears of one sort and another. For different reasons, neither had slept a wink. Addy had woken the Fowick vicar and his wife and pleaded with them to look for her daughter in the vicinity of the Church Hall. She had also roused the Commanding Officer of the troops stationed at Alnwick, who was eventually able to report that a Lieutenant Tony Welch – unpropitious surname – had gone AWOL, and nobody knew where he was. She had finally alerted the local constabulary and extracted a promise that the Missing Persons Bureau would be advised about Miss Forester immediately.

Addy cried with relief, but said two things that turned Eve's unusual smile into a tearful grimace. She mentioned the county-wide search and that she must call it off, and she let slip the two words, birth control.

Eve howled at her: 'You've spoilt everything.'

'Oh darling, please – I didn't mean to – what have I spoilt?'

'I've been with a wonderful man, the only man I could ever look at after Guy, and he loves me so much he's broken all the military rules for my sake, and you've behaved as if I were an escaped prisoner, and you've made it sound squalid.'

'I'm sorry, dearest – please forgive us for being worried, please forgive us for loving you.'

'Well – I can't live here any longer, I've thought it for months, and I'm sorry too, but I'm not going to.'

'Oh dear! We shall be sad without you. Still, it's for you to choose – you're not our prisoner, Eve, you never were.'

'I'm getting married.'

'My darling!'

'I am, Mother – you can't stop me.'

'How exciting! Goodness, what thrilling news! I long to know every detail, but could you just wait for me to do a couple of telephone calls?'

She did three, to the Reverend Ralph Jones, to Tony's CO, and to the police.

'Now!' she said, having recovered a degree of composure and as if to invite confidences.

'I can't tell you details,' Eve replied with a rebellious sob.

'Of course you can't. I wouldn't expect you to. But are you happy?'

'I was before I walked in – I would be if I wasn't worried that they'll shoot Tony for staying out late with me.'

'No, darling, they won't shoot him, I promise, but he may be confined to barracks for a few days. Does Tony deserve you?'

'I don't deserve him.'

'That's modest of you – I can't quite believe it. Listen, I think I ought to wake your father to tell him you're engaged, even though he hasn't had much sleep. Will you come with me, darling? But you must be tired, too – would you rather go to bed? We could break the news together when you've come down to earth.'

'Will you tell him, Mother?'

'If you want me to.'

'He won't be cross with me, will he?'

'No, darling – why should he be?'

'Tony's determined to come and talk to him.'

'That's honourable.'

'We can't wait, you know. How can we wait in the middle of a war?'

'No, darling, I do understand. Your father will work out the practical part with Tony. He and I only wish for your happiness. You're exhausted, sweetie, and no wonder – why don't you grab a little sleep now, while I let him sleep on?'

'I'm sorry, Mother.'

Addy kissed her by way of reply.

Later, before lunch, Eve, looking frightened, joined her parents. Rufus, coached by Addy, hugged her and opened one of his last bottles of champagne. He congratulated her and asked a few friendly questions; Eve answered that Tony had been brought up in Pinner, Middlesex, that Mr Welch Senior was a pharmacist and Mrs Welch a working nurse, and that as yet Tony had not decided what career to follow post-war, although he was keen on cars and might go into that sort of business.

Rufus then asked if or when Tony would be shipped over to France to join the Allied armies there.

'I can't bear to think – soon – that's why we can't wait.'

'Well, tell him I look forward to meeting him and having a chinwag.'

The meeting occurred as soon as Tony was allowed out

of his camp. He was a small neat chirpy individual whose speech was largely composed of slang phrases. He was impressed by Forest Court and called it 'a bit of a bonus'. He had 'dropped a clanger' by not 'clocking in' for 'lights out' after the Fowick dance, and had duly 'got it in the neck'. He was sorry if he had 'caught the aged ps with their trousers down' by 'popping the q' to their 'dearly beloved', but she was such a 'smasher' that he had 'taken the plunge' and, ever since 'the old Adam' had found his Eve, had been absolutely catapulted on to 'cloud nine'.

Rufus escorted Tony into his study: it was like a St Bernard with a terrier puppy. While they talked, Addy braced herself to revert to the subject of birth control, and the particular advantages of family planning when a couple were young and poor and at risk from all the fighting. Eve at least listened to her this time round, and might have been influenced by her mother's reference to the example set by Conrad and Peggy Saunders.

The men emerged. Tony had agreed to pronounce sentence. He told Eve that they had her parents' blessing provided they 'hung on' till the war was 'in the bag'. Her father, he explained, 'knew his onions' and prophesied that peace was 'just round the corner'. When peace 'broke out' he would 'fix himself up with a living wage in Civvy Street' and 'slip the ring on her finger'. The 'top secret' was, he added, that his 'bunch' had received orders to go and 'hammer the Hun' on the day after tomorrow, so there was not a 'snowball's chance in hell' of getting the 'wedding bs' rung.

Eve cried, but Tony comforted her manfully and took her off in his car to dine in Fowick.

Rufus and Addy shared the opinion that they had done all they could do to serve the cause of common sense. Tony was likeable, although how Eve could compare him with Guy amazed them; but he appeared to be even more childish than she was, and the Foresters clung to the hope that she would have grown out of him in a matter of months. They had no doubt, first, that their teenage daughter should not marry the first teenage man to propose to her after a few hours' acquaintanceship, or, secondly, that they had to look as unlike spoilsports as possible. The biggest risk they ran, Addy realised and warned Rufus, was that Tony would get himself killed: in which case she was afraid Eve would not forgive them.

She was caught in a web of conflicting hopes and fears. Gone was her self-assured decisiveness, and gone her steadiness under a kind of fire. She could not mourn Conrad and Guy as she meant to, she had other preoccupations. She could not concentrate on Rufus, and seemed to have no time for Ian and Faith. It was not that she cared for Eve more than for anyone else, it was rather that she had not cared for Eve enough and was now desperate neither to let the girl ruin her life by marrying Tony, nor to ruin her own life by having prevented Eve's marriage to a pip-squeak who had died before showing that he had feet of clay. She had been harried by guilt over a sin of omission, and was now additionally harried by deeper potential guilt over a sin of commission, or any rate a mistake.

Tony had to live, so that Eve could see him in his true colours. Tony must not die, and always be seen by Eve through rose-tinted spectacles.

Addy found it difficult to live with her daughter's reproachful attitude, and dreaded to be her daughter's enemy for ever. She could not defend herself – she had guided Rufus in the matter, and it was common knowledge that the wedding might have been organised. For the first time in her life she felt she was a failure, that she had failed Eve and was failing everybody.

But her prayers were answered. The war was drawing to a close, and Tony broke his leg climbing on to a tank and was sent home to convalesce in the very hospital where Addy, and sometimes Eve herself, worked. The intervening period produced the desired effect: Eve had been taken aback by the unexpected reunion with her fiancé, and after a month of seeing him daily she made it clear that the engagement was off by asking her parents' permission to live at Walkers Row and look for a job in London.

The war was won. The sad air that Addy breathed now bore a scent of victory. She would seize her opportunity to make reparations and mend fences.

She then received Theo's telephone call about Ian.

'Theo!' she exclaimed with pleasure – he was one of the people to whom she owed debts of time and communication.

'Addy,' he said in a broken voice, 'I'm the bearer of very bad news.'

'Tell me!'

'Ian's had an accident, he's been involved in an accident.'

'Is he hurt?'

'Worse.'

'Oh God!... Theo?'

'Yes, I'm here.'

'What happened?'

'He fell on to the electrified line in the Underground.'

'That's impossible.'

'Yes – but he did.'

'How do you know?'

'They came to see me. He'd been having lunch with me in the office. He had my name and address on a piece of paper in his pocket.'

'Oh yes, you were talking to him about careers.'

'Exactly.'

'Was he all right with you?'

346

'Yes.'

'Why, Theo?'

'Nobody knows.'

'I must go.'

'Yes, my dearest.'

It was unbearable. It was the last straw. But she had to bear it, even though she believed her back was finally broken. She had to talk to Rufus, and they had to talk to Eve and Faith, and inform friends and employees who were their friends, and make arrangements and do the necessary. She had to find out more from Theo, and then she would have to tell and retell herself the story backwards, from the end to the beginning.

She coped, as usual. The funeral took place at Fowick Church, and was also a Memorial Service for Ian's two brothers. Rufus held his head high throughout, but Addy wore a thick black veil and bowed her head low.

Ian was unlike her older children, and when Faith arrived she was like Ian. It was always noticeable: Ian lacked the physical proportions of Conrad and Guy, and of their parents for that matter, his head was a little too heavy and his legs were on the short side. And his hair was not his crowning glory, instead of Conrad's close-fitting cap of shiny brown curls and Guy's softly wavy golden mantle Ian had uncontrollable spikes. Even more marked were the differences of personality and character. Ian was reserved. To put it less politely, he was wary, unresponsive and cold. He preferred not to be cuddled. He was apparently self-sufficient. Almost every adjective descriptive of the other boys was inapplicable to him. The one thing they had in common was charm, different types of charm, but, in Ian's less obvious case, charm nonetheless. He had a wistful smile. He was born to be sympathised with. His appeal was to hearts of the softer kind.

Faith was his friend at once, he was closer to her than to

his other siblings. They played together, they had mysterious games of their own invention that they played – Ian's age debarred him from the games at which Conrad and Guy excelled. They were an extraordinarily private little pair, often seemingly like strangers in the midst of the active, talkative, humorous and accessible family of Foresters. They sniggered together at inexplicable jokes. They sat together, wide-eyed and watchful, their faces mostly expressionless, but suddenly transfigured by innocent smiles fraught with wistfulness.

Conrad devised and wove them into mystical fantasies. They were changelings. They had been discovered under the traditional gooseberry bush. They were baby wizards, devil's spawn, children of the man in the moon, werewolves in the making. When they were toddlers and only allowed to mix with older folk after tea, Conrad called them *les visiteurs du soir*.

The difficulty for Addy was that she was always needed by Rufus and, more or less, by their three older children, and seemingly not needed by Ian or, later on, by Faith. She was maternal, fond of and touched by Ian, but felt rebuffed, superfluous, and had no time to spare, after attending to the others, to study him, to please him, and overcome his resistance. She knew she should, she wished she had, she was ashamed to wonder if she was being a bad mother, but she did not, she never had the chance to give him her undivided attention, and his smiles at her tightened the screw of her guilt, which created another obstacle between them.

It struck her that she had given birth not to a male child but to a vicious circle. When Faith joined in, the negative image that occurred to her was the maypole – she was it, she was the maypole, and her two youngest were dancing round her and tying her up with their ribbons.

Peacetime was peaceful for the Foresters. Addy looked back on it and marvelled at its peacefulness. None of them had died, and, although she had struggled not to be complacent, she never imagined the horrors in store. Life had been such a powerful idyll then that Ian and Faith had not been able to mar it. There was room in her world, in her all-embracing universe, to accommodate them in theirs. Everyone fitted in, they were forced into a single and singular unit by the pressure of the general mood of happiness.

If only, Addy prefaced her recollections now. Objectively, she understood that her grief would be more tolerable if only she were able to spare herself. She was against regrets, she thought guilt was futile and did no one any good. She could see that in fact guilt clouded the issue and militated against common sense, reason, logic and experience. But the truth and the whole truth was that the older she grew, and the more affected she was by sorrows, she simply could not stem her regrettable guiltiness. If only she had known, if only she had been more perceptive!

She talked seriously to Ian before he left home for his first boarding school. She had asked Rufus to tell the boy the facts of life, and to warn him against improper school-masters and so on. Rufus refused, he said boys had to learn to fend for themselves, and he was not going to speak gibberish to any pre-pubic person. This theory had probably suited Conrad and Guy, who were large for their age, strong and savvy, but she was concerned for the welfare of Ian and tackled the task herself.

'Darling, do you know how babies are born?'

They were out of doors. She was sitting on a garden seat, and had detained him as he bicycled round.

'Yes,' he replied.

'How do you know?'

'Eve told me.'

'How did Eve know?'

'Guy told her.'

'Oh. Do you understand it?'

'Yes.'

'Don't bicycle away for a minute, Ian. Are you feeling all right about going off to school?'

'Yes.'

'Do you think you'll miss us all and be homesick?'

'No.'

'I'm so glad. You're such an independent fellow, I do admire that. I just wanted to ask if you understood that a schoolmaster can behave a bit funnily with a young boy?'

'How?'

'What?'

'Funnily by making jokes?'

'No, darling, no – by hugging and kissing boys.'

'Oh that!'

'You would tell us, or tell your brothers, or tell the head-master, if you were ever worried about that sort of thing, wouldn't you?'

'Maybe.'

'Why do you say maybe, Ian?'

He shrugged his shoulders and asked: 'Have you finished?' And he bicycled away before she could think of the right answer to his question.

On the day of his departure for school he showed no emotion: which was yet another difference between him and the older boys. He was also different in that he stuck to the middle of the scholastic road, he was neither very good nor very bad at lessons and at games. In the holidays he seemed to be content in the shadows cast by Conrad and Guy. He was polite to his parents when he had to talk to them, his so-called shyness excused him from having to take notice of grown-ups in general, and he whispered to and sniggered with Faith. He received rather scant attention from his mother partly because he indicated that he did not want it; but in the retrospect of bereavement she blamed herself for failing to reach out to him across the barrier of his self-containment.

Ian reacted characteristically to the death of Conrad. He expressed no grief, he kept his distance from the mourners who cried and held hands and embraced one another. But Addy saw, almost with relief, that he was not impervious – his face was white for weeks and his smile was permanently more wistful.

At the time of Guy's death he was fifteen. He had been closer to Guy than to Conrad – all young people loved Guy's good humour and unflappability, just as older people loved him also for his intelligence and glamour. Ian took the news badly – who could take it well? He was at school, and his headmaster suggested to his parents that he should cut his term short and be with his family. When he arrived at Forest Court, Addy said something to him that, a moment later, she knew was a mistake, and that haunted her in due course.

She said under pressure of emotion, and to fill the void of one of his silences: 'You're our all in all now.' What did the phrase mean? It was an ungrammatical cliché. But its meaning was far too clear to comfort Ian – how could she have placed such an impossibly heavy burden of responsibility on his narrow shoulders?

Whether or not on account of that sentence, changes occurred in the boy; but they passed unnoticed either because everybody was changed by the loss of Guy, or because they were attributed to puberty. He began to cultivate fitness – he walked for longer distances than Faith could manage, and went for equally lonely runs up and down the hills of Northumberland and Aberdeenshire.

There was an episode that surely shed light on his future or lack of future. Again the red deer strayed on to Beltran land, and Rufus received an invitation to participate in the cull of two or three stags. He was about to refuse, he announced that he had grown too old to stalk or to shoot beautiful animals, even if for the good of the herd, when Ian pleaded for the job.

Rufus was surprised and commented: 'I didn't think you liked shooting.'

Ian replied: 'I don't mind.'

'Have you shot with a rifle before?'

'I've joined the Rifle Club at school, I've done a lot of shooting lately.'

'I didn't know that.'

'It's not important.'

'Well, it is, actually – I don't want stags wounded.'

'I won't wound them.'

'You're not offering in order to relieve me of a duty? That gamekeeper could see to the whole business.'

'No, Father – please let me.'

Ian shot the stags, and Mr Fraser praised his marksman-ship and his physical endurance.

At sixteen, Ian broached the subject of his military service – he could join up in fourteen months, and he was trying to decide between the RAF and the army. He appeared not to consider his parents' sensibilities in the matter. He reverted to it repeatedly. He assumed that he would have to fight, and made the extra assumption that they would wish him to do so. Vengeance was never hinted at, although Addy was particularly frightened that he was motivated by feelings twice as vengeful as Guy's had been. She held her tongue, she prayed, and did her best not to beg him to be a coward.

But it was already 1945, and every day that passed proved more conclusively that the war was drawing to an end. Rufus and Addy breathed metaphorical sighs of relief mixed up with other feelings, and Addy tackled Ian head-on when he showed dissent from the celebratory national mood.

'Don't be disappointed, darling – please be glad for all of us that soon there'll be no more danger and misery.'

'That's not logical, Mother.'

'Well, you know what I mean, and you know who I'm thinking about specially.'

'I'll be in the army whatever happens.'

'Of course, darling, but an army at peace, that's what I'm praying for.'

Later, a few weeks before Ian was due to receive the King's shilling, Addy mentioned the boy's attitude to Theo Edmunds: 'Naturally Ian wants to be like his brothers, but he seems to be put out when I can't encourage him to go and take appalling risks.'

Theo said that Ian would definitely not be in time to fight the Germans, he would become part of a temporary army of occupation. And the Allies would wish to reduce expenditure on their armed forces – Ian should not count on a lifelong military career, he might well be 'axed' for no good reason as so many servicemen were after the First World War. He should be thinking of an alternative post-war occupation, and, as he was Theo's godson, Theo proposed to ask him to lunch in the City and suggest a possible future job in business.

Addy was all for it.

Then she had to comfort Theo by assuring him that Ian's death was not his fault, it was hers.

And perhaps, she reiterated, it really was an accident, although Theo had given him no more to drink than a glass of beer.

Faith aged fifteen reacted violently to the accidental theory.

'Ian was determined to be as brave as Father and Conrad and Guy,' she insisted. 'And he was a hero, too.'

Addy cried in her husband's arms.

'It was such a horrible way to die.'

'So are deaths in battle.'

On another occasion she asked: 'Will we survive?'

'If you don't I won't,' he replied.

'Oh but I will,' she said. 'I promise to – after all we have so much to live for.'

EPILOGUE

It was 1950, five years after Ian died and the war ended, seven years after Guy was killed, nine years after Conrad's death.

Rufus was sixty and no longer in the best of health. He was going deaf and had a gammy leg. His heart seemed to have been weakened by attacks upon it of one kind and another. Needless to say he was a bad patient, he was bad almost on principle. He took the view that ill-heath was anti-social, and behaved as always and as if nothing was wrong with him. He refused to diet, put on weight because he was not so active, continued to smoke and curtailed none of his duties.

Heart trouble is supposed to fray tempers. The antithesis applied to Rufus. His size and his silences combined with his medals had made a formidable man of him, notwithstanding his benevolence. Now he smiled more often, and more sweetly, and his gentleness was plain for all to see. He even talked more, making a joke of his hardness of hearing, and almost boasting that he was coming apart at the seams.

'I wish you wouldn't,' Addy sometimes said. 'Be well for me, please. I'm nowhere near ready to do without you.'

He would apologise – they believed in apologising to each other – and reply: 'Likewise, my love,' and add that he was not intending to let her down, he was really not playing ducks and drakes with their future, he was just flying the flag.

And she would comment, 'I know,' and kiss him and let the matter drop.

They had learnt in a hard school the lesson of living for the day.

Addy at fifty was as strong physically as ever, although her lustrous dark hair had turned white. She had almost secretly taken over a lot of the work on the estate previously done by Rufus. She would spend a couple of nights at Beltran Castle or at Walkers Row apparently on impulse, but in fact to supervise repairs to the roof in the first case and in the second to meet a plumber. She insinuated an oar into farm business when she could do so tactfully. Her instructions were followed not only because the Forester family was noted for its fairness and commitment to its employees, nor because of its sacrifices in the war, but because she was sensible and looked so straight and searchingly into the eyes of whoever she spoke to and smiled at.

She had changed, of course – her war had changed her. She had never been noticeably complacent, although she had been born with a silver spoon in her mouth, married well and happily, and was the mother of five more or less outstanding children; but she clearly took even less for granted. She was on the receiving end of a mystery – why she had had to lose her three sons, all her sons – and by force of circumstances and by choice she bowed her neck and her knee before the ruler of her fate. She went to church regularly nowadays, and Rufus, no doubt for similar reasons, accompanied her even when he was not officiating as a church warden.

She would place flowers on Ian's grave on his birthday and at Christmas and Easter. She wrote the names of her three boys on the card on Ian's Christmas wreath. People had asked the Foresters if they would like to have a memorial of some sort to Conrad and Guy in Fowick Church, and some had volunteered subscriptions. But Rufus and Addy declined: Ian had his grave, and the other two were commemorated in the Roll of Honour of local Northumbrians carved on the cross in the marketplace.

Addy was not saddened by her churchgoing, she did not blame God for what had happened. Her steady and almost life-long cheerfulness left little room for improvement, yet Faith, her youngest, once expressed surprise that she seemed to be boosted up by Matins.

'Do tell the vicar, darling – he'll be so pleased,' Addy responded laughing.

'Well, I feel flat as a pancake after chapel at school, and at Fowick I'm haunted by memories of Ian's funeral. How on earth do you do it?'

'I don't do anything – it's not an accomplishment, and nothing to be proud of – it's religion's fault, and what Fowick Church is there for. Besides I'm still an optimist, oddly enough.'

'Odd's the word,' Faith echoed in her sharp dry way.

She was nothing like any of her siblings. Now, at twenty, she differed from her late brother Ian, who might have been the twin of her childhood. She was still plump, in fact altogether large, and not good-looking – she had inherited none of the looks of her parents. And she was not clever academically, but her humour had a cutting edge. The contrary thing about her was her kindness to animals in general, including human beings, and her father and mother in particular. She lived in a tiny cottage on the Forester land – it had been used by the shepherd at lambing time – and worked as an assistant in the Veterinary Surgery in Fowick. She had four rescued dogs, two rescued cats and a rescued parakeet, and had said she was against men and marriage until she rescued a young male trainee vet called Timmy.

To put sisterly differences in a nutshell, Eve was all that Faith was not. Eve, aged twenty-five, was a minor celebrity, wife and mother. Guy's death, the loss of the one she adored, had hardened her heart, whereas similar losses had softened the heart of Faith. She had rebounded from the arms of Tony Welch, or, rather, bounded upwards in social terms and into the homes, villas, yacht and luxurious lifestyle of the Anglo-Greek tycoon, Maurice Pandros.

Her engagement to Maurice, and the part of her marriage that would take place in a Greek Orthodox church in Greece, were revealed to her mother in a telephone call from New York.

Addy swallowed and tried to sound pleased.

'When can we meet your Maurice, darling?' she asked.

'I don't know, Mummy – he's frightfully busy – he's not a hayseed, like us – I'll do my best to bring him to the Court.'

'Your father would like that. Where are you now, Eve?'

'I'm with Maurice – not at the moment, I'm alone – he's wheeling and dealing somewhere – I'm staying in his apartment here – it's so grand – on the thirty-fourth floor!'

'Are you happy?'

'I feel like Cinderella – everything's so new and exciting – I'm spoilt already.'

'Darling, would it be possible for you to be married at Fowick as well?'

'Probably not in church – maybe in a Register Office – we'll have to wait and see.'

'What's he like, Eve? How old is he?'

'Thirty-something – he hasn't told me.'

'And handsome?'

'He's so frightfully rich, Mum – I'm in another world – that's the point.'

'We'd love to see you both as soon as you can manage it, darling.'

'Sorry – I must rush,' Eve said.

Addy told Rufus, who summed up all their analysing of,

360

and agonising over, Eve's rejection of her family and its values by saying: 'I don't understand.'

Eve did bring Maurice to Forest Court. It was a flying visit, they stayed for two nights: an English wedding was out of the question for the time being because he had been married before and his Greek divorce was not finalised. He was an agreeable man with a shining brown complexion – Faith was scolded by Addy for calling him oily. He did not seek the permission of his prospective parents-in-law for what he was doing and aimed to do to their daughter. Instead he as it were paid for her with a huge tin of caviare that must have cost a few thousand pounds – Faith said she preferred fish paste.

A contingent of Eve's family attended her wedding in Athens. But Rufus and the senior Ameses succumbed to food poisoning, Addy spent most of the trip in the travel agency, rescheduling their flight home, and Faith somehow found out that well-bred Greeks did not as a rule marry girls who had been willing to live with them in sin.

At least Eve was not left standing at the altar, and looked stunning in her nuptial finery. For the next two years her relations only saw her in photographs in glossy magazines. But she managed to fit a baby in between social engagements and beachcombing, a boy, Stavros Conrad, and in the early months of 1950 she paid another visit to Forest Court, minus husband but with Stavros and his nanny in tow.

The child was obviously more Greek than English, and what was also obvious before long was that his mother was not very maternal.

One night Addy and Eve had a heart-to-heart after Rufus had gone to bed. It was Eve who did the detaining by asking if Addy was tired.

Then she lit a cigarette restlessly and said without preamble: 'My marriage won't do.'

She answered questions thus: 'I hardly ever see Maurice, not that I mind much... He's been unfaithful to me already, I know... He'll finish with me soon – he can shake off loads of wives – all his Greek friends are able to... It'd all be more of a mistake if it wasn't for the money – I'm rolling, you know.'

'How sad!' Addy volunteered.

Eve corrected her: 'Not for me – and why should you be sad?'

'Sad for Stavros, darling.'

'He'll survive. We'll all survive. Who cares? I don't. There's nobody in my life, there never will be anybody, like Guy.'

Eve cried then, they both cried on each other's shoulders, then Addy asked: 'Is that why you called Stavros Conrad? We thought you might have called him Guy.'

Eve shrugged her shoulders.

'You'll have to forgive Guy for dying,' Addy said gently, 'and not forget him, not forget anything, but remember he was your brother. If he'd lived, he'd probably be married by now and have children and lots of responsibilities. You will care for somebody soon, perhaps even for Stavros.'

'I loved him so,' Eve sobbed, referring to Guy and to justify herself.

'That's how I loved my sons.'

'Oh well ... oh dear!' Eve wiped her eyes and blew her nose. 'I suppose I should say a big sorry.'

'No need, darling.'

'You're right. You always are – it's really annoying. I mean right about Guy – he was in love with a girl – I was jealous of her. What a muddle!'

'You'll have to untangle your web.'

'Okay.'

Shortly after Eve's departure, while Rufus and Addy wondered if she had benefited from their reunion, Theodore

Edmunds rang to say in a strange quavering voice that he was unwell.

'What is it?' Addy wanted to know.

'Too difficult to tell you.'

'I'm coming south, I'll be with you tomorrow,' she said.

They had communicated less and less. Addy had been so grief-stricken during the war, Theo had been so important and busy, and travel between Northumberland and London was problematical. Peace posed other problems: Theo was older and tireder, Addy had to take care of Rufus, Faith was still her responsibility, and she was seldom at Walkers Row – there had been talk of selling it. Theo remained her admirer, friend and, as he called himself, 'adviser of last resort'; and his letters were as fond as ever. But she had not known he was ill.

In the hospital he was in a private room, and comatose, wearing an oxygen mask. Addy bit back tears, and again fought to rise above her selfish feelings of guilt, because she had not been good enough to him. She stroked one of his bony white hands, and in the course of her two-hour vigil the following exchanges occurred.

'Thank you,' he managed to whisper.

She bent and kissed his hand by way of answer.

'Are you in pain?' she asked.

He shook his head minimally.

'I've left you everything,' he said.

'Oh no, Theo!' Her exclamation was a plea that he should not talk of dying.

'You will use it well,' he said, and she replied, 'Thank you, Theo.'

At last he mouthed the words: 'Goodbye, dearest.'

She declared distinctly: 'I love you,' and tiptoed away.

He expired that night – a nurse had warned Addy that he would not pull through. His wish was to be buried in Fowick Church, near the Forester family plot. Addy accompanied the coffin northwards. Three Foresters, Rufus, Addy and Faith, and as many friends from London, were the mourners at his funeral – he had no living relations.

His estate, according to solicitors, was large, and Addy wondered what to do with it.

Rufus urged her to do nothing in a hurry, Faith told her to give the money away.

'It's not needed,' she said. 'Eve's got too much, and I want no more.'

Eventually she handed out largesse to needy friends who would accept it with grace, and put fifty per cent in a charitable fund for distribution to local causes.

She discussed 'testamentary dispositions' – another solicitor's phrase – with Rufus and Faith. It was agreed that Eve should inherit Beltran and Faith Forest Court, and each should have half the available cash and the valuables.

When all was signed and sealed she remarked to Faith as they pottered round the garden of the Court: 'You were a funny little girl, both sorts of funny, you and Ian were as close as Eve and Guy were, and there seemed to be no admittance of outsiders. But you never can tell about anything, and certainly not in a family – now you're my comfort and joy. I've been such a favourite of fortune in so many ways – no, really! – but I've never forgotten what poverty is and how hard its hardships are. You're the same as me in that respect, I believe – you're not a hypocrite, you like not to have to count your pennies, and nonetheless you remember all the poor ones. I've been thinking of that girl Eve mentioned, Guy's girl, and hoping she's all right. Theo's money is still burning a hole in my pocket, and I'd love to shower some on a deserving stranger. Do you happen to know that girl's name?'

Addy drew a blank. Faith had no relevant knowledge or information. But some weeks later an extraordinary coincidence in human form happened to the Foresters.

364

She was a pretty woman in her later twenties. She had walked up the drive and rung the front door bell. It was afternoon. Addy asked whoever was there to step in through the open door. They met in the hall.

The visitor immediately cried, shed tears and covered her eyes with her hands.

Addy at length extracted the information that she was Peggy Saunders, Conrad's girl, not Guy's, who was now overcome by the badness of her behaviour, dropping in uninvited, and then blubbing.

Addy, tearful too, showed how delighted she was by the visit, and led Peggy by the hand to meet Rufus, who embraced her when he had mastered her identity. Faith was stuck at work, and Rufus' deafness ruled out triangular conversation, so Addy put forward the idea of a little walk, and Peggy said she would love that.

Time was limited. Peggy was on holiday with her fiancé, Joe, and Joe would be returning to fetch her from the bottom of the drive in an hour and a half. Addy offered tea, or alternatively a tour of the garden; but Peggy shyly wondered if she could walk into the hills – she was wearing stout shoes on purpose – she had heard so much about those hills from Conrad.

They set off together, and Addy congratulated Peggy on her engagement to be married.

Peggy explained haltingly: 'I'm staying with Joe's parents in Newcastle. I specially wanted to see you again if I could. I'm so sorry I didn't keep up with you after Conrad... I hadn't the heart. And then I read about your Guy and your Ian and I was afraid of making things worse for you... But now I'm glad I came.'

Addy said how much the visit meant to her, and thanked Peggy for having disregarded the conventions.

'I couldn't help crying when I saw you again, you brought back all the memories, but I'm happy at last, I am honestly, and happier still that you're not sad about me and Joe. He's very good to me, and I do love him, and we'll be all right, I'm sure – but that's not to compare him with Conrad.'

Addy reassured her.

Peggy continued: 'It was so short, you know, our romance, five months and four days, but we packed so much into the time, so much of ourselves, all of me or nearly. The danger and anxiety added to the loveliness – it was like poetry – and I couldn't look at anyone else for seven years afterwards. I've known Joe for two years, and – what can I say? – it's prose, and perhaps none the worse for that.'

Addy spoke of Conrad's enthusiasm for flying and for fighting for his country.

'Yet he was peaceful with me. We made a little island of peace for ourselves in the middle of the war. We had nothing but tenderness, and fun and laughter. Sorry, I'd better stop before there'll be more crying. He made me laugh at the names of these hills, perhaps he invented the names, one hill called Old Hen, and Pudding and Pie and Top of the World.'

'We've just climbed Old Hen,' Addy said. 'Peggy, I hope you'll bring your children here one day.'

'Could I? Conrad thought his home was the best place, and now I can see why. But I'm going to have to economise in the family way. Joe's an only child and his mother's not well, he has to support his father as best he can, and my father had an accident last year and my mother's in difficulties. We have to lend hands in households miles apart and contribute otherwise, and Joe himself isn't strong, he had TB when he was a boy and it left him with one leg shorter than the other. He's a printer, he works in a small printing business and I do temping as a secretary.'

'Conrad told me you sprang from a farm in Yorkshire.'

'That's right. We were well-to-do before the war. But when Dad was in the army and I was away from home, mother got in a muddle and we lost our land and most of our money. Now my parents live in a bungalow in Worthing in Sussex. Joe and I will manage very nicely, we'll do better by helping each other, and our dream is to have a shop somewhere. I've nothing to grumble about any more, and I've my time with Conrad to look back on. I just meant to say not too many children.'

Addy said she understood, and that they had surmounted the hill called Pudding and Pie.

'Where's Top of the World?'

'We're nearly there.'

'I'll be so pleased to have been on the Top of the World with Conrad's mother.'

'Don't be alarmed by the question I want to ask, Peggy – would you accept a gift of money?'

'Oh Mrs Forester...'

'Don't refuse me, please listen!'

'But I didn't come...'

'I know that. I'm offering because you might have been, because I wish you were, my daughter-in-law.'

'Oh Mrs Forester!'

They stopped walking, and Peggy more or less collapsed once more on Addy's shoulder.

When they resumed walking, Addy said: 'Now, my dear, prepare yourself for another quite agreeable shock! I'd like to give you a large sum of money, enough to ease your lot, my wedding present to you and Joe with no strings of any sort attached. It's money that is mine by accident, funny money, I think it's called, and superfluous to the requirements of my family and our charitable interests. I can't think of a better home for it than you two – and Conrad probably warned you about my impulsiveness. So there you are – don't be too grateful and embarrass us both – and remember if possible never to feel beholden.'

Peggy expressed her gratitude charmingly, then inquired:

'How can you be so strong and calm after all you've been through?'

'Wait till you're a mother and you'll know the answer,' Addy laughed. 'When Ian died I thought it was the last straw. I had suspected Conrad's death would break my back, and then more so that Guy's death would. Ian's would without a shadow of doubt, I thought. But you see, it didn't. I am aware that last straws can be the end of everything, but I believe they're rare. To die of grief must be extremely difficult. Reality and logic can save the skins of most people who are not mental. I loved and I believe was loved by three remarkable people, my sons, for twenty years, I loved each for twenty years, which is wonderful – you had Conrad for no more than five months. I was left with an adorable husband, two daughters, three houses, money galore – comparatively speaking I was still in Easy Street. It would be very wrong of me not to be as strong and calm as I'm able. Forgive such a long speech. Incidentally, where we are now is our highest hill.'